42 MILLION TO ONE

A Political Thriller Inspired by Real Events

HAL MALCHOW

Double M Publishing

Published by Double M Publishing
Potomac, MD

ISBN 978-0-578-73797-3 (paperback)
ISBN 978-0-578-73798-0 (ebook)

Library of Congress Control Number: 9780578737973

Printed in the USA

First Edition July 2020

To the following individuals who have
been heroic voices in speaking out
to protect American democracy.

Sue Halpern
The New Yorker

Kim Zetter
The New York Times and *Wired.*

Alex Halderman
University of Michigan

Author's Notes

This book is a fictional story that takes place against the background of real events. While the characters and the plot are creations of the writer, many of the incidents relating to voting machines, their vulnerability, and the likelihood of manipulation represent real events.

The South Carolina primary in which an unknown candidate received 59 percent of the vote against a candidate mounting a credible challenge to the incumbent took place in 2010 in the Democratic senatorial primary contest between Vic Rawls and Alvin Greene. This primary contest is recreated in Chapter One. Coverage of this event is provided in the Bibliography.

The incidents demonstrating the ease of voter machine and voter registration website hacking at the Def Con Conference in Las Vegas took place in 2017 and 2018. Coverage of these events is provided in the Bibliography.

The statistical probabilities that the differences between exit poll predictions and actual results were due to chance were based upon a comparison of initial exit poll releases with actual election results in 301 elections taking place between 2004 and 2016. These probabilities can reflect many factors, including weaknesses in exit poll methodology. A comparison of exit poll results with public polling averages (realclearpolitics.com) shows that the two methodologies produce similar results but that exit polls, on the average, provide better predictions of actual results. The title of this book, *42 Million to One*, reflects the actual statistical probability that, across these 301 elections, the shift toward Republican candidates could be due to random chance. This probability is not the probability of voting machine manipulation. It is simply that the differences between exit poll predictions and actual election results cannot be the product of random chance.

These probabilities (P-values) were computed by Greg Huber, chairman of the Political Science Department at Yale University. Anyone wishing to check or recompute these figures can review or download this data at halmalchow.com/80milliontoone/exitpolldata/.

The statistical probability that the shift from exit poll data to Republican advantage in actual election results was rounded up to 42 million to one. The actual number is 41,735,024 to one.

Events involving the *Washington Post*, the *New York Times*, and other media outlets are strictly fictitious. Voting machine companies described in this book are fictitious, although the use of substandard paper to make the punch cards that were used in the 2000 Florida presidential election were based on management decisions made by Sequoia Voting System, which was purchased by Dominion Voting Systems in 2010. Polling reported in this story is likewise fictitious, although efforts were made to approximate public polling on most issues.

"Everything begins in mysticism and ends in politics."
Charles Peguy

Part One

1

Lucy Gilmore

One summer night in Charleston, South Carolina, I saw something I was not supposed to see. I wasn't even looking. That is God's truth. But I saw. And the next thing I knew my whole world was turning upside down.

My name is Lucy Gilmore. At the time this story begins I was 25 years old and a reporter for *The Washington Post*. I had attained this lofty position at a young age after, as a cub reporter in Rock Hill, South Carolina, I uncovered graft in City Hall and was fired by my editor, a close friend of the mayor. Jobless but determined, I dug through the city dump to find the documents I needed and took them to the *Charlotte Observer*, which ran the story. The whole triumphant martyr thing was cause for celebration in newspaper circles. A job offer from *The Washington Post* followed.

Okay, that's all good but that's not the story I am here to tell. I've got a better story, much better. It begins in Charleston, South Carolina, on primary election day in 2018. You see, my uncle, my beloved uncle, Vince Rawlings, was running for the United States Senate. I drove down from Washington, D.C., for his primary election night party.

His Republican opponent was Jim Mintura, a pompous Tea Party incumbent senator. Vince had never run statewide. He had been a circuit judge. But in a recent SCIndex/Crantford poll Vince had pulled within seven points of Mintura even though hardly anybody in South Carolina even knew who my uncle was. So Democrats, while still skeptical of his chances, were starting to talk my uncle up.

The primary was a whole other matter. Vince was basically unopposed. Basically. He had an opponent named Barry White. White spent no money, made no campaign appearances, and had no website. I later learned that his filing fee of $10,400 was paid anonymously. His campaign strategy seemed to be to hide in his house and hope no voter would knock on his door. So all we thought about that night was the upcoming fall campaign against Jim Mintura. The celebration was held at eight that night at the Southend Brewery, one of these new brew pubs that had gotten pretty popular. It was a refurbished warehouse and when you walked in the door the first thing you saw was a big row of stainless steel tanks telling you their beer was fresh. Vince's party was on the second floor, one cavernous room that overlooked the harbor. We retreated to the back corner of the room and gathered around one TV.

In most victory celebrations, the candidate waits in a suite several floors up and, when the outcome is clear, he or she makes a grand appearance, a sometimes gracious speech, and, of course, regardless of the outcome, thanks all who had given their time and money for the campaign.

But Uncle Vince was right there in the room chatting, giving hugs, glowing in anticipation of the small victory he was about to achieve. I walked up behind him and tapped his shoulder. He turned, opened his arms, and consumed me in a huge hug that I was, frankly, damned proud to receive. He stepped back and looked at me with a large smile.

"Lucy, you look great. Congratulations on getting that job at *The Post*. No one deserved it more." Then he paused and his smile spread. "How are those Cubs doing?"

Okay, I am a Cubs fan. Holy Jesus. I am a huge Cubs fan. But more on that later.

"Not as well as you are going to do tonight, Uncle Vince."

I thought back to the year my father died. I was 12 years old. My mom was cold and distant. We were no help to each other. For months, I could hardly leave my room.

But Uncle Vince stopped by the house at least twice a week. He talked to me about life and adversity and how if I could not get my dad back at least I had to make him proud. He told me I was special, and he described to me the great person I might become. Gradually, at his urgings I found my feet again.

As I looked at Uncle Vince, I retrieved my handkerchief—I always carry one—and wiped my eyes.

Boy oh boy, there we all were: me, Uncle Vince, and about 40 friends, waiting to cheer, celebrate, and raise a glass honoring the first step on his journey to the United States Senate. All eyes watched the TV screen waiting on the first returns.

The first 12,000 votes were reported at 8:41 p.m.: 4,800 for Vince, 7,200 for his opponent, Barry White. Those were surprising numbers, but this unknown candidate was not going to beat Uncle Vince. Then came a second report and a third.

With half the vote counted, White had 52,289. Uncle Vince's total? 33,483. How could Barry White be winning? No one in the room had even heard of this guy.

Vince's campaign manager leaned over his laptop, scanning returns.

"Something's wrong," he said. "Something is very wrong."

A group of supporters surrounded his computer screen hoping for an explanation. Geography told us nothing. Except for Vince's home county, White led almost everywhere. That couldn't be. The manager stood up and scratched his chin, confusion darkening his face.

An assistant ran to the table.

"Walter," the assistant said, referring to the manager. "I got a call from the Secretary of State's office with some surprising information."

"What?" the campaign manager asked.

"We may be losing in almost every part of the state, but in half the counties we are winning the absentee ballots with 80 percent. Overall, we are winning the absentee votes by 11 points. Does that ever happen?"

"Never," he answered.

The manager kneaded his brow. Then his face went white. "Oh my God," he said, almost in a whisper. He left to talk to Vince.

* * *

As the returns poured in, I was as confused as everyone else. So I sought out some people I knew to be well informed in all matters of South Carolina politics. Slowly, some pieces of the puzzle began to emerge.

First, if White was winning the polling place ballots and Uncle Vince was winning the absentee ballots, what was the difference? The difference was that the absentee ballots, in most counties, were counted by hand. All the other vote totals came from a machine.

Second, South Carolina had bought all these new voting machines statewide. All our machines were computers where the voter touched the screen to indicate a choice. You put your finger on the candidate you support and, voila, that candidate gets your vote. But because there were no paper ballots, there was absolutely no way to know if the computer was delivering an honest count.

Let me tell you. It gets worse.

There were reports from voters across the state that they had pressed the button for Vince, but the machines showed Barry White as their choice.

All this was making me queasy. By the end of the night my hopes and Uncle Vince's candidacy lay on the floor waiting for the broom and dustpan to lift them away.

* * *

The next day, political pundits of all stripes weighed in to explain the result. Some of these so-called experts suggested that ballot position was the explanation. Barry White was listed first on the ballot and that explained everything. But I researched that issue. There were serious academic studies of the effect of being first on the ballot. The effect varied, depending on how much the voters actually knew about the candidates. But even where the voters knew nothing, the effect was pretty small.

Then there was the "Can't Get Enough of Your Love" theory, referring to the famous song sung by the legendary R&B singer, Barry White. According to this theory, voters entering the voting booth had confused Barry White the candidate with Barry White the singer and had cast their votes to send the wrong Barry White crooning up I-95 to Washington, D.C., even though Barry White the singer had been dead for more than a decade.

But once you discarded these theories you faced a set of disturbing questions. Why were the machine counts different from the hand counts? Could these voting machines have actually been rigged?

I called a longtime political reporter at the *Post*, Bernadette Simpson, someone who would know about vote counting, stolen elections, and enterprises of that sort.

"Bernadette, I need your perspective. I am down here in South Carolina and there are some things about this Democratic Senate primary that don't feel right. Do you know anything about programming voting machines to change the count?"

"Not a thing but it would not surprise me. This country has had a pretty long history of vote fixing but not much in recent years, at least not that has been caught."

"Enlighten me."

"In 1960, Mayor Richard Daley of Chicago voted the cemetery to help John Kennedy carry Illinois and enter the White House. In the 19th century the corrupt political machine, Tammany Hall, once voted 55,000 votes in a precinct with only 41,000 voters. Lyndon Johnson had apparently lost his 1948 race for US Senate when a box of 'lost' ballots suddenly appeared, giving him just enough votes to reverse the outcome. These are just a few examples."

"But all that was 50 years ago, at least."

"Boss Tweed didn't have our technology. Maybe with computers he could have gotten thousands more votes."

"How easy is it to manipulate the machines? It can't be easy, can it? I mean, if they could, then any scummy politico could..."

"Sounds like a theory, but that's not my expertise, Lucy. I'm afraid I don't know."

I had a lot to learn.

In the meantime, Vince Rawlings smelled the same rat. He hired a computer expert to examine the machines. He also filed a protest with the South Carolina Democratic Committee.

* * *

I went back to Washington and went to work. The more I learned the more my stomach turned.

I talked to a computer expert who worked with voting machines. Could you program a voting machine to change the outcome of an election?

"Sure can. It takes three lines of code. Two lines adjust the vote counts any way you want."

"What is the third line for?" I asked.

"The third line erases all three lines on election night so that if someone wanted to check the code, all evidence of the crime would be gone."

So there it was. If you inspected the code, all evidence would be gone.

2

Sheldon Klumm

My name is Sheldon Klumm. For three years, I worked for Election Day, Inc., a company that manufactures and services voting machines for more than 40 percent of the nation's polling places. I am a programmer. Voting machine programmers don't actually have to be good. For the most part, you just fill in the blanks—candidate names, the office they are running for, the date of the election, and the stuff the counties need to put a ballot in front of the voter. But I knew my stuff. I was good.

I had been on the job about six months making okay money. One thing I liked was that a lot of times there were no elections going on. So I spent that time doing what I like best, playing video games and wondering if I should stick it out at Election Day, Inc. Then my career took a big turn.

I got a call from the boss, Jasper Rittendom, to visit him in his office right away. I wasn't too nervous about the meeting. I had a cousin who was married to Jasper's niece and sometimes he would call me "cousin" in the hall. Besides, I could program circles around the rest of the staff. I figured they needed me to develop some proprietary programming language so no one could know what in the hell was going on inside our machines. Maybe they wanted to move our stuff to a new operating system that would be more efficient than all that Windows stuff we were mostly using. They were probably looking for some magic. Magic is what I do.

7

I was wrong. Completely freaking wrong.

I got off the elevator on the fifth floor, the top floor of our building, and was ushered into the big office. And there was Jasper Rittendom, our CEO. He was skinny with uncombed hair that would have been distracting if he had more of it. He also had these bug-eyes that sometimes wandered the room like searchlights that have lost their pattern.

Oh, I almost forgot. He also had that friendly, jump to his feet and shake your hand manner, which he probably had developed by schmoozing all those second-rank politicians. You wondered what he had to do to get the business. You wondered but never asked.

There was a second person in the room and that was a surprise. Chase Davenport, chairman and major stockholder of Election Day, Inc. Chase Davenport would not have flown in from West Palm Beach, Florida, to compliment me on my work. I knew right then and there that something was up.

Unlike Jasper, Chase had a stylish appearance, fine suits, a military polish to his shoes, and a head of hair so orderly you wanted to pull on it to see if it was real. As I entered, he grinned at me and nodded but did not get up.

Jasper waved his hand at a seat next to Chase. Jasper's office was neat and orderly but bore none of the ornaments of success. An oak desk nicely stained but shaped by a carpenter, not some fancy wood artist, sat against the far wall. A window looked out onto the street, with an unremarkable view of Omaha. At the center of the wall, behind his desk, was a large color photograph of the 1997 Nebraska Cornhuskers national championship football team. It was signed by the coach, Tom Osborne. I took my seat.

I sensed a nervousness in the room. Jasper looked at Chase. Chase looked at me closely and then nodded to Jasper. Then Jasper asked a surprising question.

"Sheldon, have we ever talked politics?"

"Not that I recall," I said, blinking.

"Well, do you have leanings?"

I could smell the rat already and he was a stinker. They were big Republicans and, frankly, if their ethics were so high how could Election Day, Inc. be so successful in this political world? I didn't care. I did not care about politics one bit. My gigs were video games and writing poems. But I also know that if you want to get ahead in life, a little ass kissing is sometimes required.

"Well, I am a strong Republican," I lied.

"Then you have probably been thinking about the upcoming presidential election."

I nodded. Maybe two minutes in the last month.

"Well, as you know it's going to be a pretty important election," Jasper continued. "And I think you understand the things that could happen if the Republicans lose."

"Yessir, I do," I answered, surprised that my two minutes were not a waste.

"You know we have a good business here and we don't want to let things get out of hand. But if we could push a few votes in the right direction, we could change the course of history."

I looked back and forth between my two bosses. Chase leaned forward and spoke.

"Sheldon, you have been a great employee here. Frankly, you are a star. But we think you can play a much bigger role in this company. Of course, this is a completely private conversation, you understand."

"I do," I said. The nervousness of my bosses was delicious.

"Sheldon, I think you understand better than anyone else that our risk is low. These Touchpad 3000 voting machines are selling like hotcakes and they keep no paper record of anyone's vote."

"Right," I interrupted. "If there are no paper ballots then the only records are the counts that come directly from our machines. They are the final word and no one can prove our results wrong."

Chase nodded at Jasper. Jasper smiled. I had thought ahead! But if you're like me, staring at a computer screen with not much to do, you think about a lot of things.

9

"And it only takes two lines of code to change the vote counts," I continued. "And another one to erase the code on election night so if someone gets suspicious and wanted to check the code, it would not be there at all."

Don't think I was some mastermind. This was pretty simple stuff.

Jasper and Chase were nodding their heads, delighted that I had considered these issues.

"And besides," Jasper explained, "why would anyone be suspicious? If we changed the counts by 10 or 20 percentage points, yes. But what if we only nudged the percentage four or five points? They have polls. The polls don't always predict the outcome. As long as you don't get greedy, why would anyone be suspicious at all?"

"And something else to consider," Chase added. "If they looked for the code, they would not find it. But they have no right to look at the code anyway. The Digital Millenium Copyright Act protects our intellectual property."

"Let me reiterate," Chase summarized. "A big part of the strategy is never to be greedy. Just shift the vote four or five points. Never more. Democrats will still win elections. Republicans will still lose elections. In most elections the winners will be the same. We would just be giving the good guys a little nudge."

I leaned back in my chair, considering this invitation. "Who knows about this?" I finally asked.

"Three people: you, me, and Jasper," Chase responded.

"That's all?" I asked.

"We can't let anyone else know," Jasper added. "We thought long and hard about which programmer we could trust with this assignment—someone who won't make mistakes, someone who cares about our country, a patriot we could bring into this partnership, just the three of us."

"So what is the offer?" I asked, getting to my point of interest and it wasn't politics.

Chase nodded at Jasper.

"Of course, if you accept this partnership there will have to be some changes in the way we do things. For one, we would create a new position, director of Programming Quality Control. You would have the last look at any programming before we ship to the counties. You would place the vote shifting code on the memory cards. You would not be part of the programming staff. You would report directly to me."

"And there would be other benefits," Chase added.

"Yes, yes," Jasper continued, "the salary for the new position is $120,000 per year. There will be some specifics in the contract, especially covering confidentiality of your work."

I smiled. They were almost doubling my salary.

Then Chase looked at me in a fatherly way and provided reassuring words.

"Sheldon, the other side has been stealing votes and elections for centuries. Lyndon Johnson voted ghosts down there along the Rio Grande. Mayor Daley in Chicago voted the cemetery." He turned and pointed to a voting machine standing against the wall.

"Sheldon, do you know what that machine is? That machine is a thousand cemeteries marshaled for the good, saving our nation from socialism and moral decay."

So here I was with this big decision. Maybe I should have taken a stand. But if I didn't take this big raise, someone else would. And did I care who won these elections? Not one bit. I was not even registered to vote.

So I looked at those thousand cemeteries sitting in that fancy black box and thought about how well an undertaker gets paid. It was safe. It was easy. I had to wonder: How could I turn it down?

3

Max Parker

You may have never thought about what it is like to run a campaign. That's my job. I run Democratic campaigns and it's exciting work. Since almost all campaigns take place in even-numbered years, a guy like me has to improvise in the odd years. I make a little money consulting, and every now and then a lobbyist might pay me to talk to someone in Congress I helped elect. I am not part of a big firm. Guys at the big-time firms spend the odd years in the Bahamas. I never made the big time.

Then I got a call from a nobody congressman named Jeffrey Scott.

He wanted to talk about *his* presidential campaign.

I almost fell out of my chair. Jeffrey Scott was a second termer who had struggled to get re-elected in a conservative district in rural Oregon. I liked him. He was likable. But as he explained his plan, my first mission was to restore his sanity.

"President, you say?"

"That's right. And you're just the man to get me there, Max Parker."

No money, no name recognition, and no support. It was as if he were saying he could walk on the field at the Super Bowl, at halftime, down 77-0, and win the whole thing.

That is not how life works. And face it. This guy was no Tom Brady.

Jeffrey Scott did not look like a president. Where was that Roman nose, those square shoulders, those eyes that looked into your soul and told you that you were the most important person he'd ever met? Jeffrey Scott was barely 40 years old. He was scrawny, five-foot-six, with big feet, a little pudge in the midsection, short curly hair, and freckles. Freckles for God's sake. If he was cast in some White House TV series, he would be the overaged intern—the one who dropped a steamy bowl of southwest red chili right into the president's lap.

But shit, did he ever have a plan.

"Voters are sick and tired of all this partisan bickering. They want a calming voice to bring this country together." He was nothing if not earnest.

"And let me guess, you're that voice?"

"That's right."

"That's a nice thing to say, Jeffrey. But the fact is that the only thing Democrats and Republicans really agree upon is how much they hate each other. I think you'll find the polling supports that."

"Of course, the hatred is growing," he answered. "But no one is showing them another way. The field is full of all these people saying the same thing. But my message is different and that's why I'll stand out. Voters want to know it's possible to come together."

I told him that being nice never got you on the news. Being provocative, going on the attack, reaching for the jugular, smearing the other guy, fairly or unfairly, that was what gave those greedy journalists a story. You had to tell America how bad your opponent really was.

Jeffrey Scott just smiled with a calm presence like some Buddha who knew I would be saved.

"Words aren't that important. Not really. It's what you *do* that matters. You can't tell voters what to think. You can only show them what your beliefs look like in action."

13

Like I said, the guy was earnest in a Howdy Doody kind of way. But if he really believed that, he would be lucky to get re-elected back in Oregon. It's just not the way politics works out in the real world.

And after I told him his ideas were crazy and that he needed a psychiatrist more than a consultant, he made the most remarkable statement of all.

"I need you to run my campaign, Max."

"No can do, Jeffrey." I looked at my watch for an excuse.

"Who are you working for now?"

"Nobody."

"Max, if you are right, this campaign won't last more than two or three months. You can take the money and find something better. No one will blame you for losing a campaign that never had a chance to begin with."

He was right about that. My money was a little low. The Iowa caucuses were almost a year away, but my bills weren't. Two or three months could float me through an otherwise uncertain patch. Besides that, it was a presidential campaign and that was something I'd dreamt about.

So, against my better judgment, I decided I'd do it, but I didn't come out and say it right away. I wanted him to make the case on why anybody would take him seriously.

"Where did you go to school, Jeffrey?"

"Williams College. Majored in psychology and economics. Got my JD from the University of Oregon. Graduated third in my class."

"Oregon have much of a law school?" I'd hoped, though I knew better, for him to rattle off some Ivy League pedigree.

"It's accredited."

"Let me guess, after you finished, you gave Portland a try?"

"No. I left Eugene and headed south on I-5 to Roseburg, where I grew up. Had a window in my law office that let me see the Umpqua National Forest."

"And then?"

"And then what?"

14

"The part where you got into politics."

"County commissioner. Caseload was a little light and my dad—who everybody loved because he was one of the only doctors in town—told me that maybe it'd be a way to get out the word that I was back home. Then I won. As a Democrat." He laughed. "If you know the town, you'd know how funny that was."

* * *

The next day, Jeffrey was in my office going over his short career. He had just been elected commissioner and fortunately for Jeffrey, the Douglas County Board of Commissioners faced a crisis. For the better part of a hundred years, the county had relied on timber revenues to sustain its services. But Douglas County, once the "timber capital of the nation," was not cutting much timber anymore. Clear cutting had decimated much of the forest land. Environmentalists had managed to restrict harvesting in the national forests. There were solutions but few could be considered because the animosity between loggers, federal employees, and environmentalists had grown to a level where no one was speaking at all.

But Jeffrey Scott had the magic Douglas County needed. He went to the timber companies to find out what it would take to make a deal. He went to the environmentalists and did the same. By the time he was finished he had achieved what no one thought possible. He had forged a deal that increased timber harvests, improved management of the forests, and put the environmentalists in charge of making sure everyone followed the rules.

The *Oregonian* did a large feature story on the deal and Jeffrey's role. It was entitled "The Little Commissioner Who Could." One year later, he was elected to Congress, as a Democrat, by a margin of three votes.

"Sounds like you were living the dream."

"Yeah, it wasn't too bad. But then the rafting thing."

"The rafting thing?"

"Oh, I thought you knew." He swallowed hard, his Adam's apple more prominent than it had been.

Years earlier, Jeffrey took his wife and young daughter on a rafting trip in Idaho. It was still spring, and the water was high, too high to see a log lodged between the rocks. The raft struck the log and flipped in the air, discharging its passengers into the rapids. His wife and daughter never made it to shore. For the last seven years, he had lived a solitary life. A repentant monk.

But now he was running for president of the United States, unknown, untested, no family, and his only accomplishment was that he had settled a local forest spat.

And for some reason, I'd agreed to run alongside him.

God help us both.

4

Lucy Gilmore

As soon as I got back to Washington, I called Vince.

"Did your computer guy find any issues with the voting machines?"

"Lucy, he wasn't allowed to look."

"How can that be?"

"Apparently, the Digital Millennium Copyright Act bars inspection of the machines. What is inside is their intellectual property. No one is allowed to look, not even election officials."

Can you believe it?

I called our political editor at the *Post* and asked for a meeting. Sometimes I get a little intimidated by a big meeting. You see, I am only four-foot-ten inches tall. And it can be hard enough for a woman to get listened to, much less one who is so short she needs a pillow on her chair to reach the keyboard.

But the day of the meeting, for some reason, all these anxieties had disappeared. Here I was, a reporter. I worked for one of the top newspapers in the United States of America. And I had a story.

Could it get any better?

The story was that our elections were being stolen. Rigged. And what better example than a completely invisible candidate getting 59 percent of the vote against a candidate who was within seven points of unseating an incumbent United States senator. Motive: Senator saving his skin. Weapon: Voting machines that can be rigged. Crime: Invisible candidate gets 59 percent of the vote.

What was I missing?

So there I was sitting in the office of Brad Aaronson, the star political editor at *The Washington Post*. He had broken the story about Jack Belimi, a lobbyist who had made a fortune representing Indian tribes and then crossed the line between influence and bribery. Brad wrote a great book about how we got into the Iraq war, sure to be a loser but made worse by Americans who knew nothing about the country we suddenly owned. He wasn't my boss. I covered local politics in the DC suburb of Prince George's County, Maryland. But he was nice enough to see me and listen to my pitch.

His door was open, and he was hacking at the keyboard.

"Lucy? So nice to see you."

He had soft brown eyes that clashed a little with his salt and pepper hair. He was always in a hurry but in a relaxed way, calm, but if you were wasting his time, he started glancing around the room. Anyway, he was always nice to me. He complimented my story on Rock Hill corruption. He told me I had a big future at the *Post*. For a 25-year-old, still with stars in her eyes, that was all it took. I loved him.

Now I had his attention. He looked at me directly with a little respectful half-smile and waited. "Brad, I have a pretty big story. Did you read about the election in South Carolina?"

"Yeah, I saw something about it. Barry White, the singer, won another Grammy."

Not a good answer. But I continued.

"Well, that is what they are saying but, listen, Barry White, the candidate, made no appearances, raised no money, has no website. Someone paid his $10,400 filing fee anonymously. But he got 59 percent of the vote against a guy who was giving Senator Mintura a race. How could that happen?"

"I don't know."

"Well, I know. They recently installed these new voting machines. Have you read about these voting machines?"

"A little. Bring me up to speed."

"The ones in South Carolina are basically computers. Computers can be hacked. According to experts the machines are easy to hack. Three lines of code and you can change the vote count any way you want. I believe those computers were programmed to give White the election." I looked across the desk into his blank stare.

"So has someone inspected the machines?" he asked.

"Rawlings, our candidate, hired a computer expert. It seems that internet copyright law prevents any inspection of the code, even when the election produces a highly suspicious result."

"Really?"

"Really."

"Well, that does potentially sound like a big problem. But if you want to do a story, we need to prove something."

"The proof is the impossibility of the result."

"That's an opinion. It seems to me we need some facts."

"Well, here's a fact," I answered. "The absentee ballots. The ones counted by hand. Rawlings won the absentee ballot count by 11 points. Barry White won the machine count by 18 points. That never happens."

"Hmmmm." That was all he said. So I continued.

"Well, the fact is that we can never get facts. You can't inspect the machine and you can't look at the code. There is no way to question the number. It appears on the screen when the polls close and that is all you have. If someone cheats, if someone codes the machine to change the counts, there is no way to disprove them. It seems to me that this is exactly the story we need to write. Our democracy is completely vulnerable. Wouldn't you agree?"

"I think this is a problem. I don't think we have a story, not yet. Let me ask you something. What is your relationship with Vince Rawlings?"

"He's my uncle."

"Lucy, don't you think that should disqualify you from writing the story?"

"I guess so," I answered, swallowing my disappointment.

"I have to say this is a pretty touchy subject. We now have these voting machines in almost every single precinct. If you say our voting machines are rigged, you are saying that our whole democracy could be a fraud. You can't say something like that just because the results of one election look strange."

"What if it is a fraud? What if this is happening everywhere? Don't you think that is the most important and desperately urgent story that this newspaper could do?"

"Lucy, this is not your turf. 'What if' is not a story. I will have someone write something up that says people are wondering about the result. But saying that voting machines are being rigged—without evidence—is not a story that is ready for prime time."

Two days later, a three-paragraph story reported that the State Democratic Committee had rejected Vince Rawlings's protest and awarded the nomination to Barry White.

5

Sheldon Klumm

The cold slime rose around my waist. A fog billowed through the landscape, darkening the mood and concealing dangers that awaited. The cattails trembled and a water moccasin parted the reeds, his head raised just above the surface but passing me without notice.

Breathe deep. Breathe deep.

My hands gripped a weapon, a macro-blaster 496—not a rifle, not a bazooka, but something in between, a shooter that launched large bullets that exploded on impact. I had earned this master-piece of annihilation by reaching level 8 in Beserker 5, the game that unfolded before me.

I waited. Above me was a wooden bridge, not a bridge really but a few planks of rotting wood laid over this putrid swamp. Here was where the elf will cross. I bent forward, concealing all but my head beneath the muck. If seen, if discovered, the elf would lower his bow and drive his arrow between my eyes and through the back of my skull.

I peered between the planks. In the distance, I saw a faint rustling of leaves. The elf appeared, dancing along the path. I imagined the elf was reliving victories he had enjoyed at my expense. It had happened, but not in recent days. But not this time. Not never again.

I ducked back into my hiding place. I was camping, which means instead of attacking I awaited my enemy's moves. Some gamers look down on camping but sometimes it is better to lay low. I look down on losing.

I rose again to inspect the trail. The elf was gone. Did he leave the trail? Was he crouched, readying his attack?

I feared he had sensed my presence. Perhaps he was drawing his bow. My muscles were tense. In my stomach I felt the churn of gravel and mud. The first to strike. The first to win. That is my creed. I counted to three. With all my strength, I exploded through the planks, sending them into the air. The elf stood in the trail. The elf drew his bow. He lowered his aim. His arrow fired but my macro unloaded first.

The bullet detonated and the sound echoed off the mountains on all sides. There was no elf, not anymore. Only his tiny remains raining down from the sky.

Woot! Woot!

I hated the elf, that pointy-eared, pansy, girly creature. When I began playing Berserker, I got to choose which creature I would be. I could have been an elf or the wild-eyed Norseman or even the zombie that lived in holes he dug with his extraordinary claws. No, I chose to be an orc because the orcs are the most primitive, the most disgusting, the ones we all want to lose. But I don't lose. Hardly ever anymore. I am a gamer, a video game wunderkind, a master of the cyber realm.

And nothing excites my joys and emotions more than being rained on by the body parts of an elf I have exploded into the heavens.

Oh, and let me re-introduce myself. I am Sheldon Klumm. You met me already. I work for Election Day, Inc. I am the programmer they assigned to help Republicans win elections.

I know that you are thinking two things.

First, you are thinking *Sheldon, you are a slimy, scumbag Republican, stealing our elections and wrecking our democracy.* My answer is: Politics—who cares?

You are also thinking, *Sheldon, why do you waste your life playing video games?* My answer is I am unfit for the real world. I am fat and socially awkward. I am the guy who makes the girls go "EEEWWW!" But in my cyber world I am a hero. I am a star. Hero or dork? Which would you choose?

So maybe I should tell you a little more about myself since I am a big part of this story. I am not your usual thirty-something guy with a girlfriend and who hangs out with the guys. I have not had a date in three years. Of course, it is hard to get a date when you are parked in front of a gaming console morning and night. But it did not start with gaming.

It started with girls, and the first girl involved in this mess was my mom, a single mom with a bad temper who imagined my every misdeed. I was her only child and she peered into every aspect of my life. She looked at my emails. She searched for me on Facebook and MySpace (I was not present). And while most mothers live in fear that their children will succumb to the temptations of drugs or pre-marital sex, mine feared that I might be a nobody who never knew the joys of intoxication and carnal delight.

Unfortunately, that was exactly who I was.

To lift my life, she enrolled me in a ballroom dancing class, sent me to football practice, and volunteered me for the student news-paper, a document I still have never read. Each initiative ended in failure. Each initiative drove me deeper into my computer. And it did not take long for my mother to conclude that I was a hopeless failure and a personal humiliation, an assessment she stated almost every day.

By the time I was in tenth grade, I was pretty shy with girls. Well, let me put it another way. I was terrified. And to make matters worse, I am five-foot-six inches tall and weigh 275. I was not much to look at and they weren't looking.

Oh, I am not a virgin. I did get laid twice in college. But since then I have hardly had a date.

So back to my better life—my life inside a computer. I am a *connoisseur*. I collect the great video games. I have Pong, that prim-itive first video game where you moved a paddle up and down to strike a ball and send it back. I have Space Invaders, where you slide left and right, hide behind barriers, and shoot aliens out of the sky. I have Pac-Man, Donkey Kong, Super Mario Bros., and some special cult games that those champion gamers would not recognize at all.

Collecting, playing, all that's great. But a few years back something even bigger happened. Someone had the idea that in addition to letting you play the game, they would let you change it. A gamer like me could download "mods" for different parts of a game and those mods let you change the dialog, change the characters, and even change the story itself. It's called "modding." I know programing. It is easy for me. So I am morphing these games all the time.

Take that asshole at Election Day, Inc., Oscar Billick, who talks about how fat I am and whispers jokes about me behind my back. I put his face on an evil vampire and then I changed the story so that the vampire likes only pig blood and crawls into the muck every night for dinner. Hilarious.

Did Oscar ever see himself wallowing in the slime, guzzling pig blood? Of course not. Oscar is not cool enough to know Vampalooza.

I also changed the background music. You want a dark mood? Who can compete with Beethoven's *Ninth* or Wagner's *Die Walküre*?

But for me the big fun is dialogue. I am a rhymer. I convert the dialogue to poetry. At the beginning of the great game Skyrim, a dark-throated executioner says to the prisoner, "You started this war and plunged Skyrim into chaos and now the empire is going to put you down."

In my version the executioner says:

> Deeds of greed, deeds of woe
> Seeds of chaos did you sow
> Our great kingdom you unhinged
> Now your crime will be revenged

Sylvester Stallone or Shakespeare? Why even ask?

6

Lucy Gilmore

Okay, my employer deep-sixed my story. Voting machines fraud does not measure up.

So if you want to understand what was going to happen next, maybe I should share a few things about me, Lucy Gilmore.

Let me start with this statement. I have a dark side. It shows up in a number of ways. I am a crier. I sob at sappy movies and fourth cousin weddings, old songs, and, sometimes, when my Cubs lose.

I am also visited with dark views of myself and the world around me. Churchill called it his black dog and most of us call it depression. Mine is no moderate condition. Sometimes I spiral downward into black spaces filled with self-recrimination and despair.

But don't give me your sympathy. What underlies this sadness is something that can change the world.

Consider the people with depression who have done great things—Abraham Lincoln, Charles Darwin, Winston Churchill, Marie Curie, Martin Luther King, and on and on. And when you consider them you start to understand that some people just have deeper emotional currents. Those currents do make you sad. They can also make you obsessed. In a real way, they produce a madness, an unyielding determination that is blind to the dangers standing between you and the goal you pursue.

Was Darwin afraid people would accuse him of toppling the entire Christian religion? Hell no!

So most reporters might have left that meeting with Brad Aaronson and thought, *Okay, move on. Pick your battles. Don't make them mad.* Not me.

I saw a crime. I am sure of it. And Brad Aaronson's opinion does not matter.

Not one fucking bit.

So I have been digging. If we have equipped our polling places with voting machines that can be hacked, rigged, and manipulated with little risk of detection, well, how in the hell did that happen? The answer won't surprise you.

Congress got involved.

This story began with the 2000 presidential election. You may recall that the outcome of that election, in which Gore won the national popular vote by a half-million votes. The electoral vote was decided in the state of Florida where the official vote count showed George Bush the winner by 537 votes. Five hundred votes out of almost six million cast. But there were big problems with the count.

In Broward County, one of the largest Democratic counties in the state, a poorly designed "butterfly ballot" confused many voters. In a number of counties, the use of punchcard ballots produced "hanging chads." Hanging chads happen when pieces of the punch card are partially separated but still remain attached. Were they votes? Were they not? With Bush clinging to a tiny lead, Republicans said "no." Democrats said "yes." Meanwhile, the secretary of state of Florida, Katherine Harris, surreptitiously purged from the voting rolls enough Democrats to change the election outcome four times over.

Although evidence suggested that Al Gore actually received, or would have received with proper counting, a larger number of votes, the contest moved to the courts and, ultimately, the United States Supreme Court. There were five Republican appointees. All five voted for Bush. The four Democrats voted for Gore. George W. Bush became president of the United States.

The furor over this election and the fumbling of its count resulted in some serious international embarrassment. Now, Americans may not care a hoot for the opinions of Frenchmen or Egyptians. But no one wants to become the butt of jokes across the globe.

Want some examples?

In observing a closely contested election in France, one pundit said the frontrunner was leading by a "chad." Another German observer suggested that his government had a secret strategy to win the election. Import American voting machines! Finally, one British journalist proposed that all Americans should be banned from serving as international election observers because obviously Americans did not know how to run elections at all.

These insults stung because, in the opinion of the vast American citizenry, our democracy was the greatest in our world. After all, we INVENTED democracy! Those Greeks may have tried it out but look at them now! But no amount of hubris could obscure the fact that American election officials were looking like the Keystone Cops after a long night at O'Leary's Tavern.

Something had to be done. Something bold. Something decisive. Something that would correct these problems for good. And in this case, we did what we always do in matters of national crisis.

We appointed a commission. The National Commission on Federal Election Reform.

It was actually a good-looking effort. It was co-chaired by Jimmy Carter and Gerald Ford—two former presidents who were so honest they could not be re-elected at all.

And when the commission issued its report, it called on every state to adopt a statewide system of voter registration, maintain centralized voter lists, and provide for provisional voting for voters who believe they are properly registered but can't prove it on the spot. It also recommended that the states and federal government take additional steps to ensure the voting rights of all citizens and to enforce the principle of one person, one vote. In other words, buy some voting machines that actually work.

So the Help America Vote Act, or HAVA as it was called, was signed by President Bush at the end of October 2002. To implement this law, President Bush appointed the Election Assistance Commission and a chair, Dr. DeForest Soaries. In addition to all those reforms, the law provided for more than $2 billion to "update voting equipment."

Now, even in politics, $2 billion is a lot of money. And that money went to local election officials, politicos, insiders who would understand a favor and know how to repay. Suddenly, this whole matter was no longer about election security at all. From across the nation, election officials sounded one unanimous cry.

"Show us the money!"

And the Congress, with a haste barely witnessed since the bombing of Pearl Harbor, pushed all that money right out the door.

But Dr. Soaries protested. "Now wait a second," he pleaded. "What about standards?"

Don't think he wasn't right.

Voting machines had become computers. And with computer technology came all kinds of problems these election officials had hardly considered at all. Without standards, these decisions were left in the hands of election officials at the state and local levels. Some states had centralized systems where the secretaries of state designed the systems and, to the extent they thought about it at all, prepared defenses.

In other states, election administration was a local matter, sometimes delegated to hundreds or even a thousand local jurisdictions. These officials might be a retired fireman without a high school diploma, an insurance salesman, or a city councilman who had lost his job in the last election. Most are surely good people but ill-prepared and underfunded to defend our voting machines from all those hackers who want to decide our elections themselves.

So were these issues important enough to merit the attention of the American Congress? Would it make sense to research how voting machines might be corrupted? Was the security of our democracy an important enough reason for delay?

No way.

Instead, Congress directed Dr. Soaries to send $2.3 billion to the 50 states to buy equipment, even though the equipment was not ready to be bought. He begged Congress to let him do the research before they sent the money.

But Congress said "no."

Here is what DeForest Soaries had to say about this tragic episode:

"The politicians don't care. Washington believes that the machines can't be that bad because, after all, the machines put them in office. If they won the race, how bad can the machines be?

"Instead of setting standards for all voting machines, specifying the minimum-security measures necessary to protect our democracy, no standards were written at all. *Recommendations* would come two years later. After all that voting machine money had already been spent!

"So here is what I learned. We really don't have a sense of how sloppy and how raggedy our election process is.

"The crux of the Help America Vote Act was not really to repair voting but for members of Congress to be able to boast that they were responsible for X number of dollars going back to their states without regard to whether it made sense or not. We have no standards for voting equipment in this country.

"I sent $2.3 billion in federal money to state governments to enable them to buy voting equipment, but the voting equipment was purchased with the money even before the voluntary standards were written.

"Why would you ask an agency to allocate $2.3 billion to the states to buy equipment for which there is no research and no standards? That's just stupidity.

"We train casino workers better than we train election workers."

What can you say? Nothing blinds the eye like $2.3 billion.

We have standards for toasters, but for voting machines? None at all.

Paper ballots had spoiled the 2000 election.

Computer voting was on its way.

And computer voting, largely unsecured and unregulated, plagued American elections for the next 16 years.

7

Max Parker

I have to say that the whole thing was embarrassing. My candidate, Jeffrey Scott, announced his candidacy on love, peace, and reconciliation. Not exactly in those words but that's what it added up to. Here we had something north of 100 million angry voters, the Democrats, thinking that the Republicans were a bunch of Hannibal Lecters who wanted to restore black people to the servant class to have them bringing Republicans mint juleps while they sat in rocking chairs on the front porch of their new McMansions. Meanwhile, Republicans saw Democrats as modern-day Bonnie and Clydes who would steal their money and give it to the poor, who would then buy more drugs and, when the money ran out, go back to robbing their homes.

My candidate was making peace offerings. These voters wanted war.

Anyway, three months after my candidate hired me, the first big event of the campaign was approaching. The presidential debates. But there were two Democratic debates. Jeffrey was in the wrong one.

The incumbent Republican President, Webster Miller, was not running. There was no Democrat frontrunner. So every Democrat who ever got a C+ in their 11th grade civics class suddenly thought they might make a great president. At the moment, there were 27 announced candidates for the Democratic nomination. And since you could not put 27 candidates on stage at once, there were two debates. The first debate was held in prime time in New York, featuring the 10 candidates with the highest polling. Seventeen million people would watch that debate. The second debate featured the next 10 candidates with the lower polling numbers, none of whom were getting five percentage points. This was the also-ran debate. It was held in Trenton, New Jersey. If we were lucky, 600,000 Americans might have watched.

And what about those other seven candidates? Well, some of them had yet to find 25 supporters. They probably met at the Texas Palace Mobile Home Park in Abilene, Texas, for a shouting match and unsupervised brawl.

Unlike the big frontrunner debate, which had two hours of time, the tier-two debate was only 60 minutes. You could call it the losers' debate if you wanted but the truth was that the participants were a pretty remarkable group.

There was Tom Stanton, senator from Arizona, six-four, trim, with a chiseled face and a jaw like the overhang of a western mesa. He was smart and an effective insider in the Senate. The key word is "insider." That is why he was second tier.

Then there was Rex Bilbray, governor of Georgia, who made a fortune sailing against the wind. He looked at Home Depot, a big Georgia institution, and walked away in disgust. What made a hardware store great? All that extra staff sitting around most of the time with not much to do but when you needed help, they were on the case. Sometimes they even knew your name. There was nothing better than a good neighborhood hardware store, so he built or bought a chain of them all with a local name but together with the buying power to get their inventory at competitive prices.

Then there was Mildred Clark from California, who built Security4U, one of America's biggest online trading companies. She had money but big business meant low poll numbers in our primaries. There were other second-tier stars. Oskar Okoye, the African American mayor of Austin; Juliet Brown, a smooth-talking congresswoman from the Bronx who, among other things, was ready to dismantle most major corporations and pay big reparations to the descendants of slaves. Sell *that* in Alabama.

Finally, the most colorful of the bunch, Stan Jankovich, former mayor of Cleveland, and running for president for the third time. He was about three feet tall and was married to this beautiful and towering redhead who would need binoculars to look into his eyes. But you have got to hand it to him, he had a following and a gift for words. In one debate he actually said:

"I am running for president to enable the goddess of peace to encircle within her arms all the children of this country and all the children of the world."

This is the kind of oration that makes some in my party weep with joy. But to a professional like me, his gifts were a lot more like that orange tie you got for Christmas rather than a bottle of passable scotch.

So these were some of the candidates, and then there was Jeffrey, whom I have already introduced and who, if his level of support had been two-tenths of a percentage point lower, he would have been shouting to be heard in that trailer park down there in Abilene.

The debate was in the Arm & Hammer Arena, not a large venue but there was no overflow crowd. Those in attendance were mostly donors but not the $100,000 donors who filled all those seats in the main event in New York City. These were $5,000 and $10,000 donors, glad to be here because they were junkies but suddenly aware that $5,000 does not buy the kind of access it used to.

Candidates were positioned based on their polling numbers with the winners occupying center stage. Jeffrey had the spot on the far right.

There were three moderators, who the media B-team would pose questions to the candidates: Steffan Kingsley of NBC News; Sarah Jones, a reporter for *The Washington Post*; and Sybil Jenkins of MSNBC. Steffan welcomed the audience and read the rules. No answer could be more than one minute long. Right. That's like telling Wall Street tycoons to keep their deals under $50. Then rebuttals, no more than 30 seconds. There was only an hour, so by my calculations, counting overtime answers, moderator posturing, and candidates shouting for more time, each candidate got two questions. One of those questions would be about whatever scandal or inconsistency the moderators could dig up. Well, since Jeffrey was not saying anything likely to excite the voters, it wouldn't matter much anyway.

The questioning began. What were the questions? Did someone ask about Social Security whose insolvency was 15 years away? Of course not. Medicare? Its demise was even closer. Not a word. What about the ballooning budget deficit? Well, the Republicans had already given away the money in tax cuts and Democrats had big plans for all that money that was no longer there. Anyway, all that deficit talk was a downer. No, the questions were a game that goes all the way back to Watergate, when the world discovered that politicians were corrupt, and the press ascended into their role as the citizenry's first line of defense against these lowly curs.

The initial question from Steffen Kingsley went to Tom Stanton, the senator from Arizona who polled highest among these also-rans with an impressive four percent.

"Senator Stanton, you have been praised as a Senate insider, someone who makes deals and works behind the scenes to make government work. But many in this country believe that our government in Washington is not working, that we need an outsider as president because we need someone to shake things up. Are you capable of bringing that kind of change?"

Well, yes, Senator, when did you stop beating your wife? But then this game had been going on for a half-century or more. The politicians are practiced as well, and they have the advantage. They don't have to answer the questions at all. Stanton replied.

"Thank you, Steffen. Sometimes it is not the loudest voice that makes the biggest difference. But as president I will raise my voice for the issues that define who we are in our nation. A middle class, fairly paid and receiving its rightful share of our nation's wealth.

Strong and effective measures to curb climate change. Vigilance against discrimination based upon race, gender, or religion. The right to a college education for every citizen regardless of financial means. The Republican Party has served and lifted the wealthiest among us, and our nation has taken a wrong turn. I will fight to undo these wrongs and bring back the American dream."

Next, Sarah Jones took her shot at Mildred Clark, whose sin was her own economic success.

"Ms. Clark, your company is certainly an American success story. But I have to ask, Security4U has been the subject of three sexual harassment lawsuits, nine lawsuits for gender and racial discrimination, and your company has been criticized for paying you $23 million per year. If that is your record as a corporate leader, how can you assure Americans that you as president will run a nation that provides opportunity for all?"

Mildred Clark may have been new to this game, but she had the best coaching money could buy. And who would not have expected this question?

She spoke briefly about all the women and minorities holding high positions in her company, then pivoted to her main issue, defining capitalism in America. "People like me are getting an unfair share and it's got to stop."

Then there were the controversial issues. Juliet Brown got a tough question about paying reparations to the descendants of slaves. Why should a descendent of a Union soldier be taxed for a sin their ancestors had fought to stop?

Governor Bilbray of Georgia was asked about his previous opposition to gun control. How can we trust you to keep your promise to do more? Of course, he could. If elected, he would not be living in Georgia anymore.

On and on it went until Jeffrey Scott was the only candidate yet to be questioned. Jeffrey had been quiet in the House, almost invisible. He was as clean as a whistle. Sybil Jenkins began with a smirk, as she delivered the question that would surely finish this young upstart's career.

"Congressman, you are a second-term congressman who has hardly spoken out on any national issue. You are last in the polls among the candidates here tonight. Why are you qualified to be president and why are you even running?"

Jeffrey smiled as if he had been pitched the sweetest, slowest softball ever to come across the plate.

"Thank you, Sybil. Here is my most important qualification. I am willing to say some things tonight that no other candidate has the courage to say. Our government in Washington is broken. Congress has not passed a budget on time in 30 years. Medicare is on the verge of bankruptcy and Social Security is not far behind. It's great to talk about tax cuts, but all we are doing is using the credit card to juice the economy and pass the bill to our kids. And that's not all they get.

"They will inherit a climate that may be barely livable. Why can't we solve these problems? In America we have become two angry mobs, so different on issues and so angry at each other that we can no longer even talk. We need a president who can turn down the heat, begin real conversations, and find the common ground. We need a president who can help Americans understand that a hero is not someone who makes righteous speeches about unyielding principles. Success in a democracy is about finding a majority. The hero we need in America today is a president who can start a national conversation and build majorities to address problems so difficult that they have not even been mentioned on this stage tonight."

For a moment there was silence in the hall. Truth, bluntly spoken, is uncomfortable. But after the pause a small applause rose up in the hall, tentative but firm. His words were memorable, but they left one question unanswered.

How?

* * *

After the debate, I met Jeffrey at the hotel bar.

"How did I do?" he wanted to know.

"Jeffrey, I think you stood out. You told them to park their dreams. You told them to listen to Republicans. And you told them their retirement was dead unless Washington can do something it has not been able to do for the last 30 years.

Jeffrey smiled. "I knew they needed something different. Max, your problem is that you spend all your time reading these polls. You ask people what they want, and they want a free lunch."

"My point exactly," I answer.

"But even though they want that free lunch, even though they raise their hand and ask for it, even demand it, they have lived in this world, some of them for a long time, and they also know something else."

"What is that?"

"There's a catch. There's always a catch, and if it sounds so great it might not be true. Sometimes the greatest tragedy is getting what you want."

"Jeffrey, you are making all this too complicated."

"Maybe so. But these voters are confused. They are reacting to some sentence read to them by an interviewer in India working for a buck-50 an hour. Max, there is a difference between a politician and a leader. A politician mimics what the voters said in the poll. A leader shows the voter something she hardly considered. He lifts the voter. He empowers her. He holds her hand and leads her to a new and better place.

"Anybody can read a poll. A leader changes the poll."

Right, I thought. And even if all that were possible, how could an inexperienced candidate, whose supporters were so few they could be counted on an abacus, who looked more like a delivery boy than a president, how could this man be the one to deliver the miracle our nation needs?

That question was soon to be answered.

8

Lucy Gilmore

Okay, so Congress had its way. It launched the computer age of voting. Therefore, the next thing I needed to learn was how easy would it be to get inside one of these machines and change the votes. How do you hack a voting machine? Do you need rare tactics and superlative skills? Or could just about anyone do it?

To find all this out I needed an expert. I needed a hacker. We have people at the *Post* who help with these things. They asked, "Black hat or white hat?"

I smiled. "Black hat, of course."

So here was my guy. He was about six feet tall and as skinny as a cat burglar in a prison break. He had an earring in his ear (only the left one) and a ring in his nose. His hair was dark and stringy and he had a goatee that barely covered his pale white skin. His name? Are you ready for this?

His name was Z-Doo.

It wasn't his real name, of course, but when you hack for money, secrets, or the joy of destruction, you don't have a real name, at least not one you would share with a reporter for *The Washington Post*. I told him my interview was completely off the record and that all I wanted to learn was about voting machines and how easy they are to hack.

He responded with a smile, almost a sneer, and said, "If you want to know about how easy it is to hack voting machines, Miss Gilmore, all of that is a matter of public record."

"What do you mean?" I asked.

Apparently, there is an annual hackers conference in Las Vegas.

It all started with a gnarly group of computer nerds who didn't shower so much, used bad language, and got together every year to trade secrets and plot the collapse of major American institutions. Well, that was 25 years ago. Now, it is something else. The Def Con Conference. It is hackers. It is anybody with a network who is scared as hell of getting hacked. It is white hats, black hats, and everything in between. The conference takes place at Caesar's Palace in Las Vegas. And listen to this: 22,000 people showed up last year.

Holy Jesus. Who knew?

So at this conference are events and forums covering all sorts of topics. And in 2017 somebody decided it would be fun to set up an event called "Voting Village" where hackers were invited to hack voting machines. Everything would be fair game. They placed on the floor versions of all the voting machines currently in use. Anyone could walk in the door, pick one out, and try to hack it. Anyone!

"So what was the result?" I asked Z-Doo, a little afraid to hear the answer.

He straightened in his chair, puffed out his chest, and with a glimmer in his eye, answered, "Those machines were like Custer at Little Big Horn. Not a single one survived."

"None?" I gulped.

Within two minutes three of the machines were goners. Two minutes! Within a few hours every machine was under hacker control. These hackers were not briefed. They had no information on the architecture or programs of these devices.

"Can I tell you some really bad news?" Z-Doo asked.

"You mean it gets worse?"

Z-Doo just smiled and explained that many of these machines contained security defects that had been identified as long as a decade ago, yet hundreds of them were still in use. Many of these devices were touchscreen machines that keep no paper records. So if someone managed—"managed" being a word that overstates the difficulty—to control these machines and change the vote counts, then there would be no discovering the crime or the culprit.

"Did you hack one?" I asked Z-Doo.

"Too easy," he snickered. "Did you hear about the kids?"

"Kids?"

"The next year they invited children to hack state voter registration sites."

As Z-Doo explained it, the Voting Village invited 39 children aged 8 to 17 to take a crack at hacking simulations of state voter registration sites.

"One of them, Bianca Lewis, wore a T-shirt that said, 'No Time for Barbie, I've Got Hacking to Do,'" Z-Doo explained. "These kids were told to pick a state and go to work. The first one to break through, 11-year-old Audrey Jones, did so in 10 minutes. Before the day was done, 35 of the 39 children had successfully hacked one of the state websites."

When I first heard about hacking voter registration sites, I thought, *Who cares? You can buy a voter list.* But then I learned that hacking a voter registration site allows the hacker to remove the names of voters most likely to vote the wrong way. Want to hurt Democrats? Remove 20,000 African American voters selected randomly across the state. Want to hurt Republicans? Erase the membership roster of the Heavenly Hills Country Club and 25 other clubs promoting similar social intercourse.

These voting machines, these voter registration databases, they are the walls protecting our democracy. They are walls of straw, and it doesn't require a wolf to blow them down. It's hard not to wonder if a hummingbird with asthma might do the job.

So my next thought was this: Who would benefit most from this Voting Village? That one's easy. Election officials. Right? By understanding how easy it was to hack their machines and enter their websites, surely they would be better prepared to defend our democracy.

I asked Z-Doo, "Were there any election officials in attendance?"

He laughed out loud. "What do you think?" he answered.

It turns out that Def Con invited 6,600 election officials from all over the nation to come and participate in this investigation of their work. Barely 100 attended. Invitations were sent to the 51 secretaries of state or equivalent positions in the 50 states and the District of Columbia.

How many attended?

Only one. Alex Padilla of California.

9

Max Parker

When Jeffrey Scott told me what he had decided to do, I thought he was crazy. His idea was so strange, so stupid that I refused to even help.

He wanted to attend the Tea Party Nation meeting in Orlando, Florida, and speak to them about "common ground." He asked for an invitation. He did not even get a reply, but I am sure their laughter was so loud it was heard in at least six foreign nations.

Since they would not let him speak, he decided to go to their meeting, set up a podium with a mic and portable speaker on the sidewalk, and talk to the participants as they entered the building. His main topic? How we reduce the number of abortions in America.

His choice of the Tea Party Nation was, to me, an astounding failure of political judgment. Common ground? The only ground that interested these Tea Party zealots was somewhere they could bury Democrats, every single one. But Jeffrey Scott was not interested in my opinion. He was polite. He was respectful, as I presented all my arguments, every one backed by polling, news reports, and the conventional wisdom of the day. He smiled with the patience of a saint, and said he understood my concerns but explained that he was going to do this anyway.

What had I gotten into?

Jeffrey got on a plane, flew to Orlando, and brought a video photographer with him.

* * *

There he stood, behind a podium with a "Jeffrey Scott for President" yard sign neatly taped to the front. He planted his podium directly in the walkway leading to the entrance of the Amway Center, the 6,000-seat arena where the Tea Party activists were assembling. He spoke into a mic connected to a small square speaker that stood at his feet. His eyes were respectful, his words full of passion.

"I am a candidate for president who believes that even though we don't agree on many issues, we can still work together to achieve progress."

As he spoke, a security officer approached to ask him to remove his podium. As he was making his request, Scott's video guy put a hand on the officer's shoulder and told him that to remove a presidential candidate was likely to become big news. It was better for the meeting if he let him speak. So he did.

The sidewalk was crowded with thousands of activists making their way to the meeting. Few recognized Jeffrey Scott. Most walked by thinking him some crackpot. But a few stopped to hear his message.

Now Jeffrey Scott was speaking about abortion.

"Abortion is a great moral issue of our day. Most of you believe abortion to be the murder of a child and I respect your right to hold that belief. I, along with millions of other Americans, believe that the issue of when life begins is a religious one, as to which each American must be given the right to make a personal decision."

A smattering of boos arose from the audience.

"But we can all agree that we must act to reduce the number of abortions. We can find common ground in making abortion less necessary."

The reaction was mixed. Some onlookers seemed interested. Others were distrustful.

"Murder is not a choice," came a cry from the audience.

"More money for Planned Parenthood! Is that what you want?"

But Jeffrey Scott was hard to rattle. He said simply, "You want to save these babies. You want to stop this murder. We have been screaming at each other for decades. What if we worked together? What if we had a conversation. We could save lives."

"No birth control for little girls!"

The shouting grew. Jeffrey Scott could hardly be heard.

His video staffer looked at Scott and signaled to cut his speech. But Scott would not be silenced. He waited for the shouts to quiet and began again.

"We can share a goal. We can save these babies."

Suddenly, through the air came a brick, striking Scott squarely in the face. He dropped to his knees. The crowd surged forward to see. The lone security guard ran to call for medical help. The brick thrower, Luigi Romano, ran, almost unnoticed, from the scene.

10

Lucy Gilmore

I start every day with the same routine. I go to the *Bleed Cubbie Blue* message board, check on the score, and trade comments with my fellow fans. The best part of the day, unless they lose.

A lot of people ask me, "Why are you so fanatical about the Chicago Cubs? You have never even been to Chicago. They are better now but have a long history of losing. What's all this about?" It's about the Billy Goat Curse. Let me explain.

You see, 70 years ago, a wealthy tavern owner in Chicago brought his goat to a game. The goat, his name was Murphy, smelled so bad they threw them both out. The tavern owner placed a curse on the team. He said they would never win another pennant. No one thought much of his threat at the time. But for the next seventy years, guess what? The did not win a single one.

Sure, it's nice if your team wins all the time. But money can buy great players and great players make it look easy, and what's the fun of that? But what if your team is battling not only against limited talent and mismanagement but against history itself? What if the past is filled with ghosts that haunt every game, explain every shortcoming, and darken every glimpse of the future?

Heroes are not the ones who collect a big check and make everything look easy. Heroes are the players who struggle against the odds, who overcome their demons and who find a path to victory that others dismiss. It's not the people with a head start who change the world. It is the unexpected victory that turns the world on its head.

So, of course, in 2016, when the Cubs won the World Series, it was one of the biggest days of my life. That old curse was dead. And it was dead because if you believe, if you battle your demons, if you stick to your mission and never give up, one day your victory will come.

At least that is what I believe.

But this particular morning I was thinking about another mission. I was thinking about the Def Con conference and what I had learned. Voting machines massacred by second-rate hackers. Children breaking into state voter registration sites. Election officials absent. One secretary of state in attendance.

But these absences, disappointing though they were, paled in comparison to the most shocking absentee of all.

The voting machine companies.

So here were these hackers making their products look like the most pathetic attempt at technology since the Hindenburg fell from the sky. You would think the companies would be embarrassed. You would think they would be scared. You would think they would be working night and day to discover and correct the flaws in their very own work product.

You would think.

But there was not one single representative of any voting machine company in attendance at the Voting Village.

Not one.

It wasn't because they did not know what was taking place. In the midst of the Voting Village fiasco, they sent a message to their customers. Listen to this.

"Physical security measures make it extremely unlikely that an unauthorized person, or person with malicious intent, could ever access a voting machine."

Ever? Puh-leeze.

So there are three companies that dominate the voting machine business: Election Day, Inc., in Omaha, Commonwealth in Canada, and a smaller company in Austin. Election Day, Inc. and Commonwealth have about 80 percent of the market.

When Congress held a hearing to question these companies about the shortcomings of their products, two of the three leading companies refused to even attend.

Their message? "We are above supervision. We are above Congress. We are above the law."

We pay them billions of dollars and what do we get?

Sitting ducks.

And a big Bronx cheer.

11

Max Parker

I got the call. It was Jeffrey's number. I feared the worst.

I saw a news report from Orlando and had been calling frantically trying to get through to somebody in the hospital and find out what was going on. He had been hit in the face with a brick for Christ's sake. But now, with all these privacy rules, you can't learn a thing about any friend or relative unless you are one half of a pair of Siamese twins, separated at birth, and you can prove it over the telephone.

Jeffrey's wife and daughter passed away several years ago, his parents were dead, and all that probably meant was that his condition would remain a state secret long after this hospital was bulldozed to the ground.

"Jeffrey, thank God you are alive. How bad is it?"

"Well, it hurts a little. This guy broke my cheekbone and I've got a crack in the orbital lobe of my skull. They put in 11 stiches and my eye is so swollen it may be a week before it opens. They are going to try to keep me here for a week but there is no way. This is our opening."

"Opening?"

"Yeah. We are tracking down the guy who did it. I am going to pay him a visit."

I panicked.

"Jeffrey, lie back down until your brain settles and you come to your senses. Punching this guy would not look good and you can't do it in your current condition."

I heard a chuckle at the end of the line. Jeffrey was apparently so amused that his face was aching from his smile. He could hardly wait to share his plan.

"I am not going to punch him, Max. I am going to forgive him. I am going to show America, and the world, not by words but by deeds, how we bring our country together."

"What if he has another brick?" I asked, a little incredulous.

"I am not worried about that. I am going to his door and offering him forgiveness. Maybe he will hit me, but it is a chance I will have to take."

* * *

By the time he called me, he had already begun his move. He had directed our press secretary, Darla O'Leary, to post the video on social media. Within 20 minutes, we had the name of the brick thrower, Luigi Romano. She called the big hotels and found out where he was staying. A $20 tip produced a room number. Within 15 minutes Jeffrey Scott had changed clothes, quietly departed the hospital, and was on his way to Room 329 of the Hilton Garden Hotel in Orlando, Florida. The press was informed that Jeffrey Scott and his assailant would be making a joint announcement in the lobby of the hotel.

This was the craziest thing I had ever heard or seen in my entire political life.

All I could do was smile.

12

Sheldon Klumm

I am sitting behind my new desk in my new office and for once I am not playing video games. Instead, I am reading the latest edition of *Edge*, one of my favorite video game magazines. This month's issue is full of articles I can't put down.

"Osidian shrinks its ambitions as it makes its Xbox first-party debut with Grounded"

"Valve's digital card game Artifact 'reboot' is so large, it's internally being called Artifact 2, says Gabe Newell"

"High seas steampunk meets avian action in The Falconeer, a gorgeous aerial shooter about 'dealing with your past'"

Does life get any better?

But as I pored through this magazine, I ran across an ad for Play NYC, a video gaming convention that was expected to draw almost 10,000 gamers. They had 165 exhibitors and would feature 147 games. Look at these events.

Exclusive BOSE AR Debuts

Rats, Roaches & Unreal Engine 4

Hot Pepper Shedoza

Dogfight! With Pretrocore Games

So freaking awesome!

Could I miss this? Certainly not. I checked my calendar. Oh my God, this expo was the same week as our voting machine expo in New York. If I could get Jasper to send me, I wouldn't even have to pay.

* * *

I entered Jasper Rittendom's office. He was poring over paperwork.

"Mr. Rittendom, I have an issue worth discussing."

Jasper looked up. His eyes wandered the room.

"Shoot."

"Fred Randolph in sales was talking to me. He said sometimes at the voting machine events the customers are asking about programming. I thought you might need a programmer on the scene, just in case, and I am happy to volunteer for the New York Expo."

"That's strange," Jasper answered. "I thought they mostly ask about theater tickets, dinner reservations, and booze."

"Well, mostly, I suspect. But you never know when a big customer might need to hear from a programmer. We are getting some bad press. All unfair. But there is nothing more reassuring than an answer delivered in language they can barely understand."

"Sheldon, that's what I like about you. You are always thinking ahead. Book a flight. We are staying at the Exclesior."

Woot! Woot!

Of course, the bad news was that I would actually have to show up for our expo. I figured 35 minutes. Tops!

13

Max Parker

There they were on the television screen, standing side by side. Luigi Romano, the Tea Party brick thrower, and Jeffrey Scott, candidate for president. Luigi was a little nervous, looking from side to side, probably worrying if the police might enter the room and carry him away. But Jeffrey was his usual Buddha. All calm. That soft smile and tone of voice that told everyone who saw him that he was a man with love in his heart.

And, of course, a bloodied bandage covering half of his face.

"Mr. Romano and I are here to say that our conflict is over. Mr. Romano has apologized to me and I have forgiven him. What happened this morning speaks to what is happening all across our nation every day. Americans have become angry at each other—so angry it has become difficult to talk. And without talk there can be no hope to save our country.

"In politics the best way to get things done is to learn from each other, to share ideas and find agreement. Can we rescue Social Security without compromise? Can we slow climate change without a thoughtful exchange of ideas? Can we find common ground without first honoring our differences?"

Then Luigi spoke. "When I heard the knock on my door, I was terrified. I thought it was the police ready to take me away. But instead, there stood Jeffrey Scott. I was afraid. I was sure he wanted revenge but instead he offered me his hand and gave me forgiveness."

"I believe abortion is murder. Jeffrey Scott believes it to be a choice. But in a short conversation, without raising our voices we were able to agree on ways the number of abortions might be reduced. But I also learned a lesson far more important than the issues we shout about. I learned that if we can get beyond our differences and find forgiveness in our hearts, America just might become a better place. Thank you, Jeffrey Scott. Thank you so much."

Then both men turned and embraced.

Suddenly, I knew that Jeffrey Scott was a genius. I also knew something else.

Congressman Jeffrey Scott was a nobody no longer.

14

Lucy Gilmore

I was googling for voting machine stories and look what I found. In 2014, Terry McAuliffe, the governor of Virginia, on election day, walked into a voting booth and pressed a button to cast a vote for his friend, Senator Mark Warner. The machine recorded a vote for Senator Warner's opponent. He tried again, and once more that machine displayed a vote for the wrong candidate.

Can you believe it? He is the number one guy in Virginia, but that voting machine was talking back!

Finally, the machine recorded the vote he wanted but you have to wonder. How many times, all across America, did a voting machine record the wrong vote? The answer is that voter testimony about machines changing votes has surfaced in Texas, Mississippi, Georgia, North Carolina, Ohio, Pennsylvania, Tennessee, Colorado, Florida, Virginia, South Carolina, and Illinois. There are cell phone videos recording these events.

So what did these voting machine companies have to say about these issues? They pointed out that, at least in some cases, voters get a paper ballot they can check. Some of the cases. And listen to this.

A study by Georgia Tech Professor Richard DeMillo and Marilyn Marks of the Coalition for Good Governance establised that "in actual polling place settings, most voters do not try to verify paper ballot summaries, even when directed to do so," and that "among those voters who attempt to review their ballots, a statistically significant fraction...fail to recognize errors."

So the question as to these malfunctions, that could be deciding elections all over America, is this. Were these incorrect votes the product of faulty machines or malicious programming? Well, many voting machines are so poorly built that the answer is actually hard to know.

Listen to this.

Many of our voting machines, which are not subject to any national quality standards, are manufactured using the cheapest parts available with little quality control. In 2007, Dan Rather did an hourlong program where he described these problems.

His story began with a report on a 2006 congressional election where the Democrat, Christine Jennings, lost by a few thousand votes. Voters reported that when they pressed Jennings' name, the machine recorded no choice. Hundreds of signed affidavits documented the problem. Those affidavits were supported by the vote count. In one Florida county, Sarasota, 13 percent of the voters cast no ballot in the congressional vote. In the other two counties, which leaned more strongly Republican, the drop-off was less than three percent.

One possible explanation for the poor performance of these machines, according to Rather, is shoddy workmanship. He took his crew to the shanty towns of Manilla in the Philippines where the machines used in Florida were manufactured. There, workers complained of rushed schedules, low wages, and poor quality control. In fact, one worker demonstrated the company's quality control check. He held the machine with both hands and shook it to listen for loose parts. The same worker pointed out that the shaking test was the only quality control check and that it was performed on only a small fraction of the machines. Workers at the factory were paid, on average, less than $3 per day.

Later, a new manager was sent to the factory to improve both quality and production. He identified problems with the touchscreens, which were manufactured by a company in Minnesota. According to the new manager, between 30 and 40 percent of the touchscreens failed their quality control standards. But instead of fixing the problem, the voting machine company continued using these substandard components.

The Rather report also demonstrated how a major voting machine company may have caused the "hanging chad" problem that clouded the 2000 presidential election. Over the protests of their employees, the company management chose to manufacture punch cards using a lower quality, and cheaper, paper. Employees testified that the poor quality of the paper explained the punch card problems in Florida that year. Can you imagine? Our selection of the president of the United States decided by a company decision to save money by manufacturing substandard punch cards.

Did any of these companies pay for shortchanging Americans? Was there any penalty imposed for putting our elections at risk? To my knowledge, the only consequence was that they made more money.

A voting machine company can sell the cheapest, lowest quality machines to any state or county. The Republicans have blocked all legislation that would have set uniform quality standards to protect our democracy.

Their argument? State rights.

The right of States to leave our elections undefended.

Is that in the Constitution? You gotta ask.

15

Max Parker

Every newscast in America showed the Jeffrey and Luigi show. It had everything an audience could want. A dark deed. Reconciliation. Love. Forgiveness. And even suspense because the audience, having witnessed what happens when Republicans and Democrats get together, were sure Jeffrey would pull out a semi-automatic Glock and blow Luigi's brains out. And those who don't watch television news saw it because it was shared, 15 million times, by Americans who could not believe that courtesy and respect had mysteriously returned to American politics even for a 10-minute moment.

The whole episode did more than propel Jeffrey Scott into the limelight. He suddenly surged to 18 percent in the polls. Not first place. Not second place. Third place. But compared to last place, number three was feeling pretty damned good.

As I was considering this stunning development, Jeffrey walked into my office.

"Jeffrey, I guess you saw the new poll. I've got a question for you. How much did you pay Luigi to throw the brick?"

"Minimum wage."

"You cheap bastard."

"It's called fiscal conservatism, my friend."

"So you paid him $7.50."

"In Florida, it's actually $8.46 an hour, but then it only took 10 seconds to throw the brick."

I was laughing.

"Seriously, Jeffrey, did you think something like that would happen?"

"I thought something might happen. And the worse it was, the better for the campaign. We needed something. You can't get luckier than a brick."

When is a brick in the face your lucky day? Well, one thing was becoming clear. Jeffrey Scott was cut from a different cloth.

* * *

There is nothing like a surge in the polls to change your world. The rats were swimming *to* our ship.

Do you know how hard it is to find a good fundraiser when 22 candidates have already skimmed the cream? Well, all of a sudden, it was not so hard at all. Once we hit 18 percent, it wasn't me doing the calling.

"Max, this is Weston Sims. Look, things aren't going so well with the Briley campaign. I was wondering if you were looking for a fundraiser."

"We sure are, Weston. When can you start?"

The truth was that we hardly needed a fundraiser. The money was pouring in. So were the phone calls—people volunteering, people wanting jobs, people asking how to give. And journalists who would not have returned a call one week ago were suddenly begging for interviews. We had a staff of five. Now we needed 55.

We found a new headquarters. Fifteen thousand square feet—seven times what we had before. All those guys selling computers and desks and surge protectors…they were all over us. We were not up to speed but we were 20 percent there. Progress in small bites.

The other problem was debate prep. This time we were not in the second-tier debate. Jeffrey was breathing on the neck of number two. In the last debate, not a single other candidate was even caught looking at Jeffrey.

Now things had changed. This time candidates would not just be looking at Jeffrey. They would be shooting at him and the ammunition would be live. Jeffrey had a target on his back. He was the guy on the rise, and he was an easy target because he was advocating the biggest sin in American politics today.

Compromise.

Primaries are decided by what is known in politics as "the base." Who is the Democratic base? They are, frankly, a bunch of neo-socialists who want to ban the internal combustion engine, tax capital gains at 40 percent, break up Google, and guarantee jobs for every American – whether they want them or not.

But now that you know where Jeffrey stood in this race, let me tell you about all those other schmucks running in the first tier.

In first place was Lewis Ladner, a fire-breathing populist senator from the state of North Carolina. He was checking in at 27 percent in the polls. His favorite address was Wall Street. He had a line. A good one. "Congress does not regulate Wall Street. Wall Street regulates Congress." Democrats jump out of their chairs every time he says it.

Those one percent of the population who own all the wealth and earn all the money? Lewis loves them as well. He loves them because when he gets on stage, he brings his baseball bat and beats the crap out of them. They are responsible for poverty, home foreclosures, cruelty to animals, meningitis, homelessness, prescription drug prices, and college tuitions that no one can afford. His list would be longer, but in a debate, where you only get one minute to answer, you can only blame the one percent for so many things.

There was a reason why Lewis Ladner was in first place. Lewis understood something about politics. Politics is all about emotion. Some political scientist down at Emory University did some research about politics and the brain. His name is Drew Weston. He put all these sticky things with wires on people's heads and then handed them something about politics to read. Then he looked at his computer to see which parts of the brain processed political information.

Well, the minute an individual reads the word "vote" or "candidate" or even "government," the whole frontal cortex, the part of the brain that processes reason and other advanced thinking, actually shuts down and the amygdala starts shooting fireworks. The amygdala is one of the more primitive parts of the brain. It deals with emotions—fear, anger, love, and hate. It was probably guiding human behavior long before early man learned to add two and two. Apparently, and unfortunately, it is still guiding political behavior today.

Next there was Christine Holloway. If you were measuring candidates by their qualifications, she would have been in first place going away. She started out as governor of Pennsylvania, a moderate who was re-elected by a big margin. She was in the Senate until she got appointed Treasury secretary. She had a master's in economics from Wharton. But qualifications ain't what they used to be. Hell, in Alabama, a guy who preyed on high school girls, stole from his charitable foundation, and got thrown off the Supreme Court for not reading the Constitution, all of those things, and he still got 48.5 percent of the vote in an election for US Senate. Why? Because he was not a Democrat. Who cares if you are a Rhodes Scholar? You don't need an IQ of 50 to take orders from your party leaders.

Anyway, Christine Hollloway was whip smart, middle of the road but a little cautious. And being cautious was not all that helpful in this create-a-moment internet news world. She was also African American, which, in the Democratic primaries, added to her luster. She was running about 20 percent in the polls.

After that the field fell off. There was Jake Stillman. Openly gay, married to a man, Harvard MBA, governor of Vermont. Then there was Howard Rimmler, hedge fund operator, billionaire (aren't they all?), whose lead issue was climate change. There was a governor from Montana who had actually been shot by a right-wing lunatic but wasn't making gun control his big issue, probably because he didn't want to be shot again.

Other candidates included Clark Hammerschmidt, a pretty boy senator from Wisconsin. Women hoped he would stay on the

TV screen all night, but if he did he would wear out his welcome because his rap was a little on the light side. Next, Senator Grace Tiller, a policy wonk from Massachusetts with 500-page plans on every conceivable issue. Now that we were raising money, I could hire a researcher to read them. Thank God.

Is that enough?

What has America become? It's kind of like a banana republic where 20 would-be dictators are all planning a coup but no one is good enough to pull it off.

Anyway. Enough of my ranting. Let's get to the event.

* * *

The second debate took place in Cleveland, Ohio, at the Rock and Roll Hall of Fame. Once again, a room full of donors. The moderator, Chuck Laguens of ABC. The questioners, Cindy Brumfield of Facebook and Janet Blake of PBS. Each candidate had two minutes for an opening statement. Lewis Ladner, leading in the polls, got the first shot.

Ladner did not open with a smile. His expression was angry. His eyes said we are rudderless on a sea of tragedy and our boat is taking water. Ladner was a robust man, with a body shaped like a hogshead barrel, stout with spindly legs. His suit, not a designer model, sagged across his frame, wrinkled and loose. His still brown hair was too long, falling over his ears on the side, and he had a small scar on his left cheek, the story of which he was known to tell in various versions in bars all along the primary trail.

He leaned forward and began with a tremor in his voice.

"In America, the middle class is fighting to survive, and that struggle is not going well. In the last 30 years, your income has stayed stagnant while the price you pay for essentials, food, gas, clothing has inched steadily upward. Meanwhile, almost all the wealth our nation has created, wealth we all helped create, is being taken by the richest one percent of Americans.

"All this money owned by the top one percent has now entered our political system, corrupting its rules and bribing our leaders to give the super-wealthy an even greater advantage over those who have little or nothing at all. Our children's path to progress is blocked. Blocked by tuition rates that place a college education beyond the means of the average American family. Meanwhile, fraud has become a business model and greed a religion.

"My campaign is not about a few new policies. It is about taking back our government. Prying it from their greedy little hands. It is about breaking the billionaires' power so that Americans can earn a fair and comfortable wage. It is about giving you affordable health care and giving your children a fair shot at the American dream. My campaign is about more than righting wrongs. It is about rewriting the rules so that every American can share in our nation's success and no one class of Americans will be allowed to rig our system, cheat their workers, and use our government to feather their own beds at your expense. Change. Big change is what the Lewis Ladner campaign is all about."

The applause was thunderous. He knew how to do it.

Next came Christine Holloway, her business suit perfectly pressed, her hair perfectly coiffed, her posture formal and stiff. Unlike Ladner she smiled, a nice easy smile that seemed too nice given all the anger these voters felt.

"Ladies and gentlemen, I cannot compete with the eloquence of the esteemed senator from North Carolina. If Americans were choosing an orator, the good senator might win hands down. But we are not choosing an orator; we are choosing a president.

"My preparation for this office includes eight years as governor of Pennsylvania during which I was re-elected by a large margin. It includes seven years as a United States senator and three as secretary of the Treasury. I know what it means to govern a state, to pass a bill in Congress, and to help lead an administration. I too am alarmed by the state of our economy in which the rich get richer and the rest of us struggle.

"I am calling for A New American Capitalism that will demand more taxes from Americans who make the most money, less taxes on those who don't, and changes that include access to college for all Americans, Medicare for all, new initiatives to slow climate change, a higher minimum wage, and, yes, generous paid family leave for working Americans. I have the experience, I have the vision, and I have the best chance of any Democrat at this event tonight of beating the Republicans in November."

Well, no surprise here. Ladner talked about the voters. Holloway talked about herself. You don't have to wonder why he was ahead.

Now for the curveball. My candidate, Jeffrey Scott. We practiced this opening many times. I was always telling him not to lower expectations. By the time he finished compromising with Republicans, expectations among our Democratic audience were below sea level.

Jeffrey Scott was standing at the podium, as calm as if he was discussing the weather with an old friend. He looked better. We sent him to a tailor and got him a new suit. Somebody who actually knew what he was doing was cutting his hair. He no longer looked like an intern. Some of it was the aura of running third in the polls. But did he look like a president? Not close.

But there was something dramatic about Jeffrey Scott that night. It was the bandage, no longer bloody although adding some blood was discussed. But big and white and still covering half his face, it was a badge. A badge that said this man had courage, this man thought differently, this man was not like the others.

"For the last three weeks, Americans have been asking me questions. They want to know why I would go to a Tea Party convention, to the enemy camp, and talk about reconciliations and compromise. They want to know how I could forgive someone who struck me with a brick, breaking my cheekbone, cracking my skull, and requiring surgery to repair. They ask: Why would I leave the hospital against doctor's orders to approach Luigi Romano and achieve reconciliation? I did these things because if we want to end the culture wars, to calm the hatred and to heal the distrust that divides our nation, we need a president who leads by example.

"We need a president who thinks differently, acts differently, and can take the extraordinary steps it will require to calm the conflicts that are crippling our nation. And when I am president, I will tackle the hard questions that will be barely mentioned in this debate tonight. I will take measures to rescue Medicare from imminent financial collapse. I will find a way to rescue Social Security that is headed for bankruptcy over the next 15 years. I will take a hard look at how we reduce our national debt because if we forgive student loan debt only to saddle our young people with a mountain of government debt, what have we really accomplished?

"I am a Democrat, but we will need Republican ideas to move forward on these issues. Maybe they will improve what we do, maybe not. But they will give us a real chance to actually pass legislation and implement solutions to our toughest problems. The greatest danger facing our nation is not Republican or Democratic ideas. The greatest danger is inaction, paralysis, and gridlock that has crippled our democracy for a decade or more."

This time, Jeffrey Scott won real applause. Not timid or hesitant but not unanimous either. After all, who is in this audience? They are the soldiers of the culture wars. And Jeffrey Scott was telling them to put down their weapons and go home.

Well, there were other nice opening statements. Jake Stillman, the 37-year-old openly gay congressman from Virginia, spoke about young people, the debt we are leaving them, the climate they may have to endure. He was refreshing, practical, and a little outside the normal political blather. But appealing to millennials is a good way to finish last. Their voting turnout in a Democratic presidential primary? Fifteen percent.

Grace Tiller talked about her plans, and to her credit she showed how she would pay for everything: numbers, taxes, and expenses—all of it. But that's all in the frontal cortex. Reason. Thoughtfulness. Advanced thinking. If you don't address that little old primitive amygdala that processes love, hate, anger, and totally ballistic out-bursts of rage, you make it hard for the voter to even remember what you said. Dr. Tiller, who has a PhD, made a lot of sense but garnered few actual votes.

Well, you know what comes next in a presidential debate. Questions about the great problems facing our nation? No way. Opportunities to offer a vision guiding America to a brighter future? Not if you actually answer their questions. No, the next round of questioning was more akin to what happened in Soviet times when you were summoned by the KGB to a small room with one light bulb and a folding metal chair. Here was Janet Blake with the first question to Senator Ladner.

"Senator Ladner, your Republican opponents call you a social-ist. The programs you propose would require massive tax increases. You may be leading in the primary polls but many Democrats indi-cate they will have difficulty voting for you in the fall. Wouldn't your nomination result in certain defeat for the Democrats in November?"

Well, not exactly like a KGB interview. She did not pull out the rubber hose. But while those media types may be as sleezy as we are, their skills are far behind. Here was Ladner's answer delivered with the sweetest smile you ever saw.

"Thank you, Janet. In American politics today, being attacked by Republicans is about the highest compliment a national leader can obtain." Laughter and applause. "I am proud that in this cat-egory of Republican criticism I lead every candidate in this debate and I do so by a wide margin." Applause and laughter. "But Janet, there is something else everyone has to understand.

"We are not talking about adjusting the carburetor to fix an automobile that can still back out of the driveway. We are talking about rebuilding an American economy to serve the middle class of this country, to give their children a chance at a better life and to curb the one percent that would drive this country to destitution and despair just to add a few hundred million to their investment accounts. Big change does make some people nervous. But big change is what America requires.

"My support is growing. And the more voters look at our situation, the more voters will be ready to right what is wrong in this country and restore our nation as a land of opportunity—for everyone—that it once was."

You gotta love Lewis Ladner. She threw a tomato at his face and he handed her back a good-looking club sandwich. Not how it always happened at the KGB.

The rest of the questions were in a similar vein. Stillman, of course, got asked how in the world Americans were going to elect a gay president and whether his husband would join him on the campaign trail. Cheap. Christine Holloway was asked if the financial markets collapsed would she do the same things Obama did or would she handle it differently. If she said different, she would diss Obama. If she said the same, she would endorse policies that, while wildly successful, were wildly unpopular as well.

This was the "gotcha round."

One problem with Jeffrey Scott is that he is clean, at least as far as I know. One of my favorite books is Robert Penn Warren's *All the King's Men.* In it, Willie Stark, the character based on Huey Long, turns to his campaign aide, Jack Burton, who has suggested that someone is clean. Wille says to Jack, "Jack, there's something on everybody. Man is conceived in sin and born in corruption." I believe it. But whatever sins Jeffrey Scott has committed, word hasn't reached me. His question from the moderator, Chuck Laguens:

"Mr. Scott, I appreciate your making this appearance despite the horrible injury you endured. Forgiving your enemy was a beautiful gesture and the result has been a surge in the polls. But a president has to be tough. He has to be feared by our enemies. Do you think you can be tough enough to keep America safe?"

Boy, was that a curveball but a good one.

"Well, Chuck, you have to be tough to take a brick in your face." Laughter. "To be president you also must be smart. You have to know when to stand firm and when to reach out. I know our enemies in Russia, Iran, and North Korea. Dealing with these enemies requires strength and resolve.

"But here at home, our problem is we have become our own worst enemies. Our two political parties are at war while neither has the votes needed to do anything about our problems. If we want progress on the urgent, almost catastrophic problems facing us down the road, we had better calm the waters and find peace at home. That is why I went to the Tea Party convention and offered an olive branch to the other side. In the end, Luigi Romano and I showed Americans that if we can calm down and talk to each other with respect, we can find common ground."

"Congressman Scott, with all due respect, Luigi Romano is not Senate Majority Leader Steve Shaughnessy. Some say finding common ground with one of the most partisan members of Congress is a difficult, if not impossible, goal."

"Chuck, you are right. Luigi Romano sat down with me as a matter of individual conscience. Steve Shaughnessy may be a partisan. He may have a base that will applaud his rejection of any Democrat. But I am confident I can bring him to the table. Because when I lay out, in an honest and urgent way, the problems facing our nation, his absence from the table will exact a large political price. I promise him this. If he won't come to the table, I will lay the pending collapse of Social Security and Medicare at his feet."

Big words but there was calm in his voice and ice in his eyes that said he meant business. His message was forgiveness for the repentant, but the sinners would pay. To this crowd Shaughnessy was a villain. A Darth Vader of the political world. His submission was a delicious thought. The crowd erupted. Jeffrey Scott might sometimes sound like St. Francis of Assisi. But he was willing to be the executioner as well.

The rest of the debate was predictable, at least until they got to the questions submitted by ordinary citizens on Facebook. These were no gotcha questions. They were the questions about Social Security,

Medicare, and the budget deficit—and all of the problems that have become, frankly, in politics, too difficult to address. Forgotten, at least until Grandma starts getting smaller Social Security checks 15 short years from now.

Jeffrey was in fine form. He thanked Facebook users for bringing us back to the real issues, issues that the media had discarded. He pinged the media for their focus on candidate shortcomings and small offenses. He got more applause. Overall, he was different, honest in a frightening but admirable way. He had distinguished himself from the pack.

A big accomplishment. A start. But would it be enough?

16

Sheldon Klumm

There I was in New York City, all ready to check out the video game exposition at the Javits Center. Ten thousand people. I could hardly keep my underwear dry.

But before I could feast on this cornucopia of dazzling cyber adventure, the old world reared its ugly head. I was expected, since they were paying for the trip, to make a few token appearances at the voting machine exposition. The exposition is an annual event where all the voting machine companies go to show their shiny new machines, and all these election officials show up not because they are interested in the machines but because we buy them theater tickets, meals at fancy restaurants, and lots of booze. As I understand it, these characters can really drink.

Okay, time to get my geek on. At this exposition I was standing around some of our machines and answering questions. There were maybe a few hundred American election officials in attendance, but I noticed some European visitors as well.

Did you know that most European countries don't even use voting machines at all? England? No. Netherlands? No. Ireland? They tried it and quit in 2010. Germany? They tried it in a small way, but their Supreme Court ruled voting machines unconstitutional! So freaking unbelievable.

But many of these visitors were from Eastern Europe and, unlike the Americans, they actually knew something about our stuff. In fact, they knew a lot.

Instead of asking about restaurant reservations and show tickets, they wanted to know what programming language we used. They asked which states our company serviced, when we did the programming, and what security features our machines used. And most surprising of all, some of them even asked about me.

This man walked up to me, his name was Ivan Kosolov. He said he was "Eastern European" but he sounded kind of Russian. When I told him I was the final quality control officer for the voting machine programming for Election Day, Inc., he got excited. He asked me if I finalized the programming for all our 28 states.

"That's my job," I answered.

Then he asked about specific states. He knew all our states and what equipment they used. I told him I looked at all the code before it went to the states. It would be hard for anyone to cheat, at least someone other than us. And Ivan was being really nice so before he left, I invited him to our Election Day, Inc. reception at 6:30 at the Plaza. He raised his eyebrows at that one. A voting machine company from Omaha doing an event at the Plaza. He promised to show.

* * *

For a guy who grew up in Mulberry, Ohio, the Plaza is something to see. I like the entrance with those six columns and red carpet and that fancy overhang that lets you get out of your car and not get rained on. Everywhere columns, chandeliers, and marble floors. A big step up from anything in Omaha, that's for sure.

I walked into our reception, thinking I would make a token appearance and then head to the Javits Center and check out some games. And as I looked around who do I see but my new friend Ivan Kosolov, and standing next to him was probably the most beautiful woman I had ever seen in my whole life—maybe three lifetimes if I could get them.

Oh my God!

I walked across the room to thank Ivan for stopping by but I could not take my eyes off this woman and could only stutter when I tried to speak. I can barely describe this pinnacle of beauty. She was a little tall but not too much, maybe five-foot-seven. She was blonde, not that dirty blonde you see so often in Omaha. Her hair was almost white. She wore it in a way that reminded me of the '50s. It rose at the top of her head and curved downward almost in the shape of a heart. The face? OMG! She had these eyes that had a horizontal shape, two perfect lines, long lashes, and right there in the middle of each, a perfect circle of sapphire blue. Her lips followed the same straight line but were tempered by their round, plump shape. She could not have been 30, but she could not have been 20 because there was a worldliness about her that said she had been a few places. She looked at me and actually smiled.

Maybe most guys would see a woman like that and leap across the room like an Olympic broad jumper about to set a new world record. But me? My feet were nailed to the take-off board.

But Ivan had his eyes on me and gave me a big smile and squeezed my shoulder. This woman looked at me like I was the most interesting person she had met all day.

Ivan turned to this stunning blonde and said, "Nadia, this is the man I was telling you about. Nadia, meet Sheldon Klumm. Sheldon, meet Nadia Fedorov. Nadia is studying American voting machines and needs someone to help her along."

"P- P- Pleased to meet you," I stuttered.

"Oh, the honor is all mine, Mr. Klumm. May I call you Sheldon?"

"Yes," I said but in a voice that suggested I had just sucked the air out of a helium balloon. My knees were shaking, and my real voice had fled the scene.

"I'll leave you two to talk." Ivan turned and left me with a wink.

What was I to do?

But Nadia sensed my nervousness, terror in fact, and proceeded to bring calm to my condition. She asked how I had risen to such a respected and important position. She asked about Omaha and where I grew up and what sports teams I liked. I told her the Dodgers because their color was the same as her eyes. So stupid! But she laughed as if she thought it was the funniest and most flattering compliment she had ever received. She told me she was from Ukraine and worked for the state in their new Department of Elections.

"We will buy thousands of voting machines," Nadia said.

So I told her all about our machines and that paper ballots were a relic and that the new touchpad machines were what she wanted. She listened intently and nodded at all I said.

Then she reached over and put her hand on mine and said, "Why don't we get away from this crowd and go someplace quieter, more intimate?"

The word "intimate" had the effect of my body being touched by a pair of live jumper cables. Was she coming on to me? Wherever this was headed I was sure to fail. But she took my hand and led me from the room to the restaurant downstairs. At the entrance, the maître d' nodded at Nadia and led us to a table where two candles burned, in the back corner of the room. And when the waiter arrived, Nadia ordered a fancy French wine I could not even pronounce, and I ordered "the same" because surely any wine I knew had no place in this restaurant. And after she finished her foie gras and I downed my burger, she leaned across the table and said, "Sheldon, would you like to have some fun?"

Fun. Another jumper cable word. I suppressed a scream. But what could I say? *Go away, you homely bitch?* I nodded, my mouth open, my eyes showing all the calm of a man who has encountered an angry cobra and has five minutes to live.

"My room is upstairs," she whispered.

She took my hand and guided me out of the restaurant and to the elevator. As the doors met, leaving us alone, she turned, pressed her body against mine, and planted a long, wet kiss on my lips. As she pulled back, she gave me a smile as if my kiss was a new and profound sensual experience.

In the room, I faced my moment of truth. I had not had sex with a woman in a decade. And why would she want sex with me? I was confused, baffled, but mostly terrified.

She undressed me slowly as I nervously waited for little Pedro to rise to this extraordinary occasion. She removed her own clothes and her body was like a chiseled Venus, her breasts ample and with nipples rising upward to attention. Her shape was an hourglass, her legs only slightly thin, her shoulders delicate and white.

And what was my reaction? Little Pedro only sagged, his head drooping in a posture of shame.

But Nadia hardly blinked. She knelt before me and began licking Pedro like he was Reese's Peanut Butter ice cream on a stick. And after a long wait Pedro rose, perhaps in a bewildered effort simply to understand what the hell was going on. Nadia nudged me back onto the bed and slid me inside. Ten seconds later we were done.

Then, to my utter surprise, she laid at my side, stroking my chest, and said in her beautiful Ukrainian accent, "Sheldon, you are such a beautiful and interesting man. Can we see more of each other?"

17

Lucy Gilmore

I was waiting at the reception desk for my meeting with Peyton Bailey, king of the Democratic mail consultants and pioneer of the database targeting that has taken over American politics.

Peyton was less an innovator than a shrewd observer who acted on what he saw. In the late '80s and early '90s, database marketing was transforming the retail transaction. Millions of catalogs and letters pitching credit cards, insurance offers, and probably even mail order brides were dropping into homes across America.

What was making these mailings so successful? Data. Data and its statistical analysis could predict who was likely to buy from your catalog and how much that customer might spend. To support these efforts giant databases were assembled estimating the income, race, length of residence, marital status, number of pets, and hundreds of other data points for more than 100 million households.

Bailey was fascinated by the new marketing and thought, *Why not politics?* So he pitched this new approach to targeting, wrote a book, and became an evangelist for the new methods. It took him 12 years to win adoption but now he was a star. And if you work for the *Washington Post* you can always get an interview with anyone— unless, of course, the guy you want is the subject of some scandal or criminal proceeding.

I walked into his office. He was in his 60s and had beady eyes that sparkled when he talked. He left his desk to sit across the coffee table and begin.

"I want to start by denying all involvement in the scurrilous events you are investigating." He had a soft southern accent.

I laughed. "Mr. Bailey, I am investigating scurrilous events, but I am sure you are not involved. I need your help to get to the bottom of it all."

"Well, tell me more."

"I have come to believe that voting machines are being manipulated to change the outcomes of elections in this country."

I then described election night in South Carolina almost two years ago. I described the Def Con Conference that demonstrated how easy it was to hack these machines. I walked him through the barriers to proving my claim.

"You have looked at more voting data than probably anyone in politics," I continued. "Somewhere in that data there must be clues. Let's assume that the Republicans are fixing the numbers. Is there anything in the election returns that would suggest something is going on?"

Bailey's eyes twinkled and his right hand massaged his chin. For a moment he was silent. Then he spoke.

"First, I would not be surprised if you are right. Those Republicans, many of them, are ruthless.

"Second, there is a way to look for problem elections. All of the major elections now have exit polls. The exit polls use big samples. They only poll people who actually vote so there are no undecideds or non-voters in the mix. If there is a big difference between the exit polls and the actual results, that would be a clue that something was going on."

"Where would I find these exit poll results?" I asked.

"Well, that is a problem. The National Exit Poll, which is hired by most of the major news networks, publishes their initial findings shortly after the polls close. Then, when the returns come in they adjust their numbers so they match the actual vote count. Seems like cheating to me but it appears no one is complaining.

"You would have to find the initial exit polls results and not the ones they still publish today. If the actual election results were very different from the first exit poll prediction, that would be some evidence that something is going on."

"Where do I get those numbers?" I asked.

"They might be hard to find."

"Can you help?"

"Maybe," he answered. "It would be in service to democracy itself."

I was holding my breath.

"Let me see what I can do."

I hurried home, hopeful but not optimistic. Maybe someone else would have these numbers. This was a new lead. It was something.

When I arrived at my apartment, I had an email from Peyton Bailey. In the attachment were initial exit poll predictions from 301 Senate, gubernatorial, and state presidential elections from 2004 to 2016.

* * *

There was no point in sleeping that night. I went online and found the actual election returns for each of the 301 races. I entered them into an Excel spreadsheet and compared predictions with the actual results. It was a little confusing. In many races the exit polls were spot on. But there were other races where the Republican candidates outperformed the exit polls by three, four, and even five percentage points. Some races shifted to the Democrat but there was definitely more Republican movement.

Not most but a significant number.

In the 2014 governor's race in Wisconsin, the exit poll showed Walker losing by .3 percentage points. On election day he won by 5.7. A six-point shift.

In the 2004 Ohio presidential race, exit polls showed Kerry a two-point winner. When the votes were counted, Bush won by two points.

And in the 2014 Kentucky Senate race, the incumbent went from an exit poll lead of seven points to an election victory margin of 15 points.

I tried to grab a couple of hours sleep before work, but it was hard. My head was full of numbers. Frustrating numbers that were whispering in my ear.

How to make sense of them I did not know.

18

Max Parker

Right after the second debate, we went into the field and polled Democratic primary voters. The results were reported in a campaign meeting and conference call in our shiny new offices not three blocks from K Street, the notorious location of lobbyists and power brokers.

There were so many new faces that we needed introductions.

"Can we go around the table and each person tell us your name, your role here, and the strangest thing you have ever done?" I said, opening the meeting.

I always like the oddball question to loosen up the group. This one got nervous laughter.

"Greta Simmons, MCQ Research. Pollster. I once cheated on a Latin test in college."

"Stephanie Little, Political Intelligence. Research. I once went to a costume party in Manhattan dressed as Mother Goose."

"Jones O'Leary, political director. I once voted for a Republican."

Raucous boos from around the table.

"Only kidding," Jones added.

And so the staff continued until all had finished. I opened the meeting.

"All right team, this is the first full meeting of the leadership staff of the hottest candidate in this race for the Democratic nomination. And a few weeks after listening to some of the dumbest ideas I have ever heard, I would like to pronounce Jeffrey Scott as one of the smartest candidates I have ever met."

Chuckles.

"Now, what we have all been waiting for, Greta is going to share the results of our post-debate poll. Very interesting numbers. Greta."

"Right. Interesting candidate, interesting message, interesting numbers. Let's start with the horse race."

Greta, short, round, 50ish, with curly hair, perfect eyebrows, and eyes that dart around the room. She had the energy of popcorn in a souped-up microwave. She grabbed her clicker. The PowerPoint appeared.

"This poll was conducted only among potential Democratic primary voters. Numbers across the electorate will be different." She snapped. "Ladner: 31 percent. Holloway: 20 percent. Scott: 19 percent. Stillman: 7 percent. Rimmler..."

"One percent!" someone shouted, using Lewis Ladner's favorite two words to refer to our hedge fund manager who was certainly worth billions.

"Okay, okay," Greta responded, smiling. "He has four percent. Everyone else is groveling around at one or two. If you believe the public polls, we have hardly moved at all. But our numbers show some strength. Among our supporters, 72 percent say their support is very strong, the best number among the three leaders. Ladner's voters like him a lot. He is at 69 percent, very strong. Holloway's strong support is tepid: 55 percent."

Greta moved to the central question in the race.

> In thinking about the race for the Democratic nomination for president, do you prefer someone who stands by principle and opposes the Republican agenda, almost across the board, or do you prefer a candidate who reaches out to

Republicans and compromises to shape legislation that can actually pass?

"Principle? 57 percent. Compromise? 38 percent."

Stephanie, with our research firm, raised her hand. "Well,
if more people want someone who will fight for principle, why is
Scott's favorability higher than his unfavorable?"

"I think it is because people like him for who he is as a person.
He's different. He's honest. But when push comes to shove will they
vote to give him the nomination? That could be a bigger lift," Greta
added with the tact of a pollster who had assuaged candidate egos
for the last 25 years.

Quiet around the table.

"Another thing we tested was compromise in real life. Let's
start with Social Security. Here is the question."

> Right now, Social Security is projected to
> become insolvent in 15 years. Imagine that the
> Democrats and Republicans sat down and com-
> promised on a plan that could extend the current
> program for an additional 20 years. The plan
> would bolster the program with more money
> now and allow citizens to voluntarily put up to
> 10 percent of their Social Security withholding
> in qualified private investment accounts. The
> plan would increase the retirement age by two
> months every year until it reaches 70.

"Anyone want to guess the level of support?" Greta asked.

"Sixty-two percent," Maxine Mendelsohn, the fundraising
director, estimated.

"Seventy-one percent," Rick Sampson offered.

Greta paused to let the tension build. Then she delivered the
figure. "Forty-three percent."

Looks of dismay across the room.

"The number is not as grim as it sounds," Greta continued. "Compromise involves hard choices by everyone involved. The undecided on this question is actually 28 percent. So the opposition is only 29 percent. But it underscores the difficulty in front of us.

"Underneath these numbers lies an aversion to an older retirement age. That is the killer, especially for those who are not already in the program. That people would even consider this plan is a little surprising to me."

So there we were. Good news: We were barely out of second place in a large field of candidates. Bad news: The whole idea of compromising with the enemy was making Democratic voters nervous. Politics is the business of telling voters what they want to hear. Jeffrey was telling them something else and a lot of them didn't like it.

19

Lucy Gilmore

Sometimes a girl needs a drink. And sometimes she needs a guy…if he's the right guy…and she can find him. I am not much on the bar scene. I'm also no net lizard. I tried internet dating. A lot of times you get this online cyber chemistry that disappears in person. A lot of times the guy shows up and looks like the pictures he posted were 20 years old.

So it was Friday night. I was alone with all these election numbers that I could barely look at anymore. Time to step out on the town.

My destination was the Showtime Lounge. It sounds like a big extravaganza with a giant band and maybe some Washington, DC, version of the Rockettes. But it is not. It is a dive. A hole in the wall with character.

The bar is located near the hip U Street district, but from the outside, it looks like it belongs in a neighborhood headed in the other direction. It is painted white with one window and "SHOW TIME" painted in blue letters from the '30s after they ditched all the art deco fonts and reverted to a more desperate look.

You open the door and are confronted with bizarre, big-eyed pen and ink portraits of jazz musicians all over the walls. Every Sunday for the last 15 years, customers have been entertained by a punk band, Granny and the Boys, the name surely derived from the fact that "Granny" is now 84 years old.

You can't make this up.

I sat down at the bar and ordered a sangria.

The place was buzzing and they were having music later that night, but there were still some seats at the bar. One of them, the one right next to me, was suddenly occupied by a small Asian guy with some spikes in his hair and eyes that were slightly crossed. But cross-eyed or not, his eyes had sparkle and I noticed there were other seats, but he picked the one next to me.

He looked at me and said, "Pick a song and I will play it for you." He paused. "It's on me."

I smiled. The jukebox is free.

"How about 'Ocean Eyes,' by Billie Eilish?"

He did a double-take. It's a song about a guy who melts a girl with his ocean eyes.

He recovered and smiled. "Good choice," he said. "Save my seat."

When he returned I heard his story. His name was Binky Wong. I asked him where he got the name Binky. He explained that he was born in Taiwan but came here at age three. His Chinese name was Bingwen so his mom started calling him "Binky" for short.

"You should not pick an American name until you've been here a year," he explained, but his smile showed he did not care one bit.

He liked Indian food and baseball. But when I mentioned the Cubs, his eyes narrowed. Dodgers fan. He had a master's from UCLA and worked at the National Institute of Health as a "biostatistician." In a more polite way, I asked what the hell was that. He explained that he used advanced statistics to predict the behavior of tiny pieces of DNA.

You gotta respect someone who works at a job too complicated for you to understand.

Then it was my turn and my story and I gave him the basics. He asked where I worked, and I told him the *Post*. His eyes lit up. Then he asked me a question, not the usual question about best stories or biggest stories but a question more personal that gave me a window into who he might be.

"What was the story, out of everything you have written, that has meant the most to you personally?"

I gulped. My eyes watered. I answered.

"I haven't written it yet."

And I don't have to tell you what we talked about for the next hour.

So, as the band struck up and conversation got harder, he leaned toward me with this expression of hopefulness and mirth and said, "Why don't we go back to your place and look at those numbers?"

Such a cheesy line but I loved it. And I was liking him too.

We went straight to my apartment. And when he left the next morning, he took all those exit poll numbers and promised to return with more numbers still.

"Statistics is the measurement of knowledge," he told me. "Give me a few days and I will tell you what you've got."

* * *

Three days later, that Binky was at my door, a bottle of wine in his hand. He opened the wine and poured two glasses. Handing me mine he said, "You are going to need this."

As we sat down, he pulled out a stack of papers and said, "Let me start by explaining p-values.

"P-values are used by scientists, lawyers, sports teams, pollsters, law enforcement, and even drug companies. Let's say you are doing a drug trial. In your treatment group, half of the participants show improvement. In the control group, only 10 percent do. The p-value looks at sample sizes and differences and computes, scientifically, the likelihood that those differences could be due to random chance."

I was fascinated.

"Really? So let's take an example from my data. In the 2014 Wisconsin governor's race the exit poll shows Scott Walker losing by a half percentage point. But on election day he wins by almost six. Can you tell me the likelihood that he won honestly?"

"Not exactly." Binky was getting a little nervous.

"The p-value just tells you the likelihood that the difference was due to random chance. The actual cause could be voting machine manipulation, it could be flaws in the exit poll methodology. It could be anything. But if your p-value is low it means the difference is probably not accidental. It says something is probably going on.

"But since you bring up Walker, I should tell you that the difference between the exit poll prediction and the election day result was not random chance."

I waited.

"There is a four-tenths of one percentage point probability that that difference could be due to chance."

Holy Jesus. What a guy!

"But overall, there is a lot of variance in the data. It does not look like all the elections are being rigged. But there are definitely some suspicious numbers.

"You asked about John Kerry in Ohio in 2004. The odds that Bush would outperform the exit polls by four percentage points? Less than a percentage point."

He handed me some papers. "Here are all the elections ranked by the likelihood that the result could be due to random chance. I will send you the excel file."

I had one question I had been waiting to ask.

"So Binky, overall across all these elections, what is the difference between exit poll predictions and Republican performance at the polls?"

"Only one percentage point."

My heart sank. Proof was ever elusive. But Binky came to the rescue.

"What if one in five elections are manipulated," he explained, "and looking at the data the number is probably even less. But let's say one in five elections were rigged and the average rigged election shifted the margin by five points. And let's say the other four elections averaged out to no shift at all. What is your overall shift? One percentage point. Exactly what this data shows."

"But if it is only one point, how confident can you be that something is going on?" I asked.

Binky smiled. "Yes, that is exactly the question. If the shift is only one percentage point how confident can you be that the number is real. If the number is real it is evidence that something is going on."

"So," I interrupted, "what are the odds that this Republican shift could be due to random chance?"

"Lucy, you have a sample of almost six hundred thousand interviews. That huge."

"Give me the number."

"Lucy Gilmore, the probability that that one percentage point is the product of random chance is 42 million to one."

20

Max Parker

The key staff was a little disappointed. The poll showed growth, spectacular growth, from nothing to third place. A lot of Democrats liked Jeffrey Scott. But voters were conflicted. They were human beings, goddamnit. They supported compromise but did not want to give up a thing.

Let's face it. The politicians don't want to deal with the really tough problems and neither do the voters. Talking about what it takes to fix Social Security is a trip to the dentist for two root canals. Let Grandma worry about Social Security. Let the grandbabies deal with the debt. The problem is that if you are over 50 you *are* grandma. And there are so many millennials that if they ever actually caught on to how badly they are getting screwed, they might actually vote. If they did, they would rule the world.

Or at least what is left of it.

For Jeffrey Scott and this one election there was a big problem. How do you get from 20 percent to at least a third of the voters, which is basically what you need to win the Democratic presidential nomination? The unmistakable message of the poll was that there was no clear path to victory.

We should have been discouraged but the staff had not figured the hopelessness of our situation and the consultants were not down. They get paid win or lose, and they kind of liked Jeffrey because he was fresh and different. Fresh. Different. But not president.

So when in doubt, struggling for solutions, what do you do? You call in your media consultant. Ours was a man named Casmir Zielinski.

Casmir was not my choice for this job. He was Jeffrey's choice. A quirky choice. He had never done traditional TV advertising for a big statewide race. His specialty? Internet viral video. But since Jeffrey believed that old-fashioned TV ads were dead, Casmir got the job.

Casmir was tall, with a head of bushy red hair and bright blue eyes. He was not yet 50 years old. His family emigrated from Poland when he was 16 and he had a sly smile with a gap between his two front teeth indicating that he did not make it to America in time to be herded into the orthodontist office. His late arrival resulted in another issue. Studies show that people who have a lot of confidence never lose their accents, and Casmir must have believed he was God himself because even though he had been in America almost 30 years, I could hardly understand a word he said. But when I could understand him, I was usually impressed. He had a different take on the world.

For all his unusual ideas, he had a calm demeanor that suggested that his unconventional tactics just happened to be the most sensible and ordinary course of action any campaign would take. But Casmir would scare most campaigns shitless.

The meeting was me, Jeffrey, and Casmir. We were seated in Casmir's office, a big office with six chairs, a nice walnut desk backed by a battered leather chair. Most consultants cover their walls with photographs of their candidates inscribed with messages attributing all their success to the genius of this advisor. Not Casmir. He had a sly sense of humor.

One day he went out to the Capitol Mall where you can get your picture taken with cardboard cutouts of America's most famous politicians. So Casmir had his picture taken with cardboard versions of Ronald Reagan, Bill Clinton, Hillary Clinton, Dick Cheney, and four or five more. Then he wrote his own inscriptions and hung the photos on his office walls. The Cheney inscription was the best.

> Casmir, you filthy pig! You are filling Congress
> with communists and traitors. When America
> collapses in ruins it will be all your fault. Dick
> Cheney.

You gotta love the guy. He was mooning his entire profession.

We were barely seated, and before anyone could say anything or discuss the meaning of the poll or outline our strategic objectives, Casmir popped a rhetorical question, delivered with a sparkle in his eye.

"Deed you know that you kanz photoshop a veedeo?"

"No," I snapped, believing, foolishly, that strategy comes before technique.

But Jeffrey was intrigued. He knew. He looked at Casmir eagerly, expectantly, and said, "Tell us what you have in mind."

Casmir paused for effect.

"Braveheart," he finally answered.

I looked at Jeffrey and Jeffrey looked at me. Jeffrey's expression was far more optimistic.

We waited.

"Leet me show you," Casmir began.

"Our problem is thees. Our nation is in war. We hate Reepublicans. Reepublicans hate us. Compromise in abstract is fine but in deetails is appalling. The price of peace too high. Our job in thees campaign is to make war more untheenkable than peace. Am I right?"

I nodded. Jeffrey nodded. If nothing else, Casmir may have dropped a few articles and at least one verb but presented our problem in an elegant way.

"Watch thees."

He clicked on his remote and a giant TV screen came to life. The scene was borrowed from some ancient movie. Two medieval armies with swords, spears, and those big spiky iron balls on the end of a chain are racing across a field to hack one another to pieces. There are thousands of them. Thousands and thousands, one side dressed in red, the other side in blue. And as they run, they scream. The sounds of ancient warfare, the roar of battle, almost hysterical in an intensity that makes you want to pull back from the screen. The two armies collide. Thuds, hacks, it is almost unbearable to watch. Camera cuts to two warriors wearing iron helmets and breastplates. They trade blows with giant swords. But there is nothing medieval about the faces of these men. They are familiar. One is the face of Webster Miller, the incumbent Republican president who is not seeking a new term. The second is Lewis Ladner. The contest is brutal, with sword blows severing limbs and splattering blood.

Voiceover: "Washington, D.C. Two parties at war. And what is the result? Social Security is going bankrupt. Medicare insolvent in five years. Middle-class income stagnant. Our younger people inherit a gigantic debt. Who is losing this war? You."

Cut to photo of Jeffrey Scott. Jeffrey Scott will work with Republicans and Democrats to solve your problems.

Cut to two warriors, not Miller and Ladner, but ordinary warriors, one in red and one in blue. Each holds a mug of grog. The mugs come together. Clink. They smile.

Vote Jeffrey Scott. All we are saying is give peace a chance.

I howled with laughter. Jeffrey was all smiles. Casmir was showing Americans the price of our political wars in a dark but comical way.

"Casmir, I love it. How many points?" I asked, referring to the gross rating point, measuring how many times a typical viewer will see the ads in a week.

"Zeero," says Casmir.

I was confused but I looked at Jeffrey. He understood.

"We are going viral," Casmir explained. "The ad is funny. People will share it. Besides, nobody watches paid TV spots anymore. No one unders sevendy eenyway."

He was right. In the last election, candidates for president and their allies bought $6 billion in television ads and the poll numbers hardly moved. Half of Americans now watch almost no television on the major networks. Among those who do, most have DVRs. Much of what they watch is recorded and the ads are skipped.

These TV ads are dead. But the political consultants have barely noticed.

"So let's do it," I said, happy to save the money—although at the moment, we had more than we could spend.

"Done," said Jeffrey.

Thus ended the shortest media ad meeting in the history of presidential politics.

* * *

Jeffrey's sense of humor never ceased to amaze me. His idea? Release the video at a re-enactment of the Battle of Towton in which troops fighting for the House of York and the House of Lancaster vied for the English crown. It was the bloodiest battle ever fought on English soil, and of the 50,000 soldiers who participated, 20,000 lost their lives. Peasant soldiers, dead on the field.

Not wanting to second-guess my candidate, whose wisdom was proving so much better than my own, on Jeffrey's suggestion we recruited several medieval war reenactor clubs to restage the battle on an open field in Spotsylvania County, Virginia. Prior to the battle, Jeffrey made a short speech.

> America is engaged in a great political war.
> And like the Battle of Towton 550 years ago, the
> casualties are enormous. Social Security and
> Medicare face financial collapse. We are leaving

our children a mountain of debt that will compromise their ability to fund schools, deliver health care, provide secure retirements, and protect their nation against foreign threats. The list of problems, frightening and unaddressed, is long. There is another choice. Washington is full of warriors fighting a battle no one can win. We need a president who can make peace. We need a president who can take the best ideas of both parties and mold them into solutions that Congress and our president can actually pass and put to work for our nation.

All I am saying is give peace a chance.

On Jeffrey's lapel was a blue button, a peace symbol in the middle. He raised his hand and dropped it, signaling the battle to begin. Among the soldiers were many wearing the masks bearing the faces of President Miller and Lewis Ladner.

* * *

Whoever heard of the Battle of Towton? The whole idea was silly, like a Monty Python skit injected into the presidential campaign. But this event gave television news shows the things they craved. It was visual. Two armies of ancient warrior bearing ancient weapons, bearded and unwashed. Washington ridiculed in an uproariously funny way. The two biggest names in American politics, the president and Lewis Ladner, lampooned as medieval cretins fighting a battle no one could win.

The event led every television newscast in America. It became the number one topic of talk shows. "Senator Allen, Jeffrey Scott has compared our partisan conflict to medieval battles no one can win. Do you agree?" Suddenly, the political question facing Americans was more than Democrats versus Republicans. It was also war versus peace.

Three days after the re-enactment of the Battle of Towton, Casmir's viral video, released on that day, had been viewed by 23 million American voters.

21

Lucy Gilmore

"Mr. Aaronson, several months ago, I visited with you to talk about voting machines and the election in South Carolina."

"I remember that, Lucy. I understand that you have uncovered more evidence. I appreciate your efforts. Tell me what you've got."

"I have data that indicates some voting machine manipulation over the last 12 years. I think we need to run an article that says analysis of election returns in hundreds of statewide elections between 2004 and 2016 indicates that some tampering may have taken place."

Bruce Aaronson, political editor for the *Washington Post*, looked at me, curious as to whether he had the story of the century or a reporter who had just returned from an alien visit in Roswell, New Mexico.

"Can I show you some slides?" I asked.

He nodded and I moved my chair to the side of his desk and positioned my laptop in front of him.

I clicked and a chart appeared. I explained.

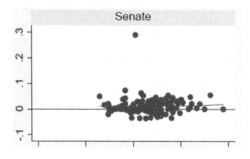

"This chart shows every Senate race from 2004 to 2016 for which an exit poll was taken. The line in the middle represents the exit poll prediction. The dots below the line, and there are not many, show races where the Democratic candidate did better than the exit poll. Those above the line are elections where the Republican candidate exceeded his exit poll numbers. Do you see the pattern?"

Aaronson looked at me. "Well, there certainly is a pattern."

"Take a look at the governor's races, 2004 through 2016."

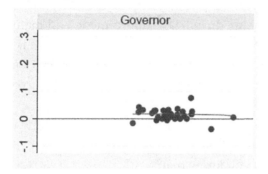

"Again, in almost all of the races, the Republican candidate is getting more votes than the exit poll predicted. Now, the presidential numbers are a little more complicated. But still, there is a tilt toward the Republican candidates but much smaller than in the other two categories. And don't forget, this represents presidential results in all states, not just the battleground contests.

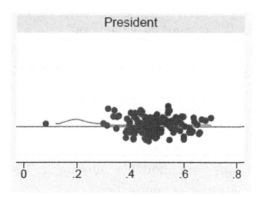

"Mr. Aaronson, how much do you know about sampling statistics?"

"Not a lot."

"Have you ever heard of a p-value?"

"Never."

"Well, in comparing the results of experiments in two samples, statisticians often compute p-values. P-values use the sample size and the difference in results to compute the probability that those differences could be due to random chance. P-values are widely used in science, medicine, law enforcement, and many other fields. If you are looking at two results and the sample size is small and the difference is small, then the p-value might say that in 90 percent of the cases like this one the difference would be due to chance."

"Okay."

"Mr. Aaronson, these differences I have shown you in campaigns across America are not due to chance."

"How do you know that?"

"Because I had someone compute these probabilities. I have the p-values. Do you want to hear these numbers?"

"Of course." Aaronson rubbed his forearm across his face. Stared at the chart. "What are the presidential numbers?"

"Overall, based upon results in 141 state contests, there is only a three percent chance that the difference between the exit polls and Republican performance could be due to chance."

"Well, that is not so alarming. We certainly can't run a story based upon that. What about the governors?"

"So you saw the chart and how their candidates outperformed the exit polls. The odds of that happening by chance are 24,332 to one."

Aaronson's jaw dropped. "That is troubling. What are the odds on the Senate differences?"

"More than 150,000 to one."

Aaronson was uncomfortable, turning in his chair as he absorbed all this surprising information.

"Lucy, this is all interesting. No doubt about it. But someone once told me that the bigger the story the higher the standard of proof. If what you are alleging is true, then a number of elections over the last 12 years have been rigged."

"Well I need to point out that not every election is being rigged. Many election results match the exit polls perfectly. So if you average all of them out, the difference is small. Overall, Republican candidates outperform the exit polls by an average of one percentage point."

Aaronson looked suddenly bored.

"Well, that's nothing."

"Mr. Aaronson, it is something. If you look at the data, most elections are completely clean. So if one in five elections were rigged and the one tainted was changed by five percentage points the data would show a one percent shift. But our measurements are highly accurate. We have almost 600,000 interviews in our sample. So what are the odds that this one percentage point difference is due to random chance?"

"Lucy, I have no idea."

"The odds are 42 million to one."

Aaronson looked out the window into the press room, his eyes glazed in thought. For a moment he was silent. Then he spoke.

"That can't be right!"

"You can have your own statistician run the numbers to check. I believe the number is right. They were computed by someone who does statistics that are a lot more complicated than exit polls."

"Maybe the exit polls have a Democratic bias," he suggested.

"Well I looked at that. I compared the exit polls with public polling averages. The exit polls are clearly a better predictor of election outcomes.

"Mr. Arronson there are some very suspicious outcome. Scott Walker in 2014 in Wisconsin? A lot of people say his re-election was fixed. Well, if you look at the exit poll and his election day numbers, here is the chance it was honest: four-tenths of one percentage point."

"Lucy, calm down. All these numbers are fine but we have no witnesses. We don't have fingerprints. No memos or emails. All we have is statistics."

"Mr. Aaronson, I am not saying we should run a story saying that these elections were rigged. But I've got a lot more examples than Scott Walker. What if we say that an analysis of election returns shows some cases of highly improbable outcomes. Vote counts five and six points bigger than the exit polls. Less than one percent probabilities these outcomes could be due to chance.."

"Well, I can't run this story about a one percentage point shift no matter what the odds."

"I know this evidence is not perfect. I wish we had better evidence. Do you know why we don't?"

"Tell me."

"Because they can write code that isn't even there. It self-erases on election night. Manipulating voting machines is the safest crime in America. Our job is to shine a light on corruption. Even the bare suspicion of corruption. When we do, maybe someone will come forward. Democracy dies in darkness. Isn't this what we say? Isn't our job to shine the light?"

"Lucy, I think you need to calm down. Solid statistics is not solid proof. If you can get me additional proof, I know the paper will be a lot more comfortable. Let me go upstairs and talk it over. You may be on to something. Let me figure out what else we need to run a story. I will get back to you."

Two days later, I got a call from Aaronson.

"Lucy, no one is ready to do this story. Give us one of three things and we can let you run with it."

"What things?" I asked.

"An actual witness to the manipulation, an audit of paper ballots that differs from the machine count, or the vote changing code on a machine actually used in an election. And one more thing.

You've got a beat in Prince William County. We can't take you off that work to chase this story."

Statistics were not enough. Not even 42 million to one.

22

Sheldon Klumm

Beexelbub's forest was dark and filled with gloom. From above, birds of all sizes and colors sounded a deranged chorus of cries, whistles, screeches, and long, hollow caws. Here the Angel of Darkness ruled and her bootlicking elves defended against all intruders. On that day the intruder was me. My trusty macro-blaster was level in my hands, ready to turn left or right to find my aim and litter the sky with elfin snow. I saw movement. Only the rustle of leaves, but I knew.

Bee Doo Eep Bee Doo …

My phone rang. Sensing my distraction, the elf seized his chance. He rose, unleashing an arrow that found the center of my forehead and left my brains oozing slowly from the back of my skull.

His smile was too much to bear.

Goddamnit! Who was freaking calling me? I had not lost to the elf in two years, one month, and 26 days.

I opened the call, my anger rising.

"Who is calling?" I almost shouted.

"It's me, Nadia."

Oh my God! Nadia Fedorov, the most beautiful woman ever created in the human species, was calling Sheldon Klumm, dork, dweeb, geek, fat, and untouchable by any respectable woman. The laws of the universe had surely been altered.

I blinked in disbelief. I was nervous. Afraid. But I felt joy as well.

"Sheldon, are you all right?" she asked, wondering at my silence.

"Oh no, I was just a little surprised. I-i-it's great to hear from you. I had a great time in New York."

"Not as much as me," she softly cooed.

What could I make of those words? Part of me wanted to celebrate an unmatched blissful moment that left me trembling in joy. But part of me worried. How is it possible that this woman could actually be interested in me? I might not believe but could I protest her words? Certainly not.

"Sheldon, I am coming to Omaha. Tomorrow."

"Nadia, that's wonderful. I don't know what to say."

"Say you will meet me at my hotel. Room 300 at the Magnolia. Two o'clock."

"I—I—I'll be there," I answered in a stutter with my helium voice.

* * *

The next day was the longest of my life. I turned on my PlayStation 4 but that did not last long. I was beheaded by a Norseman and incinerated by a dragon hiding in a tree. I won't tell you the third thing that happened, but it involved an elf. The humiliation ran deep.

I turned off my PS 4 and waited four whole hours without looking at a screen. A record. Perhaps a sad record but two o'clock finally approached and I exited my apartment.

The elevator ride to the ground floor of my apartment building lasted another eon. On each floor, it seemed, some rude neighbor appeared, slowing my progress.

"Hello, Sheldon," said Miss Willoughby, an 80-something tenant on the fifth floor. "Are you all right?"

I realized that my car key was in my mouth.

"Oh, just fine," I answered, slowly extracting the key.

Finally, the elevator door opened into the garage and I ran. I would be in Nadia's arms in no time and, indeed I was, despite my swerve from the road that removed a neighbor's mailbox from the ground.

The Magnolia was built in the '20s to look like some palace in Italy. It is made of gray stone, none of those bricks they make from ugly Iowa clay, and sits on Howard Avenue, where it rises four stories and takes up the whole entire block. Walk inside and there is marble on the walls—all the walls.

As I entered the hotel people turned and looked at me and, suddenly, I realized I was actually running through the lobby instead of strutting with my chest out like you are supposed to do at a fancy place like this. I slowed down, smiled, and waved at the onlookers as I moved with a more appropriate strut.

Soon I was standing at the door of Room 300. I knocked. I did not wait long. The door opened.

She stood before me, even more beautiful than I remembered.

She was wearing a black lace-up corset with see-through panties that weren't actually panties but black strings supporting a triangle so small you could cover the whole thing with the ace of diamonds. I had never even seen such clothes, if you could call them that.

Her deep blue eyes were accented above and below by long black lashes. She smiled, and unlike most of us it was not her lower lip that curved but her upper one, revealing her large, white teeth.

She tilted her head, waiting for me to speak, but I had no words and, if I tried, I would surely utter the disconnected syllables of a man without language at all. But my pitiful state hardly mattered because I soon learned that Nadia was a patient, understanding woman. Without saying a word, she walked to me, took my hand, and led me up the stairs into the bedroom loft. She began unbuttoning my shirt, giving my chest little kisses along the way. Then she removed my pants and she stroked Pedro, who, once again gripped by stage fright, lowered his embarrassed head.

But Nadia knew what to do. She dropped to her knees, stroking him, whispering to him, kissing him, and placing him in her mouth. Soon, he stood proud and waiting. She pushed me to the bed and mounted me, her glorious breasts rocking above my eyes.

A few moments later, I lay at her side. And despite my hasty finish, she was looking at me, not as if I were a failure, but rather Don Juan reincarnated to spread his gifts of pleasure to all womankind.

She touched her hand on her cheek and spoke. "Sheldon, I am thinking of you every day. Do you think of me?"

Once again, words tumbled over one another and my mouth moved without sound, but finally I summoned my answer.

"Yes."

"Then we should think of how to be together. Maybe?"

She spoke with her eyebrows high, as if wondering if I might actually say no.

"Yes," I stammered.

She looked into my eyes, her palm stroking my cheek. "We can be good together, no?"

"Yes," my simple word breaking to pieces in my throat.

I was swirling, a vortex of pleasure, desire, love, and, perhaps most of all, a disbelief that any of this could truly be happening. But against my doubt stood the words of a woman with whom I could have barely imagined standing in the same room with me, much less sharing a bed. Her soft voice with its strange accent melted my heart. In the end, we humans believe not what is proven or rests on any notion of life as we know it.

We believe what we want to be true.

23

Lucy Gilmore

There I stood, face to face with the bitter truth.

I know I have uncovered evidence of a deeply evil crime. I had proven, with 42 million to one odds, that votes were being moved. But could I convince my editor to share this information with the American public?

No.

And what were my next steps? There were no next steps. No witness was going to come forward. If he did, he might face a lifetime in jail. You can't get code off a machine. Right? And what would happen if I went to a county election official, told him his voting machines were rigged, and demanded that he round up volunteers to hand-count the ballots?

Right.

I knew what was happening. Rigging a voting machine was too easy. The payoff was too big. And the chance of getting caught? One hair above zero.

There was a bottle of bourbon in the cabinet. I took a drink. I cursed myself. I drank. I cried. I wished I had never been born. Next thing I knew I was awake. The first rays of sunlight were whispering at the window. And I surely had the worst headache in the nation's capital.

* * *

I have already spoken to the darkness in my soul. When things go bad, I am visited by a melancholy I know like an old friend. It begins as I tell myself what a worthless, pathetic, disgusting excuse for a human being I happen to be. I am not just telling myself these things. I am believing these things. It is like I have fallen off a cliff sucked downward by a gravity I am helpless to withstand.

My descent is powered by self-reproach. My mind is filled with taunts, my own brain telling me that I rank among the lowest human beings who ever lived. My heart pitiless, convinced of the surety that what I am suffering is what I truly deserve. My soul, absent, a witness unwilling to look.

The descent can last days, weeks, or, as in the case of my father's death long ago, feel like it would never end.

But on that day, that morning, I landed. I had hit the ground. And when you have lost all self-esteem, all self-worth, and all hope, the landing is not so hard. You weigh nothing because all that you value about yourself is gone. You open your eyes. You blink. Then you remember the one piece of precious knowledge that is salvation for all you have endured.

What is left to lose?

I went to the kitchen and made myself some coffee. I gobbled some aspirin. Then I looked around this small, dingy apartment and I considered all the ways I had failed. But as the black cloud lifted, I could see matters in a better light. I knew I had been unjustly unheard. And these thoughts gave rise to a new emotion.

I became angry.

I may be the only one who knows, I thought. *I may be the only one who understands what is happening in America.* Anger is the antidote for despair. Slowly, my strength began to return.

24

Max Parker

It started as just another crazy idea. Jeffrey wanted to find a Republican candidate for president, tackle a tough problem, and issue a joint statement showing how Democrats and Republicans could work together to find solutions.

My question was "Where the hell are you going to find the Republican?"

Jeffrey admitted that it was a tough problem, but he wanted to try. So I sent messages to the managers for all of the leading Republican candidates offering Jeffrey's idea. It was like Typhoid Mary inviting the gang to Thanksgiving dinner.

You can't blame them, really. They had 20 candidates too and the biggest issue for most Republican voters was which candidate hated Democrats the most. So my invitation, as they say, was *off message*.

Well, sometimes if you can't get a sirloin steak, you order Vienna sausage, and our Vienna sausage was a fast food magnate named Billy Brown. Brown had made his fortune in burgers—the Flash Burger. The "Flash" referred to the service. "Where you get your burger in a flash!" Of course, speed has its tradeoffs. The burgers were pre-cooked and heated in a microwave in a secret location in the back of the building. Once hot, they were covered with cooked onions that buried the flavor shortcomings of the meat. In fact, you might not be sure whether the meat was from a cow, a horse, or even a hefty rodent raised on some tropical farm. Ingenious!

Some snooty burger gourmets ridiculed Billy's products. "Gut bombs" was the prevalent nickname. But the masses aren't so choosy. Billy Brown was a very rich man.

He was also bored, and since solving problems such as the rapid preparation of ground beef is excellent training to be president, Billy announced his candidacy to be leader of the free world.

Fortunately for us, Billy Brown was headed nowhere. His 10, 10, 10 tax plan (10 percent personal income tax, 10 percent sales tax, and 10 percent corporate income tax) was going nowhere. One commentator called it the "Rin Tin Tin" plan. The label stuck and at one debate a spectator began barking as Billy described his plan. The spectator was removed but that was little help to Billy Brown, who was more polished at the microwave than the microphone.

As they say, desperation is the mother of invention, and so our partnership was born. His campaign manager, Ricardo Gomez, called me on the phone. "Max, I think we can work something out but first I have three conditions."

"Shoot."

"First, not a word about this project until we are ready to release. Total secrecy. Otherwise, we get accused of plotting with the other side."

"Got it."

"Second, if we don't reach this bipartisan agreement on whatever issue we choose, and word does leak out, we reserve the right to attack Jeffrey Scott as a flamethrowing liberal who would not budge in his desire to expand government and bankrupt taxpayers."

I was laughing out loud. "Ricardo, I think the First Amendment covers that one."

"Just so you know."

"What's number three?" I asked.

"If we do get an agreement, we reserve the right to attack you on other issues."

"Just so we know."

"Right. Look, here's the deal," Ricardo continued. "We want this event, if it happens, to be the product of hard negotiations between two adversaries. If Republicans think we are in bed together, we are dead."

Billy Brown was already dead, but I held my tongue.

"That works for us," I announced.

"Good. Let's get started."

* * *

Two days later, we held a planning meeting attended by Jeffrey; our issues director, Jane Abid, a Columbia economics grad who joined us after we got hot; three or four members of the research staff; and me. This was Jeffrey's show. He called the meeting to order and then, as usual, jumped right in.

"This campaign is about getting things done. No party, thanks to that ridiculous filibuster rule, will ever have the votes to do anything alone. We have delivered rhetoric about finding two-party solutions. Words. This negotiation is time to prove it we can do it."

"You have two sides here with very different viewpoints," Jeffrey continued. "If we want to get an agreement, we have to understand what it is that the other side wants most. Can I hear some opinions?"

"To save Social Security," one researcher offered.

Jeffrey, who was nothing if not polite, restrained a smile.

Jane Abid stepped in. "They opposed Social Security, although that was many years ago. They opposed Medicare. I think they don't want to be blamed for killing these programs."

Jeffrey leaned in. "But if all they want to do is not get blamed, they can dodge the whole issue just like they are doing now. What is it that will get them an agreement that will make Republicans cheer? That is what we want."

At the end of the table, a young man who could not have been 23, whose name I later learned to be Greg Schultz, spoke.

"A victory for them would be to control entitlement spending without cutting benefits."

"Exactly!" Jeffrey replied, almost shouting. "And how do we make that happen?"

"Probably by raising the retirement age," Jane answered. "But we need a lot of work to figure this out."

"They also want to privatize Social Security," Jane added.

"We could give them a little," Jeffrey chimed in.

"So here is what we need. We need a plan that can at least control if not cut entitlement spending and maybe have a small option to put some of your money in the market. We need to figure out how that happens. And when we start talking, we lead with some of what will make Billy Brown look good."

"Well, saving Social Security is the easy part," Jane chided. "Making Billy Brown look good is really hard."

Laughs all around.

* * *

The negotiations with our new ally went surprisingly smoothly except that Billy Brown insisted upon being present by phone or in person in every discussion. No wonder he was in last place. But since he knew so little about the subject, he did not put up a fight. He basically agreed to the plan we outlined.

> **Raise the Retirement Age:** We gave the retirees lots of options. You could postpone until 80 and get a huge check. You could retire at 55 and get a little one. But beneath these options these age thresholds moved two months higher every year.

Investing Your Retirement Savings: Our deal let people put 10 percent of their withholdings into the stock market. Only conservative investments—one of seven qualifying index funds.

Controlling Entitlement Spending: We take withholding that is privately invested off the books. That lowers entitlement spending. So does raising the age.

Taxing Benefits: If Social Security approaches a level of insolvency risk, the system's finances will be replenished by a surtax on Americans making more than one million per year.

In this deal was a lot of compromise. But since compromise was not the fashion of the day, there was plenty to shoot at as well.

* * *

We tried to get one of the big senior citizen organizations to introduce Jeffrey and Billy Brown and praise their work in finding bipartisan solutions. Nobody would touch it.

That was no surprise. Raising the retirement age, investing withholding in the stock market, and an automatic tax increase? Something for everyone to hate. The senior citizens' groups had their own plan. Same retirement age. No money in the market. And borrow what we need, which, of course, means that young people will pay for the whole thing.

Besides that, these groups are more about collecting checks and less about solving problems. If you solve the problem, why would anyone send you another check? But if you stand on principle to block all those disgusting compromises, the checks keep pouring in.

* * *

Our event to announce our bipartisan plan featured a senior from Terre Haute, Indiana. Brandy Gillespie had all the energy of an eight-year-old packed into an 80-year-old body. Her hair was white and cropped tight to her head. Hey body trim and even athletic. As she looked at the camera her eyes had this "get outta my way 'cause I am about to cause some serious trouble" expression that probably made even the cameraman nervous as hell.

"While they lie shivering in their little rabbit holes, afraid to face the biggest crisis ever to confront older Americans, our hard-earned Social Security is headed for bankruptcy," she said, her voice rising in anger.

Oh, she was so hot.

She was a grandmother raising an autistic grandchild who was way out on the spectrum. She was an Army nurse who had served in Vietnam. And when they started cutting meals on wheels in Indiana, she organized the Ancient Hoosier Alliance that filled the capital with so many walkers, crackly voices, and shaking fists that they brought that legislature to its knees.

Anyway, today, she was ours.

"Let me tell you something about the biggest crisis facing America, an imminent crisis, a crisis that will put 40 million seniors on the breadlines. This crisis is being ignored by almost every major candidate for president. Did Lewis Ladner even utter the words 'Social Security' in any of the last three presidential debates? Did he?"

A sea of crackly voices rose to a resounding "No!"

And after calling roll, shouting the name of each major candidate except our guy and Billy Brown, she continued her blistering condemnation of America's failure to act.

111

"And when someday soon, sooner than you think, I will go to my mailbox to get my Social Security check, my retirement income I worked too hard to earn, and I will discover that my check is not there, there will be one reason and one reason alone.

"The cowardice of every one of these so-called leaders, these candidates for president who sit silent while catastrophe approaches. And why are they so fearful? They are fearful because there are no easy answers. They are fearful because saving Social Security might require unpopular measures. They are fearful because, God forbid, to shape a solution that could actually become law, they might have to talk with human beings who belong to the other political party!"

Then she praised Jeffrey Scott and Billy Brown and outlined our plan.

After the press conference, we previewed Casmir Zielinski's new video. This one would run as a TV ad, which makes sense because seniors actually watch broadcast television.

Picture: Senior woman.

"Darling, where is my Social Security check?"

Picture: Senior man.

"Honey, didn't you hear? Democrats and Republicans could not agree on changes to save Social Security. Now it's gone."

Picture: Gone.

Announcer: "Partisan politics is wrecking America, but Jeffrey Scott and Billy Brown have a bipartisan plan to save Social Security."

Picture: All the other candidates.

Announcer: "Politicians without solutions?"

Picture: Gone.

Picture: Dissolve to Scott and Brown.

Announcer: "Jeffrey Scott and Billy Brown can save Social Security."

This event and this ad had three consequences.

Democrats and Republicans attacked the plan for giving too much to the other side.

Billy Brown moved six percentage points in the polls, prompting three other Republican candidates to contact Jeffrey Scott and offer to do an event.

Jeffrey Scott moved two points in the polls, into a tie for second place.

25

Sheldon Klumm

Dear Beautiful Nadia,

I wake in the morning with you in my heart
You are a Venus so gorgeous to see
You are a vision of dazzling art
And you're speaking of love just to me

My body is trembling
With thoughts of our love
Your passion, your beauty
Looking down from above

I will follow you anywhere
To the ends of the earth
To Egypt or Burma or
Or Paris or Perth

And I can't help but wonder
Can it really be true
That we have a future
That is me and is you

Until we meet again…

The man who loves you like no other,

Sheldon

26

PBS Newshour

"This is Marge Banos, with the *PBS Newshour*.

"Important news on the legislative front. Senate Majority Leader Stephen Shaughnessy announced today that there would be no movement on the Election Security Act, a proposal that seemed to have some bipartisan support.

"The act would require the use of paper ballots in all federal elections. The reasoning is that if voting machines are hacked or malfunction, paper ballots can be hand-counted and give us the ability to detect hacking or other manipulation to shift votes from one candidate to another. The act also encourages random audits of voting machine results to check for hacking or any programming that alters results.

"Senator Clark Hammerschmidt of Wisconsin, a Democrat, criticized the decision, saying, 'Without paper ballots the Russians can move in, hack our machines, and change the counts and it is unlikely that anyone would ever know.'

"Senator Shaughnessy said that the legislation was dead because he would not move any bill that in any way diminishes the prerogatives of state election officials to make their own decisions about our election security.

"The bill was opposed by the Secretaries of State Association."

27

Max Parker

There are a few things you should know about the Iowa Caucus.

First, these people think because they own the first delegate selection event in the country, that they have been anointed by God to select the next president. They go to speeches. They knock on doors. They endure and inflict the largest onslaught of advertising, door knocking, phone calling, and emailing experienced by any voters in America.

Remember those bomb shelters they sold back in the '50s? There are voters in Iowa who would buy one just to evade the campaign.

Second, even though Iowa is an increasingly conservative state, the Democratic caucus-goers are pretty liberal and not much in the mood for compromising, moderating, or any kind of foot shuffling on any major issue. Especially on any liberal do-or-die issue. And don't ask me for the list. It is pretty goddamned long.

Third, and I repeat myself, these people believe they have been anointed by God to select the next president.

And all that points to some big problems for Jeffrey Scott, who has spent less time in Iowa than any other candidate. The reason is that, before he took off, Jeffrey Scott could not draw a crowd of homeless people with an offer of a free steak dinner. And it should not be surprising that my candidate, the reach across the aisle and get things done guy, is not exactly setting Iowa Democrats on fire.

In Iowa, our strategy is simple. Get enough votes to survive.

So there we were in the middle of the Iowa winter, and my candidate was slogging around in 20 degrees below zero weather hoping that his fingertips didn't break off shaking hands with voters who had a hard time knowing this was no summer day.

The intensity of this campaign was remarkable. A candidate might appear at a rally in Sioux City, Iowa, a town of barely 80,000 people, and 7,000 might show up to hear him speak. They can stay home and get movies, watch hockey games, eat a home-delivered dinner, or drool over the most twisted porn any excitable man can imagine and what do they do? They go out in the bone-chilling cold to hear a politician paint a never-gonna-happen vision of their future.

Go figure.

But this was the problem. Lewis Ladner was packing them in all across the state. Medicare for all. End income inequality. Remove all CO2 from the atmosphere. And on top of that, correct every injustice ever fostered upon minorities or the female gender.

And Jeffrey Scott's message to voters?

Get real.

Nevertheless, we had made progress. In Iowa we were running 15 percent in the polls. If we got that on caucus night, we'd survive. But these icy winds can shift pretty fast.

If politics is about emotion, how do we fire up these voters? Here was Jeffrey Scott on the stump.

"How many people here think our democracy is working?" No hands were raised. "Social Security will be insolvent in less than 15 years. And to hear the candidates talk, to hear them lay out their vision of the future, you would think that Social Security was a vile and forbidden phrase because no other candidate will utter those words. Climate change: No progress. No legislation. Income inequality: Big speeches and no action. Democrats want more spending; Republicans want more tax cuts. Both sides have gotten their way and our young people will carry the heavy yoke of government debt the rest of their lives.

"We have become two Americas, two Americas who are separated by deep divisions and even different facts. And, frankly, the only thing we all share is anger at the other side.

"I want to share with you a truth. A truth that is surely a painful one in our supercharged world. Democracy is about creating majorities. It is about talking to people who don't share the same viewpoint and finding a way to shape a solution they can all support.

"Here are my qualifications to be president. I won't lie to you about what is possible. I have dreams for America, but I understand my dreams may not be real solutions in the world we live in. I will be a president who is focused on the most critical mission a president can undertake. I will build majorities, the majorities we need to rescue Social Security and Medicare, lessen the debt we leave our children, to combat climate change and to give middle-class Americans a larger share of our nation's wealth.

"The dreamers in this presidential race are a dime a dozen. Their dreams are beautiful, and they stir me as well. But America, with so many crises looming, cannot afford a dreamer. We need a doer. We need a president who can build majorities, who can find a way."

Jeffrey, on the stump, had passion. You could feel his belief.

But America loves a dreamer. And in Iowa Jeffrey's message remained "get real."

28

Lucy Gilmore

So what do you do when you find yourself a failure in life?

You call an old friend.

That friend was Sarah Jeffords, my old roommate from college. Sarah was a blogger in Wisconsin. Her blog, Save our Democracy, was about all the ways the Republicans were suppressing our votes, especially in Wisconsin.

"Sarah, how's life in cheese land?"

"Pretty damn good. These Republicans are giving me plenty to write about."

"I'll bet. Listen, I've got something you should know."

"You getting married? Or even better, getting laid?"

"I've got something bigger and you are not going to believe it."

"Try me."

So I went into my spiel. Exit polls. Election results. Red shifts, p-values, and Scott Walker's re-election.

"Goddamn, girl, you've been doing some homework."

"I am going to send you the paper. But listen to this." Then I dropped the number on her. Forty-two million to one.

"Holy shit!" Sarah answered. "Listen, Lucy, I want to put this on my blog."

"I can't. I have a no-compete clause in my contract. I can't write for another publication while employed at the paper. I would need approval from the *Post*."

"Why aren't they running this story?"

"They aren't the paper they used to be. Don't even get me started."

"Well, write it up for me. I will publish it all anonymously. No name. They will assume I wrote it."

"They would know it came from me. I showed them the numbers."

"They can't fire you. You are doing great work there. And look at this story. If they fired you for putting this out, they would look like a chicken shit shadow of the paper they once were."

"They don't want me near this story. But let me think about it. I think you are right. There is no way they could fire me for trying to save the right to vote."

29

NBC News

"This is Caleb Bankston with NBC News.

"With reports in from 90 percent of the polling places across the state of Iowa, it is clear that Lewis Ladner is the big winner in the first presidential selection event. Ladner is currently pulling almost 40 percent of the ballots. Christine Holloway is finishing second with 23 percent of the vote. Jeffrey Scott is trailing with a disappointing 12 percent.

"I am joined now by Martha Simpson, NBC's White House correspondent. Martha, what is your take?"

"Well, this is certainly an impressive showing for Ladner, who leads his nearest rival by an almost two-to-one margin. There has been a lot of speculation about whether the party is moving to the left. These results are a dramatic affirmation of that movement."

"And what about Holloway?"

"Holloway has accomplished her first objective, which is to fend off Jeffrey Scott and become the clear alternative to Ladner. She has a lot of support among Democratic women and those who want a more moderate nominee. But she has also been criticized for a lackluster campaign and a failure to truly energize voters. Now, I do think most voters will begin to see this as a two-person race. If you don't like Ladner's flamboyant style and his liberal agenda, Holloway becomes your choice.

"And, Jeffrey Scott certainly had a disappointing night. Who thought you could win a Democratic caucus by telling voters you have to get along with Republicans? Not sure who came up with that strategy?"

"So Martha, how would you characterize the Scott candidacy at this point?"

"Frankly, Caleb, he looks like toast to me."

30

Max Parker

Yeah, Iowa sucked. But before the media could put the final nail in Jeffrey's coffin, their attention was pulled to a 35-year-old photo that turned the campaign upside down.

The photo was everywhere. In newspapers. On television. Plastered across the social media universe.

Two students at a costume party. One dressed as a Klansman. The other with a face colored with black shoe polish, dressed as a black minstrel of another age. The photo was published in the year-book of the University of Tennessee School of Law. Underneath the photo was Lewis Ladner's name.

It may have been an old photo but the outcry was as if it had been taken yesterday. Ladner denied that the photograph contained a picture of him, but due process of law has no application in politics. The statements of outrage began with Larissa Guinn, chair of the Democratic National Committee.

"Leaders are called to a higher standard, and the stain of racism should have no place in the halls of government. Lewis Ladner should step aside from his campaign so the public can heal and move forward together."

Christine Holloway weighed in with these words.

"These images arouse centuries of anger, anguish, and racist violence. They have erased all confidence in Lewis Ladner's ability to lead. We should expect more from our elected officials, especially from a candidate for our nation's highest office. Lewis Ladner should end his candidacy immediately."

Then Ralph Brown, president of the NAACP, joined in the chorus.

"Racism has no place in the White House. Democrats should not be asked to endorse it. I call on Senator Ladner to withdraw now."

All across the nation, politicians large and small scurried to align themselves against racism by condemning Ladner in the strongest words.

But Jeffrey Scott did not share these views. We advised him to at least be silent. There was no point in confronting this tsunami of condemnation. But Jeffrey would have none of it.

He arrived at the small New Hampshire rally, where most in attendance were reporters who had been briefed on what he would say. As I waited for him to begin, I remembered a scene from long ago: 1972. Edmund Muskie, front-runner for the Democratic nomination, delivered a tearful defense of his wife, who had been savaged by the local paper. Tears. That ended his candidacy. Our standards have surely fallen. But here was Jeffrey, taking on the entire Democratic Party of the United States of America. Would this be his siren song as well?

Jeffrey began his statement, standing in the snow, his words becoming clouds in the air.

"Racism has no place in politics or in society. But the rush to judgment against Lewis Ladner is a terrible wrong as well. No one has proven that Ladner is actually in this photo. But even if he does appear in that photo it is not a reason for his candidacy to end. This picture was taken 35 years ago.

"And if he committed a wrong long ago, in his youth, is it not better to ask what kind of man he has become? Is it not more important to ask what has he done with his life in the three and a half decades since? I know Lewis Ladner. He has fought for the civil rights of all Americans. He has been an eloquent and outspoken voice against poverty and injustice. He deserves to be judged by his long and honorable career that contains not one whisper of prejudice. And if indeed he is pictured in this photo, which no one has proved, he has earned our forgiveness many times over.

"These condemnations remind me of another episode deep in the past when a US senator wrecked careers and smeared individuals with an equally insidious label. He did so often with feeble, even refutable, proof. He did so based, not on an understanding of a person's life and work, but based upon single episodes deep in the past. His name was Joe McCarthy. Communist? Racist? These labels ought not to be lightly applied. In the name of political correctness, the Democratic Party is looking a lot like Joe McCarthy today.

"I urge Lewis Ladner to stay in the race."

Jeffrey's statement launched yet another wave of outcry, but this time mostly from the other candidates. The national Democratic chair called Jeffrey's statement an "oblique defense of racism itself." Clark Hammerschmidt, the senator from Wisconsin said, "Anyone who defends racism is no better than the racist he defends."

But on social media, a different outcry began with voters tweeting support for Jeffrey Scott and his defense of the very man who stood in the way of the nomination he pursued. By calling on his opponent to stay in the race, he demonstrated something beyond the guilt or innocence of Lewis Ladner. He demonstrated a personal integrity and courage uncommon in his profession.

Support in social media was encouraging but social media does not always reflect public opinion. The New Hampshire primary was five days away. There Jeffrey Scott stood in opposition to almost every major voice in the national Democratic Party. I got our pollster, Greta Simmons, on the phone.

"Greta, what do you think?"

"Well, that was a pretty gutsy statement our guy made."

"Do you think the campaign is over?"

I could feel her smile miles away. "I think it might help."

I liked Greta. She was not full of rules and formulas. Give her a problem and she would actually think.

"Well, we need a poll," I replied.

"National or New Hampshire?"

"Jesus, that's a tough call. But I don't think the reaction will be much different."

"Well, there are no African Americans in New Hampshire. We need that read."

"Got it. When can we get numbers?"

"Two days."

"God bless you, Greta Simmons."

31

Lucy Gilmore

What's a girl to do? I have a story and my paper won't run it. So I decided to give the story to Sarah's blog. Even though the blog post would be unsigned, Brad Aaronson would know it was mine and he would be pissed. That is, if he ever saw it. But I was a rising star at the *Post*. They had just finished running my five-part feature on the problems with Prince George's County schools. There was some talk of nominating it for an award. I am good at this and they know it. It is hard to believe they would fire me for putting important information anonymously on a small blog. But you never know. Aaronson is a coward.

So I wrote it all up and gave it to Sarah. It was a little nerdy. There were a lot of numbers but it created a stir, especially regarding stuff about Scott Walker. Sarah's website has almost no audience at all. But people shared it. In the end it was viewed by a few thousand people.

That might have gone unnoticed at the *Post*, but the mainstream press picked up the blog post. In fact, the Associated Press ran a blurb paraphrasing my post by saying that a comparison of exit polls and actual elections results suggests a high statistical probability that some voting machines are being rigged and this has been going on for the last 12 years. If that is the case, some major election outcomes were probably altered. The article noted that the blog post was unsigned but the research was reportedly provided by a reporter from the *Washington Post*.

Shit! There are no secrets in Washington, DC. And I admit, I was talking about my numbers all over town.

Once Aaronson was alerted, I was back in his office. He had a copy of the text of my post in his hand. I looked him in the eye. I was not afraid. There was no way he could fire me for releasing information America needed. And, by God, he may have small testicles, but I was the kind of reporter who made this paper great.

I had just taken my seat. He looked up and spoke solemnly. "Lucy, you know you have a contract that requires the approval of the *Post* for any outside writing."

"I do."

"This post in saveourdemocracy.org was written by you, was it not?"

"It was."

"It has been a long time since the *Washington Post* has been associated with conspiracy theories. I respect your research but as we discussed, it is incomplete. Appearances are important and you have associated this paper with large and unproven events."

"I bet no statistician could show 42 million to one odds that the aliens actually landed in Roswell," I shot back.

Boy oh boy, did he get mad. I got a speech about the paper and its great history, a speech about proof, what it is and what it isn't, and a speech about how the *Post* had been implicated in big charges.

And when he had exhausted his anger and outrage, it was my turn to fire back.

"Mr. Aaronson, I did something this paper was unwilling to do. I shared evidence about an issue on the level of Watergate itself, if we might speak to the fine history of this newspaper. We had almost nothing when the Watergate story began. But Ben Bradley was braver than you. I wrote this blog because sharing this information is exactly what great journalism is about. And I did it because the great *Washington Post* would not meet that same standard."

I went too far. I knew it. But I still did not expect what came next.

"Lucy Gilmore, you are a great reporter. You have done impressive work here. But we all have rules we have to honor. Given your opinion of our paper and our standards, I think we will all be better off if we part ways. I am terminating your employment. Please clear out your desk by the end of the day."

32

Sheldon Klumm

Every day, I rise from my bed and grab my phone and read the texts from my darling Nadia.

"Sheldon, I am thinking of you, aching for you, feeling your hands on my body."

"Sheldon, do you think I could be a good American? I know it's hard to learn Ukrainian but my English is good. We could live in Florida in a big house with a giant bed, 10 dogs, and eat steak every night."

"Sheldon. I am so wet. I can taste you in my mouth, 5,500 miles away."

But while these love messages filled my heart, they were not enough. It had been five weeks since Nadia has visited Omaha. Five freaking weeks. But on this day, Nadia was arriving once more. In two hours, Nadia would be in that big room in the Magnolia where you have to climb the stairs just to get to crawl into the sheets. The bed. The altar. Oh my God!

* * *

I was standing at the door of Room 300, our room, the room where I celebrated the most joyous afternoon of my life. I was nervous. Even though she has told me I am handsome, even though she has spoken of her love almost every day, I was still fearful. But bravery would have its reward.

I knocked.

The door opened.

There stood Nadia, her breasts gazing at me like two large and adoring eyes. Her skin, from her little toes to her perfectly shaped face, glowing with welcome. My eyes darted up and down the hall, worried that someone in the hallway might see.

But she took my hand, pulled me inside while the door closed behind me. We floated up the stairs. We were on the bed. This time it was different.

For the first time, without the slightest assistance, little Pedro rose to attention. This time, unlike the past, my climax was not immediate and I actually lasted two minutes and maybe even a little more. And when we were done, proud of my performance, I felt the exhilaration of an astronaut tumbling weightless through space, feeling no past or future, only limitless bliss and breathtaking joy.

Nadia rose from the bed. There was a bottle of champagne on ice and she poured two glasses.

"To us!" she toasted.

"Forever!" I answered.

And she smiled a soft, knowing smile. "Sheldon, I must talk to you about our life."

I nodded.

"Sheldon, do you want to do this job forever?"

"Well, it is a good job. I like it. But one day, maybe, I would like to program video games."

I noticed a hint of irritation on her face.

"But Sheldon, a good life costs money. If we want that mansion in Florida with 10 dogs, where you will never have to work again, we need some gifts and I know where to get them."

I was puzzled. I liked the not-working part but was confused. "Gifts?" I asked.

"Sheldon, you tell me no one looks at your code. How much would someone have to pay you to program the results of the presidential election in any way they direct?"

"Well, I am already doing that for the Republicans."

"But what if they wanted to elect the Democrat or what if they did not know you were already helping the Republicans? How much money would you charge?"

"Well, that is a big election. People would pay a lot of money for that."

"Sheldon, how much?"

I paused and thought. I never paid attention to politics other than setting up the voting machines. But I knew those candidates were spending a lot of money. I took a guess.

"Millions, I guess."

Nadia smiled. "That's right, my darling. I could get you two million, maybe more. And some for myself as well."

"So between us, four million dollars?" I asked.

"Maybe more."

I never followed those campaigns. But four million sounded like a lot of money to me. I smiled. "Well that would take care of that house and 10 dogs. Easy!"

33

Max Parker

I am doing what I always do. I sit in my office, three TVs on the wall, and I am flipping the channels, checking for news. Suddenly, there is Lewis Ladner on CNN, his head sagging, shoulders slumping, leaning into the mic. I turn up the volume.

"This is a sad day for me but a sad day for our democracy as well. Our politics has become not a search for truth, but a quest for defamation, disqualification, and vilification. In recent days, I have been accused of appearing in a racist photo taken 35 years ago. It does not matter that I was not in that photo or that not a single soul has produced evidence otherwise. This photo was introduced, not to prove that I am a racist, but to raise a mere accusation that would drive me from this race. But this photo, fairly or unfairly, has taken its toll.

"It has cost us millions in donations and withered our support in the polls. I would prefer to fight on but with Super Tuesday approaching we no longer have the money or support to compete. Therefore, I must reluctantly announce that I am no longer a candidate for president of the United States.

"I do have one additional thing I wish to say. I want to thank Jeffrey Scott, who had everything to gain from my departure, for standing alone, in my defense, and for labeling my accusers for who they are. I have learned in this campaign that Congressman Scott possesses integrity that is rare in this profession."

Holy shit! He's out.

I called Jeffrey on the phone.

"He's out!"

"I know."

"And New Hampshire is just five days away. I think we are back in this thing. We will at least finish second."

"Max. First. We are going to finish first. Do you think his voters are going to vote for someone who led the lynch mob that hung him from this tree?"

"Maybe. She might have gotten lost in the crowd," I answered.

"His voters will be pissed. And no amount of love, inspiration, idealism, or gratitude can trump a pissed-off voter headed for the polls."

34

Lucy Gilmore

Did you ever try to find a job in a dying industry?

One of my first calls was to the *Denver Post*. The *Denver Post* is more than another big-city newspaper. They are, or were, a great newspaper that has won five Pulitzer Prizes including one for its coverage of the Columbine shooting. Their work is respected throughout the industry as journalism meeting the highest standards of our profession. But the *Denver Post* was bought by a hedge fund in 2010. They cut the newsroom from 300 reporters to 70.

The situation was so bad that the editors actually published a protest in their own paper asking, "Who will save the *Denver Post*" and attacking the hedge fund that had cut its staff. The rebels were dismissed. Needless to say, the staff that remained at the *Post* found my inquiry about a job to be quite humorous.

So I was on the phone to the great papers, the *Boston Globe*, the *Los Angeles Times*, the *Philadelphia Inquirer*. They all asked the same question. "Why would you leave the *Post*?" I would mumble something about leaving because of "disagreements." But my explanation was generally greeted with silence. So then I would describe our "disagreement," which is that I had the biggest story of the decade and that the *Post* would not touch it.

They already knew. At least they knew the *Post*'s side. Word gets around.

So I tried the second-tier papers. The *Fresno Bee*. The *Akron Beacon Journal*. The *Louisville Courier-Journal*. You don't want the whole list. So far? Not even a nibble.

But the day after I was fired, I had gotten a call from Sarah Jeffords, my old roommate who ran the Save Our Democracy blog. She was apoplectic. She did not know how the Associated Press had found out I wrote the blog post. I assured her that these things happen. I had been talking about my numbers all over town. It would not be hard for someone to figure it all out.

Then Sarah made an offer. She had no money to pay me but if I wanted to come to Wisconsin and work on my story, I was welcome to live at her house for free. She cooked a lot so I might get some free meals. Mostly, I would have time to get to the bottom of this mess.

"Lucy," she said. "You want to show how our democracy is being dismantled? Then come to Wisconsin."

I had a severance check from the *Post* and they did treat me right. I had no job offers.

And, of course, I had my mission.

I packed my bags and moved to Wisconsin.

35

Max Parker

"Greta! You have numbers?" I asked, nervously. I had been pacing the room waiting for her call.

"You better believe it."

"Fire away."

"For starters, Max, they are better than either of us suspected. Fifty-six percent think Ladner should not have withdrawn from the race. And here's the big number. Sixty-three percent of African Americans say he should have stayed in."

"Holy shit!" I answered. "Okay," I added, "that means that the numbers among white voters were a lot closer."

"White voters split almost evenly on staying in the race."

"Who would have thought?"

"But here is the best news. Democratic voters see Jeffrey's call for Ladner to stay in the race as a great positive. Of those who wanted Ladner out of the race, almost 40 percent think more highly of Jeffrey for asking him to stay."

"Why is that?"

"We asked voters to use one word to describe Jeffrey's defense of Ladner. The top three words were 'courage,' 'honest,' and 'racist.'"

"Two out of three ain't bad," I quipped.

"'Racist' had the lowest frequency of the three. Under 15 percent."

This news was so good I almost did not want to ask the next question. "What about the horserace with Ladner out?"

"Are you sitting down?"

"I can't sit down. I might wet my pants."

"Holloway 25 percent. Scott 32 percent. No one else more than 10."

"God Almighty damned."

* * *

You know it. I know it. Politics is a profession full of phonies and liars. And nothing brings these characters out from behind their rocks faster than a turning tide.

I was seated in a small suite at the Courtyard Marriott airport in Manchester, New Hampshire. It was 5:30 in the afternoon and there was a line outside the door. A congressman, four county chairs, a national committeeman, three mayors, 10 state legislators, and the goddamned coroner of Belknap County.

Jeffrey was sitting on the couch receiving these well-wishers who, five days ago, would not have nodded good morning if they were stuck with Jeffrey on an elevator that broke down between floors. But word of the exit polls showing Jeffrey in the lead had New Hampshire politicians, big and small, lined up to make their bows.

Listen to a country chair who helped Holloway. "Congressman Scott, we've been working hard for you in Grafton County. It's about time we changed how we do politics in Washington."

A state senator who worked for Ladner but stayed neutral after his withdrawal: "Congressman Scott, I doubt that the Oval Office has ever hosted a leader quite like you."

Then there was Alexander Lodge, congressman from New Hampshire, a member of the Ways and Means Committee, a New England patrician and a snob who would not have recognized

Jeffrey, a member of the lowly small business committee, if he saw him on the House floor.

"Jeffrey! Is a congratulations too early? It has certainly been a privilege to serve with you in the House."

Finally, I had to clear the room. If we won that night, Jeffrey had a speech to make, probably the biggest speech he had ever made. But before he picked up his legal pad to make notes about what he would say, he turned to me with a smile.

"Whaddya think?"

"Win or lose, I never thought we could get this far."

"We are going to win tonight," he answered. Then he offered a sly smile that could have meant he was kidding but I was not so sure. Then he added, "I knew it all along."

* * *

Pandemonium.

There is rule in politics. Always book a room that is too small for your crowd. If you draw 1,000 supporters and the room holds 1,500 then all people notice is the empty space. But if you 1,000 people and the room holds 500, they pack in tight and the crowd becomes a sensation.

Well, we have 5,000 supporters and a room that holds 500 people.

Who knew? When we booked this room, I figured our crowd would be zero because Jeffrey would no longer be in the race.

The event was downstairs, but the crowd had already filled the room, packed the hallway, filled the stairs, clogged the lobby, and spilled out into the parking lot. We did not book security or rent extra cops. But there are cops on the premises dealing with the clogged streets, frustrated supporters who can't get in and the SUVs blocking every sidewalk within a mile of our event. To make matters worse, the ground was covered with a foot and a half of new snow.

I grabbed three policemen, handed them $20 bills, and told them to escort anyone with a camera into the room.

The hotel was a typical Courtyard Marriott, square with light brown bricks and a gray shingled roof. Inside, if you could get inside, and down the stairs was the room where our celebration would take place. TVs lined the walls. CNN. MSNBC. PBS. WMUR in Manchester. Even Fox. Jeffrey insisted. And no matter which channel you chose, there was a show going on.

I love to watch these media people. Everyone says they never give politicians an even break, but that view is too simple. These media types have an agenda and their agenda is the story. An example of why politicians are lying, slimy, subhuman creatures is a good story, at least in their view. But if you give them something that surprises, inspires, and shows the world in a different way, they will not only run with it, they will add six shots of steroids and blow it up beyond all factual basis.

So even though Jeffrey Scott was leading in the late polls, that information was completely ignored. The story was "American politics has been turned upside down! A completely unconventional candidate has won a shocking victory in the New Hampshire primary."

A few examples.

"A political earthquake." CNN.

"A stunning rejection of how business is done in Washington, DC." Fox.

"Politics will never be the same." CBS.

Those media people don't often hand out halos. That night, Jeffrey Scott had one, a big one, shining right behind his head.

But, as my dad used to say, all blessings are mixed. Jeffrey Scott may be a momentary saint but we still had to get him through the door in time for the TV people to have his speech for the 11 o'clock news. Is there a back door, a fire escape? Jeffrey had been in front of the hotel for 20 minutes. People wanted to thank him, congratulate him, or just touch his sleeve on this magical night.

Finally, a staff person appeared with a hotel security guard who took us to the back, down a poorly lit stairway, and to an emergency exit where the guard pulled a key, opened the door, and actually pushed Jeffrey into the room. The people were standing wall-to-wall so I took my cue from the guard and started pushing Jeffrey forward. The supporters pressed us on all sides, and as they realized that the candidate had entered, they raised a cheer that spread across the entire room.

Applause became a chant.

"Jeffrey. Jeffrey. Jeffrey."

Suddenly he was on the stage. There was no podium. He never likes a podium. He had the mic in his hand. The air was electric. Heads bobbing up and down not so much to see but because the crowd was filled with an energy they were unable to contain.

Jeffrey was still on the stage, calm with a soft smile. He was absorbing the moment that few politicians will ever know. Then he looked at a TV screen showing the vote. He had 48 percent. Unbelievable.

He turned to the crowd. "I see we have 48 percent of the vote."

A raucous cheer.

"I guess that means we are only three percent short of a majority who believe Washington needs a change."

Laughter. Not big, but it quieted the crowd and Jeffrey started to speak.

"There is nothing more precious to this nation, more precious, more essential, more central to our essence as a people, than having a democracy that actually works. But today in Washington, we are witness to the failure of our government, and if we do not repair our government the consequences are beyond imagination.

"Our retirement programs are headed for bankruptcy. Our climate is changing and the evidence, none of it good, is all around us. Yet we cannot agree on a single solution that can be passed by Congress to slow the rising temperatures on our planet. If we had a penny for every speech any politician has made about income inequality, we could feed the poor, enrich the middle class, and place the American dream within the reach of millions more Americans. But not one serious piece of legislation to address this crisis has been enacted into law. It is time for words that are difficult and painful but are nevertheless true.

"Our democracy in America is broken. And today, the voters of New Hampshire have made a statement.

"They have said that, like all Americans, we are fed up with all the shouting in Washington and believe that it is time for real conversations about real solutions to the urgent problems facing our nation.

"They have said that they are fed up with politicians who demonize one another for long-ago offenses instead of offering forgiveness, forging partnerships, and understanding that creating good deeds in the present are far more important than reliving the sins of the past.

"Most importantly, they have affirmed that all Americans are fed up with partisanship at the expense of progress and purity at the expense of finding common ground.

"Tonight, we have won a first victory. But there is a long road ahead to win this nomination. There is an even longer road to win this election and bring fundamental, transformative, and lasting change to our government in Washington.

"And before I close, I want to make a request of each and every American. Tomorrow, I want each of you to make a gesture of unity for our nation. If you are a Democratic, I want you to find a Republican friend and give him a hug. If you are a Republican, find a Democrat and do the same. In so doing, we can all say, each and every one of us, that we are not enemies. We have differences. But those differences do not mean we cannot be partners in saving America.

"I thank the voters of New Hampshire for their voice. I look forward to carrying this campaign to every state in our nation."

As Jeffrey spoke of the hugs, supporters in the audience exchanged glances, wondering about his unusual request. As usual, this was Jeffrey's idea that he shared with no one, including me. But when he finished, the applause was thunderous. It was an enchanted evening no one would forget.

The victory was sweet, I won't deny it. But I wasn't drinking the Kool-Aid. I thought of our polls and what they said about our chances. People like principle. They want to rally to the flag. We were lucky in New Hampshire. The frontrunner fell. But can a call for more practical politics actually touch the emotions of millions of voters and win an election in America?

I still did not know.

36

Nadia Fedorov

I am sitting in the offices of the Internet Research Agency in St. Petersburg, Russia, and I am waiting. This agency is the pride of Russia. It handles cyberattacks on foreign governments. It influences foreign elections. It creates fake news, automated social media, and all kinds of other tricks and gimmicks that eat at the foundations of modern democracy. It is what Russians do better than anyone else in the world. Maybe the only thing.

And you know what? Here I am, ready to deliver the biggest decision in the entire world, and I have been sitting in this fucking chair, waiting, for the last 20 minutes.

Can you believe it? They are paying hundreds of millions of rubles to the finest hackers on planet Earth and what for? My "boyfriend," Sheldon, is going to hand the US presidential election to any candidate they choose. I have all the respect in the world for those cyber wizards that can view, explore, and manipulate any website in the world. But just because my skills are as old as Cleopatra doesn't mean they don't still work. And sometimes a good piece of pussy puts all that fancy cyber shit to shame.

But here I sit, waiting. Finally, a middle-aged woman, fat and dowdy, summons me to the conference room. *Where, I could ask, is Vladimir Putin?*

We walk down a long hall. The conference room is small with paneled wooden walls opposite a large window that looks out over the River Neva as it snakes through the middle of this town.

There are six chairs, mine with the rest occupied by men. At the head of the table is Vasily Kusnetsov, head of the Internet Research Agency, the department charged with screwing American elections. I am introduced to the other four, three of whom were cyber big-wigs, which, of course, has nothing to do with the strategy I employ.

Kusnetsov has a chiseled face with a perfect chin and small but forceful eyes. But before I can flirt, he gets right to business. "Ms. Fedorov, I understand you have a contact in America who programs voting machines."

"Yes, you might call him a 'contact.'"

"What would you call him?"

I smile. "You might remember that you guys sent me to the voting machine conference in New York to do a little fishing. He's the fish I caught."

Chuckles around the table.

"And what is this man's job?"

I can't believe it. I provided all this information in writing. The lazy schmuck did not even bother to read it.

"He is the quality control programmer. He reviews all programming of all voting machines for a company that handles 40 percent of the voting machines in America."

"Which states?"

"Wisconsin, Michigan, and Pennsylvania, for starters."

A murmur rises from around the table. Heads nod.

"It is really a perfect situation," I continue. "They are already cheating, tilting the numbers. The company gave him the job to insert the counting code at the very end of their process. They don't even look at it because, if things ever got out, they want to be able to say they never knew. He could elect Mickey Mouse, if he was so inclined."

"Oh my." Kuznetsov can barely believe our luck. "How much money does he want?"

"He wants $150 million. Nothing less. Deposited in 450 bitcoin wallets. I have the numbers in my purse."

Kuznetsov pauses, pondering the transaction.

"I think you need to understand the situation," I add. "This guy is fat, ugly, and, frankly, a little afraid of all women. I am not even sure he has been within three meters of a really great-looking woman—much less taken one to bed." I give the boys a little wink. "I promised him a wedding and a honeymoon after the election. There will be no double-cross here. He can deliver this election. And will."

One of the cyber guys asks, "Are you really going to marry him?"

I look at him like he had just flunked preschool.

"Okay," says Kuznetsov, summarizing the meeting. "$150 million is a lot of money. I need to take this upstairs."

Right, I think, *$150 million to choose the president of the United States of America?*

Nobody understands real value anymore. These guys would have refused Thomas Edison $100 for a patent on the lightbulb.

37

ABC News

"This is Daniel Phillips, with *ABC World News Tonight*. Two days ago, in his victory speech in the New Hampshire primary, Jeffrey Scott called on Americans to hug a member of the other party. Did he actually launch an interparty festival of affection and goodwill? Cindy Bishop has our report."

"Thanks, Daniel. Well, it was certainly one of the most unusual requests we have heard from a candidate in a long time." Video shows Jeffrey Scott.

"Tomorrow, I want each of you to make a gesture of unity. If you are a Democrat, I want you to find a Republican friend and give him a hug. If you are a Republican, find a Democrat and do the same. In so doing, we can all say, each and every one of us, that we are not enemies. We have differences. But those differences do not mean we cannot be partners in saving America."

"Well, what happened? Here is Liz Watson, Sheboygan, Wisconsin."

"Well, it was a little weird, but I know three people at work who are Republicans and I gave them each a hug. They were a little surprised but when I explained, they all hugged back. One said she had never hugged a socialist before. I think she was kidding."

"And Sam Bronkowski, Denver, Colorado."

"My mom is a Republican. I gave her a hug. First time in a month."

"Some voters have used Scott's invitation with ulterior motives. Listen to Beth Hahn, Arlington, Texas."

"I saw this guy and he was sort of hot and I asked him if he was a Democrat. He said he was so I gave him a hug. We are going out this weekend."

"Some refused. Here is Ralph Billings from Tacoma, Washington."

"Hug a Democrat? I would rather kiss a skunk."

"Some have videoed their hugs and posted on Facebook."

Video of man and woman wearing elephant and donkey masks. They enter into a mad, passionate embrace.

"Here is another from Cheyenne, Wyoming."

"Meet my friend, Bill. He is a big-taxing, baby-killing left-wing socialist. But I love him."

"Meet my friend, Anne. She is a fascist, Mexican-hating, Bible-toting extremist who wants to put cameras in your bedroom. But I love her anyway."

Bill and Anne raise tiny American flags.

"And here is one more."

Video shows a sofa with an inflated elephant and an inflated donkey. A guy appears on the left with a hairpin and pops the elephant. A woman does the same to the donkey. Suddenly, they are both tangled together on a couch in a passionate embrace.

"Daniel, I think this hugging epidemic is spreading. It may be a little silly…"

"But, Cindy, at least they aren't poking each other's eyes out. And some of them are pretty funny."

"That's right. The campaign is posting the hug video of the day on its website. It's worth a visit if you want a laugh."

"Democrats and Republicans having fun together. What's the world coming to?"

"Who knows? This is one strange campaign."

38

Lucy Gilmore

Sarah kept calling and asking when I would arrive in Madison. When I finally got there, I found out why.

Sarah's house was not really in Madison; it was a few miles outside of Fitchburg, which was south of the city. Houses were cheaper there and since most of the occupants were working on campaigns, it was what they could afford. Sarah made almost no money blogging but had at least enough family money to pay rent. The house was a big house, two stories and wide. But it looked rundown like one of those frat houses that had seen one too many toga parties.

All the lights were on. Strange.

Before I could knock, Sarah opened the door and devoured me in a big hug, which was not hard to do since she stood almost six feet tall. Waiting behind her were eight to 10 people. They were all in their 20s and most were raggedly dressed, but they looked at me like I was someone special. One of them held a hand-lettered sign that said, "Welcome Lucy Gilmore!"

I even got a cheer, which gave me a tear—well, more than one of those.

It seems my blog post made me something of a hero, which was nice because after being canceled at the *Post*, and having no success finding a job in my real profession, I was happy to discover I had some fans, even if you could count them on two hands.

"Will someone get Lucy a drink?" Sarah yelled.

Most of these people lived in the house. There was Joel Tifton, who described himself as a cyber-security consultant, but someone else described as a hacker. Two people had jobs canvassing for the Democratic Party. There was a data geek who did targeting at the campaign headquarters downtown. All of them, every single one, had read my blog.

"You are a hero!" said one.

"Sister, you nailed it," said another.

Sarah handed me a drink.

"Here you go, darling. It's a French 75. It will crumple your panties."

I laughed. "After nine hours on the road, a beer could have done the trick."

Sarah and I sat in the corner. I did not bring up my firing at the *Post* but described my unsuccessful job search. I started to cry.

But Sarah, who had seen me cry often enough to know not to panic, was giving me another message.

"Don't you cry over some sorry ass job you did not get in Akron, Ohio. Not getting those jobs is the best thing that could happen to you. You are onto something. Something big. And you need time to get the proof. This is Wisconsin. I've been chasing these bastards for two years and one thing I know. They are fixing these elections. It's all right here and the presidential election is just three months away."

"You think we can crack this case?" I asked, hopeful but not with conviction.

"Babe, they think they're gonna get away with it. What they don't know is that Lucy Gilmore just arrived in town."

39

Nadia Fedorov

They have the offer. $150 million to choose who will lead the biggest economic and military power in the world. Is that a bargain? It's like buying a Rolls-Royce for 75 cents. But tell me, does Mr. Vasily Kusnetsov, chief in charge of fucking foreign governments, call me back and say, "Nadia, your offer is so generous. Why don't we give you $200 million instead?"

No.

In fact, he does not call me back at all! Two weeks and no call. Why you ask?

I know why. Because Vasily Kusnetsov is a bureaucrat and in Russia being a bureaucrat can be a dangerous profession. There he sits at that table with four other bureaucrats talking about the grand prize, the World Cup, the climb to the summit of Mount Everest itself. And what are the other four thinking? Are they thinking I am part of the team that could reach the pinnacle of achievement? Will I be a part of choosing the leader of the greatest democracy on Earth? No. They are thinking, "How can I fuck Vasily Kusnetsov and get his job."

Where is the love of country? Where are the higher ideals?

So Kusnetsov is thinking how do I get this deal done without his deputy running over to the Kremlin and saying that Kusnetsov wants to give $150 million to an unreliable slut? It's a tough problem. I understand. But as you Americans say, "This is no time for softball," especially when you have the programmer for 40 percent of America's voting machines prostrate at your feet and licking your toes.

I decide Kusnetsov needs a call.

"Vasily," I ask, "do we have a deal?"

"Nadia," he answers. "What you have accomplished is amazing. The whole American election on a platter. You deserve the Hero of the Russian Federation Award! Unfortunately, we cannot give the award without publicly acknowledging your role in stealing the election."

"It's okay, Vasily. The money will do."

"Nadia, I am working on the approvals for the money. If it were up to me, you would be sitting in your new home in a golden bathtub full of thousand-dollar bills. But things are not always so easy."

I am silent. Waiting.

"Nadia, the powers that be have to look at their options."

"Options?" I ask. "I have options too. What would Turkey pay to pick the American president? Or India? Or..." I take a long pause, building drama as I prepare to name-drop the next possible customer.

"Or China?"

I feel the shiver at the other end of the line.

"They might pay a billion, wouldn't you think?"

"You don't know those people. Do you think they will drop that kind of money on a Russian who works for the Service of Special Communications? They would laugh you out of the room."

"Me? Yes. But I know middlemen." I am bluffing here but he can't be sure. "I know people they know and trust. They are negotiating as we speak."

"Nadia, you are forgetting something important. You work for us."

"Would you like me to resign?"

"That is not your option."

"Well, Vasily, tell me what you plan to do. Are you going to shoot me? Burn my apartment to the ground? Drop my cat in sulfuric acid? Who are you kidding? I own the guy who programs 40 percent of the voting machines in America. Sometimes I wonder about you, Vasily. You are nowhere near that stupid. You know who holds the cards here."

"Okay, Nadia," he replies in an icy voice. "Let me work on the money. I just need some time."

"Two weeks," I answer.

Never underplay your hand.

40

Max Parker

Success in politics has many consequences. It brings money, press coverage, and adulation, and paints your candidate with a charisma far beyond his natural gifts. But political success always comes at someone else's expense. And coming out of his surprise upset victory in New Hampshire, an array of big guns, funded by Holloway supporters, turned their fire on Jeffrey Scott.

Across South Carolina, the next major contest, the airways were flooded with TV ads attacking our bipartisan plan to save Social Security.

The TV screen went dark. In the shadows, huddled together, were a man and a woman, at least 80 years old. Their clothes were tattered, actually patched in places as if a trip to Goodwill was beyond their means. Their hands, all four of them gripped together as if awaiting the certain arrival of the apocalypse itself. The voice-over began.

"1929, stocks lost 90 percent of their value. Black Monday, stocks lose 20 percent in one day. The 2008 financial meltdown— stocks lose half their value. Who is crazy enough to risk your Social Security on the stock market?"

Picture of Jeffrey Scott with a goofy smile on his face.

"Jeffrey Scott, that's who. He supports a Republican-backed plan to put Social Security in the stock market. Jeffrey Scott. He's no Democrat at all."

That was only the start. We had done a joint plan for saving Medicare with Sutton Thomas, a Republican senator from Iowa, also running in the second tier of the Republican presidential race. There was nothing easy about that plan. The doctors and hospitals opposed fee cuts. No one wanted to raise payroll taxes. It was a simple problem. Get more money, lower costs, or both. Of course, we did both.

The ad began with a picture of a senior couple, looking 200 years old with fear on their faces.

"Medicare, the lifeline for older Americans. But Jeffrey Scott's Republican-backed plan calls for deep cuts in Medicare spending. Doctor fees cut so low your own doctor may refuse to give you care. And working Americans pay higher taxes."

Older woman leans forward, anger on her face.

"Jeffrey Scott, we don't need your Republican plan. We need to keep Medicare as we know it."

Of course, Medicare as we know it has one foot in bankruptcy. But these voters have not been going through the ledger.

There was an ad on free college. Again, Jeffrey had shaped a bipartisan plan that included work-study, means testing, and grade requirements. The message? Jeffrey Scott has joined with Republicans in opposing free college education.

Thank goodness only half the voters were still watching broadcast TV. If they were watching Netflix or Amazon or Hulu, they would not see these ads at all. But the attacks were backed by a blizzard of mail and in internet ads as well and in the sermons delivered in black churches all across South Carolina.

Where are these ads coming from? Not from Christine Holloway's campaign but from the Citizens to Save Your Retirement, a super PAC funded by Holloway supporters, and other super PACs as well. Donors can write million-dollar checks to these groups. And there are people who will write those checks because despite our upset victory in New Hampshire, most believe they can curry favor with Holloway, who has the inside track to the nomination and the White House itself.

Each day, I was on the phone with our pollster, Greta Simmons. Each day the message was the same. Jeffrey's lead was evaporating. The percentage of voters who viewed Jeffrey unfavorably was growing, especially among older voters.

Big money and slick ads, almost completely untrue. And voters who never read a newspaper were running from Jeffrey Scott like sheep from the sound of a growling wolf.

Sometimes I want to say to voters, "Don't blame the politicians. Go look in the mirror first."

41

CBS News

"This is Frank Jamison of CBS News with a newsbreak on the South Carolina Democratic presidential primary. Denise Garrity is in Charleston, South Carolina, with our report. Denise."

"Thank you, Frank. This just in. CBS News has called Christine Holloway the runaway winner of this year's South Carolina primary. Currently, Holloway is getting 42 percent of the vote, compared with only 28 percent for the upset New Hampshire winner, Jeffrey Scott.

"Early polls showed the race a tossup, but an aggressive ad campaign by Holloway allies labeled Scott, who is offering bipartisan solutions, as a sellout to the Republicans and questioned whether he is actually a Democrat at all. Meanwhile, since Ladner's withdrawal, Holloway has moved to the left, wooing Ladner's former supporters. Here's Holloway."

Holloway is standing at the podium absorbing the adulation with a sly smile. She gazes left and right, occasionally nodding to someone she knows. She does not raise her hands to quiet the crowd but rather waits until the screams, the shouts, and even the claps ease into the lower volumes. Then she leans forward, across her podium, fire in her eyes, and begins.

"Fellow Democrats. We have won a great victory tonight, not just for me, but for the most fundamental principles of our Democratic Party.

"We chose Medicare for all health care coverage over those plans that would hand even more of our money over to health insurance companies and Big Pharma.

"We chose keeping Social Security out of the stock market..." (Boos from the crowd.) "...over a plan that compromises away all that is good about this lifeline, this program that stands at the boundary between a decent life and financial destitution for tens of millions of American seniors.

"We chose serious measures to right income inequality, to raise the wealth of the middle class, and to make the one percent pay their fair share of taxes, a share they have avoided by handing senators and congressmen big checks to work on their behalf.

"Most importantly, we have said tonight, in a resounding voice, that progress depends on boldly imagining a better world. Progress begins by reaching for what is right and refusing to sully our proposals with Republican ideas that lie at the heart of the problems facing this nation."

Huge applause.

"And I have a promise for you and a message for Mr. Jeffrey Scott. As president, I will, from time to time, need to negotiate with Republicans. But I promise this. I will never give in on our principles. I will never compromise what is precious to this party, before we even arrive at the table to begin our talks."

To that last line, the applause was so great that you could see the banners and streamers shake.

"Well, quite a victory for Senator Holloway," Denise Garrity states. "And pretty strong words for Congressman Scott."

"Right, Denise. Do you think we have a frontrunner tonight?"

"Well, they've both won a major primary by strong margins. But it is hard for me to see Jeffrey Scott winning over these liberal primary voters with a message that tempers their dreams. If you ask me, Holloway is headed to the convention with the upper hand."

42

Lucy Gilmore

Are you ready? I hope so because it is time for a briefing on Wisconsin, my new home.

I'll start with the basics. America's dairyland, home of Harley-Davidson and a long progressive tradition inspired by Bob LaFollette, governor, senator, and one-time presidential candidate during the first half of the 20th century. Wisconsin was the first state to offer workmen's compensation, unemployment insurance, and an income tax.

Well, that's not a bad start, but now the state has taken a different course.

So let me begin with an important and relevant question. What does it take to cause someone to manipulate voting machines? It takes a deep hunger for power. It takes technical skills. It takes a shameless disregard for the idea that the vote of the people is a sacred, inviolate gift. And what does all this have to do with Wisconsin?

Meet Scott Walker.

In 2010, Scott Walker was elected governor and began an assault on the idea that everyone ought to have a vote and that the vote should actually influence the actions of government.

Hard to believe? Boy, do I have examples.

The first thing he did was to put in place the toughest voter ID law in the nation. "What's wrong with that?" you are probably asking. Well, the voter ID laws prohibited voting by any voter who

160

could not show a Wisconsin driver's license, passport, military ID, a state-issued ID, or naturalization papers. Student IDs could work but only with a two-year expiration date and student IDs are commonly issued year to year. Those liberal millennials?

Out of luck.

Oh, you can obtain a state ID from the motor vehicle department. But that requires a birth certificate. If you go on the website where you can get a birth certificate it says you need a driver's license, passport, US government-issued ID, or tribal ID. Catch-22.

Republicans, of course, claimed no one would be prevented from voting. State Senator Mary Lazich claimed publicly, "Not a single voter in this state will be disenfranchised by the ID law." But in a closed-door Republican caucus meeting, reported by someone in attendance, "Mary Lazich argued on behalf of the bill because it would diminish turnout in Democratic strongholds."

By one estimate 300,000 Wisconsin voters lacked qualifying IDs going into the last presidential election. I am always skeptical of these "estimates." In a big political argument, truth is the first casualty and it disappears on both sides. But even half that number is alarming.

So here is the question. Do Americans have a right to vote even if they can't drive a car, or afford one? The Wisconsin voter ID law was challenged in court. The US Supreme court affirmed it by declining to even hear the case.

It seems to me that this decision raises a question for our honorable U.S. Supreme Court. "What about the Constitution? The right to vote? It's in there somewhere. It must be." Maybe Chief Justice Roberts forgot to bring the document to work on the day this case was considered. Or maybe his dog ate it. It happens to homework all the time. But in Wisconsin, this voter ID business was just the start.

So here is another question worth considering. What if most voters want to elect a state legislator who is a Democrat? So they go to the polls, find the Democrats on the ballot, and voila! A majority of those elected legislators, or perhaps something close, would be Democrats. Right?

Well, you are obviously not familiar with the new math.

In 2012, Democratic candidates for the state legislature in Wisconsin got 175,000 more votes, statewide, than the Republican candidates. But the Republicans got 51 of the 99 assembly seats—almost 60 percent. So if Democrats got more votes, how did they lose the election?

It happened because the Republican leadership spent $400,000 of state taxpayer money to draw a map that packed Democratic voters tightly into a handful of districts. Gerrymandering. That way one party can get a lot more votes but still lose the election.

I don't think that was what Thomas Jefferson had in mind.

The problem for Scott Walker and his allies is you can't gerrymander a statewide election. But did that halt their assault on democracy? Of course not. When Scott Walker was finally defeated, the Republican legislature proceeded to pass a series of laws to limit the new governor's powers. The new governor, Tony Evers, a Democrat, would take office in January. But between election day and the inauguration, Walker would remain as governor. The legislature, selected from heavily gerrymandered districts, still held a strong Republican majority.

So in the lame duck session Republican legislators hurried through 40 measures to limit the power of the governor and other Democratic state-elected officials. They succeeded. Governor Walker signed the bill and greatly diminished the ability of the new governor to carry out the agenda that Wisconsin voters had elected him to pursue. The Wisconsin Supreme Court, in a party line vote, said these roadblocks to implementing the will of the people were no problem at all.

So next question. If you are willing to disenfranchise voters who don't drive, if you are willing to draw maps that allow a minority of voters to select a majority of the legislators, and if you are willing to pass laws that prevent an elected governor from carrying out his voter-endorsed agenda, would you also be willing to fix the voting machines?

And as I Google through news reports on Wisconsin elections, I come to a strange quote from none other than one of the leading national political consultants on the Republican side. Roger Stone was a top advisor to prominent Republican candidates including Richard Nixon, Ronald Reagan, Jack Kemp, and Bob Dole. In a column in *The Hill*, a Washington, DC, newspaper covering Congress and politics, Stone wrote this statement.

"There are strong indications that Scott Walker and the Reince Priebus machine rigged as many as five elections including the defeat of a Walker recall election."

Holy moley.

So suddenly I am a lot happier to be here in Wisconsin. The presidential election is only six months away. If my goal is to uncover the destruction of our democracy through voting machine fraud, I may have arrived, almost by accident, in exactly the right place. Would Scott Walker and the Wisconsin Republicans actually go so far as to manipulate voting machines to steal an election?

You make your own guess.

Me? I am going to find out.

43

Max Parker

Reeling.

That is what the Jeffrey Scott for President campaign was doing.

Our hug a Republican was a big thing and people had fun. But then *Saturday Night Live* got a hold of it and did a skit where independent voters surrounded Jeffrey and asked him who are *they* supposed to hug. Well, the guy who played Jeffrey, I have to admit he was pretty funny, puts on this big smile and says, "I've had a plan for you all along."

Then he reaches into this bag and starts handing out all those strange garments worn by nuns and monks. He says, "You shall be celibate." Jeffrey thought it was hilarious.

Me, after the initial laughs, not so much.

Our message was still a problem. Holloway was the dream. We were the reality. But a bigger problem was the calendar.

Okay, so we lost the South Carolina primary. But here was the worse news. Three days later came Super Tuesday. Here is a list of the states choosing delegates on Super Tuesday.

Alabama
Arkansas
California
Colorado
Georgia

Massachusetts
Minnesota
North Carolina
Tennessee
Texas
Utah
Vermont
Viriginia
Democrats Abroad

This is Super Tuesday, the worst idea in the history of American politics. How did this happen anyway? I'll tell you how it happened.

Southerners.

In 1988, all those southern states got together. Their goal was to have all the southern states vote at one time, early, so no wild-eyed liberal socialist would have a prayer of getting the nomination. But you know what happens when too many Southerners get together to enhance their own well-being? Nine times out of 10, they shoot themselves in the foot.

So in 1988, eight southern states, including Texas and Florida, decided to flex their muscles and have their primaries on the same day.

It was one more disaster for Democrats in a crazy campaign.

First of all, the frontrunner, Senator Gary Hart of Colorado, who had finished second in 1984, got nuked when the *Miami Herald* reported on his affair with a model and bit actress named Donna Rice. Where did this dalliance take place? On a yacht named "Monkey Business." You can't make this stuff up.

Then Joe Biden, another strong candidate, had to quit because he was stealing his speeches from Neil Kinnock, a British Labor Party leader. Listen, if you are going to steal speeches, you can't go overseas.

So with the big guys out, the race was wide open. I was barely out of high school but working for Dick Gephardt, a congressman from Missouri. He wasn't flashy but he had this earnest Midwest persona and he won the contests in Iowa and South Dakota, two of the three big early events. But by the time we got to Super Tuesday, we were broke.

Meanwhile, Michael Dukakis, the liberal governor of Massachusetts, who had no appeal in the South, had something better.

He was from Boston and he had a lot of money. So he picked out four big southern states with enough liberals to give him a chance, he bought the only TV ads voters saw, and on primary night, he got more delegates than anyone and was declared the winner.

In politics, greed is the downfall of many a political strategist. If those Southerners had set up an early primary with five small southern states, Al Gore would have won and Michael Dukakis might have been history.

But in politics like in reality television, bad ideas live on. I guess those Southerners thought that if people called it "super" they must have done something right. Now California, Massachusetts, and Minnesota, and other states as well, jumped on board this Super Tuesday bandwagon. What all this meant is that South Carolina became the key player. Win South Carolina and you are the story for the next three days, which gets you to Super Tuesday and all those delegates.

Ads? No one has that kind of money, even if the ads still worked.

So I don't have to tell you what happened. Senator Christine Holloway, who had toned down all her liberal rhetoric to woo southern moderates, walked away with five southern states, Massachusetts, and California. We won Minnesota (they are so sensible there), Alabama, Arkansas, Tennessee, and Virginia, states where talking to Republicans is not a capital crime.

But the main verdict was that everyone was crowning Senator Holloway as the certain Democratic nominee and the next president of the United States.

After Super Tuesday, Holloway had almost 1,000 delegates. We were at 600 and fading.

We had catching up to do. We needed one of those great ideas that only Jeffrey seemed to have.

Jeffrey, for Christ's sakes, speak up!

44

Nadia Fedorov

You need to understand something about these Russians. Oh, they are big and bold and want to bully the rest of the world, but at home, in dealing with each other, they are cowards.

Frankly, it is hard to blame them. They lived under Stalin, where if you winked at the wrong cat you might end up with electrodes on your testicles confessing to an assassination plot against the Party secretary himself. It's better now, of course, but they still have this culture of quiet accusation, squealing really, that keeps these meetings full of tension and intrigue.

I'm from Ukraine and not the part where they build temples to Putin.

And, of course, I am especially disgusted at the moment because Vasily Kusnetsov has not closed the deal. In fact, he is not even returning my calls. I suppose he thinks his hackers can steal this election. Maybe they don't even care who wins. There are probably other hackers who plan to steal this election. In fact, by election day there will probably be so much malicious code on those pathetic, undefended machines, they may not work at all.

But who gets the last look? Who, of all the people in the world, can look at those memory cards and erase all that other code and add in those three lines that deliver the winning margin to the candidate of our choice?

My boyfriend, Sheldon Klumm, that's who.

So I own this election and I need a customer. I have couple of contacts, not high level but still contacts, in China and I put out the word. "Call me. The American election is for sale."

So the message I get back is "not interested." Which could have meant "we don't trust you" but, even more likely, why should we care? No American president is going to do any favors for China.

So, then I put my offer out to India. Guess what? I did not even hear back. The clock is ticking.

I can't do this myself. I need a middleman. Someone who knows somebody in these countries. Someone they will trust with about the most sensitive transaction anyone can imagine. I know a few people. The Russians would sometimes send me to diplomatic events because someone with information is more likely to blab to a hot-looking blonde than some old guy with sagging cheeks and eyebrows that got electrocuted at the hairdresser.

I sit down and make a list. To be on my list you need several qualifications. First, you need connections and credibility around the world. Second, your moral standards cannot be too high. And, third, the best qualification would be that you are desperate for money.

You can imagine the conversations. I say, "Boris, I need some help on a big deal, tens of millions of dollars." That gets his attention. Then he wants to know what the deal is about. So I say, "It has something to do with the American presidential election." Then, if they are still diplomats, they are out. If they aren't, they want specifics. I can't be specific on the phone so I ask for a meeting. Risky. Risky. Not surprisingly, I got no meetings. But on the sixth call, I got lucky.

I got a tip.

I am about to give up when I place a call to Armand Paquet, the former Belgium ambassador to Egypt. I met him at some boring diplomatic event in Copenhagen. In fact, I more than met him. He remembered, of course. But when I start talking about the deal, he backs away. Just as we are ending the call, he offers me a thought.

"I have an idea. Why don't you call Howard Feldman? I hear he is on hard times."

Howard Feldman? I search my memory. Then I remember. He was the American ambassador to Switzerland. He struck me as kind of slimy. He might just be my guy.

* * *

Howard Feldman is from Blackwood, New Jersey. He rose to prominence in the waste disposal business where his company, Household Organics, not only picked up garbage but developed innovative approaches to toxic waste disposal that remain undisclosed to this day. As he built his financial empire, he also built a political empire, becoming a go-to fundraiser and money man across South Jersey.

Howard's fundraising success won him the job of chief of protocol at the State Department during the Bush administration where his job was to escort foreign leaders around the country. Later he was appointed ambassador to Switzerland but after two years he returned to his business and within a year was arrested for bribing a congressman. Then a story broke that he had illegally dumped toxic waste. New Jersey cities and towns fled his business. Within six months he was broke.

I look him up on anywho.com. Got his phone number and address. Then I peeked at his residence the way Google lets you do. He isn't even living in a house! He is living in a one-bedroom apartment in a crummy part of suburban Philadelphia.

Oh my, he is really broke. As Aristotle used to say, "the gods are with me." I dial.

"Hello?"

"Is this Howard Feldman?"

"Speaking."

"Howard, you may not remember me. I met you at an event for the Ukrainian president. My name is Nadia Fedorov."

"I am not recalling."

"No matter. I am calling you with a business proposition that I can't discuss on the phone. Can you meet me at the Philadelphia Four Seasons for lunch tomorrow?"

"What kind of proposition?'

"One that can make you money."

45

Max Parker

Never doubt Jeffrey Scott. He is one shrewd sonofabitch.

Here we were trailing in delegates by almost two to one. Christine Holloway, in most national polls, was pulling 45 percent of the Democratic electorate. Jeffrey? A measly 30 percent. Not good.

It was May and the convention was two months away. Everyone was hailing her as the nominee, and in primary after primary she was inching closer to the number of delegates she needed to win. Meanwhile, the other candidates were dropping like flies.

Tom Stanton, senator from Arizona? Out. Jake Stillman, the gay congressman from Virginia? Out. Almost everyone was out except for Jeffrey, Holloway, and Grace Tiller, the Massachusetts senator and policy wonk extraordinaire.

We needed something big. You know what Jeffrey said?

"Let's do an audit."

"An audit of what?" I asked, not understanding his idea at all.

"Her plans. Holloway has no plans. She barely has proposals and her numbers are all loose. We have carefully crafted bipartisan proposals and our numbers add up."

"Who cares?" I answered. "You can't win an election in the weeds."

"There will never be an audit," Jeffrey replies. "She will refuse. It's not the audit we want. We want her to say 'no.' We can make it a question of honesty. Voters will see her refuse to put her numbers to the test. And remember, Tiller will accept so that will make matters even worse."

I see Jeffrey's point, but I ask him who does the audit. Not a small question.

A wide, delicious smile fills his face.

"There is only one accounting firm Americans know. PriceWaterhouseCoopers, the accountants for the stars."

"But didn't they screw some things up?"

"Who would remember? They still have the gig," Jeffrey responded. "We will show pictures of Meryl Streep, Brad Pitt, and Stephen Spielberg. Who would American voters trust more than the firm of the stars?"

Once again, Jeffrey's idea was a little crazy, but what did we have to lose? I called our media guy, Casmir Zielinski, and told him to go to work.

* * *

In the meantime, Jeffrey called Grace Tiller. She was getting about 10 percent of the vote. She was out of money but these days there is no good advertising you can buy, and the big secret is that money is not so important. Now that there were only three candidates left, she was making the news and getting some attention. The blessings of the survivor.

Anyway, this was a no-brainer for Grace Tiller. Her plans were more detailed and her numbers added up, at least as far as I could tell.

So Jeffrey called PricewaterhouseCoopers and offered them the work. They were alarmed by the scope. Assessing costs and economic effects of changes in taxation was one complicated piece of work. The convention was 10 weeks away. Jeffrey explained that Holloway could not accept but that their company would be praised as the premier accounting firm in the world. He said we would pay $3 million for the work, more if necessary. After a little negotiation, we limited the plan to the budget. Tempted by the prospect of great publicity, PricewaterhouseCoopers finally said "yes."

* * *

There he stood, Jeffrey Scott, candidate for President, in front of the Bureau of Engraving and Printing, the federal agency that prints dollar bills, treasury bonds, and God knows what other strange instruments that are used to keep our government afloat.

Now in this situation there is something you need to understand. What happens when a candidate starts to run away from the pack in a presidential race? The media turns on her. It's nothing personal. Like I said they have their own interests and their interest is a good story. They don't want this race over. They want eyeballs, audience. So on this day, as we opened our press conference, we could expect them to run with our almost silly plan and make life as difficult as they could for Christine Holloway.

Jeffrey began.

"I stand here today in front of the Bureau of Engraving and Printing, the government agency that prints America's dollar bills and produces the bonds that finance our massive government debt. This debt, which will burden our young people for the rest of their lives, is only the beginning. Our retirement programs are already endangered. Meeting these financial challenges will be the most difficult, trying, and important work that our next president will have to perform.

"But before making the proposal I present today, I think it is worth noting how we reached this situation. We face a mountain of debt because too many politicians were not truthful about the costs of their programs. Too many politicians were not honest about the consequences of the generous tax cuts they advanced. Each of the three remaining candidates for president has offered proposals and suggested how we might pay for them. I call on my opponents to put those proposals to a test.

"I have contacted the internationally acclaimed accounting firm of PricewaterhouseCoopers, the accountants for the stars. They have agreed to review my proposals, the proposals of Grace Tiller, and the proposals of Christine Holloway. Then they will report to the American people on the real costs of these ideas and whether the promises we are making to the American people are truthful and accurate.

"Grace Tiller has agreed to submit her plans. I have submitted my own. Now I call on Christine Holloway to put her proposals to the same test and allow the American people to know the true costs of everything she proposes.

"Grace Tiller and I have agreed to pay for this audit. Senator Holloway will not be required to spend a penny for this review."

Had he made this proposal six months ago, it would have hardly generated a yawn. But now, with the race dying, the press rushed to get Holloway's response.

* * *

We knew Holloway would refuse and, frankly, she had justification. This audit involved very complex issues that would be difficult to resolve in the weeks remaining in this campaign. The truth of the matter is that her refusal was stupid. There were only 10 weeks until the convention. She could delay providing her plans, answering questions, and advancing the audit. She would walk into the convention with the audit still unfinished.

But she did refuse and that refusal was all we needed. Within minutes of her response Casmir Zielinski's video appeared on the internet and, not long thereafter, in 30-second ads running in the remaining primary states.

The video opened with a family of four: middle-aged mom and dad, preteen sister and brother.

"America's government debt: $165,000 per household and growing fast."

Family members become wide-eyed, turning to look at one another in disbelief.

"Why? Because politicians have not told us the truth about the costs of their ideas. Two candidates for president have agreed to submit their proposals to be audited by the most famous accounting firm in the world, the accountants to the stars."

Pictures of Jeffrey Scott and Grace Tiller.

Picture of a rabbit, a look of wide-eyed terror in its eyes, its ears pointing rigidly to the sky.

"But Christine Holloway refuses to prove the truth of her numbers."

Rabbit darts away down a grassy path, fleeing for its life.

"She refuses to allow inspection of her expensive ideas."

Rabbit stops, eyes large, ears again at attention, then darts away once more.

"She refuses to allow professionals to examine how she will pay for her ideas."

Rabbit pauses on the trail, glancing back and fleeing desperately once more.

"Nothing is more expensive than a politician who won't tell the truth. Haven't they cost us enough already?"

The camera pulls back to show the rabbit in the distance running furiously away until it is completely out of sight.

* * *

The video was hilarious. Over the next month, on YouTube, it got nine million hits. Our tracking polls showed Holloway falling. They showed both Jeffrey and Tiller gaining but still far away.

Jeffrey's idea had worked but it was not enough.

46

Lucy Gilmore

When you arrive in a new place to start an investigation, one of your first questions is where do you start? On that question I got a lot of advice. And one piece of advice I heard a lot was "Check out Master Vote."

Master Vote did not sell voting machines. But they programmed a lot of them. The voting machine companies hired them and they would do the coding, as well as sometimes dealing with the local election officials. They had gotten a lot of bad press. Their programmer, who was the mother-in-law of the owner, had little programming background and had been fired from four jobs. They were a three-person shop in a strip mall in Mason City, Iowa.

They did not do much work in Wisconsin, just one county, but they were all over the Midwest. Four or five people said they were suspect. One person told me they were fixing elections. I decided to take a look.

So I gave them a call and told them I worked for the Dane County Clerk's office and would like to talk with them about programming our machines.

"Those Election Day, Inc. people are too hard to deal with."

On a Monday morning, I set off to visit Master Vote, a four-hour drive. Before leaving, I had looked up the town. Thirty thousand people. Mason City is the birthplace of Meredith Wilson, who wrote *The Music Man*. The town also has a home that was designed by Frank Lloyd Wright, which is now a museum. But when I looked up Mason City's history on its website, the chronology listed items such as the organization of the first cemetery association, the purchase of the first pumps and pipes for the water system, and the police department's purchase of its first motorcycle.

Let's just say Mason City's history is not littered with large events.

I pulled into town and found my way to Dvorsky Plaza, a strip mall where Master Vote's offices are located. Dvorsky Plaza is not much to look at. It is home to a grimy pizza shop called Eatalian Pizza, a Pakistani general store, a payday lender, and one bigger place, a Fred's Dollar Store. Across the street is the Mason City Goodwill.

Even within this dreary strip mall setting, Master Vote does not shine. They operate in one room with three people inside. It is about the size of a shoe repair shop with partitions separating the three tiny offices. As I entered their office, a man, mid-forties, with a big smile, leaped to his feet and offered his hand.

"You must be Lucy Gilmore," he said.

"The one and only," I answered with a twinkle in my eye.

"I'm Millard Evanston, president of this company."

He led me to the presidential office, walled by faded partitions and without a window view of the parking lot—a choice, given the appearance of the lot, that I think most corporate executives would make. He invited their programmer, Sigrid Bethany, to join us. He brought me coffee and thanked me for driving all the way from Madison.

I began the conversation.

"In Dane County we are really concerned about cybersecurity. Tell me about what you have been doing to protect our voting machines from hacker attacks."

Milllard smiled, confident in his reply. "We have no exposure to hackers. None of our machines are connected to the internet."

I considered the five or six ways a voting machine or optical scanner can be entered or manipulated without an internet connection but decided to keep this interview lowkey, at least to start. One look at these offices told me most of what I needed to know about Master Vote and its defense capabilities.

"Aren't there ways someone can get inside your machines without an internet connection?" I asked.

"No." Millard looked irritated. He glanced at Sigrid, a tall, thin woman, older, with a grim countenance.

"But haven't many of these machines been found to have modems that are used to transmit election results?" I inquired.

"Those modems are hardware. We only deal with software, preparing these machines for election day. Those modems are only used for outgoing communications and they use landlines. So everything is safe."

"But my understanding is that there is no pure landline transmission. Even landline communications go through the internet at some point."

"So?"

"What about ISMI catchers?"

"What?" he asked with a puzzled expression.

"Some people call them stingrays. They are used by law enforcement, military, and spies to intercept transmissions and follow them back to the source to get access to the machines."

Millard looked at Sigrid.

"I have training in technology," she stated, tilting her nose upward, not looking at me directly. "Without an internet connection you can't get into a machine."

"What about the machine parts? Many components are manufactured abroad. It would be easy to modify those components to create access, right?"

"I don't know about that," Millard replied.

"What about USB drives? Most of these machines have them. In 30 seconds, you can completely rework the software. Most of these machines are unguarded, right?"

"That is not our part of the work," Millard answered, a glare in his eyes.

"Well, if you can't program to stop a USB intrusion maybe you could program to detect it?"

Silence.

"Is your programming 'read only'?" I asked. Read only means no one can change the programming even if they have the actual machine in their clammy little hands.

"Why would that be necessary? There is no internet connection," Sigrid snapped.

Millard interjected. "It is not only the internet. Let us describe the new things we are doing to protect our democracy in America."

Now I was getting angry. I had been a little unfair. Hardware issues were not their domain. But I saw this ragtag company, listened to their answers, and thought of how exposed we are.

I interrupted with a question I should never have asked. "Well, do you have an explanation for why Republicans always get more votes than the exit polls predict?"

"What in the hell are you suggesting?" Millard almost shouted.

"Thank you, Mr. Evanston. I have all the answers I need."

47

Max Parker

Back in the office, I was flipping channels, monitoring my three TVs. There was Christine Holloway's photo, full screen on all three. I turned up the volume on MSNBC.

"Breaking news in the race for the Democratic presidential nomination. The US attorney for the District of Columbia has filed criminal charges against Frederick Holloway, husband of Christine Holloway, the current frontrunner for the Democratic nomination for president. Mr. Holloway is charged with insider trading based upon stock transactions he directed two years ago after learning of circumstances that would adversely affect the price of stock held in trust for Senator Holloway's son."

I am thinking. I am thinking. If she is out, we are in.

"Senator Holloway's office issued this statement."

"I am saddened to learn of the charges filed against my husband, Frederick Holloway. I had no knowledge of the transactions upon which these charges are based. The stock sales were made from a trust set up for the benefit of my son, Stan Roberts. My husband was a trustee, but I had no position or involvement in its administration.

"These are merely charges. There is a judicial process that will determine whether or not these charges are true. In the meantime, these events will not affect my candidacy for president of the United States. I will continue my campaign for the Democratic nomination and ultimately for the White House in the upcoming November election. In doing so, I trust the fairness and sound judgment of both journalists and the voters of our nation."

Apparently, Mr. Holloway, a big-time DC lawyer, managed investments for a trust benefitting Stan Roberts, Senator Holloway's son. Those investments included $200,000 in the stock of Divergent Teknologies, a company that markets stoplights that can see ongoing vehicles and direct traffic accordingly.

According to the report, Divergent Teknologies was also a client of Mr. Holloway's law firm. When he learned of a bus accident in Houston that killed three students at a Divergent Teknology stoplight, Mr. Holloway dumped his stepson's stock, allegedly acting on inside information and the likelihood that the stock price would fall.

Then came the posturing.

Jessica Harrison, chair of the Republican National Committee, began the attack.

"These are very serious charges. These are felony offenses. I think all Americans have to ask, how could Senator Holloway have no knowledge about a very large transaction, an illegal transaction, that took place to benefit her own son? Her answers are not credible. She should withdraw from the race."

Next, Senator Miller Stephens, a Democrat from Massachusetts and a supporter of Grace Tiller, called upon the Senate Ethics Committee to open an investigation into Senator Holloway's involvement in this matter. Senator Stephens was supporting Grace Tiller in the race for the Democratic presidential nomination.

Then we heard that the Republican majority leader, Steve Shaughnessy, said he would convene a meeting of the Republican leadership to consider Senator Stephens' request. Cut to Senator Stephens.

"All of us should be shocked and concerned when a felony is committed by the spouse of a US senator, the felony having been committed to benefit that senator's own son. With the presidential race well underway, it is important that we look into this matter as quickly and as judiciously as possible."

The convention was only eight weeks away. But would her delegates hold? Would they risk giving her the nomination when evidence could surface bringing charges her way?

Jeffrey Scott might get this nomination. He might take the White House. And me? A second-tier campaign manager who took this job on a lark? I might be sitting in some cubbyhole right next to the Oval Office. And all those senators and governors who passed on my services will be crawling on their knees, into my office, asking if it is okay if they kiss my ass.

48

Nadia

After a 12-hour flight, a hasty shower, and a frantic cab ride, I arrive on the 60th floor of the Comcast Center where the JG Skyhigh restaurant is perched above the Philadelphia skyline with a hundred-mile view in any direction. There is no roof, only curved glass and a marvelous light that makes me feel as if I am breathing in the clouds.

I spot Howard.

He is a small man. I doubt he could peer over the roof of most SUVs. He is thin and wiry with dark eyes and his hair is curly and black. Dyed black.

"Howard," I say.

He turns to me and, like most red-blooded men seeing a gorgeous blonde with an ample bustline, gives me a hopeful look. I give him a big, wet kiss on the cheek.

"Now I remember you," he lies.

We sit at a table next to the glass where the suburbs unfold into curved highways, winding streams, and blankets of lush green trees. He glances at the scenery, but his gaze comes back to me. Scenery is not foremost in his mind.

"What is your business proposition?"

He suppresses an eagerness in his voice.

"You know foreign leaders, or can reach them, right?"

"True."

"Well, I need help selling what might be the most valuable commodity in the world."

His eyes glaze over. "Really, what might that be?"

"Before I say a word, I need to know that this conversation is completely confidential. Can I trust you?"

He does not even answer.

"Can I trust you? That's what I need to know."

"Look, I could say 'yes' but what good is that to you? If I am untrustworthy, would I say 'no'? Let's get to the point. But whatever you tell me, you can deny. Your word against mine. And I am a convicted felon. Let's get to the deal."

"Okay." I hesitate and continue.

"What I have to sell to the highest bidder is the outcome of the American presidential election."

He laughs. "Really?"

Then I explain. I tell him about the hacking that several countries would undertake. I tell him that the voting machines are already rigged by companies that do not have to submit their work to inspection. Then I tell him about Sheldon. That he has the final look at the coding. He can undo code installed by other hackers. Who gets the votes on election day? Sheldon has the final say.

Howard looks at me, his jaw ajar.

"You are serious?"

Now I am worried. It is time to talk money and I sense that I will have to give him a lot more than I had planned. But first, I ask the obvious question. "Do you have a candidate in this race? We are going to have to sell to the highest bidder."

"I hate them all," he stated with some bitterness.

I put the numbers right there on the table.

"Look, I have the ability to throw this election either way. It won't take much. The whole thing is a mess but no matter which Democrat gets the nod the general is likely to be close. I think we can get $150 million. If we do, you get $50 million. Then we have to pay the programmer. He gets two. We split that cost."

"Two? Why only two? He holds all the cards."

"He doesn't know the size of the deal."

"Well, I have to think about this." He glances around, looking for who might be listening to our conversation.

"Don't take long. This election is three months away and the programming takes time."

"I might want more than $50 million, if we have a deal."

Good, I think. He is nibbling. I knew he would ask for more.

"Well, Howard, let me sweeten the deal. Anything you get over $150 million, we split down the middle."

"Okay, let me get back to you."

"Soon," I remind him.

* * *

Three days later Howard is on the phone. I knew it. No one is more reliable than a man without morals or money. I tell him to go to a payphone and call the number of my disposable phone.

"Nadia, I have talked to two or three countries and no bites. They don't believe it will happen."

"Shit," I reply in my best French.

"I offered them an escrow. They put up the money. If their candidate wins, they move the money to us. If their candidate loses, they get their money back. That made them more comfortable but not enough."

"So the problem is that they don't believe we can do it?"

"Exactly."

"I have an idea," I reply. "Give me three days."

49

Max Parker

My phone rang. It was Casmir, our media consultant.

"Max, we should start peecking a vice president."

"Look, I know Holloway is dealing with this scandal, but a lot of it hasn't played out. It might turn out she is innocent."

"It ees not going to play out."

"What do you mean?"

"Okay, leesten. There is a Seenate ethics investigation. The Republicans control the Seenate. What do you theenk Shaughnessy is going to do?"

"Find her guilty?"

"Max, don't be an eediot. They don't want a verdict. They want a cloud. They are going to drag out the investigation right past eelection day. Leaking leettle teed bits which, true or no, will make her look gueelty as hell. So when voters go to the polls they have to ask themselves, 'Is she gueelty or no?'"

I had to admit, Casmir's logic made sense.

"Max, for her it gets woorse. They are posting messages on feeminist Facebook pages saying powerful white men in the Deeemocratic Party are trying to dump Holloway for what her husband did. That is the meeme. 'Don't crucify a woman for her husband's deeds.'"

"Ouch!" I answered.

"So here are our choices. If the delegates dump Holloway, the feeminists take a walk. If they don't dump Holloway, then she runs her campaign under the cloud of a straight to preeson felony. Have you seen their social media?"

"I've heard a little."

Casmir began the litany. A website listing every lie Christine Holloway had ever told. Hell, she'd been in politics since forever. She had to tell a lot of lies. An online petition, signed by millions of Republicans, some of them bots, called on her to resign from the presidential race and her seat in the Senate. A fake video, where she is talking but the computer has altered her voice to deny any involvement. But she stutters, hesitates, and looks guilty as hell.

"But guess what?" Casmir asked.

"Does it get worse?"

"No, Max, it gets better," he answered with the tone of a father explaining the obvious to his four-year-old son.

"Holloway will drop out. She has no choice and is smart enough to know it. Go find a veep."

50

Sheldon Klumm

I was sitting in my office with my feet on my desk thinking about Nadia. I closed the door and pictured Nadia lying naked in bed. I rubbed little Pedro until he was a summit in my pants stretching the fabric, begging for freedom.

Then I pictured myself mounting the most beautiful woman on the face of the planet.

Woot! Woot!

My phone rang. *Goddamnit* I thought, *I am busy at the moment!* I disconnected the call.

A minute later, it rang again. I looked at my phone. It was Nadia's number.

"I miss you, Darling," she told me. "I am so horny. I have been missing little Pedro so much."

"Oh, I miss you," I stuttered.

"Sheldon, I am arriving in Omaha tomorrow morning. Meet me at the Magnolia at 11 o'clock."

Little Pedro was back from his phone break, stretching my pants once again. It's true. It's true. She loves me so much she can't stay away.

* * *

The next day, I arrived at the room, Room 300, our suite. I knocked on the door.

There stood Nadia with her usual greeting, naked as a mole rat, two perfectly formed breasts, and those gorgeous eyes staring at me like she had arrived at Morton's Steak Restaurant in the middle of a famine for the all-you-can-eat buffet.

Does it get any better?

Nadia smiled and curled her finger, summoning me up the stairs.

The room had changed. There was now a mirror on the wall next to the bed.

"Excuse me," she said. "I want to look my best for this special morning."

Then she stood before the mirror and began to massage her breasts, smiling at the mirror with a knowing gaze. Then her hand dropped to her pussy and she stroked herself slowly, her breath becoming deeper, even frantic.

I dropped my pants, fearing that little Pedro might cost me a trip to Fred's Dollar Store for a new pair of trousers. She began to tremble, shake, and moan, all the while stroking herself with increasing speed.

Unfreakingbelievable!

She dropped to the bed, her body covered with beads of sweat. She turned my way.

"Take me, you brute," she shouted so loudly that I feared the neighboring guests might call and complain. She spread her legs to receive my offering.

Little Pedro was teetering on the brink. I rushed to enter her just as he unleashed his load. Then I lay down beside her, embarrassed and disappointed.

But Nadia would have none of my disappointment. She was soothing me, stroking my body, and telling me what a magnificent man I really was. And soon her words stirred Pedro once again and this time I enjoyed three and a half minutes of the greatest pleasure I have ever known.

And when I was finished, she cuddled with me, speaking of her love, our house in Florida, our 10 dogs, and the beautiful life that lay ahead.

She rose to sit on the side of the bed facing the mirror.

"Sheldon, would you sit next to me?"

"Of course, my love."

I seated myself at her side, looking into the mirror, and she said, "I want to go over the plan."

"Of course," I replied with a dreamy voice.

"Now which voting machines do you program?"

I was surprised by this question because Nadia knew the answer. But who wanted to argue?

"I program voting machines for 40 percent of the American voters including Wisconsin, Michigan, and Pennsylvania."

"And who looks at these programs after you have finished?"

"No one. I am the last step."

"And when you program you can change the counts to give any candidate any number of votes you want?"

"Yep," I answered with pride.

"And, Sheldon, when I call you two weeks from now and tell you the candidate I want to win, you will program these machines to make sure that the candidate I specify wins the election?"

"Anything for you, my love."

She put her arms around me and turned me back to the bed.

"Oh, Sheldon, I love you so much."

51

Max Parker

The convention was only three weeks away. The Republican videos on Facebook sites for liberal women helped fuel outrage against party leaders who suggested that it was time Christine Holloway step aside. In the meantime, their campaign to attack her integrity and to tie her to her husband's deeds had rallied Republican anger against her candidacy.

No one had produced a single shred of evidence suggesting Senator Holloway's involvement. But calls for her to step aside were growing. Guilt or innocence was no longer the question. The question was, "Can Democrats win this election with Christine Holloway leading the ticket?" Cooler heads knew the answer.

Though he knew that Holloway had become a liability, Jeffrey refused to ask her to step aside.

"I have seen nothing to suggest that she had any part in her husband's actions. Until someone proves wrongdoing, she should remain in the race."

Then, Jeffrey received the call. He put it on speakerphone so I could hear.

"Jeffrey, this is Christine Holloway."

"I don't have any delegates to spare," Jeffrey said with a smile.

"That's funny. But you may not need them after all."

Jeffrey paused, unsure about the intentions of the senator.

"Jeffrey, I am going to announce my withdrawal from the race."

"Christine, all this is really unfair. I am so sorry these things have happened to you."

"Don't be sorry, kiddo. I appreciated your words of support. But look, in our business we have to be realists. Our situation is coming apart and Democrats can't afford to lose this election. Plus, I want to say how much I have admired how you have handled yourself in this campaign. You have told more truth than the rest of us have spoken in our entire political careers."

"Well, it sounds like I've gotten everything but your vote."

"No, that's why I am calling. You have my vote. I am asking all Democratic delegates to join with me in supporting your nomination at our convention."

Jeffrey was speechless.

"My only worry is that you are a little too honest for this job. It's a dirty business. You understand that?"

"I do."

"When the horde of Tea Party mongrels mounts the White House fence, you can't be afraid to pull the trigger."

"There are ways to do that," Jeffrey replied with a smile.

"Well, I know you will figure out how. Your campaign has been a marvel to watch."

"Thank you, Christine. When are you making the announcement?"

"Get ready. I have a press conference at two o'clock."

I looked at Jeffrey. He looked at me. For a moment, silence filled the room. Jeffrey spoke first.

"I told you not to read those polls."

"Well, it did take some luck," I replied.

"Don't call it luck. Politics is full of fake scandals, fake felonies, and the real ones too. They litter the landscape."

"Luck or not, I thought it was not possible. I *knew* it could not happen. And if you had listened to all my advice you never would have made it."

Jeffrey just smiled. "I never would have made it without you."

For a moment we looked at each other. Wisdom? Luck? Who the hell cares?

We hugged and savored one of the finest moments we would ever know.

Jeffrey Scott had broken the rules. He had appealed to reason. He had lifted the curtain and spoke honestly about the situation facing our nation.

He did all of these things, things that our polling and common sense told us offered no true path to victory.

Circumstances often deliver unforeseen results. What seemed impossible had come to pass.

Jeffrey Scott was going to be the Democratic nominee for president of the United States.

52

Howard Feldman

I have been thinking about Nadia and her proposition. Her plan is to undermine the entire American democracy and rob Americans of their votes. It is a shameless and morally bankrupt plan that any citizen with an ounce of decency would refuse.

On the other hand, $50 million is a lot of money.

And guess what? I am so broke I often visit the sample trays at Trader Joe's to get my lunch.

But needing the money and getting the money are two different things. How in the world am I going to convince some world leader that this hot pussy from the Ukraine has this voting machine programmer wrapped around her finger ready to deliver the outcome of the United States presidential election?

Not possible.

The doorbell rings. There stands a Federal Express man in his purple uniform.

"Signature, please."

"I did not order any wine."

"Sir, the sender has requested a signature."

I look at the label. The package is from "Scenic Nebraska." I scratch my head and sign. Inside, I open the package and retrieve a CD. Who uses a CD anymore? But since I am in hard times and my computer is four years old, I happen to have a player.

I insert the CD and press "play."

Holy shit!

There is Nadia caressing herself in front of the camera. There is Nadia stroking herself until she collapses in this magnificent orgasm that surely sends a tremor all the way to the hotel's front desk. There is Nadia with this Sheldon character, ugly, crooked teeth, fat, and, frankly, the tiniest prick I have ever seen.

He mounts her but loses it before the second stroke. Later he is back for more. I don't know what this video is about but I plan to watch it about 35 more times. Finally, Nadia and the doofus are sitting on the bed and looking at the camera. At her prompting, Sheldon explains his job.

He explains the programming he does and how he programs voting machines that count 40 percent of the votes in the United States of America.

Then Nadia pops the big question. "Will you give the election to the candidate I want to win?"

His response is not a simple "yes." He practically crawls across the floor, sucks her toes, and says, "Anything. Anything you want."

I call Nadia on her disposable phone.

"Nadia," I say, "do you have more of these?"

"Howard, I know how to treat my partners. Are you in?"

I think for a minute. I could send this video to the Ayatollah in Iran and the supreme leader would sneak it into the bathroom, turn down the volume, and watch it 20 times.

More importantly, the story now makes sense. If you were as pathetic as Sheldon and had a woman as beautiful as Nadia, what wouldn't you do to keep her? Would he throw the American election?

One look at this video and the answer is obvious.

You would too.

53

Max Parker

The accidental candidate.

That is what they all called Jeffrey. We had challenged the fundamental gravity of politics. The punishment for such a deed is to become a mere footnote in the history of the campaign. But luck had rescued Jeffrey from the dustbin of history. Suddenly my candidate was about to be the Democratic nominee for president of the United States.

If one year ago you would have asked me to wager on Jeffrey's chances for this prize I would not have put up a dime. I would have sooner risked my money on one of those Galapagos turtles winning the Kentucky Derby.

But sometimes life is an unexpected ride.

So now we are at the event. The Democratic National Convention in Philadelphia, Pennsylvania.

Present were almost 5,000 delegates, twice what the Republicans elect, but then we are the exuberant, excessive party. To report on these delegates, there would be 20,000 journalists in attendance from all over the world. What could any of them report that the world had not already learned? To earn their hotel rooms and dinners, they would produce trivial and desperate stories like the fact that Jeffrey grew moonflowers on the tiny patch of ground behind his rented Capitol Hill townhouse. I didn't even know if it was true, but who cares?

Jeffrey arrived on Monday and checked into the Park View Suite at the Rittenhouse Hotel. I doubt Jeffrey had ever stayed in a room like this with its 850 square feet, all marble bathrooms, velvet sofas, and coolers chock full of exquisite white wine. This suite was perfect for relaxing but the rooms were like a beehive on meth. Until a few days earlier we did not know we had to pick a running mate or make an acceptance speech or deal with the 6,000 reporters who had actually requested an interview. Jeffrey did not even have a wife to pass off to the *New York Times*.

So, the running mate. Every Democratic senator, governor, and many congressmen were calling to weigh in on the choice. We didn't even have time to listen. Jeffrey convened the senior staff—Christine Holloway, Governor Bilbray of Georgia, and Senator Stanton of Arizona—to make a choice. Vetting? It would have been nice.

At the start of the discussion, Jeffrey wanted to choose a Republican, albeit a liberal Republican, if such a creature actually existed. But the warnings were clear. What if Jeffrey died? What if a Republican took the White House and appointed Republicans to the Supreme Court and cabinet positions? As these prospects were outlined you could feel the fearful shivers in the room.

Senator Stanton made the argument that we needed someone from the party's liberal wing. Let's face it, a lot of delegates were disappointed to have Jeffrey carry their banner. He had not championed their issues but championed progress instead. To show solutions, he had already compromised their most cherished ideals. He was a litmus test loser, and Democrats had more litmus tests than John D. Rockefeller had dimes. A liberal running mate would reassure the convention. Regular voters would hardly notice.

Then Christine Holloway suggested foreign policy experience would be a good thing and experience in Washington as well. After all, Jeffrey's resume was onion skin thin.

Jeffrey listened for a while, but I detected amusement. It was the smile he used when he had everything figured out but was listening out of courtesy only. Finally, he spoke.

"What if we choose Ted Maxwell?"

Maxwell was a Republican Senator from Pennsylvania. One of their last remaining moderates, a creature on the endangered species list right behind the white rhino.

"But I thought we ruled out Republicans," Stanton responded.

"What if he's not a Republican?" Jeffrey answered, his smile enlarging.

"What if he accepted our offer to be part of a unity ticket? The Republicans would pillory him as a traitor, a socialist, and a man who discarded his principles for his own personal ambition. We would let them have at him for a few days and then he would leave the Republicans to join the Democrats, disgusted by their refusal to work hand and hand to save America."

For a moment all were quiet, a little in awe of Jeffrey's plan.

"Jeffrey, that's a great idea but he will never agree to all that," Senator Holloway offered.

Jeffrey leaned into the table as if to share some precious secret. "He already did. I called him yesterday."

And so the American Unity Ticket was born. Americans loved it. The delegates hated it. We quelled the rebellion. But Maxwell was challenged by three rogue Democrats and barely won on the first ballot.

* * *

Our general election opponent was Tom Christopher. Christopher was a Tea Party senator from Texas who did not have a friend in Washington. Did it matter? Not one bit. He had led efforts to shut down the government three times. Compromise? I am sure he had never actually done it. In fact, I doubt he could even spell the word. He was a liar, a grandstander, and conservative enough to embarrass Ayn Rand.

The perfect candidate for today's internet world.

Frankly, moderation has no place in the modern Republican Party. The Republican electorate has become a mob fed red meat every day by Fox News, talk radio lunatics, and incendiary blogs. They hate their leaders. They believe cutting the federal budget in half should be easy. Why is abortion not a felony? And they wonder why America has not jailed all those scientists who have been lying to us about climate change.

The establishment Republicans used to meet at the Metropolitan Club in New York City, choose the nominee, and instruct the serfs who to support. But these people, for all their money and supposed power, are nothing anymore. The serfs are hurling mud at their limousines and blaming them for the failure to overturn international treaties banning hollow-point bullets.

All in all, though, I felt good about the race. We could employ an ancient strategy not seen in recent years. We could crowd the middle, cuddle the moderates (all 10 percent of them), and leave Christopher without room to expand his base of ignorant deplorables. It was true that the rabble has been growing. They were not 51 percent but they were getting close.

* * *

On Thursday night came the acceptance speech. There is no better venue in American politics. Thirty-five million live viewers and God knows how many more would watch the replay. In the hall were another 8,000 delegates and spectators, who had forgotten their reservations and were embracing Jeffrey Scott. They were all fiery-eyed, partisan zealots, on their feet, ready to scream approval of his every word. If someone tried to boo the nominee, he would be carried from the convention hall by angry delegates and dipped in hot tar.

The hall was filled with signs proclaiming the new ticket, "Progress Together," "American Unity," and a host of handmade signs including one that said "Kiss a Republican," which none of these delegates would actually do. Covering the ceiling were balloons of red, white, and blue. Delegates donned hats of all sorts—top hats, cowboy hats, sombreros, boaters, bowlers, and hard hats. For a tiny handful of dissenters, "Scott Free" was their button of choice, but they kept quiet and their presence was unnoticed in this sea of people overcome with endorphins, dopamine, and rare, exotic hormones that only flow in presidential election years.

The schedule was running behind, as always. Some of the warmup speakers spoke too long and some were too important to give the hook. But finally, the podium was empty and the hall quieted. Every person present knew what that meant. It meant the nominee would soon take the stage.

Senator Stanton entered the stage. At six-foot-four, he towered over the podium. He a gravel in his voice and a gleam in his eye. He was a pragmatist, an insider, and in his mind, Jeffrey's victory was a triumph for all he believed.

"Fellow Democrats, Republicans, and Independents across the nation. It is my honor to introduce to you the next president of the United States."

The crowd erupted. It took the senator 30 seconds to continue.

"The man I am about to introduce is perhaps the most unusual presidential nominee in the history of our nation. Instead of telling people what they wanted to hear, he told us the truth. He reminded us that the collapse of Social Security and Medicare was looming. He described the consequences of our national debt and ascribed its cause not only to Republicans but to our own party as well. He searched for solutions, not the lofty ambitions that make our hearts soar, but the legislation shaped by negotiation and compromise that might actually become law.

"He has broken all the rules. He has reminded us that politics is the art of the possible. He has, most of all, given us hope. Hope that our next president can give us more than rhetoric. He has given us hope that he can deliver results that can begin to heal our divisions, results that can address our most urgent problems, results that can lift up our nation and show our citizens a brighter future we can all share together."

Applause.

"And what does our opponent, Senator Tom Christopher, offer our nation? More tax cuts and deeper debt that will burden our children until their final days."

Boos.

"Medicare that will offer fewer benefits, more expensive premiums, and lower-quality care."

Boos.

"Social Security benefits will be reduced because your retirement is not worth one penny of additional taxes on the wealthiest one percent of Americans."

Boos.

"On issues like climate change, gun control, and a woman's right to choose, Senator Christopher has championed the most extreme positions in American politics and has displayed an adamant refusal to compromise or even converse with the vast majority of Americans who do not share his beliefs."

Boos.

"What future does Senator Christopher offer this nation? More partisan conflict. More government gridlock. Paralysis, impasse, pessimism, malaise.

"It is time for different leadership. It is time for a kind of leadership that we hardly imagined at the outset of this campaign. Jeffrey Scott is showing us the way out. Instead of name-calling, he is calling for courtesy and cooperation. Instead of shouting, he is calling for conversation.

"Jeffrey Scott is about more than ideas or speeches. Jeffrey Scott is about saving a democracy in peril. Our democracy. He is about saving America itself."

The crowd rose to its feet. The noise was deafening. Thousands of balloons fell from the ceiling. Streamers danced through the air. Jeffrey Scott appeared.

He raised his arms to greet the roaring mob. A few hours earlier they had grumbled about his Republican running mate. Throughout the campaign they had mocked his speeches that lectured them about the practicalities of government in our American system. Had not two late and unexpected scandals lifted him to victory, he would never have been handed this torch.

But there is something about that torch. When it sits in your hand you become bigger than you were—bigger, really, than you imagined you could be. Remember when I said that Jeffrey Scott looked more like the White House intern than a president? He was an intern no more. He was the giant slayer. He was David standing over Goliath, scowling at his fallen foe.

The human eye sees more than light. It enriches that light, it shapes that light with what the brain knows and believes. Jeffrey Scott no longer stood five-foot-six, even though a measuring tape would find him the same. He towered over the stage. And to the human eye, I ask you, who looks larger? Charles Atlas? Or the 90-pound weakling who has just hurled him into the sea?

There he stood. The accidental candidate. The unlikely candidate. But now the Democratic nominee for president of the United States. After several minutes, when the crowd had finally quieted enough to hear Jeffrey Scott speak, he began.

"Fellow Democrats."

He raised his head to look at Senator Maxwell in the gallery.

"Fellow Republican."

Light laughter rumbled through the convention hall.

"I would like to begin by speaking to the meaning of success. Early pioneers understood the need for economic aid to the elderly. They spoke out and appealed for action. But the victory, the real victory, came in 1935 when Franklin Roosevelt enacted Social Security into law.

"Harry Truman called for national health care as early as 1948. Many voices joined his cause and he is both a pioneer and a hero. But it was not until 2009 when Barack Obama moved the Affordable

Care Act through Congress that every American gained access to a doctor. Real victory was not the product of speeches. It was the product of votes in Congress, the product of hard-won legislation.

"And what about the Civil Rights Act, legislation that was blocked and filibustered for a generation by a caucus of powerful southern Democrats. Victory came in 1964 with the passage of the Civil Rights Act and was followed by the passage of the Voting Rights Act one year later.

"And who was responsible for those victories that granted full citizenship to the descendants of slaves? Lyndon Baines Johnson…"

Jeffrey paused for effect.

"…an accidental president."

Laughter.

"…who once sat with that southern caucus in opposition to those laws.

"It only takes one human being to speak to a cause. But it takes a majority to change our nation. In building majorities, we must never forget that human beings grow, change, and see things in new ways.

"Too often we confuse soaring rhetoric for great accomplishment. Too often we confuse attack and condemnation with the moral high ground. Too often we believe we were sent to Washington to preen on MSNBC instead of lowering our voices and doing the hard work of shaping solutions from viewpoints that stand in conflict.

"In Washington, we live in a culture of condemnation, mistrust, and sometimes hatred itself. My first job as your president is to bring that culture to an end.

"It is no longer enough to be a Democrat or Republican. It is time for all of us to be Americans first. But party leaders, politicians, and campaigners will not solve these problems alone. This election is a chance for ordinary Americans to step forward and speak.

"This is your chance to say: We see what is going on. Our democracy is broken, our democracy is failing us, and every person holding almost every elected office is equally to blame.

"Save our democracy. Save America. We may have fallen but we still have the strength to rise up and crawl back to the top.

"To the pessimists, the naysayers, the prophets of doom, I say look at me. Who would have predicted my standing here on this podium tonight? Who would ever have given a candidate like me with this message a ghost of a chance?

"But here I stand ready, eager, and confident that I can finish the job. Know this. Remember this. Carry this in your hearts.

"It is not too late for America.

"In America, our America, it is just time."

* * *

That night, Jeffrey Scott delivered the speech of his life. Some of us read it in advance and gave comments but the message was his, the ideas were his. Americans had not heard such a message within the reach of their memories and they embraced it. Overnight polls showed our candidate had surged from a neck-and-neck contest to a 12-point lead.

54

Lucy Gilmore

I am on my computer reading the *Wisconsin State Journal*, Madison's local newspaper. Today the coverage is about the Democratic convention and Jeffrey Scott. I don't get all mushy about these candidates. But I am in love with Jeffrey Scott.

I watched his speech online. He's not one of those noisy candidates who is playing gotcha with his opponent. He is softspoken in his own sort of way. He is focused on the problems and how we can solve them together. Give him the tough issues and he never ducks.

He speaks to what is good inside each of us and how we can restore that goodness to public life. He is about forgiveness, respect, civility, kindness—all of the things that I feared has disappeared from our politics forever.

Can anyone restore a sense of trust and community in this crazy country we live in? I don't know. There is so much hatred in America. Maybe it's all gone too far to fix.

But Jeffrey Scott is our one chance for change. And, really, I look at our country and think *we are running out of time*.

And what about that right-wing lunatic, Tom Christopher? Don't even get me started.

In the newspaper business we are not supposed to take sides, even though we do. As reporters, we can't go around endorsing candidates. But I am not a newspaper person anymore. They threw me out. So I can say whatever the hell I want. And what I want to say is that no one in politics has ever moved me more than this man, Jeffrey Scott.

I think he has a chance. He has a chance if the Republicans don't steal the election, which I know the Republicans plan to do.

My job is to get to the bottom of all this. My job is to find the truth. I feel like the whole country, the whole world really, is depending on me. You might say I have one of the biggest jobs in America.

My job is to make sure no one steals this election from Jeffrey Scott.

55

Fox News

"This is Kristin Halliburton for Fox News.

"There was much reaction to Jeffrey Scott's selection of Ted Maxwell, a Republican, as his running mate. Here is Aaron James with a report on the reaction within the Republican Party."

"Thank you, Kristin. When Scott announced his choice of Republican Ted Maxwell to be his running mate, he described his decision as an olive branch to Republicans, an invitation to begin a new conversation about our future in America.

"But, not surprisingly, Republican leaders are not celebrating his choice. Here is Tom Christopher, the presumptive Republican nominee."

"Jeffrey Scott claims he selected a Republican, but Ted Maxwell is no Republican at all. He has refused to support legislation that would bring abortions to a halt. He has voted for limits on gun ownership. He has even supported cap and trade measures to combat so-called global warning."

"Christopher added that while some negotiation is inevitable, he has no interest in discussing proposals that would abandon the party's most important ideals. Other Republicans were even more outspoken. Here is Robert White, chairman of the Republican National Committee."

"Ted Maxwell has abandoned our party. Good riddance. He was never a true Republican anyway."

"Across America, demonstrators are appearing at Maxwell speeches to protest his decision to join the Democratic ticket."

Screen shows five middle-aged white men, in jeans and T-shirts, chanting their protests.

"Traitor Ted. Traitor Ted. Traitor Ted."

"Well, Kristin, it looks like bipartisanship is off to a bad start."

"I'd say. Partisan warfare looks stronger than ever."

56

Nadia Fedorov

I pick up my new disposable and dial Howard. I turn these phones over every two days. Is that enough? Who the hell knows?

"Howard, this is Nadia. Have you got a buyer?"

"I am still working it."

"Howard, you are on the clock. The election is seven weeks away."

"Look, I am doing all I can. It's complicated. Hungary was interested in helping Christopher. They don't want all that human rights bullshit the Democrats do. Pakistan wanted to help Scott. Their foreign aid has fallen off the table since the Republicans came in. India likes Christopher because the Republicans are screwing Pakistan. And Kenya, you know they are a big recipient of foreign aid. They want the Republicans back in.

"A lot of countries know what they want but pulling the trigger is the problem. What if they got caught? And how do you move $100 million without too many people knowing? So far, no action.

"But, hey, everyone is watching your video. Again and again. It's been two weeks and I hear that in China some people still have not left the conference room."

I smile. I admit, I enjoy the flattery. Countless old, powerful men drooling over me. But 100 million bucks excites me more.

"Well, Howard, let me read you the facts of life. Programming for one state can be done in a day. Sheldon's company has pieces of

26 different states. He is doing the easy ones first. Utah, Kentucky, South Dakota. None of those are close enough to switch. Then he will start work on the battleground states. But the memory cards have to be programmed weeks in advance. Then they ship to the states two weeks before election day. He starts on Iowa in two weeks. Then the battleground states disappear one by one. If we wait too long, we won't be able to deliver 17 votes in a student council election in Bora Bora."

"Look, Nadia, I'm working on it but it ain't easy. It's not the money. It's that throwing the American election is just too touchy for a lot of countries."

"So where are your prospects?"

"I am talking to some African countries. Some of them like the idea that they can call the shots in America."

"Jesus. We'll cut the price if we have to. $100 million is better than nothing. I can explain all this to Sheldon. He will take less."

"How much is he getting, again?"

"I promised him two, but I can get him down to one. He thinks that is a lot of money."

"Shouldn't we give him more? He is the one inserting the code."

"Don't worry about Sheldon. I know what Sheldon wants. He is living the dream.

"For now."

57

Twitter

Ted Maxwell

@maxwell_ted_pa

I've had it. I joined the Democratic ticket to bring Americans together. But the Republicans refuse to even talk. I changed my registration. I am now a Democrat.

Jeffrey Scott

@jeff_scott_pres

SCOTT

Another example of why Washington is broken. Christopher can refuse to talk to me. He can refuse to talk to Ted Maxwell. He can't refuse to listen to you. You can fix Washington. It only takes your vote.

58

MSNBC

"This is Sybil Jacobs with an update on the presidential race. A new MSNBC poll shows that Jeffrey Scott has built a strong lead over his Republican opponent. With a full report, here is MSNBC political reporter Rita Savage."

"Thanks Sybil. It's been an unusual year for presidential politics. Frontrunners fallen to scandal. An unlikely Democratic nominee preaching moderation. Frankly, I think voters have been confused. But it seems they are finally sorting things out.

"According to our poll, since the party conventions, Jeffrey Scott has pulled away to an eight-point lead in the race for the White House. If the election were held today, Jeffrey Scott would receive 52 percent of the vote, Tom Christopher would receive 44 percent of the vote, and four percent goes to other candidates or undecided.

"Voter opinions are hard to change in a presidential race, so this is a formidable lead. What explains Scott's lead? Look at responses to some character issues.

"As president, which candidate will be more honest in describing the issues facing our nation?

"Scott 64 percent, Christopher 27 percent, Neither 9 percent.

"As president, which candidate is more likely to get things done?

"Scott 68 percent, Christopher 19 percent, Neither 13 percent.

"But if the race were decided on issues alone, it would be an entirely different contest.

"Which candidate most closely reflects your beliefs on issues important to our nation?

"Scott 52 percent, Christopher 45 percent, Neither 3 percent.

"These numbers indicate that Scott is winning voters on personal characteristics and likability, voting behavior not seen in recent years when partisanship and issues have driven more votes. Clearly, voters like Jeffrey Scott and his bipartisan approach.

"But in the weeks ahead, Christopher is sure to make this campaign more about issues and beliefs."

"Exciting days ahead, Sybil."

"Exciting, indeed."

59

Lucy Gilmore

Did you see the news about the Secure Elections Act? It requires paper ballots that can be hand-counted. Paper ballots are the one way we can ensure free and fair elections.

But the Republican majority leader in the United States Senate is actually blocking paper ballots. I know why and I think you do too.

In the meantime, my efforts to expose voting machine fraud are going nowhere. Word has gotten around.

I tried to get a meeting with Election Day, Inc. They never called back. I met with a Republican election official in Eau Claire. After I asked him a series of questions suggesting that the Republicans are cheating, he must have put out the word because no Republicans are returning my calls.

I don't blame him. He was a local yokel. If the Republicans were cheating, he would be the last to know.

I talk to Democrats all the time, but they can't help. I am sure that the Republicans did not send them the vote changing code for approval.

Finally, in this nation we have someone special, very special, and he could be president of the United States. He is honest. He is forthright. He is a healer.

But now I fear he is going to lose. Now I fear that his victory will be stolen.

Why? Because I still don't have the "proof." I have not exposed the crime.

60

Max Parker

My guy was ambushed. Somehow, somewhere, the Republicans dug up this old college paper written 20-something years ago by Jeffrey Scott while a student at Williams College. I can only imagine. He probably wrote it after smoking dope.

The paper questioned the basic tenets of Christianity. The creation. Jesus. God. The bread. The wine. Faith. He even hinted that the Holy Mother was not a virgin but had instead given herself over to Joseph's uncontrollable lust. I got a call from Fox News. They had this paper and needed his comments before doing the story. Jeffrey had no memory of this paper. Then Fox showed up for the interview with a hammer, a cross, and a bag of nails. Here is the interview, in part.

Fox: Congressman Scott, do you believe in God?

Scott: I do not but I have great respect for the spiritual beliefs of others.

Fox: So you believe that Christians are wrong in their belief in a higher power?

Scott: Who can say who is right or wrong? I just do not accept the Bible as received wisdom from a higher being.

Fox: So they are wrong—Christians, I mean?

Scott: I did not say that.

Fox: Well, let's talk about the Bible. You say you don't accept it. Tell Americans where the Bible is in error.

Scott: Well, the Bible says that the earth is roughly 6,000 years old. Science puts the number at four and a half billion years.

Fox: What is the proof?

Scott: Fossils. Geology. Radiometric dating.

Fox: Radiometric dating? I bet most of our viewers have not heard of that. Do you believe Jesus existed?

Scott: He probably did but he was only a man.

Fox: Probably?

Scott: Yes, probably.

Fox: So you dismiss Jesus as our savior.

Scott: Yes.

Fox: Then you would characterize yourself as an atheist?

Scott: I do not believe in God, that is correct.

I knew this was trouble.

Seventy percent of the population consider themselves Christian. The means, basically, they believe in God, and most of them think that the Bible is some divinely gifted document. They also believe, most of them, that religious beliefs represent some measurement of personal morality.

Polls also show that many Americans are open to voting for an atheist, and that number has grown dramatically over the years. But there are three things to keep in mind.

First, these elections are as much about turnout as vote choice. Keeping a godless apostate from filling the White House with pagan rituals will surely drive more of the Republican base to the polls.

Second, in the hands of our opponents Jeffrey is not only an atheist, but an opponent of Christianity. Look at these internet ads, targeted to Facebook users whose profiles indicate some Christian affinity.

Bible not true!
Says Jeffrey Scott.

Jesus not real!
Says Jeffrey Scott.

God is dead!
Scott delivers last rites.

Fox had obviously given the Republicans a heads-up. Within hours of the interview, the internet, the mailboxes, and the television networks were filled with ads portraying Jeffrey Scott, not in the act of making a personal religious choice, but Jeffrey Scott launching an all-out war against the Christian faith. So now, Jeffrey was not simply an atheist. He was out to erase the Bible, banish Jesus, and shut down churches all across the nation.

Modern politics sucks. In the old days the ridiculous, the outlandish, the totally fabricated lie never made the news except to excoriate the politician who made such claims.

Now we have the internet.

What has the internet done to politics? It has empowered ignorance. It has proliferated lies. It has decimated truth as we once knew it.

And something else. Was Tom Christopher running these ads? Of course not. The ads were run by a group called "Americans to Save Christianity." If someone wanted to give money to Tom Christopher, they could only give $2,700. Americans to Save Christianity was a "527." That means anyone could give any amount—even $20 million. That means they don't have to disclose their donors. The only restriction was that they do not *advocate the election of a candidate*. So while these ads excoriated Scott, they just never said the word "vote." The ads simply called on all Christians to band together to stop this God hater who wanted to erase Jesus from modern-day life.

Third, Jeffrey was getting a lot of votes because he was restoring civility, respecting other points of view, and bringing Americans together. Hard to square with his campaign to close churches.

You should have seen the protesters. At every one of our events, there was a line of so-called Christians holding signs. I am not sure these people had ever set foot in a church. I am sure they were paid. But they were there. They stood at rigid attention. Their faces taut. Their arms raised, erect from their bodies, holding signs, hand-lettered signs, that said:

Jesus is my savior.

The Bible is not a lie.

Nobody made up Jesus.

Jesus died for Jeffrey Scott's sins.

Save Christianity.
Defeat Scott.

And with scores of TV cameras at all of our events, these characters appeared in the newscasts every single night.

Every morning Greta called me with the overnight tracking polls. At one point we were up 12 points. But there are no sure things in politics. After a week of this nonsense our lead had fallen to four points.

Then the other shoe fell. Once someone discovered that controversial paper at Williams, opposition researchers descended on the campus, searching for more. Of course, finding student papers written 20 years ago is not an easy task. But there was one resource.

Some college professors gave the same tests year after year. Campus fraternities collected test papers that earned high grades and organized them by course and professor. So instead of having to actually read a textbook, those frat boys could simply read old questions and answers off papers that earned an "A." And guess whose papers got a lot of "As?"

Jeffrey Scott's.

Pilfered from the test files at the Sigma Chi frat house, sold to a Republican researcher, this new paper offered the opinion that Christianity and capitalism were not compatible. Capitalism was about greed, profit, and rewarding the well-to-do, the paper explained. Christianity was about compassion, forgiveness, and rewarding the poor.

Actually, if you read the paper closely, Jeffrey was praising the Christian faith, at least the New Testament part. But in the coverage, this was one more occasion where Jeffrey Scott was giving religion the Bronx cheer. Twisting the paper even further, Republicans asked whether Jeffrey's criticism of capitalism meant he was not only an atheist but some kind of communist as well. His praise for Christianity was ignored.

Now, headed into our final debate, Jeffrey's lead had dropped to two points. The story was still alive. Election day was three weeks away.

Those Republicans had manufactured an issue, twisted the truth, and turned their own defeat into a contest too close to call. I have to say these are pretty crafty campaign tactics. Given the opportunity, would I have done the same?

Don't even ask.

61

Nadia Fedorov

My phone rings.

"Nadia, I have a buyer. Sort of."

"Sort of?"

"They are still putting the money together. But I think they can do it."

"The $150 million?"

"No, $80 million. It is as high as they would go."

"I can't believe it. I fucked that fat cornhusker 20 times and all I get is $60 million?"

"$52 million, Nadia. Remember, I get a third."

"So who's the buyer?"

"The Congo."

"Why the Congo? I thought there was nothing but gorillas and pygmies down there."

"Well, Nadia, they have a lot of minerals down there and if Christopher gets elected, they are in for trouble."

"Explain."

"They have a very valuable mineral down there. Coltan. The world needs coltan. They need it for iPhones, laptops, all kinds of technology products. Demand is growing. The world can't get enough."

"But why do they care who gets elected?" I ask.

"Have you ever heard of Dodd-Frank?"

"Don't know him at all."

"It's not a person; it's a law. Remember the crash of 2008 when all those big American banks went wild and screwed the world? Well, the US Congress passed a law to get them under control. Buried deep in that bill was a provision designed to shut down militias and regulate the traffic of coltan in the Congo."

"Okay," I say. "I still don't get it."

"Christopher wants to repeal Dodd-Frank. Like all these other Republicans he doesn't believe in tying the hands of big business. I bet he does not even know about the part covering the Congo—what they call the conflict minerals part. I bet Scott, who supports Dodd-Frank, doesn't know either."

I am smiling. Both candidates not fully understanding the positions they take. And this, costing one of them the White House.

As we say in the Ukraine, it is enough to make a cat laugh.

Howard continues.

"If we repeal Dodd-Frank, the monitoring will stop, armed militias will expand, and the chaos will get worse. And if no one is monitoring coltan traffic, it will be harder for the Congo to collect taxes. Dodd-Frank did not fix these problems at all. But without that law, there is plenty of room for things to get worse."

Okay, do I care about all this? I move to the more important question.

"When are they going to pay?"

"The problem is that the government hardly functions. Keeping Dodd-Frank is worth a lot, but they are having problems pulling together the money. Their president, Mamadou Kasongo, says they can put money in escrow next week. I am not sure I believe him."

"Well, if he drags his feet, we will be down to two or three states. We could switch every one of them and still lose. And then we get nothing. Nothing! How would you feel if you gave Sheldon Klumm blow jobs and did not get a dime?"

"Nadia, I don't blame you for feeling this way. It's just this has been a hard transaction to close."

223

"You want to talk to Sheldon? He is calling me every day with one question. When? When? When? Three battleground states are already done and shipped. We are losing control."

"I will call them again today," Howard promised.

"Howard, you are making me nervous."

"I will call him now. It is hard to get him on the line and he only speaks French."

"No wonder we are having problems. Those Frenchmen never return calls."

62

Max Parker

Things are not what they used to be.

In the past, your opponent put up an ad. The ad may have called you a thief and an axe murderer but at the end of the ad, your opponent had to appear on screen and say he paid for the ad. He could lie but he had to put his name on it.

Now, there is no candidate at the end of the ad. The ad is placed by some anonymous group taking million-dollar donations. In fact, the candidates now create their own super PACs, staff them with their closest advisors, and run the same ads that they used to run except with six-figure donations and with no one to claim responsibility. That was stage two.

Stage three is the Russians. Boy, are they hammering Jeffrey. They have invaded the Facebook pages. If you have a Democratic Facebook page, say the Appleton, Wisconsin Democrats, all kinds of posts appear. Here are a few examples.

> First, he wants to put Social Security on the
> stock market. What if our Social Security was in
> the market when it crashed in 2008? We would
> all be eating dog food.

If Jeffrey Scott gets elected, Goodbye, Mother Earth! In Oregon he pushed through a deal that let the lumberjacks massacre our forests!

Jeffrey Scott picked a vice president who voted against raising the minimum wage, voted against gun control, and voted against a bill to fight climate change. If that is what we call a Democrat, I am leaving the party.

There are thousands of these Facebook pages, viewed by millions of Democrats, and they are all fed the same diet of garbage. Jeffrey was a moderate on gun control. In his congressional district everyone packed a gun. But the Facebook posts said he opposed all gun control. Then there was a video with high school kids lying dead on the ground, while Jeffrey's voice spoke to the need to be careful about limiting second amendment rights.

You won't believe what came next. There were the posts about his tragic accident on the river where his wife and daughter died. "They were on the river and the raft went under. While his wife and daughter drowned, Jeffrey Scott swam away."

Guess who put their name on that ad?

Nobody at all.

There was a video, a doctored video that showed Jeffrey talking, but a computer used his own voice to create words he never said. He is saying in the video that deep cuts in Social Security are in store. It traveled all over the internet. We screamed at Facebook to take it down. They did. Three weeks later.

Twitter was bombarded with tweets repeating all these messages linking to these videos. Strange groups appeared buying targeted internet ads. "Save Social Security. Defeat Scott." It was an onslaught of lies and distortions. Who could know all this came from Russia? No disclaimers are required for internet ads.

No one knows the effect of these ads, posts, and tweets. But I know this much. There was a study about medical knowledge. They asked people how much they thought they knew about health and medical issues. Then they asked the participants to take a quiz that measured their knowledge. The ones who claimed they knew the most actually knew the least. They believed they knew a lot because they had been feeding themselves crap on the internet.

The ones who said they knew the least, because they were thoughtful and realized the complexity of these issues, actually had the most knowledge.

Go figure.

There is no denying what is happening. The internet has empowered ignorance. The internet has empowered lies. Accountability has been erased. Anyone can play. Anyone can say anything. No one has to claim the message. In the meantime, our democracy is crumbling around us.

63

Nadia Fedorov

There is an old Russian saying. There is many a slip between the cup and the lip.

So far, I have not tasted the coffee at all.

My phone rings. It is Sheldon's number.

"Sheldon, what's up?"

"Nadia, I sent North Carolina, Colorado, and New Hampshire to the states. All three are off the table. There is not much left to program."

"What is left?"

"Pennsylvania, Michigan, and Wisconsin."

"Is that enough?"

"It should be but tomorrow I start work on Pennsylvania. I can try to drag things out, but the states are all screaming to get their memory cards. My boss is breathing down my neck. My boss, Jasper, called me into his office. I thought he was going to rag me again for falling behind. Do you know what he wanted?"

"No idea," I said.

"He wants to give the Republicans more points."

"Well, hopefully, that won't be necessary. Our buyer is trying to put together the money. I can't say what's going on. I think he is fleecing the witch doctors."

64

Max Parker

Debates are overrated. Almost always, polls show that the debates have surprisingly little effect on the outcome of a presidential election. But now, as Jeffrey Scott faced the final debate of this campaign, I was nervous. Jeffrey Scott, aided by a brilliant campaign, had entered September with an eight-point lead. But a college paper written more than 20 years earlier and an astute response by Republican operatives had chiseled Scott's lead to almost nothing. With the race neck and neck, and three weeks until election day, most observers believed the final debate could decide the outcome.

With Frank Jamison of CBS News moderating, Kristin Halliburton of Fox News and Randy Eastman of the *New York Times* joined him on the panel. Jeffrey spoke first.

> Fellow Americans, it is time to state openly and honestly what we all know. Our democracy is broken. In America we have become two tribes, with vastly differing beliefs, and each believing vastly differing facts. And while the two parties mud wrestle for power, the needs of our nation, of our people, have been postponed, shoved aside and lost.

My campaign is about transforming our culture in Washington. It is about civility, compromise, and reaching out to the other side. It is about making both Republicans and Democrats participants in our progress. The urgency for this change cannot be overstated. Medicare will be insolvent in six years. Social Security will be insolvent in 15 years, and if we address these issues now they can be solved with less pain and expense than if we continue to postpone until crisis is upon us. Whether or not you believe that humankind is changing the climate of our planet, the world is moving toward green energy and America must be a leader in shaping that future.

So how do we change Washington? There is only one way. The people of this country have to rise up. You have to rise up and say that American deserves more. You have to say to your senators and congressperson that if you can't find solutions, we need to find new representatives. You have to say our democracy is broken, our gift from the Founding Fathers is crumbling before our eyes, and we are not going to stand for it any longer.

It was an inspiring opening, but Tom Christopher was not to be outdone.

I did not run for president to tell people what we cannot do. I believe our progress depends on our adherence to deeply held principles—

lower taxes, smaller government, and a deep respect for Christian moral values.

But our progress also depends upon leaders who inspire trust. And any candidate who says he can bring us together but spends time attacking the Christian faith is a leader who invites deeper divisions, deeper distrust, and more dysfunction than even what our government experiences today.

My opponent has made a virtue of compromise. But I ask you to think of our greatest presidents. Washington. Jefferson. Lincoln. Roosevelt. Each of these leaders is remembered for championing great principles, the unity of our nation, freedom and liberty, ending slavery, and championing progressive reforms. And how many times have you heard historians or even voters say of these men, what we admire of these presidents is that they knew how to trade horses.

A president is a leader. A president must inspire a nation to reach for great goals and lofty ideals. You can find horse traders at any county fair. What we need in the White House is a real leader.

The first question came from Kristin Halliburton of Fox News. She asked of Congressman Scott, "Do you think religion has an important role in American life and do you still hold the viewpoints expressed in the papers you wrote as a student in college?" Scott was visibly uncomfortable. Surely, he was expecting this question and had prepared, but his answer reflected otherwise.

"First, let me say that these papers you refer to were written more than two decades ago by a college student who was still formulating his views on the world. Of course, I believe that religions, all religions, have an important role in guiding us both morally and spiritually in American life."

At this point, Tom Christopher interjected.

"Does that mean you have changed your position on Christianity? Do you now accept Jesus Christ as your savior?"

Scott responded.

"I do not but I have a greater understanding, respect, and appreciation for the role Christianity plays in our world."

Christopher.

"But at the same time, you don't believe a word of it. You deny Jesus, you deny the Bible, and then come to this debate and say otherwise. There are two words for this rhetoric. The first is liar. The second is hypocrite."

Christopher had drawn the first blood of the debate. Then came a series of questions from the *Times* reporter, Eastman. The first challenged the budget estimates of both candidates. Christopher's budget, according to a leading think tank would have, through his tax cuts, added a trillion dollars to the deficit. Christopher responded with typical Republican rhetoric.

"My budget proposals will shrink the deficit. That is because my tax cuts will grow the economy, grow tax revenues, and increase the incomes of all Americans."

According to the same think tank, Scott's budget understated its impact on the deficit by $50 billion. But his question put him in the same category with Christopher. To the voters, the dollar amounts, though vastly different, were all the same.

Then came the red meat: abortion, immigration, and gun control. Here Christopher was on the defensive but instead of hitting him for extreme positions, Jeffrey Scott patiently explained how compromises might be reached, generally offering the outlines of a plan that contained something to displease everyone.

But the killer came in the final questions, again from Fox News anchor Kristen Halliburton. Here is the exchange.

> Halliburton: Congressman Scott, you have almost no experience in foreign policy and I would like to gauge your knowledge by asking a few easy questions about our world leaders. Who is the president of Sweden?

> Scott: I don't know.

> Halliburton: I know that was a hard one. Let's do an easy one. Who is the prime minister of France?

> Scott: Of course, Emmanuel Macron.

> Halliburton: Wrong. Macron is the president of France. The prime minister is Edouard Phillippe. Well, I know these questions are hard for a candidate who has barely visited the State Department. So let's move closer to home. Who is the foreign minister of Canada?

> Scott: (Long pause.) Is it Christopher Foster?

> Halliburton: No, Congressman. The foreign minister of Canada is a woman, Chrystia Freeland. By the way, Congressman, have you actually ever set foot in the State Department?

> Scott: I have not.

Halliburton: Senator Christopher, you have a minute to rebut.

Christopher: I will let the Congressman's words speak for themselves.

It was a bad night for Jeffrey Scott. He stumbled to explain his religion. And worse, millions of people watched that night, the next morning, and even the following day, as Jeffrey Scott struggled to find the names of some of the most important leaders in the world.

The impact on the race was profound. Scott entered that debate with a slight lead. Four days from election day, polling averages showed him three points behind.

65

Lucy Gilmore

What is the least celebrated holiday on record? Bosses Day. October 16.

But at our group house near Fitchburg, we were not treating this holiday lightly. Sarah had posted a really funny set of instructions about how to become boss. Its feature was Scott Walker and it showed all of the down and dirty things he had done to get power and keep it. In the middle of the page was Roger Stone's quote about how many elections Walker and his top aide had stolen.

But a blog post was not enough for a day so special. To mark the occasion, we held a banquet. We might have preferred steak, two inches thick, or some elegant French souffle. All that was beyond our means. So Daria, the door-to-door canvasser, stopped by Costco where you can get a package of bratwurst, Johnsonville Bratwurst, the best, for $9.99. Without the beer, the whole meal might cost $2.15. Of course, we might eat one bratwurst, but the beer was another matter.

The dinner was okay but, as usual, the company was great. I had grown to love these people, young, penniless (you won't believe what they pay in campaigns), but with one big aspiration to save the whole world.

And God knows it needs saving.

The dinner talk was about, what else, the upcoming election. People would vote two weeks from now. Daria and Jep were doing door-to-door canvassing, which, in this day of high-strung politics, could lead to slammed doors and name-calling with a colorful vocabulary. They always had good stories. Jep said that he met a woman who answered the door in big pink bloomers wanting to know who was running. Who is running for president? She must have been locked in a closet for 18 months.

There was another voter Daria found who said he liked Christopher because he would keep immigrants out. He had a foreign accent. And you wonder why this country is such a mess.

Then the conversation turned to the last debate. Everyone was pissed about all that Bible stuff. Not that any of our crowd had been to church in at least 10 years. On the other hand, everyone was worried because Jeffrey Scott did not know who was president of Sweden.

"Doesn't he get briefings?" Daria asked.

But as I munched on my brat, the man I wanted to talk with was Joel Tifton, computer guy, rumored hacker. I was getting nowhere in my search for evidence of voter machine fraud but on that very day, Bosses Day, I had an idea.

I moved down the table and took a seat next to Joel. "So, Joel," I began. "If a hacker can get inside a voting machine to insert malicious code, can a hacker get inside a voting machine and look for code that someone else inserted?"

I was pretty proud of myself for coming up with this strategy, but Joel was not encouraging.

"Well, yes and no. You can get inside. You can look. But some of these memory cards have several hundred thousand lines of code. You might be looking for a month. And if you are looking for that long, your chances of getting caught are pretty damned good."

"Damn," I responded.

"It is much easier, much safer, to drop code on the card than to actually look for something that is already there."

"I guess," I answered. "If you did get caught it might be hard to prove you were in there saving democracy."

"That's true. But let's say you hacked into the machine and actually found what you are looking for. How do you prove it was there?" Joel continued. "Take a screenshot of the code? Sure, you can do that but anyone could fake that picture. I am not sure that anyone would count that as proof. Also, if you had access to the machine, you could put the code in there yourself. Then take the screenshot and blame someone else. How can you prove you didn't?"

More frustration. More dead ends.

"Well, I guess I am fucked," I answered.

"Lucy, there is only one way to prove the existence of the code."

"And what is that?"

"Steal a machine."

66

Nadia Fedorov

It is over. By now Sheldon has certainly programmed all states and his company has shipped the memory cards. $52 million vanished. Kusnetsov, that lowlife sonofabitch, probably hacked all those machines and Sheldon has erased their code. At least, that makes me smile.

For about a half second.

My phone rings. The disposable. Howard.

"Too late," I greet him.

"Nadia, don't tell me this. Our new buddy, Mamadou Kasongo, he just wired the dough."

"What took him so long? Really, I have to call Sheldon. I think it is too late."

"I hope not. But if we can still insert the code there is one more issue."

"What?" I ask.

"He wants in on the escrow. He gets $10 million of the $80 million."

"I thought it was his money anyway."

"It's government money. The foreign relations budget. Don't ask me to explain the accounting. I am sure they don't publish an audit."

"Greed. It's really appalling!" I reply, shivering with disgust. "So now I am down to $46 million. Do you know how much money that is for every time...?"

"Stop! You might want to focus on not getting nothing."

"You're right. I know you're right," I answer. "Let me check in with Sheldon now."

* * *

"Sheldon, we have the money. What's left?"

"I sent Michigan yesterday and they were chewing my ass for being so slow. I have one state left. Wisconsin."

"I'm no geography wiz. Where is Wisconsin? That does not matter. Is Wisconsin enough?"

"Well, the election is pretty close. Wisconsin is a medium-sized state," Sheldon responds. "It might make the difference."

Well, why not? The escrow moves the money if Scott wins. If he doesn't win, no dough. We still have a chance. What do we have to lose?

"Ok, fix Wisconsin good. Give Jeffrey Scott extra points. Lots of them. If we don't win it, you and I are going to be living in a two-room shack with one flea-bitten dog."

67

Lucy Gilmore

The first whisper of winter had penetrated the evening. Outside, there was the sound of rainfall, a drizzle, the quiet murmur of nature at night. Inside our house the rooms were warm but you could still sense the cold, the way the outside touches the windows and sends those little slivers of cold dissolving into the room. It was 1 a.m., the morning of election day.

I opened the front door and frigid air hit my face. It was only 32 degrees, but it was the first 32 of the season. A month from now, in Wisconsin, 32 would feel like a summer day.

All day I paced the house. I tried watching a movie on Netflix. I tried reading a book. I tried taking a nap. All I could do was sit in a chair, stare at the carpet, and wait.

I opened my car door and cranked the engine. I should have been nervous. I should have been afraid. But right then I felt that every single day of my life had been nothing but preparation for what I was about to do.

In the journey ahead, there were many possible outcomes. There were many risks and some of them could have ended my life as I knew it. But I didn't consider these possible. I believe there is a right and wrong and sometimes there is a guiding hand that protects those who, at great personal risk, pursue the right.

That night, I had serenity in my soul.

I turned my car toward Madison and then worked my way to Highway 181. The road travels through central Wisconsin, open fields and forests. There were no vistas that night. The sky was black and all I could see was my headlights piercing the darkness and my wipers clearing away the rain.

My destination was Theresa, Wisconsin, a village of 1,200 people an hour and a half away. I chose Theresa because it was the only village in Dodge County where people voted at a school and a school would be easier to enter than the Town Hall where more security might be present. My target was Theresa Elementary School.

As I entered Theresa, I was greeted by a colorful sign showing a row of cheerful buildings and the words "Theresa Community Welcomes You." Downtown was just a few blocks long. There was a restaurant named East Desert First, a Widmer's Cheese Cellar, and a big bar called The Pioneer Keg. The elementary school was south of downtown on the same main street.

The school was a simple red brick building, with the shape of a longhouse but square. At one end was a recreation room, not exactly a gym but serving that purpose on rainy days and long winters.

I pulled into the parking lot. Empty.

I came prepared. I had scouted this school a few days earlier. The door to the rec room was locked with a chain that wrapped around the two door handles. My goal was to get inside to the place where people would vote and where those votes would be counted. To do so I needed to break the chain. *How do I do that?* To find out I consulted Doctor Google.

The most common way to break a chain is a bolt cutter. The problem with a bolt cutter is that I am four-foot-10 inches tall and barely weigh 90 pounds. It requires muscle. If I were a man, I would be a great bully magnet, harassed by the versions looking for easy prey. The next favorite technique is the hacksaw. It takes longer and is noisier, but I was in luck because I could saw slowly and the sound would be muffled by the rain.

I put on gloves, gripped my shiny new saw, and exited my car. I walked to the back of the school, half seeing, half groping my way in the dark. But when I came to the rec room, my jaw dropped. It wasn't even locked. The chain was hanging loose. On the night before the election, actually election day itself because it was after midnight, the door to the polling place had been left unlocked. I wondered, *How many times and in how many polling places is this happening across America?* Too many, I was sure.

I entered the room and took out the tiny flashlight I brought to find my way in the dark. But when I tried to click it on, no light appeared. I struck it against the wall. Still no light. It was complete blackness inside. I was about to find out what it meant to be blind and feel a room with my hands.

I started by the door and crept along the back wall. I came to a table with two chairs and two laptops. This is where the voters checked in. This is where voters who didn't own a driver's license were told they couldn't vote.

I continued past the check-in table and reached the corner. I turned to the left, took two steps, and turned left again, groping my way in a line parallel to the first. Open space. I touched nothing. When I reached the opposite wall I turned again, following a line parallel to the last. I bumped into a metal frame, which fell over with a loud clank. I froze. I listened. Could someone have heard? When I felt safe, I dropped to my knees and explored the floor with my hands. I felt a hollow metal frame. It had a curtain. All around there were pencils that had scattered across the floor. A voting booth. I lifted it upright, putting most of the pencils in their original place.

On the same line, groping more carefully now, I discovered two more booths. I was more than halfway across the room. In Theresa and across Wisconsin, voters use paper ballots. Then those paper ballots are put into an optical scanner, which counts and reports the votes. I was guessing that the scanners were in the back corner and I felt my way there.

I touched a box-like machine. My hands explored its shape. Its top felt about 20 inches square. There was a feeder where the paper ballots were inserted. From the floor to the top was about 30 inches. It was an Election Day, Inc. 5000 Scanner. I knew. That is what they used here. There were pictures on the internet.

There was some kind of door on the front of the scanner that required a key to open. There was a plug in the back. I pulled it loose. I wrapped my arms around the machine and lifted. It must have weighed 45 pounds and, as I returned it to the floor, it slid. Wheels. I told you. The guiding hand had put wheels on this machine.

The sound of a siren reached my ears. I froze. Police? In this town at 2 a.m.? Maybe it was the highway patrol. My serenity was gone. Sweat beaded on my forehead and rolled down my face. But the siren faded away. There was silence again.

I took a deep breath. I collected myself and began to push the scanner across the room to where I thought the door was located. Without light my exit was clumsy. I toppled two voting booths and one chair. The noise, I was sure, in my now frightened state, would wake every neighbor within two blocks of the school. Finally, I reached the door. I was outside. I looked back at the loose chain with the lock hanging open on the ground. I threaded the chain and snapped the lock.

I thought to myself with a smile, *I hope they didn't leave the key inside.*

Driving home, I was super cautious keeping below the speed limit by at least ten miles an hour. Driving so slowly at 3:30 in the morning made me the most suspicious car on the road. But since there were almost no cars on the road there was no one to be suspicious.

I arrived at our house. I opened the trunk and under the streetlight looked at my prize for the first time. It was almost brand new. Black without scars or blemish.

Beeeyeuditfull!

I lifted the machine out of my trunk and pushed it up the walkway to the front door. It was now almost five o'clock. I set the machine in our living room and seated myself in a chair. I stared at it for a long time. I named it "Bonnie" after the female half of Bonnie and Clyde. This scanner has a memory card. On that card, a secret. The secret is the three lines of code that says "change the count."

I thought about today's election. On this machine, is code giving Christopher extra votes? If Christopher wins, I have the evidence to show how he did it. Our long history of rigged voting machines is coming to its end.

When Bonnie had been shuffled into my bedroom, I went to my refrigerator. I had prepared for this moment. Waiting inside was a half-bottle of champagne; at my size it doesn't take much. I also had a frozen Ritter chocolate bar with whole hazelnuts. My very most favorite. What could be more appropriate to the occasion? I retrieved these refreshments and moved to the couch.

I sat for a moment and looked at the empty space in front of me. *This will not do*, I thought. So, I went back to my room and retrieved my girl, Bonnie.

I sat. I stared. I smiled. I sipped. I nibbled. I stood up and kissed Bonnie. Then I eased back into the couch and started the whole thing all over again. And again.

And for the next hour, I savored a secret no one knew and felt the exquisite joy of living the finest day of my life.

* * *

How could I sleep? It was 6 a.m. and I had not shut my eyes since the night before last. But sleep was not possible. My body was buzzing, fueled by the knowledge of what I had done. I bounced around the kitchen, cooking an omelet, washing dishes, wiping the counter, and, most of all, waiting for the one person I was desperate to see. Joel Tifton. The man who could open this machine and read the code.

Finally, at 7 a.m. I went to his room and shook him awake.

"What the hell is going on?" he asked.

"Something big. Get up and I will show you."

Blinking, dazed, Joel staggered to his feet and followed me across the hall.

"Joel, you are not going to believe what I have to show you."

"Okay," he said, blinking.

We entered my room and I pointed to the corner. "That is an optical scanner from Theresa Precinct in Dodge County. If I am correct, it should contain code shifting votes from Scott and giving them to Christopher. I am sure of it. I need you to read the code."

He stared at Bonnie, slowly comprehending all that I had said.

"Yaaaaaas!" Joel responded. A millennial word that means something like "fuck yeah!"

His hand tightened to fists and his toes lifted his body. He was almost as excited as me. Almost.

"You did it, Lucy girl! I can't believe it. You might just change this whole fucking world."

I liked the praise, but I wanted the code more. So I got down to business right away.

"Remember, there is probably code that erases the vote-changing code. You are going to need one of those RBC compatible memory card reader-writer devices that reads the memory card outside of the voting machine environment. Otherwise, the calendar clock will erase our evidence."

I had done my homework.

"I know where I can get one." He was out the door.

* * *

Joel was back 40 minutes later, memory card reader in hand.

He stood back and looked at my prize, kind of like a guy looks over a woman before asking her for a date.

I pointed at a small lock on the side.

"I think it's in there."

He looked at the lock and asked for a paper clip. After two minutes of arduous probing the door popped open.

"I think you're better than those Russians," I offered.

Joel smiled. "Not a talent I knew I had."

Then came the security seal. This was a 20-minute exercise. When he was finally inside, he pulled out the memory card and inserted the USB drive from the reader. Now he was squinting at the screen. After a minute or so he began scrolling, slowly at first but then rapidly, as if racing for the end. After several minutes, he looked up.

"There's a lot of code here. And this is an optical scanner. It has more code than a regular voting machine."

"Why is that?" I asked. "All it does is count."

"Well, before it counts it has to see. Did you know that 30 percent of your brain cells are devoted to vision?"

I did not.

"Scanners like this one might have 500,000 lines of code. This could take a long time."

68

Max Parker

Today America has elected the next president of the United States. Tonight, we learn who it will be.

From Dixville Notch, that tiny but clever little village in New Hampshire, we received the first returns this morning. In Dixville Notch, which has a voting population of 12 adults, the voters assemble at midnight, cast their votes, and report them immediately. So in any presidential election, and in presidential primaries as well, Dixville Notch is the first news.

Then no one hears from them for another four years.

But hear from them we did, five voters for Scott and four for Christopher. An omen. If you believe in that sort of thing.

We had decided to do our election night in Washington, DC. Some people wanted Portland, since Jeffrey is from Oregon and giving Washington a snub has become a popular tradition. Not Jeffrey. He is out to transform Washington. So we might as well celebrate in exactly the place where our work begins.

Whether we get to celebrate is another matter. Polls show us behind. The endless videos of Jeffrey unable to name the president of Sweden have done some damage. Greta's last poll, actually conducted last night, the night before the election, showed us four points down. But polls have become crazy. They vary depending upon what voodoo the pollster applies to the numbers. We were up in other polls. But I have been around this horn a few times. Facts are facts. The outlook is not good.

Our election night suite and celebration was at the Willard Hotel, where Abraham Lincoln liked to stay before he got the keys to the big house. Our suite, the Thomas Jefferson Suite, was the size of a medium-sized house. From the sixth floor you could gaze down at Pennsylvania Avenue and see Washingtonians doing their famous power stride, where their legs reach ahead in large, determined steps, desperate not to be late to a meeting at the White House, only two blocks away.

It was five o'clock. People had voted, most of them. And while volunteers chased down yet-to-vote citizens on foot or by phone, these frantic efforts were almost worthless. I didn't tell them, but the real work was done. Waiting was all that was left. The first polls on the East Coast would close at seven, two hours away.

* * *

I walked into Jeffrey's end of the suite. He was sitting in a chair, in shorts and a T-shirt that featured some rock star I'd never heard of. He had a phone in his hand and feet on the coffee table. He pressed the button and ended the call.

"Well, good afternoon, Mr. President," I said with a smile.

"The numbers don't look good," he said, glancing back at his phone. "This may be the last time you get to call me that."

"Don't worry," I assured him. "I have other names but first I have an important question."

"What?"

"Who is the president of Sweden?"

Jeffrey threw his glass of water at me.

"It's Groucho Marx, you fucker! That Kristin Halliburton doesn't know shit!" Jeffrey was all smiles.

I wondered, *If we win, will I still get to see this side of Jeffrey Scott again?*

* * *

At 7:20 returns started to trickle in. There were five states in the East that closed polls at seven. Virginia, Vermont, Florida, South Carolina, and New Hampshire. We crushed Christopher in Vermont. We got crushed in South Carolina. New Hampshire, Florida, and Virginia would be close. They would take a while. Has anyone ever called Florida before midnight?

In our suite we set up an electronic board. States. Number of electoral votes. Percent of vote reported. Vote counts. And, at the top, total electoral votes.

What a fucked-up way to elect a president! All these states and their different numbers of votes is ridiculous. People should elect a president. One man (or woman), one vote. But who is going to change it? If you put actual democracy to a vote on the floor of the Senate, no one would ask, "Why not have a real democracy?" Everyone would ask, "Will the Democrats or Republicans get the advantage?" No assortment of opinions would ever give you the two-thirds majority you need.

A big round of eastern Democratic states closed their polls at eight. Massachusetts, Maine, Connecticut, Delaware, New Jersey, Maryland, and Rhode Island—also Georgia and North Carolina at 7:30. Now, returns were pouring in. Our board could barely keep up.

But things were breaking our way. New Hampshire? Declared for Scott. Virginia, not called but a lead with most of northern Virginia, the Democratic stronghold, still to report. Florida, not called but looking good. But we lost Pennsylvania and North Carolina. I looked up at the board: 60 for Christopher and 63 for us, but that was missing New York, which closed at nine and has 29 votes; and if Virginia came in like I expected, we were ahead 102 to 60. Florida was another 29. But even with a big lead now, this election was going to be close. The South and Midwest were another cup of tea. Then came those cowboys out West. Except for the Pacific Coast, ouch!

I was as nervous as a tap dancer in a minefield but what could I do? I couldn't even pray. My candidate has no God!

An hour later, the South and Midwest had weighed in. The South was solid for Christopher. In the Midwest, Iowa went for Christopher and so did Ohio. But Michigan went our way and get this, they were calling Wisconsin for Scott. Our own polls had showed us seven points down in that state. No poll showed us ahead at all. This could be the difference. I guess sometimes people see the light at the very last moment. I love those fucking cheeseheads!

The count? Christopher 147, Scott 195.

* * *

I entered my candidate's suite. He was still in his goddamned shorts.

"Don't you think you should get dressed?" I asked.

"Not until I know," Jeffrey answered. "I don't want to jinx it."

"Did you see Wisconsin?" I asked.

Jeffrey smiled. He is a Packers fan.

"We might win this," I offered. "We have a chance."

Jeffrey went back to his notes, his speech if he won.

I looked at Jeffrey and thought of his ordeal. Long days. Short sleeps. Some people calling him Satan. Others calling him the second coming of Christ—you know, that mythical one. Running for president can twist your mind. Millions of people believing and saying things with no reference to anything you are or could possibly be. And yet, underneath it all, you are a human being with all the insecurities and frailties that implies.

"Jeffrey, can I ask a personal question?"

"Sure."

"You been through this ringer for 18 months."

"Yeah?"

"You are a single guy. Did you ever get laid?"

"Come here." He motioned with his hand. I edged closer and he cupped his hand, leaned into my ear, and whispered in perfect deadpan.

"Once. Remember Paris Hilton?"

I smiled.

"Well, you are a politician. You were headed for hell anyway."

* * *

I was back to the board. Returns were coming in from the West and I have to say the West is pretty predictable. Idaho would not vote Democratic if the Republican plowed under last year's potato crop. California would not vote Republican if the Democrat burned down the Hollywood sign. There were only three states really up for grabs. Arizona went Christopher. We took Colorado and Nevada.

Do you know what that added up to?

Christopher 262. Scott 276.

We won! I couldn't fucking believe it. How did this happen?

Jeffrey Scott was going to be president of the United States.

We lost the popular vote by three million. Who cares? I am rethinking that whole electoral college issue.

Those Founding Fathers were geniuses. They had it right all along.

I thought of my own career. I was a nobody. The only reason I am standing here today is because when Jeffrey Scott came to me with his totally ridiculous idea of running for president, I was too nice to say "no." In politics it does not happen often but tonight one nice guy finished first.

I walked into Jeffrey's room. He had put on a suit. I smiled.

"You know, Jeffrey, you looked better in cutoffs."

"Don't talk that way to the president of the United States."

He said he was kidding. But I might never do it again.

69

Lucy Gilmore

I was nervous. Polls showed Christopher leading Jeffrey Scott by four points. So first of all, polls said more Americans supported the Republican candidate. And second, even if Scott got more votes, he might lose because the machines are fixed.

But then I had Bonnie. I had the proof.

The Democratic election night event was at the beautiful Monona Terrace, a convention center on the lake that was designed by Frank Lloyd Wright. The gigantic Lakeside Exhibition Hall, which looked out on the water, hosted the overflow crowd.

I arrived early. Our house, which contained three campaign workers, was fully represented. Sarah asked for predictions. One by one everyone predicted Scott but when the turn came to me, I said Christopher. Frowns all around. But never bet against someone with two ways to win.

Wisconsin was another matter. Polls showed us between five and eight points down. We would have to win without our home state. In my heart, I truly believed that there was no way Americans could reject Jeffrey Scott, who had appealed to our decency, our goodness, and our humanity. He had done more than ask us for better policies. He had said to the American voters that we, all of us, had to become better human beings as well.

As the eastern states reported, the race looked close. You knew the Northeast was going to vote Democratic but our margin was fragile. Then the Midwest returns started coming in. And the first Wisconsin returns showed Jeffrey Scott in the lead. A huge cheer arose in the room because the unexpected triumph is the sweetest of all and also because those packing the hall feared they might not get to cheer again. And when Wisconsin was called for Scott, I raised a toast to our three campaign workers in the house and gave them all the credit.

One by one the states reported until, finally, late into the night, Jeffrey Scott was called the winner.

There he was on the giant screen, addressing the American people. There was much of his speech I will surely forget but these words I will always remember.

"My fellow Americans, Americans of all beliefs, it is time to look not to the conflict that surrounds us but to a deeper place. To our hearts. Because if we look into our hearts, we will see those precious qualities that have been abandoned in politics today. Forgiveness. Respect. Partnership. An honest search for truth. These qualities make us not just better citizens. They speak to our own humanity. And underneath the anger and raging words, these are qualities, if only we can find them, that each of us share. They speak to who we are, what we share, and who we can become together. My mission as president is to help each of us to find our better selves. And when we do we just might learn that the enemies we thought we had were never our enemies at all."

Not everyone cheered. To some the idea of partnering with the other side was a difficult idea. But his words spoke to me and many others as well. Across the 10,000 who packed this room, many were moved by a politician who had rallied our deeper humanity to his cause. Tears flowed across the room, and mine most of all.

Part Two

70

Sheldon Klumm

It was the day after the election and my phone rang.

Nadia.

Our new life was about to begin. Marriage. The house in Florida with 10 dogs. When I got off the phone, I was going to quit my job. I was going to find Nadia, put her in my arms, and never let go.

In our new life, I would do more than play video games. I would write them. I would program them. I would become a star. The life before me was beyond anything I ever imagined.

"Nadia, my love. We did it."

"Sheldon." Her voice was even. Not angry but businesslike. "We need to talk. I need to explain how you get your money."

"I don't care about the money. When are you coming to Omaha?"

"Let me explain the money. Do you have a pen?"

"Okay, let me find one. Go ahead."

"I am going to read you a long code and I need you to read it back. It is the code for a bitcoin wallet. That is where you will find your money."

Bitcoin. I got it. Nadia was always one step ahead. But her voice had become cold.

"Nadia, what is the matter?" I asked.

"Listen to me, Sheldon. I am sending you a new passport with a new name. You may need it. If someone discovers the coding you are going to be suspect number one."

I laughed to myself. "No one can find the code. It self-erases. Besides, no one has the legal right to look inside the machine."

"I know all that, Sheldon. But there are serious players in this game. You never know."

"Look, Nadia, I don't care about the money, or the passport or any of that. You can tell me what to do when you get here and we find our house in Florida."

A long pause followed. Then Nadia spoke.

"Sheldon, there won't be a house in Florida. I am never going to see you again."

My life was over. I became dizzy. I could not think. I could not form a word.

"And another thing, Sheldon. We had to cut the price. I could not get the two million."

I still could not speak.

"It's going to be $500,000. That's all I could do."

71

Lucy Gilmore

The day after the election I picked up my copy of the Wisconsin State Journal. There on page three was this headline.

Voting Machine Stolen From Theresa Precinct

The article went on to say that when they opened the polling place one of two optical scanners was missing. Sheriff Hank Stillman was quoted as saying that he suspected that the machine had been stolen by Democrats to create longer lines and discourage voting in a Republican precinct. "I want to thank Theresa voters for dealing with this inconvenience. Thankfully, turnout in Theresa was higher than ever."

* * *

Joel had told me that finding the code might take a long time and long time was right. Every day, I would pass Joel in that house and every day he would tell me no progress. He was checking one line of code at a time.

November passed. December passed. I was losing my mind. It was like I had won the lottery but the check never arrived.

Finally, just after the New Year, Joel appeared at my door, his head tilted downward. He glanced nervously to the left and right, not looking at me directly. His was not a triumphant expression. I assumed that he had finished and found no code.

Before he could speak, I asked. "Why so sad?"

"I found the code."

"That's great!" I shouted, leaping to my feet.

"You're not going to like it," he answered.

"Why?" I asked

"It changes the votes all right. From Christopher to Scott. If this code is on every machine, then Scott did not win the election at all."

72

Max Parker

It was a day when the snowflakes danced, large flakes swaying pendulously in the air to a music you could feel but could not hear. On the ground, people joined the dance. Their movements were individual, skipping, twirling, rising to their toes to see the people, thousands of them pouring onto the National Mall. Although the sun still lingered beneath the horizon, its soft, emerging glow revealed a gathering multitude, assembling six hours early, to stand and watch the new president begin his work. Today was Jeffrey's day, Inauguration Day for the new president of the United States.

It did not matter that he had lost by three million votes. He was the remarkable candidate. His was the astonishing win. His triumph had grown in the telling. His victory was a victory for our kinder instincts, for the better angels of our nature. He was the president who would bring us together. He was the president who would tell us the truth, respect his opponents, restore decency and goodness to our land. Maybe, just maybe, he was the president who would make democracy work once more.

I am what many would call a political hack. I have been hardened by the rough and tumble of my profession. But this day, this ceremony, this great moment of democracy has melted the cynicism from my heart.

* * *

Jeffrey, Ted Maxwell, and his wife began mid-morning with the traditional coffee at the White House with the outgoing president, Webster Miller, and his wife, Betsy. Then into the limo to head for the Capitol and the ceremony itself.

The west face of the Capitol is lined with steps going up toward the dome and then turning to the left and right to the Senate and House chambers. Every step was filled with chairs, and dignitaries from Washington and throughout the world were taking their seats. Across the one and a half miles of the National Mall, no patch of grass was uncovered. But the most remarkable presence was what no camera could see. People have feelings. Those feelings radiate into the air and touch those nearby. And hundreds of thousands of people, inspired, hopeful, moved, all at once radiated emotions so rich, so fulfilling, that though invisible to the eye will be burned into their memories until the very last of their days.

Jeffrey Scott, the two-term nobody congressman from Roseburg, Oregon, walked down a long blue carpet and took his place beside Daniel Crawford, the chief justice of the Supreme Court. Crawford was past 80 and frail and he almost did not make the event. He had a heart condition and two weeks earlier had a pacemaker installed. His doctor had urged him to stay home. But he would have none of it. He looked at Jeffrey with a gleam in his eye that said, "I may be a Republican, but I am glad you are here."

Normally, the president's wife holds the Bible, but since Jeffrey had no wife his six-year-old niece, Tiffany, held it for him. The Constitution does not require a Bible. John Quincy Adams and Theodore Roosevelt did not use one. But after this campaign, we knew that a gesture to Christianity was in order.

He repeated after the chief justice the simple oath.

"I do solemnly swear that I will faithfully execute the Office of President of the United States, and will, to the best of my ability, preserve, protect, and defend the Constitution of the United States."

He stood before the huge crowd roaring its approval with another 40 million watching on television and the internet. He waited, savoring this moment. Then he began.

"Republicans, Democrats, Americans of all parties and beliefs, the future of the American democracy is in our hands. To save it, we must act together.

"When our Constitution was first written more than 200 years ago, our new government was called a great experiment. That experiment would test whether men and women of different backgrounds and different views could come together, find agreement, and lead our nation forward.

"For many years, almost two centuries in fact, our American democracy was celebrated as a success story and a model for our world. But in recent years, we have lost our way."

Then the new president spoke to the failures of our governments and his priorities in the coming days. First, find a compromise that could save Social Security. Second, rescue Medicare. Third, raise middle-class incomes.

As ambitious as these goals were, they would be made even more difficult because Republicans held a three-vote majority in the House and a four-vote majority in the Senate, and the Senate was led by Steve Shaughnessy, an unyielding partisan who was exactly the problem President Scott had just described.

The speech was short. Its message was simple. He closed with these words.

"Finally, I want to say that I am well of aware of the difficulties we face. Changing the culture of Washington means changing the behavior of our leaders. It means asking our senators and representatives to put aside partisan goals and put the American people first. To succeed, I need the help of every American.

"For the last decade, few institutions have been held in lower esteem than the Congress of the United States. But year after year, we re-elect our incumbents at a staggering rate. If we do not ask more of our leaders, change will never happen. To succeed, to save our democracy, to save our country, we need not just better leaders, we need better voters as well.

"So I ask all Americans to expect more, to demand more. When you see your congressperson, ask why we have not rescued Social Security or Medicare. Ask why we have no effective background checks to buy guns. And when you ask these questions you are likely to hear how legislation under consideration does not meet their principles in a perfect way.

"Well, here is the number one principle. If we don't fix Social Security and Medicare, older Americans will lose income and access to care. If we don't restrict gun sales, more people will die. If we don't reform our economy to help the middle class share in our success, our children will be less likely to go to college, to get a good job, and to share in the American dream.

"My fellow Americans, the enemy is not a lack of principles. The enemy is inaction. The enemy is delay. And the enemy is our own tolerance of leaders who would rather posture, pontificate, and blame than join hands and move our nation forward.

"This administration will be about partnership. I will bring Republicans into my cabinet. I will ensure that successes achieved together will be successes shared by both parties. But what I am demanding of our leaders in Washington, you the voters must demand as well. Help me hold our leaders accountable. Help me restore respect, civility, and compromise inside our nation's capital. Because only by saving the precious American experiment can we save our American future as well."

Wet eyes. Loud cheers. Warming hearts and faces beaming with hope. Jeffrey Scott had again carried the day.

From the podium, Jeffrey was shuttled inside to Statutory Hall for the traditional Congressional Leadership Luncheon. Several hundred people, congressional leaders and guests of our own, were crammed into a great open area populated by two statues depicting heroes from each state. It is an odd assortment. Rosa Parks and

Jefferson Davis. Mother Joseph and Brigham Young. Will Rogers, Huey Long, Robert LaFollette, and Sacagawea.

Tables were covered with acres of potatoes, string beans, navy bean soup, and champagne. At the luncheon, Jeffrey graciously apologized to members of Congress for advocating their dismissal and thanked them for serving him lunch anyway.

Then came the great parade. Marching down Pennsylvania Avenue were 1,000 people from all 50 states. Civil war reenactors. The Tupelo, Mississippi high school band. Cadets from the Virginia Military Institute. A gay band with six-colored flags. New York Police Department Emerald Society Pipes and Drums. The Boy Scouts. The Rural Tractor Brigade. In all, 68 bands, 39 floats, and a bunch of things that don't belong in any category. Thankfully, the president's car was at the front so he could reach the reviewing stand and watch.

Next, we were shuttled back to the White House for a shower and change, and then we are on to 10 inaugural balls. Ten! Jeffrey was the first bachelor president since Grover Cleveland. Cleveland was alleged to have fathered an illegitimate child, and his opponents marched through the streets chanting, "Ma, Ma, where's my Pa? Gone to the White House, haw, haw, haw." Fortunately, Jeffrey had not encountered such episodes.

His date was Barbara Dixon, a gorgeous journalist for a paper in Akron. When you are running for president you meet a lot of journalists and I guess this one caught his eye. Jeffrey was in his new tux (I am not even sure he owned one before). I was told Barbara was wearing a Green Rhinestone Silk-Chiffon Empire Plunge Grecian Gown. Don't ask me what that means.

It was a long, beautiful day, one I never imagined. I headed for bed. Tomorrow there would be 10,000 incoming calls from every human being who gave us money, volunteered, or had "urgent" business with the government. Fifteen thousand appointments to make. Decisions, I am sure, about questions I had no idea existed at all.

I talked to the outgoing White House political director. His words? "There is no hell like the first day in the White House."

73

Lucy Gilmore

How would you feel? I got up one morning and discovered that the man I loved and admired more than any person in politics today had stolen the election.

I believed in Jeffrey Scott. To me, he was America's great hope. I was shattered. I was broken.

In fixing these voting machines, Jeffrey Scott had betrayed all those beautiful words. He had soiled the hopes and dream he had inspired across America. I was angry. Bitter. Heartbroken. I staggered to my room and soaked my pillow in tears.

But as I finally started to collect myself, I began to wonder. What if it was not him?

Could it have been the Russians? No. They were helping Christopher. Could it have been the Chinese or the Iranians or the North Koreans? They all had the ability to attack our elections. They all had interests that might be advanced by one candidate or another.

How could I know? I couldn't.

And if I presented my evidence, then Tom Christopher would become our president, a president who wanted to criminalize abortions, dismantle environmental protections, and deregulate big business so the one percent got not just 90 percent of the money but surely all of it. Every bit. Everything I wanted, everything I hoped for America would be gone.

But though I was torn, I knew this. Democracy, our right to a fairly counted vote, is more important than one election, one candidate. I knew what I had to do. Even if it made Tom Christopher president of the United States.

My television was on. There was Jeffrey Scott delivering his inauguration message. There he was offering peace, restoring decency and humanity into a political system poisoned with hate. Then I knew.

There was no way that Jeffrey Scott could have, would have, fixed this election. That was not who he was. But if I turned in my evidence, who would be blamed? He would be blamed.

And the great American experiment, the healing of our nation, would come to an end.

So there I was. I could hold onto my code and give this man a chance to heal our nation. Or I could finish the most important work of my life and rescue our right to vote. I needed to show Americans how voting machines were stealing our right to vote. But if I did so, I would destroy the president, who was our only chance to save our nation.

It is not a choice I would wish on any human being. Least of all me.

74

Max Parker

You are not going to believe this.

Jeffrey Scott, president of the United States of America, was seated in a folding chair, under a folding umbrella, in his faded blue jeans, keeping warm under a faded gray down jacket that looked like he had owned it for 30 years. In one hand he was holding his cell phone; the other gripped a steaming cup of coffee. He was seated in the front yard of the Capitol Hill townhouse of Stephen Shaughnessy, Republican majority leader of the United States Senate.

I know. This scene requires some explanation.

On his first day in office, Jeffrey Scott called a press conference. He announced that he had called on the Republican Senate majority leader and the Republican speaker of the House, Missy Turner, to join him for an all-day meeting to work out a bipartisan plan to extend the life of Social Security.

Shaughnessy, sensing an opportunity to fire up his base, responded with a press statement calling the president's invitation "Just another Democratic maneuver to raise entitlement spending." He stated that the only solution to rescue Social Security was private accounts that allowed citizens to invest their withholdings in the stock market.

Missy Turner, the House speaker, offered a more cautious response, saying that she needed to meet with House leaders to come up with outlines of a proposal that could actually pass the House. A typical Washington duck.

I brought this news to our new president, who seemed to be enjoying this job enormously. When I told him that neither Republican was dying to attend his meeting, I expected disappointment, but as you have probably figured out by reading this far into this book, Jeffrey Scott was a man of surprises. His response?

"Perfect!" He could have skipped the word. His face was pure delight.

I was baffled but knew better than to object. I leaned back and listened.

"I am going to camp out in Shaughnessy's front yard until he agrees to meet," Scott continued. "And he will make me wait because he is a gold-plated asshole and, at the end of the day, not the smartest guy in town. And, something else."

"What?" I asked eagerly.

"He is going to regret that decision for the rest of his life."

* * *

Well, as you can imagine, the shit hit the fan. The Secret Service was apoplectic. The president sitting in someone's front yard for long periods of time, his location known by the entire fucking world? They said "no." Then the chief of staff hit the ceiling. Fifteen thousand appointments to make. Every department of government waiting for decisions on their 56 most important issues.

But Jeffrey Scott would not budge. His answer: "If we don't solve the big problem all this other stuff won't matter."

It was hard to argue with Jeffrey. America had elected a president to bring us together. That president had extended his hand to the Republican Senate majority leader, one of the least popular politicians in America. And what did Stephen Shaughnessy do? He did what he has been trained to do. A Washington response that had become an unbreakable habit. He attacked.

So there I stood, on North Carolina Avenue SE, in front of Senator Shaughnessy's fine townhouse. The president was in his jeans and old sneakers, waiting in the yard, and the mob of cameras, microphones, and media personalities of all types was huge. You could not have drawn more media if a secret cult of radical nuns broke into the Vatican and murdered the pope.

And something made this episode even bigger than a mere pope murder. The media was in LOVE with the president's event.

On the lawn a continuous interview was taking place.

"Mr. President, how long do you plan to sit on Senator Shaughnessy's lawn?"

"Until the senator gets serious about helping save Social Security. Or at least until I need a shower. Senator Shaughnessy has not offered his facilities."

"Mr. President, Senator Shaughnessy has called your invitation a maneuver to increase entitlement spending."

"I like that word, 'entitlement.' Older Americans are entitled to retire, and I want to make sure that happens. But I have ideas to reduce Social Security spending. That is why I am sitting here waiting for Senator Shaughnessy to offer me a simple conversation."

"Mr. President, is Senator Shaughnessy an example of the culture of partisanship you promised to change?"

"I am not criticizing Senator Shaughnessy. I am giving him an opportunity to be part of that change."

"Mr. President, do you think Senator Shaughnessy's refusal to meet might actually result in bankrupting Social Security?"

"If we can't have a conversation, that would be the result. But I expect that Senator Shaughnessy, when he considers what would happen if older Americans lost their retirement, I believe he will meet with me, we will have a reasonable conversation, and we will find a way to solve this problem."

"Mr. President, do you have a message for the American people?"

"I do. I think the senator needs a nudge. Call his office: 202-224-2541. Or send him an email. Or a real letter. Tell him, 'Senator, don't you think saving Social Security is worth a conversation?' I think he might need to be reminded."

Oh, if you could have only seen the twinkle in the president's eye. He had his foot on Senator Shaughnessy's neck and the senator was too dumb to say "uncle."

* * *

Day two on Senator Shaughnessy's lawn. Three things happened.

First, we installed a porta-potty on the sidewalk. We also brought in one of those lawn chairs, the long ones that you can stretch out flat and even sleep on. So worldwide, at home and in the farthest reaches of our planet, you could view pictures of the president of the United States entering a porta-potty and sleeping on a lawn chair beneath a pile of quilts.

Second, there was one mob of news people covering Jeffrey's vigil on the lawn. There was another following Senator Shaughnessy, wherever he went, wanting to know when he would actually meet with the president. Being nimble is a great virtue in politics. Ronald Reagan was once asked about his opposition to raising taxes. His answer: "My feet are in concrete." Later when the cost of his tax cuts exceeded estimates and he needed to retreat, he remarked with a smile that "the sound you are hearing is the concrete breaking around my feet."

Well, Senator Shaughnessy was not born with a nimbleness gene.

Asked when he planned to meet with the president, he responded, "That decision is under review."

Asked what he thought of the president's vigil, he called it a "cheap stunt" that "demeans America's highest office."

Asked if the president was right to camp on his lawn, Shaughnessy lashed out angrily, "Well, I will say this. Back in Kentucky where I am from, we would call it trespassing."

Third, inspired by the president's request that Americans give Senator Shaughnessy a nudge, three million Americans called his office, effectively shutting down his phones. Another four million sent emails. These communications were angry and unforgiving. The message? Meet with the president. Save our retirement. You are a fucking (insert hostile noun here).

Hearing about the avalanche of fury that had descended on the senator's offices, Missy Turner, the Republican House speaker, sent the president a message.

Mr. President, I would be delighted to attend an all-day meeting at the White House to discuss how we work together to save Social Security. Thank you for your leadership in bringing our parties together to find a real solution to this urgent problem. I know we can achieve progress on this issue.

Her statement was released to the press. In a quick flick of her scissors, the Republican House Speaker had dropped Senator Shaughnessy's balls to the floor. And when they hit, you could hear the clink all over town.

75

Sheldon Klumm

What I wondered could be true
The joy of living life anew
Now my sorrow runs so deep
That all I do is sit and weep

I want to die. Maybe a slow, painful death would punish me for the shitty and pitiful freaking life I have led.

I never cared about politics. It makes no difference to me. But I have come to understand that for money and love, I have committed a terrible crime. I was wrong. I deserve no kindness. I deserve no sympathy. I certainly deserve no love.

What is left for me? On the phone, I heard the chill in her voice. Her words were stones—stones that covered me with bruises and broken bones.

I deserve this tragedy. I am nothing. I am wretched. How low am I? I am lower than the maggots that live beneath the surface of the earth. I am deplorable, despicable, beyond the comfort of others.

Where do I go? What do I do? I cannot program voting machines. I cannot work at Election Day, Inc. These instruments have crushed my life.

In her final words, Nadia told me to go away. Take my new passport and go somewhere far away. Where?

I am not looking for luxury. Punishment is all I deserve.

Oh, God. Oh, God. I am crying again.

I believed that Nadia Fedorov loved me. But the dream was false. I was a pawn, used by her to sell the election. Then I was discarded.

Nadia, oh Nadia. What can I say?

Please come back to me.

76

Max Parker

Most of the work that takes place on Capitol Hill is about two types of Americans. The needy and the greedy.

The needy sometimes make a lot of noise but they have no money to spend. The greedy generally stay quiet and spread a lot of money around. And one reason that there are so many Americans who are truly needy is that the greedy generally get their way.

Did you know that 30 of the Fortune 500 companies spend more on lobbyists than taxes? I think you know why.

So here we were. We had been in the White House barely a week and President Scott wanted to save Social Security. And suddenly the new president was holding some cards.

The president's front yard vigil had made Senator Shaughnessy the arch-villain for every American who hates Washington. And there are a few of those.

And as we began our legislation efforts, the president, as usual, had some tricks up his sleeve.

On the day of the meeting, the president called a press conference and reported that he and Speaker Turner had had a long conversation and that she had convinced him of the merits of allowing retirees to put some of their withholding in the stock market in tightly regulated investments.

He also said that Speaker Turner had other ideas and said that if we were able to achieve an agreement that would save Social

Security, Speaker Turner should get most of the credit. A good first step, anathema to most Washington pols, easing the credit into your opponent's hands.

At the press conference, of course, Senator Shaughnessy went unmentioned.

Shortly thereafter I found myself in the Oval Office, my very first visit. Walking into that office, I almost lost my breath, and, seeing my swoon, President Scott brought me back to my senses.

"Okay, Max, are you ready to fuck Senator Shaughnessy?"

"Mr. President, I thought we already did."

"Is he upright?"

"I believe he is."

"Well, then we have to finish the job. I want you to call Michael Roberts with the Securities Industry and Financial Markets Association. Tell him that Missy and I are making a deal that would let people put up to 15 percent of their Social Security withholding in the stock market."

"Right," I answered.

"That is up to $131 billion in new securities investment. He knows the number but give it to him anyway. But tell him that the problem is Shaughnessy, who is all bent out of shape because I embarrassed him in front of the whole country. He is opposing the plan because he doesn't want to raise the amount of income subject to Social Security to $200,000. Do you know what that will cost those greedy sons of bitches? Less than $5,000 a year. And how much will they make when all that money hits the market?"

"It would be hard to count," I answered.

"Exactly. But tell Mitchell that I don't want him to lobby Shaughnessy directly. I want him to ignore Shaughnessy and tell his Republican colleagues that he is screwing them and if Shaughnessy doesn't stop the industry is going to start giving to Democrats again.

"Tell him that I am getting all kinds of heat from my own party on this issue and if he doesn't come through, he is not getting within three blocks of the White House as long as I am president."

"Anything else?" I asked with a smile.

* * *

The big meeting took place in the Cabinet Room at the White House. Present were Missy Turner, Stephen Shaughnessy, and, of course, the rest of their leadership teams and the leadership on the Democratic side. Inside the Cabinet Room is a long oval table that seats about 20 people, just enough for all those "leaders," the president, and his staff. Busts of George Washington and Benjamin Franklin fill the niches. Two portraits hang on the wall, by tradition chosen by the current president. President Scott chose Abraham Lincoln, because he brought the nation back together, and Lyndon Johnson, because he got things done. I looked up at the LBJ portrait. I love that LBJ. He seemed to smile at this august gathering.

The president began.

"It is great to have everyone here today to talk about how we are going to save the most popular program in America. I want to make a few points. First, when Social Security reaches insolvency, there is an automatic cut in benefits of 23 percent. At the White House we plan to spread the word among seniors."

Shelly Harmon, Democratic Minority Leader in the House, raised her hand.

"But isn't insolvency still 15 years away?"

"Thank you, Shelley. That leads to the second point. If we reform this program now, those reforms will cost about a quarter of what they will cost if we wait until actual insolvency takes place."

The number was a stretch but produced many nods around the table. They knew. That did not mean anyone was going to do something about it.

"If we want to do this now, here is what it will take. First, we propose allowing taxpayers to invest up to 15 percent of their withholding into highly restricted equity investments, index funds basically. Second, we want to gradually raise the retirement age by two months every year but offer more options that incentivize waiting longer to retire. You can still retire at 62 but the money will be less. In fact, you can retire at 55 but the money won't be good. If you wait until 75, the money is more. Third, we want to raise the amount of income subject to Social Security withholding from $132,000 to $200,000.

"So no one likes to pay for anything. That's the bad news. The good news is we can fix the problem and share the credit."

"Mr. President," Shelley Harmon, Democratic minority leader of the House, was speaking. "We are getting a lot of heat on these issues. AARP, as you know, is adamantly against these individual accounts. And raising the retirement age as well. I don't know how many votes we can produce for any proposal that includes either feature."

Marvin Hudson, the Republican Senate majority whip, interjected. "Raising the income subject to Social Security withholding is a tax increase. There is no way Republicans can vote for that." Beside him sat Shaughnessy, who nodded his head, glaring at the president.

In this modern era of politics, our government is like a bus. The president is in the driver's seat. He has the steering wheel, the accelerator, and a brake. But the bus is filled with interest groups, labor, business, Big Pharma, small business, Wall Street, Silicon Valley, and a lot more. There are no empty seats. And every one of those interests also has a brake.

The lobbyists for the seniors' groups were crawling across the capital like roaches in a garbage strike. No stock market! No raising the retirement age! The Chamber of Commerce and tax groups were screaming, "No tax increase!"

All that opposition was predictable. You see, these groups are not actually in the business of solving problems. They were in the business of collecting dues and making their members so happy that they send them more money every year. And the best way to make those dues payers happy is to loudly demand what their members want, which is more money, lower taxes, and unreasonable ideas about what they deserve from the government.

But the president had expected these protests and he was ready.

"Okay, so my party won't give in on raising the retirement age or allowing stock market investment. Republicans won't raise the income subject to withholding. Do we have anyone offering compromise?"

Missy Turner said she could live with this outline, that it would be a hard sell to her caucus but that she could produce enough votes to pass it, if it had full Democratic support.

"We can't deliver what you are asking," Shelley Harmon, the House Democratic minority leader, responded. "I may not be able to produce a majority."

The president looked across the room and smiled. He knew how Washington worked.

"I am disappointed but not surprised," he said, his lips pursed, his eyes intense. "I think we need a little public education. My scheduler will contact you. We will reconvene in six weeks."

* * *

As the participants exited the White House, they met a horde of reporters asking about the meeting. After Senator Shaughnessy's humiliation, most attendees offered a positive spin, saying that there was frank discussion, there were differences, and that they had scheduled another meeting to seek an agreement.

But the president, who accompanied them, set a different tone.

"The meeting was extremely disappointing. Both parties clung to old positions, positions that are inadequate to solve this problem and save Social Security. Therefore, I am making a special request of America's seniors.

"Here is what happens If we fail to save Social Security. The law provides for an immediate 23 percent reduction in benefits. I am asking seniors to volunteer to accept a 23 percent reduction in benefits for one month. At the end of the month we will send you a check for the amount of that reduction. Then we will fly all the participants to Washington, DC, all expenses paid, to enable you to report to our Congress on what it was like to receive a check reduced by 23 percent.

"We will take the first 500 volunteers. Seniors can sign up at dontcutmycheck.org."

I wondered who in the hell would take a pay cut, especially on those paltry benefits, even if they got their money back after a month. But people were mad. It was one more Washington failure. And this time their Social Security checks were at stake. Plus, there was that free trip to Washington.

Three hours later, more than a million older Americans had volunteered to participate.

77

Sheldon Klumm

I quit Election Day, Inc. I left Omaha. It was time to heal. And there is nothing like a drive across the American West and $500,000 in your pocket to begin mending your soul.

The landscape is littered with cactuses and I have an idea. Maybe I can make a video game about cactuses. I love those saguaros, those big ones with the straight trunks that rise up high and sprout arms that look like they are waving at you as you drive by. Then there are the prickly pears that look like some creature with an awful disease that wasted away all body parts but their ears. Maybe in my game those ears can hear everything in the universe. Then they inform the government.

Well, maybe not. I have to work on that one.

My destination is Los Angeles, California. There are 19 video game companies in LA including Electronic Arts, PlayStation, Riot Games, and Naughty Dog. With all this money, I could wait five years, knocking on doors, filling out applications, and bribing receptionists just to get the job of my dreams—a programmer, a developer, or a concept creator for a company that makes games.

Nadia may have cheated me. She may have used me. I may be no more than garbage and trash. But I have money and this money is my chance to find my dream. I admit, being a programmer of video games may not be quite as good as fucking Nadia Fedorov every day. But if you want to know how weird I am, programming video games is starting to feel close.

And something else. I intend to enjoy that money, money I have never had. I am going to stay at some great hotels and eat great meals. My soul needs repair. And for the first time in my life, I have money to pay for it.

I pull off I-40 to Flagstaff. My hotel is the Radisson Country Suites. I was looking for the best hotel in Flagstaff. Somewhere where I could spend some of this $500,000, sleep in a great bed, and get deep tissue massages. After all, my tissue is pretty deep. But the best I could do was the Radisson at $159 a night. Well, I won't have to go cheap in LA.

I checked into my room and hooked up my PlayStation. I loaded a new release, *God of War*. At 2 a.m. I was fast asleep.

78

Max Parker

If you want to make a point with voters, it's a good idea to get visual. And what better visual than your own frickin' grandmother sitting on the couch impoverished and angry about it?

In early April, those 500 seniors streamed into Washington, ready to tell their stories about living on a Social Security check that has been reduced by 23 percent. And since the average monthly check is $1,372, that means living on barely $1,000 per month.

How does anyone do that?

There was Primadeen Melrose from Sweetwater County, Wyoming, about 20 miles west of Green River, the county seat. Primadeen had a few things to say about living on 23 percent less money.

"Well, I ate a lot of Vienna sausages, which lose their charm after the third time in one week. I had to turn down the heat and use more blankets. I bought cheaper cat food and then my cat ran away. I think somebody in Congress needs to fix this problem."

Then there was Manuel Lopez, who lives in Queens. He showed up with a cast on his foot and a crutch. Because he could not afford the subway, he had to walk and slipped on the ice. He said otherwise it wasn't too bad. His wife, Romina, still got her check in full.

"I was a kept man," he bragged.

Buela Necaise of Wiggins, Mississippi, also had a few things to say.

"Primitive. We ate a lot of beans. That's the cheapest food you can buy. But me? I ran out of diapers. Not pretty. Then I cut back on my Alzheimer's drug and after that I forgot to take it at all."

Nobody died. There were a few broken bones, some cases of the flu, and a handful had their power cut off. Many lowered their thermostats, shivered in the cold, and ate food they did not like. There was not a desperate tragedy among them. What these 500 men and women had accomplished was simple.

They brought the crisis from 15 years away to now.

In the hands of our media consultant, Casmir Zielinski, the tragedies grew. In front of his camera, these 23 percent victims expanded their stories and Casmir added a new twist. Here is Milton O'Leary from Walden, Colorado, gradually turning red and redder as he speaks.

"I could not take my grandson out for ice cream. We ate ramen noodles every night. No restaurants. No movies. And we fell behind on our bills. Who could live on a thousand dollars a month? And why are we even talking about all this? Because those sorry bleep bleep members of Congress who make $200,000 a year, get free health care and a $2 million pension can't get off their duffs and fix our Social Security! I say fire 'em and make them live on our income!"

Then there was the quarter video. It opened with a picture of a quarter. Twenty-five cents. The announcer says:

"What if you could fix a problem for 25 cents now but if you wait it will cost four times as much? Who would wait?"

Picture of the US Capitol. A dunce cap lowers over the dome.

"Congress wants to postpone fixing Social Security even though fixing it now costs one-fourth of what it will cost to fix it later."

Picture of senior couple, raggedly dressed, sitting on a worn-out couch, eyes wide with alarm.

"What if Congress can't find four times as much money? Then Social Security checks get cut by 23 percent. Can you afford a 23 percent pay cut?"

Both seniors scream. The announcer adds, "America can't afford to wait. Call your senators and congresspersons. Tell them to fix Social Security now!"

My favorite was the "trade places spot" with Rebecca Sims of Turlock, California. Rebecca is about 90 years old and weighs 82 pounds. You wonder when she had her last meal.

"Did you hear about the 23 percent Social Security pay cut? That's what happens when Congress can't get its act together and fix Social Security. That's why I support the Trade Places Act. For one day, seniors all across America will receive a congressional salary. Just one day. It won't cost so much. But members of Congress have to live on a Social Security check with a 23 percent cut."

Rebecca pauses for a moment, her face glowing with pleasure.

"For the rest of their lives."

The ads and the videos were paid for by Americans to Save Social Security. Democratic donors put up the money, some in large undisclosed amounts. The president made no fundraising calls. He knew nothing about it at all. Me neither. I will swear it under oath.

I probably don't need to tell you what happened. When you are 24 years old you barely pay attention to politics. You are having too much fun. But when you are 74, living on that paltry Social Security check, stuck in front of a television set all day long, you have plenty of time to think about politics.

Especially when you are eating Vienna sausages three times per week.

The calls shut down the congressional switchboards. An avalanche of emails filled inboxes. Callers who could not even leave a message got angrier still. The number one message?

"Pass the Trade Places Act."

79

Sheldon Klumm

I pulled up to the entrance of the Chateau Marmont, 8221 Sunset Boulevard, Hollywood, California. My car, a 2011 Volkswagen Beetle, was stuffed with every belonging I could fit including six gaming consoles. Before the bellhop could shoo me away, I shot him a bored expression and said, "I am checking in."

The Marmont is a castle, rising six stories in the air and sprouting turrets rising even higher. Attila the Hun would not challenge this castle. It is not only big in size, its legend is even bigger.

This is where John Belushi died. After a night of sharing cocaine with Robin Williams and Robert De Niro, he was last visited by a woman who gave him a fatal injection of heroin and cocaine. Called the most rock 'n' roll hotel in the world, the Marmont has a long history of delicious tales. It is where *Rebel Without a Cause* was conceived, cast, and rehearsed. It was the site of Helmut Newton's tragic death. It was where the director Nicholas Ray wooed the then 16-year-old Natalie Wood.

Perhaps Harry Cohn, the one-time President of Columbia Pictures, said it best. "If you *must* get into trouble, go to the Marmont."

Well, I, Sheldon Klumm, lifelong dork, man without social standing but with $500,000 in my pocket, was checking in to the Chateau Marmont.

Woot! Woot!

The carpets were thick in colors of mauve and red. Speckled through the lobbies, restaurants, and bars were celebrities small and large, some recognizable, but most just so eccentrically clothed that you knew they must be somebody big. I stopped in the bar for a white Russian and just gazed. Then dinner. Time to live high. No more burger and Pabst Blue Ribbon. I have money. My soul needs repair. For me it was Prime Filet Mignon, Oregano Butter, and Asparagus.

Glowing from my meal and proximity to the rich and famous, I scurried up to my room to get down to business. I had interviews coming up. I would need to know all the new releases. I hooked up my Xbox and played until my drowsiness took over and I was slaughtered by a mutant orc.

80

Max Parker

Two weeks after those seniors assembled in Washington, we hauled all those congressional "leaders" into the Cabinet Room for a new meeting. Two things had changed.

First, all the congressional leaders were pissed. The president had broken a sacred law of congressional conduct. Do not deal with a problem today that you can postpone until tomorrow. Social Security bankruptcy was 15 years away but the president had made it present. Present! The very idea!

They were also mad because they got the blame. All of them, even if they had supported the president's ideas. But, after all, complete inaction is a shared sin.

The second thing that was different was that these leaders were not parsing their vowels and shuffling their feet. Now they had no choice. Something had to be done.

The president began the meeting with three pointed questions.

"Everyone in this room knows we have to raise income or cut costs to reach a solution that saves this program. Who in this room is unwilling to change the retirement age rules so that we add two months every year until we reach 70?

"I think 70 is too high," said Shelly Harmon, the House Democratic minority leader. "My caucus can't support that."

The president fixed his eyes on Congresswoman Harmon and spoke slowly and with emphasis on each word.

"When Social Security was passed, life expectancy was 60. Today it is almost 80. When the program began, there were 159 workers for every Social Security recipient. Today there are less than three. You don't need a math degree from Cal Tech to understand why the program is going bankrupt. Ms. Harmon, what is your proposal to bring this program back to financial health?"

"I understand," she stuttered. "I was saying it is a hard sell."

"And doing nothing is an easy sell?" the president responded.

"Not anymore," she answered, a tinge of resentment in her voice.

The president looked around the table. "Okay, who here is willing to report back that we could not save Social Security because we were unwilling to raise the retirement age for full benefits? Remember, you can still retire at 62, but you don't get as much money. You can even retire at 55 although you would probably starve. And you can get more money if you wait until 75."

No one spoke at all.

Then the president went to the next question: Raising the amount of income subject to Social Security withholding. Looking straight at Senator Shaughnessy, the president said, "Stephen, I am fully prepared to walk out of this meeting and report to Americans that we could not get an agreement only because Republicans are trying to protect the rich. Is that what you want?"

Shaughnessy glared back without speaking.

"I will take that as a no. So we have two of our three issues settled. Does anyone disagree?"

No one objected.

Then the president turned to Congressman Harmon. "Are the Democrats, in order to get an agreement, willing to allow individuals to voluntarily place up to 15 percent of their withholding into secure, highly regulated index funds."

Harmon answered, "No."

The president rose and leaned across the table toward the congresswoman. There was a gleam in his eye that said he had been waiting for this moment. "I am going to say something here that needs to be said. The interest rate on a 30-year Treasury Bond is two and a half percent. The average annual return on the S&P 500 over the last 20, 30, 50, even 80 years is 10 percent. Why are Democrats blocking allowing workers to voluntarily choose a much better deal?"

"I know why and you know why," the president continued. "Because we can win votes by scaring seniors. No one has to do this. Anyone who wants to, anyone stupid enough can take their two and a half percent in Treasury Bond interest. No one is required to use the market at all. But those who invest their 15 percent will have a better retirement."

"Much better," the president added.

The Republicans beamed. Even Shaughnessy offered a feeble smile.

"Are you ready to kill the deal over this issue?" the president continued, glaring at the minority leader. "Because if you are, I am going to say exactly what I just said and I will state, as a Democratic president, that my own party is responsible for the collapse of these negotiations.

"So are you in or out?"

"I have to talk to my caucus," the minority leader answered.

"Of course, you have to talk to your caucus. Are you willing to tell your caucus that you support this deal and lobby them to support it as well? If you answer is 'no' then I am ready to declare failure and lay it at your feet."

A long silence ensued. All eyes looked at the minority leader. Finally, she answered. "Okay, I will advocate. But I can't promise votes."

The president smiled. "I can handle the votes. What I need to be able to say is that this room and everyone in it has compromised for the good of America, reached an agreement, and that Social Security will be saved."

His statement did have a nice ring to it. The whole room was nervous. The interest groups would fight back. But the president had raised the cost of failure and no one wanted the blame. The president could declare victory. And the declaration would be the biggest victory of all.

* * *

Outside on the White House lawn, the president gathered the congressional leaders to make a statement.

"I have met with the leaders of both parties in both houses of Congress. Fixing Social Security is not easy. It requires many compromises from both Democrats and Republicans. But there are three elements to the solution."

The president recited the three planks in the plan and continued.

"Our agreement does make changes to Social Security. Not all changes will be popular. But in making those changes we have done two things. First, we have rescued this retirement program from looming bankruptcy. Second, we have maintained the dollar amounts of all benefits and those benefits will continue to be subject to cost-of-living increases on an annual basis.

"This agreement is evidence that we have a new day in Washington. Democrats and Republicans can work together to put our nation first. I especially want to thank the Republican leadership for their partnership in this agreement. They deserve every bit as much credit as members of my own party."

Following the announcement, interest groups moved to lobby Congress to kill the deal. Unions and the AARP opposed raising the retirement age. The Chamber of Congress and anti-tax groups lobbied to kill the provision raising the amount of income subject to withholding.

But the onslaught of ads and videos in the aftermath of the deal left opponents with no chance. In one ad, the rescue of Social Security was hailed not only as a victory for the program, but a victory for democracy itself.

Man: I am a Democrat and I am proud of our new plan to save Social Security.

Woman: I am a Republican and I am proud too.

Man and Woman: We are proud because we did it together. We were partners, we compromised, and together we saved retirements benefits for every American.

Woman: Once we stopped shouting at each other—

Man: Once we actually talked—

Man and Woman: We proved that anything is possible if you put America first.

Announcer: It's a new day in Washington. Support it. Thank your representatives for putting you first.

While many members of Congress grumbled, the presumption of support created a trap. Victory was presumed. Both parties were on board. And to oppose the plan was to oppose not just the bill but the new way of doing business in Washington.

The president had tackled the gridlock that had gripped Washington for decades and walked away with a win. The bipartisan plan passed by substantial margins in the House and Senate.

And across America, citizens began to wonder. Could this new president really change Washington for good?

81

Sheldon Klumm

There I stood, just inside the entrance of the Hollywood location of the G Star Raw Store, a place where hip Hollywood types go to buy hip Hollywood casual clothes. I stand out like a dead cactus in a flower show.

How I did I end up here? Yesterday, I had my first video game programmer interview. The company was Riot Games. Riot created *League of Legends*, a blockbuster hit, and a few other successful games. Their offices were in West LA and their floors were filled with trendy furniture and staff dressed like it was the weekend at the clubs. Me? I showed up in brown slacks and a white long-sleeve, button-down shirt.

Well, after a long wait, I was called into the office of Delbert Dugger. I wondered if his name was real. He had no desk. He worked on a sofa with his feet on the coffee table and his laptop in his lap. He was wearing shorts, running shoes with no socks, and a T-shirt that said "Muse." I was not sure whether it was the noun or the verb.

Anyway, he looked up at me, a dweeb in my dorky midwestern interview attire, and smirked. Then without greeting, because after all you don't have to greet someone you aren't going to hire, he motioned me to a chair and asked, "What's the haps?"

Not being sure what he was asking, I said I really wanted a job programming games.

He stared at my brown pants.

Then we had a short conversation about programming, and when I told him we used languages that worked in Windows, he was not impressed.

"Windoze," he commented. "Not good."

Then I talked about modding and he perked up, a little, but a pair of brown slacks in Hollywood seemed too much to overcome.

He thanked me for my time. And said, "I'll be back in touch."

It was clear I needed some better freaking threads, and that is why I was standing at the entrance of the G Star Raw Store looking like I was trying to find Walmart but wandered in there by mistake.

"May I help you?" The store attendant was staring at my pants.

"I need some new clothes. I just got here from back east and people dress different here. I have some job interviews in the video game business. Can you help me out?"

He was still staring at my pants.

He finally looked up. "Sure. You want to look like a video game programmer, right?"

I nodded.

"Follow me." He took me to the jeans section where I bought already torn jeans for $115 a pair. Size 40 but still tight. Then shorts. Like the jeans, their store was filled with "slim fit" models. I bought three pairs of something that looked like cargo shorts. Finally, T-shirts. I bought two plain and, remembering "Muse," I bought a red T-shirt emblazoned with the word "Reckless" across the chest.

Am I reckless? Maybe not, but I think it is okay to fake it in LA.

82

Lucy Gilmore

Was I wrong to wait? I was not. The new president had proven that we could all work together. He had saved Social Security. And this accomplishment proved more than his great leadership that was bringing Americans together again. It proved that there was no way that this man, so decent and respectful and honest, could ever have fixed his own election.

I gave Jeffrey Scott his chance to save America. Now it was time to save our right to vote.

I went to the website for the *New York Times* and looked at some of the reporter bios. I needed a political reporter. I picked out a reporter named Phyllis Breeland and give her a call.

"Breeland."

"Ms. Breeland, my name is Lucy Gilmore. I was a reporter at the *Post* and am between jobs. I have a story regarding the last presidential election."

"Fill me in."

"Well, I would rather not do this on the phone. There are parts of this story I need to show."

"Can you give me the elevator pitch?"

"Let's talk in person. You will be really glad we did."

Reluctantly, she agreed to meet the next day at her desk on the press floor at the *Times*.

* * *

I brought Bonnie with me, pushing her through the front door, up the elevator, and down the hallways of the 11th floor. Finally, she and I found ourselves parked in front of Phyllis Breeland's desk. She was tall and slender and had worn out eyes that said she had been around a long time. Her hair was hort and black but speckled with gray.

She said hello and looked at me, one eyebrow slightly raised, waiting for me to reveal the election story I would not describe on the phone. I sat in a metal chair with hardly room for my knees because all these desks were crowded together—same as at the *Post*.

Ms. Breeland looked at the scanner, squinted her eyes, and asked, "What in the hell is that?"

With one of the sweetest smiles I have probably ever worn, I replied. "Ms. Breeland, this is an optical scanner, an Election Day, Inc. 5000 Scanner that counts paper ballots in the state of Wisconsin. Inside of this scanner is a memory card. On that memory card are three lines of code that shift votes from one candidate to the other."

I leaned over and handed her a copy of Joel's notes.

"Here is the location of the code on the memory card and a transcription of its contents. Not only does this code change the counts, it is programmed to self-erase after the votes have been counted."

There was an uneasy moment while Ms. Breeland stared at me, unsure of whether any of this was real.

"You said it switches votes from one candidate to the other. Which direction?"

"It switches votes from Tom Christopher to Jeffrey Scott."

Phyllis Breeland gasped.

"You are a reporter, right? With the *Post*?" she asked.

"I was," I replied. "That's why I am giving you this story."

She turns, looks me in the eye, and begins asking questions.

"Where did you get this machine?"

"I stole it."

"Aren't you worried about going to prison? That's a federal crime, isn't it?"

"I knew what was going on. It was the only way to prove it."

She obviously did not know about the laws shielding these machines from any internal inspection, even by the election officials themselves. I explained. Then I described my drive to Theresa, Wisconsin, at one in the morning to the elementary school where people vote.

She was impressed but the questions kept coming. She was good.

"What if this is the only machine that's been compromised?"

I explained that except for one county, all of the machines are programmed by the same company, Election Day, Inc. If Election Day, Inc. had put bad code in one place, it is likely to be everywhere, unless it is outside hacking. But if it is Russian code, why would they pick on Theresa? It would be everywhere as well.

Ms. Breeland nodded, thinking, eyes on idle to the outside world.

"One more question. An important one. This code self-erases. How in the world can we know if other scanners have been programmed in the same way?"

"Easy. You have paper ballots completed by the voter or paper ballots printed by a touchscreen machine that the voters are asked to inspect. You can count the paper ballots by hand and compare them with the results reported by the machines."

"How long do they keep these ballots? The election was five months ago?"

"Twenty-two months. State law."

"So in any precinct, you can count the paper ballots and know if the machine was compromised?"

"That's right."

Her jaw dropped. Her eyes wandered the room, half focused, her mind processing all that she had heard. Then her voice rose among the clamor of the press room floor.

"Holy shit. Holy, holy shit!"

Then she stopped, embarrassed.

"I am sorry, Lucy, I hope you are not religious."

"Don't worry. I used the same language when my Cubs won the World Series."

* * *

The next morning, after the *Times* had verified the code, I was summoned to meet with Phyllis and their political editor, Rick Middleton. He ran through the same questions Phyllis had asked and I delivered the same answers. Then he broke the news.

"Lucy, we had someone look at this code. It seems to be the real thing."

"That was quick."

Middleton leaned in my direction. "Well, we are the *New York Times*.

"Anyway, we are doing this story. You and Phyllis will share the byline. You did the work. It is the least we could do. What an amazing story. What a breakthrough. On behalf of every American I want to thank you for this contribution to our democracy. Why don't you follow Phyllis to her desk? We would like to run the story tomorrow."

On the way, Phyllis asked me a question. "How long have you known that this voting machine was compromised?"

I paused, struggling for my answer. Well, why not be honest.

"Three months. I just couldn't bring myself to be the person who made Tom Christopher president."

83

Nadia Fedorov

Have you ever heard of Sumba Island? I hope not because that is where I am, hiding out, and it seems to me that a place no one has ever heard of is a good place to hide. Oh, and another thing. You probably haven't heard of Doris Leaper either. She's rich. Really rich. Forty-six million In 38 accounts located across the globe.

Doris used to be Nadia Fedorov.

How I ended up with a name like Doris Leaper is a sad tale. Here I was in godforsaken Omaha, Nebraska, where they name their football team after those serfs who pull the leaves off corn, and I know I need a new name. After all, I directed the heist of the presidential election of the United States of America. Who knows who might come looking for poor little Nadia? If they find me, I need to be someone else.

Here's how it happened.

I opened the *Omaha World Herald*—excuse me, but there is nothing worldly about Omaha, Nebraska—and checked the obituaries. I needed a woman about my age who had bit the dust.

The problem was simple. Those 27-year-olds were not exactly dropping like flies. No one on the list.

The next day, I came up empty again. I was getting nervous cooling my heels in Omaha. On the third day, I found a woman who was 41. Opioid addict who fell in the Missouri River and drowned, which is a hard way to die because that mud pit is so shallow you can practically walk across. But I didn't bite. Those customs people would take one look at me and *know* I was far too hot to be 41 years old.

Finally, on the fifth day, a 25-year-old woman appeared. Doris Leaper. It was the shittiest name I've ever heard but, hey, it was time to wave Omaha good-bye. So, now I am stuck with this awful name.

I cried all the way to Kiev.

Not only do I have a new name. My hair is red, cut short, and spiky. It's a little weird but I have the same gorgeous tits so none of the guys even notice.

Sumba is an island barely 50 miles long. I live at the Nihi Sumba, a lush resort in the jungle where a room can cost $2,500 a night. I am staying in the Wamora, the "lush jungle getaway" in a two-bedroom villa.

Life is hard.

People around here are a little strange. They run off hiking in the jungle, which is full of mosquitoes, snakes, and, I am sure, lurking somewhere in the shadows, a Komodo dragon. I stay on the sidewalk.

The guests really like to sit around looking at birds. The other day everybody got excited to see the red naped fruit dove, a fat bird with a red racing stripe down the back of his neck. I am not into all that nature stuff. But, hey, I have met a lot of hot guys and they've been glad to meet me.

I have to say there is a lot to like about this new life. New name. New hairdo. New home somewhere no one has ever heard of. And $46 million (well, I have spent some of it) tucked away in all those investment accounts, all under different names all around the world. Who could find me? Surely not those FBI guys plodding around Washington, DC, in their shiny new wingtips.

Give me a fucking break.

84

The New York Times

Voting Machine Manipulation Discovered in Presidential Race

Discovery Could Prove Christopher the Winner

This article by **Phyllis Breeland** *and* **Lucy Gilmore**

Evidence extracted from a voting machine used in Dodge County, Wisconsin, has cast doubt on the outcome of last November's presidential election.

The voting machine contained computer code that altered the election results by switching votes from Republican Tom Christopher to Democrat Jeffrey Scott. The effect was to shift six percentage points from Christopher to Scott. If the code was present on all of Wisconsin's voting machines, Christopher and not Scott would have actually won the state.

A Christopher win in Wisconsin would have reversed the outcome of the election and handed Christopher a victory in the electoral college.

Wisconsin Republican Chair Oscar Arneson called for a complete audit of statewide returns.

"This almost unthinkable attempt to steal a presidential election has been exposed and, hopefully, thwarted. The Republican

Party calls on the Wisconsin Election Commission to conduct a full audit of election returns by counting paper ballots and comparing the hand counts with those reported by the machines."

Voting machines in Wisconsin, with the exception of one county, were all programmed by Election Day, Inc., a voting machine company in Omaha, Nebraska. Election Day, Inc. delivers voting machines to Wisconsin polling places across the state. If one machine was manipulated, it is possible that other machines contain the same malicious code.

Jasper Rittendom, CEO at Election Day, Inc., denied that any illegal code had been placed on the machines.

"We have done spot inspections of the machines used in Wisconsin and none of those machines contained the code in question."

But an examination of the code found on the optical scanner that counts paper ballots shows that the code not only included instructions that changed the counts for the two presidential candidates but also instructed the machine to erase the malicious code after the election, thereby destroying the evidence of the crime.

The code that altered the final counts in Scott's favor was discovered on an optical scanner used to count paper ballots in Theresa, Wisconsin, a small precinct that tallied less than 800 votes. The machine was stolen from the polling place on the morning of the election, so the erasing instructions were not activated.

No one has yet discovered vote tampering at any other precinct.

The White House has denied any knowledge of tampering with any voting machine during the recent election.

When confronted with Republican calls for a full audit, Max Parker, speaking for the president and his campaign, said, "We likewise urge the Wisconsin Election Commission to conduct a full audit of the reported results. If machines were programmed to report false results, Americans need to know."

As investigations get underway, the prospect of a constitutional crisis looms over the nation. There is no constitutional or statutory guidance for reversing the outcome of a presidential election. If the tampering occurred statewide, the United States Supreme Court will likely face the prospect of deciding which candidate will occupy the White House for the remainder of Scott's term.

Wilfred Jones, a constitutional scholar at Harvard Law School, offered, "If auditing shows that Scott actually did not carry Wisconsin, then we face a legal battle with few precedents and little guidance from either statutes or the Constitution. I am afraid we face an outcome no one can predict."

85

Sheldon Klumm

I turned off Hollywood Boulevard and into the strip mall. Right in the middle was a big square building made of red-painted bricks and a marque worthy of a small Vegas casino. The establishment was Jumbo's Clown Room, not a strip club but a "bikini bar" and restaurant. I was told that the offices of Untamed Mutiny were three doors to the right of Jumbo's.

Untamed Mutiny was my seventh interview since my fashion disaster at Riot Games. Programming voting machines had not been the ideal credential. So far, no one had called back.

Untamed Mutiny was a start-up. They had no game, not yet, and their office appearance suggested one may not be on the way. It looked like one of those great bar-b-que joints where the owners know nothing about marketing or washing windows but word of mouth was making them rich. The only difference was there was no line outside Untamed Mutiny's door. The front featured a large, unwashed plate-glass window and no signage except a piece of paper with "Untamed Mutiny" in 18-point Arial type Scotch-taped to the door.

I entered.

There were six desks, mostly metal, scattered across the floor filled with scrubby 20-somethings banging at keyboards. I was wearing my "Reckless" T-shirt, cargo shorts, and no socks but in this crowd I was still overdressed. I asked for Joe Sinopoli, the owner.

Sinopoli was my age, around 30. His hair looked unwashed, and for that matter so did he. But he had an intensity in his gaze that told you things were churning upstairs.

"So you want to program video games?" he asked.

"I sure do."

"How bad do you want it?" he asked.

"Worse than anything else in the world."

He smiled. "I like guys who are hungry. Hey, I looked at your mods. Interesting stuff. Where did you get the idea to do the rhymes?"

"Well, I just thought it helps to be different."

Sinopoli leaned back in his chair and for a moment looked at the ceiling.

"Sheldon, do you know what makes video games sell?"

"Cute characters, like Mario and Latios. Blood and gore?"

"Yeh, yeh, all that helps but no one really knows why one game takes off and another one sits on the shelf. I don't know about all these rhymes but maybe we do a game for kids. You know, Dr. Seuss stuff. It might work."

I was stunned. No one had even looked at my mods. This guy had looked and was thinking about how to use my ideas. Maybe I had a chance. Plus, the idea was brilliant. A video game for five-year-olds all done in rhyme.

He might be a genius.

Sinopoli leaned across his desk, his burning eyes meeting my own.

"We are on a shoestring here. I can't pay much."

I thought about my $500,000 or at least what was left of it.

"Well, how about minimum wage?" I asked. I just needed a chance.

He straightened up and gave me a strange look.

"Are you sure?"

"We can review my salary after three months." I hoped there would be three.

He paused for a moment, absorbing my offer, and then rose from his desk.

"All right, you mutineers, I would like to introduce our newest employee, Sheldon Klumm."

The staff turned to stare. I heard one of them whisper, "I thought we were broke."

* * *

I floated out of the office, my shoes barely touching the ground. My dream had arrived. I was a video game programmer. Oh my God! I could do Dr. Seuss games, take every book and turn it into a game. The kids still read that stuff. They could read the book and then want the game. It could make all of us rich. Filthy freaking rich.

Woot! Woot!

I walked straight to Jumbo's Clown Room and took a seat at the bar. I mean why not celebrate the biggest day of your life? I looked at the drink menu. The Drunken Monkey caught my eye. The menu said it had two kinds of rum, bitters, orange, pineapple, a little nutmeg, and God knows what they weren't telling you. It came in a really big glass. By the time I finished, I was plastered.

Did that stop my celebration?

Fuck, no.

I got in my car and drove back to the Marmont.

* * *

At the hotel, my celebration continued. It was two in the afternoon. I picked up my controller, My reflexes were sluggish but who cared? I launched into five hours of *Assassin's Creed*, staggering through the desert, easy prey everywhere I roamed.

Then I stumbled out of the hotel and caught a cab to Bestia, a restaurant I understood to be one of LA's finest. Goddamnit, if you can't enjoy the good life on the biggest day of your entire existence, then you are a hopeless dork. I may still be a dork but now I have hope.

At Bestia I ordered the most expensive wine on the menu and guzzled three glasses. What do I know about wine? They could have put Boone's Farm in a fancy French bottle and I would hardly know the difference. But I think it tasted great! Then I devoured the most expensive meal on the menu, Slow Roasted Lamb Neck with smoked anchovy creme fraiche sauce, little gem lettuce, and soft herbs. In Omaha, a great meal was burger with beer. But Omaha is history. My imagination is raging.

I see myself holding the *Cat in the Hat* video game, which has already sold 20 million copies. I am surrounded by photographers and reporters. How will I spend all that money? I look around at this magnificent restaurant. Bestia! Maybe I will buy this place.

One the way back to the Marmont my phone rang. Election Day, Inc. Was I taking their call? No fucking way. They called again. I blocked their calls.

But while my spirits soared, there was one thing that made me sad. There I was, enjoying the greatest day of my life and I had no one to tell the news. Not Mom, that's for sure. Then I thought there was this girl in the office back at Election Day, Inc. She was always friendly. I dialed her up.

"Hello."

"Cindy, this is Sheldon Kull. I have some great news."

There was a pause. Then she answered.

"Sheldon, what have you been up to? No one has heard a word from you. Where are you? People are looking for you."

"I'm in LA. I just got a job programming video games! Can you believe it?"

"Well, Sheldon, I know that will make you happy. Listen, I've got to run."

There was a chill in her voice. I never should have called. Bitch.

But back at the hotel, I made another trip to the bar, gazed at the Hollywood poohbahs, and imagined myself among them. Then

I was back in the room, the controller in my hand until I passed out and was murdered by some ruthless villain who did not understand that someone is entitled to pass out in the middle of the best day of his life without getting slaughtered. When did decency depart our planet?

* * *

I woke up. My head was pounding. But my smile was still there. I realized that I did not even ask Joe Sinopoli when I was supposed to start. But my call could wait. First, eggs benedict with herb roasted potatoes for breakfast.

As I walked through the lobby, I noticed groups of guests gathered around newspapers, many with shocked expressions. As I passed the reception desks there was a stack of the *New York Times* on the counter. I don't read many newspapers, the dead tree version of the news. But it seemed something was going on.

I picked up the paper and a large headline was splashed across the front page.

Voting Machine Manipulation Discovered in Presidential Race

I read the article. The crime of the century. The number one suspect was me. I was toast.

I had that passport Nadia sent. I went back to the room, packed one bag, and raced to the airport.

Part Three

86

Max Parker

According to legend, Lyndon Johnson, in one of his Texas races, circulated a rumor that his opponent had sex with barnyard animals. When one of his aides pointed out that they had no proof, Johnson said, "I know that. I just wanted to hear him deny it."

Now at the White House, before that blue podium emblazoned with the presidential seal, there stood Jeffrey Scott, as honest as an Eagle Scout in the first pew at church on Christmas morning. The president was not denying that he was a pig fucker. Worse. He was denying that he had stolen his own presidential election.

"I have called this press conference to tell the American people that I have interviewed my staff. I have interviewed my fundraisers. I have interviewed my consultants. I have been unable to identify any evidence or knowledge or involvement by my campaign in reprogramming voting machines to change the outcome of the presidential election.

"Apparently, someone has manipulated at least one voting machine and possibly more. I have called for a full statewide audit of the Wisconsin vote counts using paper ballots. This audit will identify any other machine that has been manipulated as well."

"If these audits determine widespread fraud, I will work with Republican leaders to appoint an independent counsel to investigate this matter and prosecute all wrongdoing that may have taken place."

The president was clear. He was adamant. But if someone rigged the election to put Jeffrey Scott in the White House, who would be the number one suspect?

The number one suspect would be Jeffrey Scott.

87

Sheldon Klumm

At times like these, my mother's words echo in my ears.

"Sheldon, you are a fat, lazy slug.

"Sheldon, you will never amount to anything.

"Sheldon, all you do is play video games. When are you going to quit wasting your life?

"Sheldon, you are an embarrassment to me. All my friends talk about what a worthless son I have. They may not say these things to my face, but I know they are saying them. All the time."

And as I sat in this airplane high above the Earth, her words made me smaller, smaller, and smaller, until I was sure that I must have disappeared into my first class seat.

"Champagne, Mr. Skidmore?" the flight attendant asked.

Skidmore. Elmer Skidmore. That is the name on the passport Nadia sent me. Have you ever seen an uglier name?

I looked up at the flight attendant.

"I'll have two," I answered, knowing I had nothing to celebrate but plenty to medicate. At any moment I expected my mother to walk down the aisle, look me in the eye, and say, "See, I told you so. Now you know I was right."

There are only two things that have ever distinguished my life. The first was my short-lived romance with the beautiful Nadia Fedorov. Nadia cast me aside. She never wanted that house in Florida or those dogs. She never wanted me. Never.

Then came the job at Untamed Mutiny. I was going to design and program video games. I soared with happiness and bliss. But that dream, my beautiful dream, was wrenched from my hands the very next day.

Sitting in that seat, there were things I knew. I was the most wanted criminal in the world. At Election Day, Inc. every finger was pointing at me. The FBI was on my trail. They would surely find me no matter where I hid. When they found me, they would put me in a cell, all alone, by myself, for the rest of my freaking life.

Who can blame them? Not me.

Now a new fear entered my heart. Instead of video game stardom, I would die in disgrace, nothing more than a dork, a fatso, a socially awkward dolt who wrecked our democracy for a pitiful price. My footprint on this planet would be covered with disgust, revulsion, repugnance.

I had two weeks of freedom, certainly no more than two months. Somehow, I needed to make a statement. I yearned to be remembered for something besides my crime.

88

CNN

Good evening, this is Michael Braxton with a big CNN Newsbreak. In the biggest scandal in the history of American politics, audits of the Wisconsin votes in last year's presidential election show widespread manipulation of results. And it appears that Wisconsin is not the only state conducting audits and finding fraud. For a full report, we have CNN Political Correspondent Rebecca Sentori.

"Thank you, Michael. The Wisconsin audit conducted over a five-day period has been partially completed. Every audited precinct shows an identical result. Three percent of Christopher's vote was shifted to Scott, which produces a net six-point change in the margin. If the manipulation took place on all machines, then Christopher would clearly have won the state."

"So, Christopher actually won," Braxton interjects.

"Well, Michael, it is not so simple. Wisconsin has a highly decentralized system of voting administration. There are more than one thousand local election officials, each with individual or joint authority over elections in their villages and towns. Apparently, a number of them did not save the paper ballots, as required by law. Without the paper ballots there is no way to prove the machine counts wrong. So Scott still retains a lead. But if you assume that that all of the machines were rigged, then Christopher wins.

"Then things get even worse. Worried that their own machines may have been hacked, election officials in Virginia, Michigan, and

Florida have conducted audits of their own. These are not statewide audits. They are samplings of precincts. But those audits suggest further tampering. In precinct audits in those three states, hand-counted ballots show that the machines report a higher total for Tom Christopher than he actually received."

"So, Rebecca, are you saying that both candidates were cheating?"

"No, Michael, you can't say that. What you can say is that someone was programming machines in Wisconsin to add votes for Scott, and that machines in Virginia, Michigan, and Florida were programmed to add votes for Christopher."

Braxton interjects. "So Wisconsin was rigged for Scott. Pennsylvania, Michigan, and Florida were rigged for Christopher. Do you think we will have to have the election all over again?"

"No. The only state being questioned is Wisconsin. Despite the cheating it appears that Scott still won Virginia, Michigan, and Florida. After the Wisconsin audit he still has a lead in Wisconsin. But if you assume all Wisconsin machines were rigged, including the ones where election officials lost the ballots, then Scott would definitely lose."

"So who won the election?" Braxton asks with a smile.

"I think Christopher won. But that is not for me to decide. That decision is headed for the U.S. Supreme Court."

89

Lucy Gilmore

The first thing you have to know is that there is no salary for being a hero. My story in the *New York Times* made me a celebrity of sorts. I appeared on talk shows. I was getting newspaper features and interviews. But to pay the rent, I was waiting tables.

I moved back to DC, Prince William County actually, because it was cheaper in the exurbs. I rented at Dominion Pointe, a week to week apartment building filled with just-divorced women and just-evicted men. The room wasn't much. One room with a little kitchen on one side and a toilet and shower on the other. My job was waiting tables at the Smoky Bones Bar and Fire Grill in Woodbridge. With tips, I made $700 most weeks.

In these interviews, the question I got most often was "You showed that the odds against Republican cheating were 42 million to one. But you steal a voting machine and it was the Democrats doing the fixing. Can you explain?"

Did I understand why Wisconsin was rigged for Scott? I had no clue.

Anyway, I had been dealing with all these surprises when, all of a sudden, I heard a knock on my door.

Two officers from the Prince William County Sheriff's Department stood waiting, glaring into my pathetic room.

They informed me that they had an out-of-state warrant for my arrest from the Sheriff of Dodge County, Wisconsin. They were charging me with a Class H Felony Theft for stealing a voting machine, which was county property. The penalty was up to six years in prison. They read me my rights. They explained that I would be turned over to officers of the "out of state jurisdiction" for transport to Juneau, Wisconsin, the Dodge County seat. I was handcuffed and led to their vehicle.

* * *

We arrived at the Sheriff's office in Manassas, Virginia. I was handed over to two deputies from Dodge County. One was fat, with a furry mustache and beady eyes. The other was skinny and tall with a lost expression on his face. Laurel and Hardy without the laughs. They each grabbed an elbow and escorted me to their vehicle, a Ford Transit Prisoner Transport Vehicle, which was a large white van apparently designed to carry multiple prisoners but that day reserved for only me.

They opened the back and I climbed in. The prisoner compartment consisted of a white plastic bench built into one side of the van with five seats. No windows. An expanse of white plastic everywhere you looked except for the grating between the prisoner chamber and the front seats. Each seat had a belt, not for my protection but to lock me in. There I sat, no cushion under my butt, no way to lean back. Belted in and cuffed.

My back hurt right away. It was a 16-hour drive to reach Juneau.

Disbelief. Despair. Desperation. My mind was a torrent of swirly emotions. What had I done? I had saved democracy! But apparently in rural Wisconsin that is a crime! I leaned forward, put my face in my hands, and cried.

The trip felt like a hundred hours. No window. No light. No sound except the tires on the road and occasional drumbeat of raindrops on the roof. Unable to stand or change position, my whole body throbbed in pain.

Twice I asked for a bathroom, and each time we stopped I was paraded through the convenience store in handcuffs, a spectacle that caught every eye. Rather than becoming the feature of a third parade, I wet my pants.

In my mind, the trip would never end, but finally I felt the van slow and turn. There was another turn and a stop, and when our vehicle resumed it turned again and slowed to a crawl. I heard a chant, a cry from voices in the night. Those cries were for me.

> Lucy, Lucy, set her free
> Lucy saved democracy
> Can a sheriff stoop so low
> Let our hero go!

> Sheriff Stillman shame on you
> We all know just what you do
> We all know your evil plot
> To cover up for Jeffrey Scott

As the van slowed to a stop, I heard hands slapping the sides of the vehicle. People screamed epithets at my escorts. The deputies entered the back of the van, unlocked my belt, and led me, stooping in pain, out the back door. I was greeted by a great, raucous cheer.

The protesters were everywhere, hundreds of them, shouting, screaming, beating on and pushing against the van. The crowd pressed the deputies on all sides, hissing invectives. More deputies appeared to clear a path. I was overcome with emotion. I wanted to lift my hands and acknowledge their support, but my only response was large, desperate sobs. I dropped to my knees, unable to stand.

Someone help me! Please!

The deputies grabbed my elbows and lifted me from the ground. With quick steps they moved forward to the jail, a long, modern building with an entrance of glass windows and doors. I could no longer walk, my toes dragging the sidewalk as I was carried to my fate. Two more deputies opened the door to the jail. There was nervousness on all faces. Surely no one in Juneau had encountered so many screaming citizens demanding real justice.

We moved down a hallway. There were deputies on all sides. We stopped at a desk where I was asked questions and booked, but I was so hysterical I could hardly speak.

Then I was dropped into a chair in front of a white panel, a camera on a tripod staring me in the face. My head fell into my hands, sobbing.

There was a crowd of deputies surrounding me.

"No crying in the photo," one shouted.

They viewed me as a criminal of the worst kind. A criminal so weak that she couldn't face her own medicine. A female deputy lifted my chin and wiped my face with a towel. They shot my picture, front and side. The mug shots.

Finally, I was escorted to my cell. I was gaining composure. I asked.

"Who are all those people outside?"

"Well, little lady, no one from around here. They're Tea Party nuts pouring in from all across the country."

90

Nadia Fedorov

I am lying on a table in my gazillion-dollar-a-night villa and some dude, brown-skinned with big muscles, is stroking my legs and stroking my back and massaging my ass, all while I melt into the table. If there was anything left of my muscles I would turn over, look him in the eye, and whisper, "Fuck me." But who can turn over when your entire body has been converted into warm, glowing Jell-O?

There is a loud knock on the door.

"Don't answer," I rasp.

But then there is another knock, this one louder. My face tightens. I will speak to the manager tomorrow. This guy will be on the street.

Then another knock and my masseuse, my brown man with the magic hands, walks to the door and pulls it open.

Two men storm inside.

"Nadia Fedorov."

"No, my name is Doris Leaper."

These are Russians. You always know because you can see, amidst the Western face, a trace of Asia in their eyes, those slightly slanted eyes, left to us by those rampaging Mongolian brutes. And boy was I right.

"Ms. Fedorov, we are with the KSB. We are taking you to Moscow. Get dressed and pack."

* * *

So how did they find me on some godforsaken island no one has even heard about? You have to admit these guys are pretty sharp. They think, she was in Omaha, Nebraska. She would fly back to Kiev. So they looked for people who had made the trip.

They found six people but only one female under 30, Doris Leaper. Once they had my new name it was nothing to find me in the Omaha obituaries then track me from Kiev to Cairo to New Delhi to Jakarta and then to this beautiful villa on the island of Sumba. Now I am headed for Moscow for a reason I don't know. I never should have stopped in Kiev. What a fuck-up!

Now, to make matters worse, I am traveling coach.

* * *

I am expecting an unpleasant visit. I will be hauled into Kusnetsov's office and berated for freelancing in the presidential election, even though I offered him a very generous deal. They are surely mad that Scott won. He might bring healing to their government. But now I am going to get blamed because Kuznetsov would not fork over the dough. Sometimes life is beyond unfair.

But as I am guided through the hallways of the Kremlin, my escort opens an elegant door, which takes us into a grand foyer with burgundy walls decorated with flourishes of gold. This is not Kusnetsov's office. My escort leans over to the receptionist and says, "Ms. Fedorov is here to see Mr. Nikolaev."

Dobry Nikolaev! The deputy head of government. Vladimir Putin's trusted confidant and enforcer. Could this be good news? Should I be nervous? I am led into his office, a grand spectacle of a workplace with a magnificent conference table surrounded by carved chairs with red velvet seats and a view of the Kremlevskaya embankment.

Deputy Nikolaev rises to greet me. He is tall, so tall, and slender and chiseled. He grasps my hand and looks into my eyes like an adoring father might gaze upon his favorite child. Can this be real?

"First of all, Ms. Fedorov," he begins, "I want to thank you for your work in the American presidential election. Intended or not, you have handed Russia a great opportunity. America's democracy is in crisis. And we intend to make that crisis grow."

"Yes, Deputy Nikolaev, we should definitely do that."

"You were in the middle of the transaction that reprogrammed the Wisconsin voting machines to give the election to Jeffrey Scott."

"That is correct, Deputy Nikolaev."

"We need you to make a video recounting your role and stating that you received money from a Democratic donor close to Jeffrey Scott. You need not name names."

"But Deputy Nikolaev, that will mean I could be prosecuted if I ever set foot in America again. I could not travel to America or any of its allies."

"That is true. But we intend to compensate you for this sacrifice."

My eyes light up.

"How much?"

"I was thinking five million dollars," Nikolaev suggests.

"I was thinking 10," I reply.

"Really, 10 is too much. You are doing a service for your country."

I look across at Nikolaev. There is something sexy about power. He is strong. He is a man who knows what he wants and how to get it. But I have my methods as well.

"Deputy Nikolaev, perhaps we might continue this negotiation over dinner at my hotel?"

Nikolaev looks at me closely, surprised by my brazen suggestion. Does he often see women like me? I cannot know.

"How about six?" I suggest.

He leans back in his large leather chair, his eyes taking in my form.

"I believe I would be free at six," he answers with a smile.

I thank him and am escorted away.

When closing a deal, most people need a signature.

Me? I just need a date.

* * *

While in Moscow, I learn more. I do have my sources. My little video is just one part of the campaign to screw America. Kusnetsov is mounting a huge social media campaign to convince Republicans that Scott has stolen the election. For the Democrats he is showing proof that the Republicans are lying. America's divisions are growing. Hatred and anger are rising. The decision about the election is headed for the Supreme Court, which will settle this case.

Maybe. From what I hear the KSB may have a surprise in store.

91

Sheldon Klumm

Here at the most tragic point of my most tragic life, I have one consolation. My consolation is an idea.

Yes, I know I will be remembered for fixing the presidential election. But I will also be remembered for my own video game, my first and final game that will be the work of a maestro, a magician, a creative talent who can transform computer code into a mind-blowing experience.

And if the FBI wants to find me, I am going to make them play my game. And while they do, millions and millions of people will watch, some of them cheering me on.

I may be headed for the exits, but I am going to make my exit good.

I have a name for my game. *Wrong President*. And it is going to be unforgettable.

But before I program the incredible adventure I envision, I must first take precautions.

If you are going to taunt, ridicule, and entertain the venerable Federal Bureau of Investigation, you better be careful because there are so many ways for them to find out who you are and where you are hiding. One of them is hardware.

Your computer has a couple of unique identifiers. First is your IP address, which lets internet aficionados like the FBI find your approximate location.

So if you are visiting the Omaha Craft Axe Throwing competition website, the FBI may be lurking in the background waiting to catch your scent.

The second identifier is the MAC address, which manufactures use to identify a machine based on its hardware. In my case this address can be used to tell where my computer was purchased, say Walmart in St. Louis, Missouri. Not good. If I purchased the computer with a credit card, then they learn who owns the computer and I am really fucked. If I pay cash they can look on the Walmart video cams for the date and time of the purchase in hopes of seeing the face of their suspect. And since they already have my picture, it would be straight to the slammer for me.

So instead of flying directly to my ultimate destination, I fly to Thailand and book a suite at the Oriental, Bangkok's finest digs. I pay a hotel staffer to buy me a new laptop, with cash. When the FBI sees my game, they might try and find me through my MAC address. If they do, they will know I was in Bangkok and *when* I was there. Big fucking deal. They won't know where I went after I left, which could be anywhere in the world and definitely not the same neighborhood.

That is just the start of my anonymity. There is also a way to prevent them from even finding my real IP address or any hints about my location. Have you ever heard of TOR? Have you heard of the "Dark Web"? Since you are unlikely to spend your life in front of a computer, probably not. TOR was designed for people like me, who value the finer things in life. Like remaining anonymous while being the most wanted "cyber terrorist" in America. The letters stand for "The Onion Router," so named because of the many layers of identity protection designed to confuse anyone trying to find you. All built into the network. There is no point in going into the details. Let's just say that John Dillinger, had he lived in the cyber age, could have used Tor to taunt those G-men without them ever finding where he was.

Just like me.

But enough of all this nerdy stuff. Remember Chateau Marmont? Compared to the Bangkok Oriental the Marmont is a Hampton Inn. In the restaurant, the service is so intense they practically hold your fork and put the food in your mouth. I don't know shit about wine, but I order the most expensive bottles on the menu, and they are really freaking expensive, and they taste pretty damned good. Of course a big price tag always improves the flavor of the wine. And they even have girls. This morning I had a "full body massage." Only $200! And since I am working hard to get rid of several hundred thousand dollars in only a few weeks, I guess I will have another one this afternoon.

In the meantime, my game, my masterpiece, *Wrong President*, is developing fast.

92

Max Parker

Last night, Jeffrey Scott invited me to the residence to talk. His candor was startling.

"You know I did not win that election," he told me. "I think I should resign."

"Mr. President, resigning will not fix anything. It will make Maxwell the president. Christopher would not take office at all."

"I know all that. But I was given the presidency through a criminal act. Someone fixed these machines and I did not win at all."

"Well, the same criminal act elected Maxwell. Besides, you and I both know what is about to happen. The Supreme Court is going to decide this case in a few days. There are five Republican justices and four Democratic ones. So you know how the case will be decided. I don't even know why they are hearing arguments."

"What bothers me is that the Supreme Court will be basically throwing me out," Jeffrey answered. "If I was wrongly elected, the honorable thing for me to do is to acknowledge I did not win and step aside."

"Well, if you do that, half the country will think you did it. The Republicans will get a prosecutor with a staff of 300 all working to put you behind bars. Even if you win, you will have to spend millions of dollars on lawyer bills. Do you have that kind of money?"

"I don't."

"Mr. President, let the court decide. Let them put Christopher in. Their decision will not be based on any determination of your guilt or innocence. That's what you want, right? You want the election reversed without the crime being laid at your feet."

"I guess that's right."

"So leave it alone. One day someone will get to the bottom of this. One day we will know how it all happened. But until we do, don't take a fall. Don't make yourself look responsible for something you did not do."

The president just shook his head. There were no good choices. "I guess you are right," he said. "It just seems that a person in my situation should be able to admit what happened and do the right thing."

"Sorry, Mr. President," I answered. "That is not in the Constitution and that is not how politics works."

93

Hank Stillman

My name is Hank Stillman, sheriff of Dodge County, Wisconsin. And you won't be surprised when I tell you I am catching some serious shit.

The whole country is up in arms about the presidential election. And if I have learned one lesson from all this hoopla, it is that if you are a small county with 88,000 people in the middle of central Wisconsin and everybody in this country of ours is screaming at each other, don't get in the middle of it. We may know the difference between right and wrong up here, but out there in those offices of rich lobbyists in Washington, DC, and those fancy penthouses in New York City, they aren't much interested in what we think.

The problem is that I stuck my nose in it already. My view was simple. Nobody is allowed to steal voting machines in my county. I know Democrats and Republicans have a different view of this episode. But I don't give a shit what party you belong to. The law is the law and I am going to enforce it.

So this woman, jobless and barely the size of a dwarf, breaks into the voting place in Theresa, Wisconsin, and steals one of our machines.

Excuse me, is that not a crime?

And what is my job?

To prevent and punish crimes.

So when I hear that this part-time reporter is out there bragging about how she lifted one of our voting machines, I have little choice. I arrest her. And you would not believe the disparagement, the abuse, and the out and out dog cussin' I have endured for the simple decision to do my job.

That prisoner van had hardly left Virginia when I get a call from guess who?

The goddamned chairman of the national Republican Party.

I cannot repeat verbatim what he told me because there might be children reading this book. But he called that little felon a "hero."

Then I get a call from Tom Christopher, the Republican candidate for president, who says when he gets into the Oval Office, Dodge County better not expect a penny of federal money or even one single goddamned food stamp, for that matter. Then he tells me as his first act as president, he is going to present Lucy Gilmore the Presidential Medal of Freedom!

I wanted to wretch.

My jail yard is still populated by Tea Party activists, some of whom drove all the way from California and Idaho to complain about our principled and impartial justice here in Dodge County.

I may not have some graduate degree from one of those fancy universities, but I know this. America is getting crazier every year.

I am sorry I stuck my nose in all this. I should have let that little burglar dance through the streets of America bragging that she could come to Dodge County and break the law because their sheriff is too damned chicken to enforce it. But I wasn't chicken. I did my job.

And don't tell me all this stuff about saving democracy. There is always more to the story.

I've been in this business a long time. Crime is crime. And I know a criminal when I see one.

94

Dmitri Oblonsky

Let me introduce myself. My name is Dmitri Oblonsky. I live in St. Petersburg, Russia, where I work for the Russian KSB, which used to be the KGB and is now the primary intelligence agency for the Russian state. My job is hacking.

Before you are impressed and consider me one of those Russian cyberwizards, they do exist, and can hack right into the networks of the CIA or even the American National Security Agency, I have no special magic. In fact, I was considered a lower mid-level hacker, someone assigned to looking at emails of some American law firm, a minor Finnish political party, or the bank statements of some foreign capitalist trying to do business in our fine country.

Easy. All of it.

But when I got a call to go to Moscow, I was more than a little surprised that anyone there even knew my name. But they did and I could barely believe what they had in store for me.

They wanted me to fly to Washington, DC, and hack the pacemaker of the chief justice of the United States Supreme Court! And why did I get this plum assignment? First, hacking a pacemaker requires no skill at all. The people who designed these devices only thought about the heartbeat. Security was an afterthought, or to be more accurate, no thought at all.

To hack a pacemaker, all I need is a human being with an implanted cardiac defibrillator in close physical proximity. Once I have connected with the device, I can inject, replay, modify, or intercept data. But I don't even need to do any of those things. All those exercises were beyond our requirements. I only needed to turn the damned thing off.

The two most fundamental principles of cybersecurity are authentication and authorization. Neither is present on a pacemaker. Oh, and did I mention that the data is not encrypted?

So why me? Why was I chosen among thousands of lower level hackers to fly to America and snuff this judge? The reason I got selected for this mission was my Aunt Yula.

It all started when Aunt Yula defected to America in the '80s. And once we threw Marxism in the trash bucket, it was okay for the family to visit her and her husband, Hiram, who owns the biggest tire store in Meridian, Mississippi. My dad had a job selling natural gas to Western Europe, which was a lot of money but not much selling because they were all begging for the stuff. So every year we would fly over to Meridian, a town of 40,000 in the middle of a pine forest, for some holiday called "Thanksgiving" where you eat enormous amounts of food and say "thanks" when your aunt does not offer the pecan pie for "thirds."

I also spent many summers over there. My English is almost perfect. Almost. They talk a little slow down there, so my accent is not Russian. My accent is southern. And what foreign agent would learn English with an accent that makes him sound dumb? Of course, they are *not* dumb at the KSB. They know these little tricks. Their little trick was to send me, a slow-talking Southerner, to Washington, DC.

Thank you, Aunt Yula!

I got a plane ticket and a room in a nice hotel, but not the great ones because no one wants somebody important with a good memory running into me. I checked into the Monaco, a hip place in a hip part of town with a lot of art deco furniture and an outdoor singles bar where I won't mention that I had some luck.

Those southern men have a certain charm.

* * *

My first task in this amazing assignment was to get a front row
seat, or close to it, for the oral arguments in *Christopher v. Scott*, the
Supreme Court case where these judges get to decide who is actually
the president of the United States. Everybody in Washington was
talking about this case, and a seat in the gallery was first come first
serve. The argument was three days away. So I bought a sleeping
bag and went straight to the entrance, where 12 people were already
waiting in line. I needed to be one of the first ones in line because
I needed to be in "close proximity" to my target, Chief Justice
Daniel Crawford, 84 years old with sharp eyes, a bony frame, and
a Medtronic pacemaker that kept him alive. Only one other justice
used a pacemaker, a different brand that would not be affected by
my efforts.

Sleeping in the line, on the sidewalk next to me, was Suze
Benjamin, a law student who went to the University of Virginia. I
told her I was from Mississippi and we made a deal. I would hold
her place while she got a daily shower and brought back food. She
would do the same for me.

For Suze, seeing the oral arguments in this case was the event
of a lifetime. She told me how she loved constitutional law and got
an "A" in the course. She was so excited.

"History is going to unfold before our eyes!" she told me.

I thought, *If only you knew.*

* * *

The day of the argument arrived. Wednesday morning at 9:30
sharp the security guard opened the doors. By now the line of people
waiting to watch went all the way to the street and down the block.
But I was number 13 in line and, hopefully, if all those powerful

politicos had not pulled strings, I could get on the first or second row. Hopefully. If not, I would have to return the next day, before the decision was made, and suffer through some argument about the constitutional aspects of natural gas distribution rights.

I worked my way to the metal detectors. I was sure security was tight, but it was not tight enough for Russia's KSB. To tell you the truth, these Americans are amateurs. They think they are safe because they won't let you in with a cell phone. They gave me a key to a locker to store it. But I had a second device, not really a cell phone—it wouldn't call anyone—and not really a smartphone either.

It was a small device 1 ¾ inches long, less than an inch wide, and thin. It was encased in black plastic. On one side were three fake buttons and one real one. The buttons were emblazoned with those little symbols you see on a car key—lock door, unlock door, car alarm, and another symbol I don't even understand. To anyone who looked at it, it was a car key, one of the new kinds you don't have to stick in the ignition.

My device was so well designed that I could have just dropped in in the plastic bucket and run it through the scanner. But I work for KSB and they don't do things halfway. I was wearing Ariat Powerline H2O Climbing Boots. I was wearing these boots because they have a long metal shaft in the sole of the boot running from just behind the toes to the heel. Russian technicians, cobblers actually, had altered the boots to install a second shank. And between the two shanks lay my device, hidden from any metal detector because although they can detect metal, they can't see *through* it.

And what if they found my car key hidden in my boot? If they asked, "Why are you keeping your car key in your boot?"

"In case I lose the other one," I would reply.

I took off my boots. The guards put them on the conveyor belt, looked at the screen, and waved me through. I skipped all the way to my seat.

No one was in the room except the first spectators in line. I took a seat in the second row. The justices sat about 25 feet away, right at the limit of my range. Nine big leather chairs spread out along a wooden dais backed by tall white columns in front of crimson curtains trimmed in gold. Very impressive. They should see my metal desk in St. Petersburg.

Facing the justices directly were seats for the attorneys, and behind the attorneys were the chairs where the spectators sat. Off to the right was other seating that Suze told me was reserved seating for honored guests and friends of the justices.

I leaned down and pulled open a tiny door on the sole of my boot. I retracted my keyring and placed it in my right pants pocket. It was strange that the KSB had given me this assignment because I was not performing a hack at all. What I was doing was pressing a button, the "lock door" button on my fake key ring. The key ring was programmed to locate the Medtronix device. The button tells the device to stop the heart. All the "hacking" is already built into the device so this murder could be performed by a two- year-old with a one-minute lesson. But hey, I got a trip to Washington, some great meals, and got lucky at happy hour. I won't be filing a complaint.

The courtroom was starting to fill. A few of the lawyers were now present. The reserved seats were taken, and the visitors' gallery was completely filled. At 10:00 am sharp, a woman stepped forward, banged her gavel, and announced, "The Honorable Chief Justice and the Associate Justices of the Supreme Court of the United States!" The attorneys and spectators rose to their feet. The Justices stepped out from behind the red curtain and stood behind their seats.

Dramatic!

Suze explained to me that the person making the announcement was the "crier" who then continued her shouting.

"Oyez, Oyez, Oyez."

I was puzzled. No one uses these words in Mississippi. She continued.

"All persons having business before the Honorable Supreme Court of the United States are admonished to draw near and give their attention, for the Court is now sitting. God save the United States and this Honorable Court!"

Oral arguments were opened by the appellants, which in this case was the Republican Party. They were appealing the decision of the Wisconsin Supreme Court that upheld the election of Jeffrey Scott. As it was explained to me, the power to define the selection of electors, as described in the 12th Amendment, is granted explicitly to the "legislature" and not the state government as a whole. Wisconsin statutes provide only for an audit of election returns by a hand count. Since the audit remedy was exhausted, and no additional remedy was provided, one of the Wisconsin Republican justices sided with the Democrats and affirmed the vote count as it stood.

Representing the Republicans was Baron Richardson, a solicitor general in the Bush Administration. He began stating his case.

"Mr. Chief Justice, may it please the court. In its long history, this court has addressed great injustices, terrible crimes, and crises whose resolution have reshaped our government in large and fundamental ways. But never in our history has this court resolved a constitutional crisis so tragic, so without precedent, and so perilous to our democracy itself.

"Clearly, a great wrong has been perpetrated against our election process. This wrong goes beyond the imagination of our Founding Fathers or the contemplation of past decisions of this court. In the absence of guidance from the past, it is incumbent upon this court to provide a remedy that can accurately recognize the clear expression of the Wisconsin electorate and provide guidance for the resolution of all future problems of this kind."

But Mr. Richardson's orations did not last long for he was interrupted, rudely it seemed to me, by Justice Tanya Wilson, who said:

"Mr. Richardson, we are all aware of the facts. There is no precedent for reversing the decision of the electoral college. There is no precedent for removing an elector for misconduct or other reasons except as provided by state law, which in this case does not remotely address our situation. It seems to me, given the problems in Wisconsin, Florida, Michigan, and Virginia, it is likely that voting machine manipulation may have been more widespread than we know. In my view, we have an election where the outcome is not completely clear. In that situation, where no candidate is a clear winner, the selection of the president becomes the decision of the US House of Representatives as provided in the 12th Amendment to our Constitution. Would you not find that to be a reasonable solution?"

Richardson replied.

"Justice Wilson, that is not the remedy we seek. We seek to the have the election result reversed, Jeffrey Scott removed from office, and Tom Christopher declared a winner in his place. I would add that at a time when citizens are doubting the integrity of our democracy, a vote by the House of Representatives would further diminish confidence in our election process.

"As you know, a vote in the House of Representatives is not a vote of each member. It is a vote of each state. In some cases, a majority of a state's congressional delegation belongs to one party, a party different from the party of the candidate for president supported by their voters. Two states, Michigan and Pennsylvania, have an equal number of Democrats and Republicans in their delegations. Will they be able to cast a vote at all? Finally, and perhaps most importantly, is Vermont due an equal voice in choosing our president as California, a state with 63 times its population? No, neither Constitutional language nor statutory provision requires submission to the House in this situation. Clearly, the House remedy was designed to accommodate elections where more than two candidates were receiving votes in the electoral college. To choose that remedy would only cast deeper doubts regarding the justness of the election outcome."

Another justice, Oscar Frederick, interrupted.

"A clear problem before this court is that you are asking us to reverse a finding of fact, a finding that is seems to me is wrong but arrived at in accordance with Wisconsin statutes. This court does not determine facts. This court determines law. Can you more clearly state your basis for reversing the outcome of the Wisconsin election?"

Again, Richardson responded.

"Our basis for reversing the outcome of the Wisconsin election is the equal protection clause of the 14th Amendment. Clearly, a fraud has been committed in every audited precinct. Through a failure of local election officials to preserve the paper ballots, the voters in the unaudited precincts have been denied an accurate count and, therefore, have been denied equal voting rights. The equal protection clause, as you recall, was the basis for the 2000 decision in *Bush v. Gore*."

Another justice interjected.

"Yes, but in *Bush v. Gore* that principle was used to affirm the Florida Supreme Court—not to rewrite the entire election result."

Okay, you can see why I am not a lawyer. All this back and forth jabbering. No one was arguing about who really won. What does it accomplish? It is a little interesting, mostly because this is not the way disputes are settled in Russia. Russia has more direct methods.

Anyway, I was getting bored. I looked at my watch. Forty more minutes of this nonsense. The defense had not even spoken. I pulled out my key ring. I looked up at my target. The chief justice looked like he might fall asleep in the biggest case of his life. It was time to bring this circus to an end.

Suddenly, the chief justice himself was speaking. We have manners in Russia. I would not interrupt.

"If we review the evidence here, it is clear that many voting machines, in Wisconsin and other states, have been compromised and compromised to favor different candidates. We also know that Russia was deeply involved in trying to advance the election of Mr. Christopher through fake news postings on internet sites, tweets, and other forms of cyberwarfare."

Now the chief justice was irritating me. Sure, we played around in the election. This guy doesn't know the half of it. But no one has proof we hacked their machines. I don't know if we hacked their machines. Maybe we did but this is a court of law. Where is the proof?

I was outraged at this travesty of justice. I had had enough. Everyone was riveted by the unfolding theater of this case. I raised my hand and pointed. I pressed the button with the car lock symbol.

The chief justice's eyes widened. He lifted his head and blinked. He pressed his arm to the dais, trying to steady himself. But within 10 seconds he was gone. His head fell to the table, his eyes still open but drained of all life.

A loud murmur filled the courtroom. The justice next to him grasped his shoulders, lifted him erect, and whispered in his ear. Someone else tested his pulse, looked up in panic, shook her head.

"An ambulance," another justice cried out. "Someone call an ambulance!"

People were screaming. Near the bench some were crying. Some spectators stood staring in disbelief. Others hurried to the doors. I departed slowly, not wanting to draw attention. But I was anxious to leave. There was a lot to do in Washington. *Maybe,* I thought, *I will visit the archives and take a look at this Constitution of theirs.*

* * *

Four days later, I was back in St. Petersburg. I had received many congratulations. Some at the KSB called me a hero of the state. All I did was press a button, but I had no reason to argue their point.

I dialed up the internet to check the American news. The American Supreme Court had issued its decision. No decision. Four votes for Christopher. Four for Scott. The Wisconsin verdict stood. The man who was not elected president was still in office.

Get ready, America. This shitshow is just getting started.

95

Damien Pietro, FBI

My name is Damien Pietro, special agent, FBI. Someone upstairs must think a lot of me because I got the nod to lead our investigation of voting machine hacking in the last presidential election.

Our first stop was obvious. Omaha, Nebraska, home of Election Day, Inc. Election Day, Inc., the company that sold, serviced, and programmed the voting machines used in the Wisconsin election. My partner, K. B. Denton, and I arranged a meeting with Jasper Rittendom, the company's CEO, and Chase Davenport, the board chair.

The meeting was held in a conference room on the second floor. In the halls on the walls were posters that proclaimed, "Vote. It's the American Way," "Your Voice. Your Vote.," and perhaps most ironic, "On Election Day, Stand Up and Be Counted!" Waiting for us in the conference room were the two Election Day, Inc. officials and their two lawyers.

Mr. Rittendom He was bug-eyed with scraggly patches of uncombed hair. He had a strange way of staring around the room. Davenport, on the other hand, was a smoothie, perfectly coifed hair and clothes straight from his personal tailor.

Rittendom rose to greet us, shaking our hands with a little too much enthusiasm. "Gentlemen, we are so glad to see you. As a company, we are terribly embarrassed. We want to get to the bottom of this as soon as possible."

"Well, Mr. Rittendom, that is good to hear. No one is in a bigger hurry to figure this out than we are," I answered.

I handed him our subpoena. It covered all emails, cell phone records, and company documents relating to the recent presidential election.

Mr. Davenport's attorney, Ricardo Villante, suggested that the subpoena overreached. I ignored him and began my questions.

"I think the appropriate way for us to get started is for you to explain how you think the vote changing code got into these machines. They were your machines. You programmed them."

Davenport took the lead. "Well, I would like to say there are really only two ways this could have happened. The first is that we might have been hacked. But we discount this theory. Our machines incorporate the highest level of security and would be extremely difficult to penetrate."

I had read reports from the Def Con conferences. The Election Day, Inc. machines were sitting ducks, hacked in a matter of minutes. Some of their machines contained uncorrected security flaws that were identified years earlier. They had all the security of a saloon door on Saturday night. I held my tongue.

"And what is your other theory?" I asked.

There was a long pause as Davenport and Rittendom looked at each other, deciding who would respond. Finally, Rittendom spoke.

"Well, this is pretty embarrassing to admit but we suspect that a Election Day, Inc. employee may have been bribed to insert the code."

Mr. Rittendom proceeded to explain how Sheldon Klumm had been assigned to do quality control on all programming. He said that, after the election, Mr. Klumm had withdrawn large amounts of cash, at bank branches in Omaha.

"Then he just disappeared." Rittendom turned and nodded at Davenport.

"How much cash did he take?" I asked.

"I don't know exactly. I heard it was a lot. You would know how to find out."

"Yes, I got a voice mail from him saying he was not returning to work," Rittendom added. "He never even picked up his paycheck."

"So he suddenly leaves Omaha, with no explanation, after withdrawing large amounts of money and you never contact authorities?"

"No," Davenport finally said.

"Where is he now?" I asked.

"No one knows," Rittendom said. "I don't think anyone has heard from him since."

"You say that Mr. Klumm did quality control. What does that mean?" I asked.

"He was the last person to look at the code before we shipped the memory cards."

"And he did quality control for Wisconsin, Virginia, Michigan, and Florida?"

"That is correct," Rittendom answered.

I looked hard at Rittendom and asked the key question that their answers raised. "If this Sheldon Klumm took money to rig the presidential election, why did our machines in Wisconsin favor Scott while in Virginia, Michigan, and Florida votes were added for Christopher?"

Rittendom and Davenport exchanged nervous glances.

"We have no earthly idea," Davenport answered.

* * *

I knew this story could not begin and end with Klumm. That did not answer the question of why Election Day, Inc.'s Wisconsin machines were rigged for Scott and the Florida, Michigan, and Virginia machines were rigged for Christopher.

It was a head scratcher, that's for sure. But that is what we are paid to figure out.

One thing I knew already. Those Election Day, Inc. guys were lying. Finding Sheldon Klumm was at the top of our list. Unfortunately, there were no recently moved Sheldon Klumms we could identify anywhere in the country. Also, no one by that name had crossed a border.

Election Day, Inc. gave us a picture and an ID number for his laptop. The ID number allowed us to look for that computer on internet sites. If he checked into the Nebraska Cornhusker football site, for example, we could spot him and work our way back to the location of his computer.

It was a start.

96

Max Parker

I was never prouder of my president.

There he was. The not-elected president. The cheat. The liar. The unpresident.

Among Republicans they were telling jokes. "How does the president sleep at night? He lies in bed."

There were others I won't repeat.

Remember saving Medicare? We had the votes. It was about to happen. We were about to save health care for almost 50 million Americans! But once this election scandal broke, the president became toxic. Those Republicans ran away to hide beneath their rocks.

Jeffrey Scott wanted to resign and give the job to Tom Christopher, but that was not possible. Our Constitution was inadequate to address this crisis. I guess James Madison failed to understand what computer voting might mean.

Well, tonight the president was addressing the nation on television.

"Fellow Americans. I come before you tonight to address the tragedy of last November's election. A terrible crime has been committed against our nation. Citizens are angry. Americans are shouting at one another. I am more aware than anyone on Earth that large numbers of Americans believe that I was responsible for the voting machine fraud that miscounted the ballots in Wisconsin. Many may never be convinced otherwise.

"This crisis has exposed how vulnerable our democracy has become. It has shown us that our defenses against criminal manipulation are fragile and weak. It has shown us it is not easy to identify and prosecute those who commit these crimes. This episode has embarrassed our nation. It has left Americans in a fog of despair.

"But our generation will be judged less by what happened than by how we respond. Our challenge is to bring these criminals to justice. And our challenge is to remake our election infrastructure so that our democracy can never be stolen or sabotaged again.

"To this end, I speak to you tonight about two actions I am taking.

"First, I call for the appointment of a special prosecutor, operating in an independent division of the FBI, who will lead and supervise an investigation into the voting machine fraud identified in Wisconsin, Florida, Michigan, and Virginia. So that there can be no question about White House influence over this inquiry, I invite my opponent, Tom Christopher, the man most wronged by this episode, to nominate a qualified individual to lead and supervise this investigation.

"We know wrongdoing must be punished. We knew that before these crimes were committed. The bigger lesson is that we must do more to protect ourselves against these kinds of criminal activities in the future.

"So as a second action, I am sending to Congress an Election Protection Act. Our system of election administration was created when people marked and counted ballots by hand. Many of our states administer their elections at the local level where the individuals in charge have insufficient money or expertise to defend our democracy. Those seeking to change our votes have large resources and computer skills that are rare and barely a decade old. No one can deny that the Russians, the Chinese, and the Iranians possess the ability to change our election outcomes.

"Who is defending our votes? Retired teachers, part-time fire-fighters, public citizens with fine intentions but without remote competency to meet the challenges they face.

"The Election Protection Act would protect your votes in a number of ways.

"First, it sets strict standards for any machine used to count votes in any polling place in America. These would be federal standards that apply to every state and locality. Those standards would end paperless voting. And to ensure that no vote was fraudulently added, the Election Protection Act would require audits in randomly selected precincts after any close election.

"Voter registration lists and websites will be kept in one national location that can be accessed and used by the states. The states will continue to register their own voters and update these lists. But the computer systems that hold them and protect them will be funded by the federal government and developed by the best cybersecurity experts in the world.

"Finally, every state will be required to quarantine 10 randomly selected voting machines and memory cards delivered by the voting machine manufacturer and those machines will be inspected for any malicious code.

"So long as we use computer technologies, new threats will arise, and we will need to find new ways to defend. But I do believe that these measures represent giant steps in defending our votes from manipulation by criminals, foreign or domestic. And they represent urgently needed changes that are long overdue.

"Throughout American history, there has been corruption in the voting process. Politicians who controlled the counting have stuffed ballot boxes, delivered false results, and placed the wrong candidates in office. But today, computer technology has empowered corruption in a larger and more frightening way.

"Our outdated system of election administration is no longer an adequate defense. The job of protecting our democracy must be placed in the hands of experts with money and skills equal to those who would steal our votes.

"A great wrong has been committed on our democracy. Our job is to right that wrong and ensure that it never happens again."

It was a great performance. But Americans had barely switched their channels when Tom Christopher attacked the Election Protection Act as "a federal takeover of American democracy."

He did, however, promise to nominate the special prosecutor.

97

Fox News

"This is Kristin Halliburton, with Fox News, reporting on an alarming development in our coverage of the presidential election scandal. With our report we have Dean Jacobson. Dean."

"Thank you, Kristin. In the wake of the president's call for a special prosecutor and a federal government takeover of all American elections, the Fund for Economic Prosperity, a supporter of conservative causes, has released a video of one Nadia Fedorov, a citizen of the Ukraine who claims she paid an employee of the voting machine company Election Day, Inc. to rig the Wisconsin voting machines. In the video she claims the money she paid to the programmer was given to her by a prominent Democratic donor. Someone, in her words, 'close to the president.'

"She did not provide the name of the donor. Here is the video in its entirety."

"My name is Nadia Fedorov. I am from the Ukraine and now live in Russia. Prior to the recent election, I met an employee of Election Day, Inc. at a voting machine exhibition in New York City. The government of the Ukraine was considering using voting machines and I was representing one of its local communities. The employee, Sheldon Klumm, told me that he programmed almost half of the voting machines used in America.

"While in New York, I also met a Democratic donor who told me he was close to Mr. Jeffrey Scott. This donor was deeply alarmed at the prospect of Mr. Tom Christopher becoming President. Ultimately, I acted as a go-between to facilitate an exchange of money between the donor and Mr. Klumm. The donor gave me $500,000 to give to Mr. Klumm, in exchange for Mr. Klumm's programming the Wisconsin voting machines to shift votes from Christopher to Scott.

"I did not receive any portion of that payment.

"I deeply regret my involvement in this transaction. It saddens me every day. Mr. Klumm took advantage of my own romantic attractions to persuade me to become involved. Because I will be subject to criminal prosecution for my actions, I cannot leave Russia where I currently reside. But knowing of the controversies regarding the American election, I felt it only honorable to set the record straight. A crime did take place. It was committed by Sheldon Klumm. It was paid for by someone close to the president."

Fox News continued its report.

"The Fund for Economic Prosperity said that it received the video from 'a source in Russia' but declined to be more specific. Some have charged that the video was produced by the Russian government to further escalate the controversy over President Scott's involvement. The Fund further stated that they do not know the name of the Democratic donor who paid for the rigging of Wisconsin voting machines."

"Well, Dean," Halliburton interjects. "It looks like they have nailed the president."

"That's true, Kristin," Jacobson responds. "It's great to finally get to the bottom of this disgraceful matter. Any reactions on the Republican side?"

"You better believe it. The chairman of the Republican National Committee called on President Scott to name the donor involved and to resign from office. In Congress, there have been new calls to begin impeachment proceedings."

98

Lucy Gilmore

If you've never been to jail, here is something you won't know. Leave your watch at home.

I woke up in the morning and looked at my watch: 7:13 a.m. Then, 10 minutes later, I checked again. I don't know why I kept checking. I had no meetings on my schedule. If I did, I would not have known. The sheriff had confiscated my phone.

So by wearing this watch, seeing time pass in 10-minute increments, my day stretched out into eternity. I took it off and put it under my pillow. It might get stolen. Good.

The cell was eight feet by ten feet wide. Toilet. Sink. Two bunk beds. The sheets had not been washed and my mattress felt like it was stuffed with ballast from a train track. But my pathetic apartment at Dominion Pointe had prepared me for this room. No down pillows there either.

I had two cellmates. Sally was a wild-eyed, homeless woman who could not have been a day under 65 and weighed about 30 pounds. She had mental issues and smelled bad. The worst is she sang to herself, often late at night. Her crime was that she had attacked a sheriff's deputy. But she was scheduled to be released that afternoon.

Ellie was my other cellmate. She was a meth dealer. Fiftyish, orange hair, an artificial shade, and missing a few teeth. I actually liked her. She'd been in there a few times and she had stories on the deputies. The stories weren't so good but they were better than look-ing at your watch.

A guard arrived at our door.

"Lucy Gilmore."

I looked up.

"You have a visitor."

I was led to a room with a small table and two chairs. Seated was a man in a suit. Short hair. Serious demeanor. He rose and shook my hand.

"Lucy Gilmore, I am getting you out of here."

"Who are you?" I asked, not intending to interfere with his mission.

"Franklin Messing. I am a lawyer with the Tea Party."

Franklin explained that he had posted bail: $100,000.

"A hundred thousand dollars?" I asked.

"Well, it's not like you are a common meth dealer."

Then he explained that I couldn't leave the county until my trial was finished but they had found me a place to live.

"This is about the craziest thing I have ever seen," Franklin explained. "The sheriff is nuts and the DA is afraid of him. There has been a lot of pressure to let you go. The president has said publicly that you should be released but he cannot pardon someone facing state charges. The governor would pardon you, but he can't do so until you have actually been convicted. Unless the district attorney decides to drop the case, there is no relief."

"So all this is going to trial?" I asked.

"Don't worry, we are flooded with contributions from Tea Party members all across America. You will have no legal expenses at all."

After some paperwork and dirty looks from the sheriff, Franklin drove me to the Inn at Lake Wissota, a nice hotel with overstuffed furniture, a good restaurant, and a view of the lake. That hard, nar-row jail mattress was nowhere to be found. Before me was a king bed with a mattress that surely cost a thousand bucks. So the first thing

I did was I lie on the bed, spread eagle, and make snow angels with my limbs. The mattress was soft, so soft.

Then, after a luscious shower, I went to the restaurant and ordered a steak and charged it to my room. I assumed those Tea Party nuts were picking up meals as well. If not, what were they going to do? Put me in jail?

I went back to the room and picked up the phone. I called a literary agent I'd met during an interview in New York. She told me I should write a book about my battle to uncover voting machine fraud and my triumph in doing so.

I called her and asked her to overnight a laptop. She was excited. In the meantime, I grabbed a stack of hotel stationery and started outlining the story.

She asked when I was going to be free. I told her it could be a long time.

"I am so sorry," she said.

"Not me," I answered. "The longer they keep me the more books I am going to sell."

99

Damien Pietro

This case was a head scratcher. Three states programmed to help on Christopher. One state programmed to elect Scott. One guy writing every program. Company executives were in full-scale cover-up. The culprit was missing. And the culprit, Sheldon Klumm, may be the only person who could tell us what in the hell really happened.

Before the news broke, he was all over LA. He had no reason to hide. He had credit card charges at the Chateau Marmont, Bestia, clothing stores. Luxury destinations. Big tabs. We checked bank records. His money for rigging the presidential election was a measly half million bucks. But when the *Times* published the story, he checked out of the Marmont and was gone.

So we went to work finding him. What if I committed the crime of the century and that crime was published in a headline on the front page of the *New York Times*? I would drive straight to the airport and kiss America goodbye. But we had no record of a Sheldon Klumm leaving or entering this country. So we took a look at records from the Los Angeles airport, LAX, on the day of the story.

LAX is the sixth busiest in the world. Eighty-seven million passengers depart every year and, of those, about 40,000 passengers depart for foreign countries every day.

Sheldon is 33 years old and probably traveling with a fake passport. So we looked for white males, aged 30 to 35, departing the country on the day he left town. Now we were down to 2,241. The way to get a passport is to find an obituary of a person your age, gender, and race. Then you write some government agency and get the birth certificate. You take the birth certificate to the post office. Voila! You have a passport. So we took our 2,200 suspects and ran their names against a list of recently deceased persons.

There was one match. Elmer Skidmore, who died last year in Osceola, Nebraska. He flew from LA to Bangkok that day. But Skidmore was no longer using credit cards, at least not in his name. His next flight was to Oslo. We checked hotels there; no record of anyone with that name.

Once in the EU, there is no-passport record unless you travel by plane. Travel by car, ferry, or train? No way to track. Once Elmer Skidmore landed in Oslo, he simply disappeared. There are 27 countries in the EU. But at least we are not going house to house in Timbuktu.

Is Elmer Skidmore Sheldom Klumm? Does a cornhusker husk corn?

100

Max Parker

Head for the bomb shelters. The Russians have attacked. So have the Republicans and, frankly, I can hardly tell the difference.

By now everyone has seen Nadia Fedorov tell the world that the president's best friend paid to rig the Wisconsin elections. Apparently, half the country believes it.

So next we get the fake video. You know, where they take a video of Jeffrey Scott and some crazy software scientist listens to his voice and then can make him say anything they want. Well, this video has the president say that he does remember that one of his donors was using his own money to try to rig the Wisconsin machines. "But I did not authorize it." In the video, when he gets to that line, the picture freezes and the sound repeats again and again.

Then you know what else those Russians did? They took that same doctored video, posted it on Democratic websites, and said, "Look what the Republicans are doing! Fake videos of the president. Has any American political party stooped so low?"

There is a fake news story that went to Democrats about the murder of some programmer who supposedly rigged voting machines in Virginia, Florida, and Michigan. To Republicans, there is a story about how Nadia Fedorov wants to come to the US and give testimony but the White House is blocking her arrest. All of these stories are posted on thousands of Facebook pages affiliated with Democrats or Republicans or liberals or conservatives or just plain kooks. The same stories appear instantly everywhere. But when you contact Facebook, they promise to "look into it," and by the time they pull the post the whole thing is over.

The Russians have one objective. They want to make Americans hate each other. And, sadly, it is working.

Oh, and the Republicans?

Fake polls showing a majority of Americans supporting impeachment. Petitions demanding that President Scott resign. Speculation about which of Scott's close friends paid for the rigging of the Wisconsin election. You can go online and vote for the guy you believe did it.

And did I tell you about the Twitter forest fire? It is raging, fueled by bots, trolls, and Kool-Aid drinking citizens, all ready to pack their guns, climb the White House fence, and retake our government.

Meanwhile, Democrats are still in the conference room arguing about how to respond.

101

Damien Pietro, FBI

Look, I know a Russian ploy when I see one. They have this big reputation for screwing with our elections. Their success, if they are having any, is based upon volume and not finesse. Look at that Nadia Fedorov video. The only person she fingers is that programmer but the programmer has no connection to the president.

The guy she says paid for all this goes unnamed. It doesn't take a genius to know what is going on. Those Russians are making things up to cause America trouble.

I may see the truth but these days people believe what they want to believe and half the country now thinks the president wrote Sheldon Klumm a personal check.

What can you do?

But for all these reasons, I was more than a little surprised when my partner, KB Denton, walked into my office to share his research on Ms. Fedorov.

"Damien, you're not going to believe this but at least some of that Nadia girl's story is checking out."

"Yeah?" I replied.

"First, she did visit New York City the week of some voting machine expo. Sheldon Klumm was in town too.

"Second, after that weekend, she made three separate trips to Omaha and stayed at the Magnolia in one of their premier suites.

Third, she made another trip to New York, for what purpose we don't know.

"Also, in the video she says she paid Klumm $500,000. That is roughly the amount the guy moved off Bitcoin. As the election day approaches, she changes her identity and gets a new passport. An American passport issued in Omaha."

"How do we know that?" I ask.

"Well, it is a guess but a good one. About this time, there are only four people who traveled from Omaha to Kiev. Three of them are men."

"And what about the woman?"

"She died last month, before this Nadia woman got on the plane."

"You got Miss Fedorov's new name?"

"I do. Her name is Doris Leaper."

102

CNN

Good morning, this is Michael Braxton with a CNN Newsbreak. In a major development in America's presidential election scandal, Tom Christopher has sent his choice for special prosecutor to the White House today. The man he has nominated is Cason Blake.

Blake, who has served as a US attorney in New York City in two Republican administrations, prosecuted a number of Democratic officials and earned the nickname "Cold Case Cason" for winning convictions in old cases his predecessors were unable to bring to trial.

CNN has caught up with Mr. Blake. Our legal correspondent Jane Foster is standing by with a live interview.

"Mr. Blake, this is a pretty big assignment, right?"

"You bet, Jane. Americans need answers. This scandal is tearing us apart."

"I know your inquiry is only starting but do you have a direction?"

"Well, Jane, the FBI has already begun the investigation and I need to review their work. But if someone fixed these machines to illegally elect the president, it is obvious where the investigation has to begin. It begins with the president and his campaign."

"The president says he welcomes the investigation," Jane Foster responds. "He has offered to be helpful in any way. Does that make him less likely to have actually known about the fix?"

"I have been at this for a long time. I need to talk with the staff at the FBI. I need to get up to speed about what they are learning. But here is what I know. Suspects say a lot of surprising things when they know the law is headed their way."

103

Damien Pietro

It was the strangest message I had ever received in my 25-year law enforcement career. It was a poem posted on social media and directed to me.

> Damien, Damien in pursuit
> Of the man who took the loot
> And changed the votes to Jeffrey Scott
> But now my picture's all you've got
>
> G-men, G-men looking hard
> Without clues your search is marred
> What's the question makes you glum
> Where the hell is Sheldon Klumm
>
> I have clues, yes lots of clues
> If my game to play you choose
> So let's start and have some fun
> Perhaps your quest will soon be done

At the bottom of the poem was a web address. Wrongpresident. us.

Was this really Sheldon Klumm? Why would he want to help the FBI? I sensed a trap of some kind. That or this Sheldon Klumm was one weird dude. And from what I had learned about the guy, that might be the case. But when the man you are after might be sending you a message you have to look. And besides, so far, we weren't making much progress at all.

I brought in our computer people. We set up a sandboxed computer isolated from any sensitive network. That way viruses or damaging code would be contained. Then we set up our systems to locate any traces of either his IP or MAC address and find out where the hell he was.

The techies handed me a video game controller.

"What do I do with this thing? Does someone know how this works?" I asked. We all exchanged blank looks.

Not having any guidance, I typed in the web address and hit return.

On the screen a picture of the White House appeared. It was night and light shined through the windows. The camera moved closer. In one window was Jeffrey Scott. His eyes enlarge, he exits. He appears at another window and then another. The credits appear over the screen.

Klumm Productions Presents

Wrong President

The screen goes dark and an image appears. It is Sheldon Klumm. He is wearing a T-shirt that says "Democrassassin" and cargo shorts. The voiceover begins.

Sheldon Klumm is the Democrassassin.
He spoiled the presidential election.

He is on the loose. He could be
anywhere in the world. Can you find him?

The screen goes dark again and two guys in dark suits and wingtip shoes appear. The faces? Mine and my partner, KB Denton! Where did he get those pictures? I'm not on Facebook.

The voiceover says, "G-men, do you accept this challenge?" The buttons appear. One says "Yes" and the other says "No." The "No" button is yellow.

Well, what can I do? I'm no coward. I click "Yes."

The two FBI agents appear on the screen. To the right are weapons, ancient weapons, a dagger, a sword, an axe, and a spiked mace.

"Choose your Weapon"

Blinking, I choose the sword. KB has no controller. I choose the mace for him.

The game begins with a scan of a desert littered with stone outcroppings. The scenery is beautiful. Blue skies. Golden sand. Four elephants enter the screen. They are saddled and men ride each one. The camera follows them into a village littered with palm trees and huts.

KB and I find ourselves behind the elephants. We are wearing dark suits, white shirts, club ties, and wingtip shoes. The villagers wear robes and point at our clothes. They laugh, almost hysterically. Some are actually rolling on the ground. We follow the elephants along the dirt street until we arrive at a temple with broad steps leading to a large door. At the top of the steps, the men dismount and turn to face us.

"This way," one says, motioning toward a door. We enter a large room with one chair. A throne. On the throne sits a warrior with a massive club. He speaks with a sly smile.

So begins your quest for Klumm
Unmatched evil has he done
Where he is I have a clue
But first there's something you must do

> Behind me lies a special door
> About which I will say no more
> To enter you must fight your way
> Through this warrior on this day

The warrior steps down, holding his club high. He swings at KB, who has no controller. KB crumples to the ground. I have barely learned to walk, much less swing my sword. What are all these buttons? In no time we are both dead. Howling laughter fills the temple.

The villagers swarm into the chamber and remove our clothes. The scene switches to the village where people are wearing our suit coats, ties, and boxer shorts and one man is limping down the dusty street wearing one shiny wingtip.

Everywhere people are dancing, clapping hands, celebrating our instant demise.

Klumm appears on the screen. He is also amused.

> Damien, Damien, not well done
> But this game has just begun
> You need help to get a win
> When I'm back you'll try again

We knew this about Klumm. He was a video game fanatic. Hours and hours every day. And he was also what they call a modder, a guy who changes the games.

He was humiliating us. But he was also stupid. Why would anyone want to engage in an enterprise that allows us capture his computer ID and track his location.

"Did we get numbers off the computer?" I asked in an angry voice.

"Dimitri, we were on a TOR."

I just sighed. He was covering his tracks. God knows what else we were in for. I knew one thing for sure. We were playing on Klumm's home court. KB and I were no match.

365

The phone rang. It was the director.

"Damien, I hope you know."

"Know what?" I asked.

"Your whole game is on YouTube."

"Oh my God," I answered.

"One hundred thousand views. Already."

I covered my phone with my hand and shouted into the room. "Who in this goddamned agency plays video games?" I shouted. "Find a champ and get his ass in here."

104

NBC NEWS

"This is Caleb Bankston with NBC News. Another shocking revelation in the presidential election scandal. With our story is Oren Sullivan."

"Thanks, Caleb. This story gets stranger every day. In the Democratic Republic of the Congo, a nation located in the heart of the African jungle, there was a coup during which the military ended the 10-year reign of President Mamadou Kasongo. Shortly before taking control of the presidential palace, coup leaders released documents showing Kasongo had paid approximately $70 million to Nadia Fedorov to reprogram the voting machines in Wisconsin and advance the election of Jeffrey Scott.

"Kasongo apparently feared that, if elected, Christopher would repeal Dodd-Frank and, with it, a little known provision that protects the Congo and its commerce in a rare and valuable mineral, coltan.

"The new government is cooperating with the FBI to provide evidence of the alleged payments. Nadia Fedorov has alleged in a video, believed to be filmed in Russia, that she received the money from a Democratic donor close to the president. But now the FBI has the information it needs to track the payments and confirm the new government's story. Caleb."

"Wow! If true, then our election was bought by a third world country for an amount that represents a tiny fraction of what both candidates spent to win."

"That's right, Caleb. America's election might have been stolen by a third world dictator at a bargain price. Can it get any worse?"

"Not in my imagination. Not at all."

105

Damien Pietro

The cavalry had arrived. Two guys who claimed to be serious gamers. One, Darryl Suiter, actually worked for the FBI. The other guy was his friend, Sherman. He had no job. He spent too much time gaming.

I had gotten a new message from Klumm that morning. Listen to this.

> Damien, Damien, do no fret
> Your new partners may help yet
> Join me now in our new game
> The way it ends may not be same

How did he know all this? Well, after my performance it is not hard to guess.

We start over. Darryl and Sherman don't walk behind the elephants. They run. Then they see a camel. They jump on and gallop into the village. Hey, how did they do that?

They don't wait to be invited into the temple. They storm the temple and confront the warrior. This is different!

Darryl and Sherman have the same weapons we have, a sword and a mace. But they have moves. When the warrior advances, Sherman withdraws, and Darryl moves to the side. Seeing their maneuver, the warrior charges Darryl but he spins away, striking the warrior on his back with his mace. Sherman charges forward with his sword. They are a team. One distracts and one attacks. In no time, the warrior lays motionless in a pool of blood.

I am awed. Maybe *I* should learn this game.

They open the door in the back of the temple. Little stars ripple through the air with a tingling sound.

"What was that?" I ask.

"When you win a battle, you gain strength," Sherman explains.

A small chest contains a note.

> Water, water in the sky
> The masses for their thirst do cry
> Water, water flow and glide
> To the city large with pride

I look around the room. Water in the sky? Rain? Runoff?

"Does anyone have a guess?" I ask.

Not a word.

"So Klumm is in some place where water from the sky flows to the city. Come on. Think."

But no one ventures a guess.

A little ring sounds and the word "loot" appears. Darryl presses a button and a dagger appears, which he stuffs in his pack.

They leave the temple and exit the village. In the distance a small triangle appears. Next destination.

After some time walking we come to a tomb surrounded by desert on all sides. Guarding the tomb is a creature I have never seen. It is at least six feet long and has six legs and two heads. On each head is a mask. One head wears a Jeffrey Scott mask. The other wears the face of Tom Christopher.

"No fair!" shouts Sherman. "They aren't on the same team!"

Extending upward from their heads are pointed ears. In the mouth holes you can see small pointed teeth. But mostly you can hear the noise as the heads glare at each other and cackle indecipherable nonsense. The tiny legs march forward. The heads swoop toward our agents.

Darryl and Sherman retreat. The Christopher monster moves forward and back, feigning attack. The Scott monster moves its head in a circular motion. The monster stands on its hind legs and rises into the sky. There is a whip-like quality to its movements. He lurches toward Sherman, who retreats once more. Meanwhile, Darryl takes a swipe at the neck of the Scott version. But with a snake-like motion he sinks his teeth into Darryl's shirt and drags him close. Darryl pulls his dagger and begins furiously stabbing. But it is too late. The monster has ripped off his head.

While the monster is lapping Darryl's blood, Sherman attacks, planting the mace in the back of the monster's head. Suddenly he is still. Then after a vigorous battle, the head bearing the Christopher mask lay severed on the ground.

"What do we do now?" I ask. Then Darryl presses some buttons and brings his G-man back to life.

"I thought you were dead," I say.

"I was. But you can restore your character. You just lose all the levels you earned."

"Oh." What else could I say? I had so much to learn.

Inside the tomb is another clue.

> The namesake of your destination
> Exists inside America's nation
> And every hamlet of this name
> Did Tom Christopher so acclaim.

"Research!" I cry. We need the names of cities in America that match cities in Europe where all the towns voted Christopher. What a project.

Once more Sheldon is on the screen. He is holding a controller. Behind him is a picture of the president's desk in the Oval Office. He moves his controller right stick to the left. Tom Christopher appears behind the desk. He moves it to the left and Jeffrey Scott appears. When his back and forth continues for too long, he puts down his controller and addresses our FBI team.

"Well done, Dmitri. You are getting close. But who knows? Maybe not close enough."

"See you soon!" He smiles and his image is gone.

* * *

That night several of us stayed at the office to review the game and ponder the clues. Water from the sky? What city in Europe has the most rainfall?

Reykjavík.

Is there a town named Reykjavik in America? Not a one.

We checked out YouTube. Second episode posted. The game was a hit. In all, 800,000 people had viewed one of the games.

Struggle as we did, we could not crack the case. As we were about to leave, a colleague of Darryl's stopped at the door to give him a ride. He looked at the screen.

"How do you like the game?" he asked.

I hastily turned off the computer.

"It's okay. I've played this one a million times. *Assassin's Creed*."

"Oh my God," said Darryl. "Why didn't I catch it? He's right. Our Sheldon is modding *Assassin's Creed*! He's been modding it all over the place."

"Tell me about the game," I said to our visitor.

"It's a journey game. The whole thing is about 15 hours, if you are really good."

"And where does the journey end?"

"It ends in Rome."

Rome. Fed by the aqueducts. I get that.

"But how many Romes are there in the US?"

Google delivered the answer right away. Nine.

Then we checked how they voted. Every one gave Christopher their vote.

* * *

There were 711 hotels in Rome and Elmer Skidmore may not have been staying in one. He may not even have been in Rome. But we were trying to solve the biggest crime conducted in the United States in decades. Maybe ever. FBI staff began calling.

It did not take long. We found him. The Palazzo Naiadi. Maybe the best hotel in Rome: $1,400 per night.

106

Max Parker

I was channel surfing again. MSNBC. CNN. Fox. Suddenly, he was on every screen.

Cason Blake. The Republican partisan and special prosecutor who thought his job was nailing Jeffrey Scott.

He was saying he did not believe the Congo allegations. He was saying that the Congo received a half-billion dollars a year in US foreign aid and that they had every incentive to keep Scott in power.

Did it matter that the people exposing the payoff were not in power at the time? Does it matter that they had shared paperwork confirming their story? Did it matter that we had finally gotten to the bottom of this wretched mess?

It did matter, not because Case Blake wouldn't shut his mouth. It mattered because now he no longer had a case he could take to a jury.

So Jeffrey Scott, facing widespread popular suspicion for having rigged his own election, invited his opponent to nominate the special prosecutor. Look what was happening.

They say all is fair in love and war.

Unfortunately, a few years ago they added politics as well.

107

Sheldon Klumm

I was at my computer on the TOR. I was waiting for the G-men to begin. I have to admit, my game, *Wrong President*, was hardly the masterpiece I'd imagined. All those deserts hardly fit with the theme. But when you mod you can't fix everything. My third episode was different. I had created a magnificent dragon. He had a 12-foot wing-span and footlong claws and, as I waited for the game to begin, he was floating lazily in the distance high in the sky. At the game's launch, he would swoop down, lift those G-men into the air, and carry them to an underground castle where terrible ordeals would ensue.

My fans would love it. And I had fans. I had posted our first two episodes on YouTube and, face it, when you are the number one criminal in the whole entire world, you get a lot of fans. People could go to the web address and actually play the game using the TOR browser. And for some people there is nothing more delicious than an icon of evil, taunting and humiliating the good guys in hilarious fashion.

You can't deny it, the bad guys don't always win but they always have fans.

So how many people watched that first episode? How many people howled at the villagers dancing on the sand in those dark suits, wingtips, and club ties?

I was up to a million. I was smiling. And this episode with my gargantuan dragon was sure to be the best yet. I wonder if Nadia has seen my game. If she saw my dragon, would she take me back?

But I waited. The FBI had signed into the game but something was strange. Their players were not moving. They were just standing still. Something was wrong.

I would not wait! I summoned the dragon, who swooped toward these frozen agents.

My phone rang. I didn't answer. I was not about to miss this game. But then it rang again. The players were still not moving and my dragon was about to arrive. I answered.

"Sheldon, this is Damien Pietro."

"Oh my God, I am freaking fucked."

"Afraid so," he answered. "The Italian State Police are at your door. I suggest you let them in and don't do anything stupid."

I let them in. There were a dozen burly men in helmets and puffy vests and carrying guns big enough to slaughter a herd of elephants in two shots. You would think they were arresting the Soviet army.

I was led through the lobby. I bet I was the first guest of the Palazzo Naiadi to ever be escorted through the lobby by the Italian State Police. But then I thought, *That can't be true. This place is so expensive you probably have to break a law to afford it.*

I was handed over to Damien Pietro, whom I met for the first time. I was not sure what to expect but there was no waterboarding tank in sight. He was a short, broad shouldered man with short salt and pepper hair.

Pietro had this straight-spoken, down-to-business style. And he must have been smart because it only took him two clues to find me. I expected at least two more episodes.

He had a lot of questions. There was no point in lying. I gave him all the details. Nadia giving me blow jobs, me fixing the votes for Republicans but then Nadia finally selling the election to make the Democrats win—with only one state left. I told him what I had heard about the Congo. I knew there was another guy involved in all this but did not know his name.

"Does Howard Feldman ring a bell?"

I said "no."

My story lined up completely with what the new government in the Congo had to say. It explained Nadia's movements in the states. And I was happy to learn that thanks to my testimony there would be no impeachment of the president.

After all, hadn't I caused him enough trouble already?

108

Lucy Gilmore

So this story is finally coming to a close and, I have to say, boy oh boy, has my life changed for the better. Once NBC News reported that the voting machine fraud was purchased by the Democratic Republic of Congo, the district attorney of Dodge County, Wisconsin, dropped all charges against me.

Two months later, I finished my book. I named it *Stealing Bonnie*. In the meantime, the embarrassment of knowing that the American election had been bought by some African dictator deep in the jungle made me something of a heroine. My book became a bestseller. My story in the *New York Times* won the Pulitzer Prize.

And get this. I ran into Brad Aaronson on the street and he actually apologized. Holy Jesus, was that sweet.

Other big things have happened. I am now employed as a reporter for the *New York Times*, which features me prominently on their website. And remember Binky Wong? We got married.

It's been a helluva a ride. I've got my hankerchief out just thinking about it.

Let me finish with one piece of advice. If you see something you weren't supposed to see, the safe thing is to keep your mouth shut. But if you brave the dangers, if you defy the doubters and if you stand and fight for what you know to be true, there might be a gift in store.

You might end up changing the world.

109

Nadia Federov

Okay, so you would think that a drop-dead gorgeous woman with 40-something million in the bank would be having a pretty good time. Not so fast. With arrest warrants in place in most of the civilized world, my face viewed across the entire planet, I was stuck in Moscow.

But not for long.

I found the best cosmetic surgeon in the Russian Federation, who rearranged my features in a remarkable way. And when the bandages were removed, I looked in the mirror and thought, "I am even more beautiful than ever. How is that even possible?"

I took on a new identity. This time I was no Doris Leaper. I became Anastasia Lebedev, the last name meaning "Swan" in the old language.

As I traveled the world once more, I had an idea. There were others like me. Rich but unable to travel because they made their money in forbidden ways. So I hired a talented team of cosmetic surgeons and opened a clinic for customers who needed a new identity or just a more beautiful face. And for an extra $20,000 my customers could choose their own new name and acquire a new passport as well. Those Russian bureaucrats are so cheap. Thirty dollars a pop.

My business, You Can Be Anyone, is a huge success. My clientele has grown to include the fabulously wealthy; many of whom have made their money in improper ways. And, of course, I am as stunning as ever, pursued by men, young and old, all across the globe.

110

Jeffrey Scott

We are now at the end of this story, and one thing you have been wondering is: *Why have we never heard from the president himself?* Since a lot of this tale is about me, I felt it was better left to others to tell. But I can restrain myself no longer.

Let me first report that I did not get impeached but I did not run for reelection either. Millions of people, no matter what the evidence, still believed I stole the election. So I left politics and got a TV show that honored American leaders who made compromise, accomplishment, and bipartisanship important in their careers. In campaigns across the country, those leaders I had honored proudly put their award in their campaign mailings and TV ads. I think it may have helped.

But there are issues I want to discuss that are a lot bigger than me or my TV show. You are wondering, I am wondering, everybody is wondering.

What the hell is happening to our country?

Can I point some fingers? I don't care if you say "no" —I am going to point them anyway.

First of all, the internet. Thanks to the internet, people can say vaccines give you autism. They can say that America did not land on the moon or that a major American candidate for president was running a child pornography ring in the basement of a pizza restaurant on Wisconsin Avenue in Washington, DC.

And people actually believe these things. A lot of them.

Which leads to my second point. Suddenly, instead of getting television news from three honest networks, we are getting it from 20. And the people who run these shows figured out that the way to get ratings is not to tell people the truth but to tell viewers what they want to the truth to be.

In our politics, we remain at war and our losses are unspeakable. Whatever happened to forgiveness? Respect for other beliefs? The understanding that we are all in this together?

These words seem distant in our past.

I offered forgiveness. I respected the beliefs of others. I showed our common goals.

But I failed.

Guess what I found out on the internet today? I learned that the president of the Congo was a personal friend and that I called him on the phone and asked him to come up with the money to fix my election.

The truth has become a refugee, persecuted, hunted, and abused.

That leads to my final point.

Something is seriously wrong with the American voter.

Year after year, polls show barely 20 percent of the American voters believe Congress is doing a good job. But year after year, our voters return 90 percent of them to Washington.

In a democracy, the voters are the enforcers of good conduct. But now, politicians can lie. Politicians can take large special interest contributions and sell out the voters who elected them. They can molest women, obstruct justice, and conduct themselves in ways that undermine all possibility of progress. They can do all these things with no consequences at all.

If the American voters are our moral police, they are spending their days at the Dunkin' Donuts waiting for the shift to end.

It all boils down to this. The American voter is not up for the job.

But I always have an idea. There is hope. It might even work.

Instead of patrolling the border, searching and interrogating and harassing anyone wanting to enter our great nation, instead of making people in Uzbekistan fill out a 20-page application, in English, just to get a visa to enter our nation, let's adopt a different approach.

Instead of harassment, anyone crossing our border should be greeted with a thousand-dollar check the moment they set foot in the US of A. We would provide them a free ride in a nice car to anywhere in America they want to live. We would throw in two weeks of fully paid rooms at a Quality Inn. And in every town in America, instead of getting greeted by immigration police, we would organize welcoming committees of local citizens to celebrate their arrival.

Oh, and we should throw in free passes to Disneyworld if they have kids.

And within one week of their arrival, each and every one of them would receive a personal thank you note from the president of the United States expressing our nation's profound gratitude for their decision to make America their new home.

We want to fix our problems in America, right?

We need new voters.

Those immigrants are our only hope.

Acknowledgments

I would like to thank Ben LeRoy for his wise and detailed advice in revamping this book and creating a better story. Ben, you have taught me a lot.

I would also like to thank Jonathan Simon, whose work in analyzing anomalies in election returns has shined a light on the possible manipulation of voting machines and the outcomes of our elections.

I would also like to acknowledge the following persons who read the book in advance and offered many helpful comments and observations that reshaped the manuscript.

Kathy Geraty Arnold
Kathryn Cummings
David Dekker
Wilson Golden
Scotty Greene
Cam Kattell
Judy Kohn
Tom Marking
Joyce Mordhorst
Susan Shallcross
Jonathan Simon

Bibliography

Many of the events illustrating voting machine vulnerabilities are surely surprising to most readers. As to the major topics covered, here are the sources reporting these events.

The 2010 South Carolina Democratic Primary Result

In 2010, a Democratic candidate for the U.S. Senate, who was the presumptive nominee, was soundly defeated by a candidate who made no appearances, raised no money, had no website, was unknown, and whose $10,400 filing fee was paid anonymously. The invisible candidate received 59 percent of the vote. This election story is reported in a two-hour documentary produced by Katie Couric and directed by filmmaker Jason Smith. The story of this election is recreated in Chapter One. The documentary can be viewed at www.hollywoodreporter.com/news/katie-couric-voting-issues-bush-886653.

Other coverage of the unusual election results included the following publications.

Adams, Richard. "Alvin Greene: South Carolina's Democratic Conundrum." *The Guardian*, June 10, 2010. www.theguardian.com/world/richard-adams-blog/2010/jun/10/alvin-greene-south-carolina-democrats-plant

"Democrats want investigation into surprise Senate primary winner." CNN Politics, June 14, 2010. www.cnn.com/2010/POLITICS/06/14/greene.south.carolina.primary/index.html

Shaller, Tom. "SC Democratic Primary Getting Weirder By The Hour." *FiveThirtyEight*, June 12, 2010. https://fivethirtyeight.com/features/sc-democratic-primary-getting-weirder/

Shaller, Tom. "Something Fishy in South Carolina?," *FiveThirtyEight*, June 11, 2011. https://fivethirtyeight.com/features/something-fishy-in-south-carolina/

DEF CON Conference Voting Village

Chapter 8 recreates episodes from the Voting Village, an experiment in hacking voting machines and state voter registration sites. These episodes occurred at the 2017 and 2018 conferences. Background on these events is provided in the reports issued by the conference as well as coverage in the mainstream press. Here are some sources providing a more in-depth view of these events.

"An 11-Year-Old Changed The Results Of Florida's Presidential Vote At A Hacker Convention." *BuzzFeedNews,* August 11, 2018. www.buzzfeednews.com/article/kevincollier/voting-hackers-defcon-failures-manufacturers-ess

DEF CON 25, Report on Cyber Vulnerabilities in U.S. Election Equipment, Databases, and Infrastructure, September 2018." www.

defcon.org/images/defcon-25/DEF%20CON%2025%20voting%20village%20report.pdf

"DEF CON 26, Report on Cyber Vulnerabilities in U.S. Election Equipment, Databases, and Infrastructure, September 2018." www.defcon.org/images/defcon-26/DEF%20CON%2026%20voting%20village%20report.pdf

Halpern, Sue. "Election-Hacking Lessons from the 2018 Def Con Hackers," *The New Yorker,* August 23, 2018. www.newyorker.com/news/dispatch/election-hacking-lessons-from-the-2018-def-con-hackers-conference

Halpern, Sue. "Election-Hacking Lessons from the 2018 Def Con Hackers Conference." *The New Yorker,*

August 23, 2018. www.newyorker.com/contributors/sue-halpern/page/4

McMillan, Robert and Dustin Volz. "Tensions Flare as Hackers Root Out Flaws in Voting Machines." *Wall Street Journal*, August 12, 2018. www.wsj.com/articles/tensions-flare-as-hackers-root-out-flaws-in-voting-machines-1534078801

Newman, Lily Hay. "Voting Machines Are Still Absurdly Vulnerable to Attacks," *WIRED*, September 28, 2018.

Red Shift From Exit Polls to Election Day Results

Red shifts from exit polling to election day results are extensively documented in *CODE RED: Computerized Elections and the War on American Democracy: Election 2018 Edition*, by Jonathan Simon.

387

CODE RED provides detailed descriptions of evidence of voting machine vulnerabilities and manipulation. Data on exit poll numbers were drawn from the book or its author. This book provides a detailed discussion of the statistical likelihood that shifts from exit poll predictions and actual election day results cannot be due to random chance. Actual election results were taken from public sources, primarily state election websites. Anyone wishing to check or recompute these figures can review or download this data covering 287 statewide elections from 2004 to 2016 at halmalchow.com/twobilliontoone/exitpolldata.

Voting Machine Security

Blake, Andrew. "Voting machines subject to 'staggering' vulnerabilities: Report." *Washington Times*, September 27, 2018. www.washingtontimes.com/news/2018/sep/27/voting-machines-subject-staggering-vulnerabilities/?utm_source=GOOGLE&utm_medium=cpc&utm_id=chacka&utm_campaign=TWT+-+DSA&gclid=Cj0KCQiA2ITuBRDkARIsAMK9Q7NbOB0HN1XW2UqjzfUUdUq7l-yb5IZSWhNPx-t9apBDJY2EvR0GT_MaAuqJEALw_wcB

Diaz, Alex. "Election machine keys are on the Internet, hackers say." Fox News, August 24, 2019. www.foxnews.com/tech/i-have-the-keys-to-your-voting-machine-probably

Elfrink, Tim. "'It is not letting me vote for who I want': Video shows electronic machine changing ballot in Mississippi," *Washington Post*, August 28, 2019. www.washingtonpost.com/nation/2019/08/28/mississippi-election-machine-changes-votes-video/

Fessler, Pam. "If Voting Machines Were Hacked, Would Anyone Know?" *NPR Morning Edition*, June 14, 2017. www.

npr.org/2017/06/14/532824432/if-voting-machines-were-hacked-would-anyone-know

Good, Chris. "How hackable are American voting machines? It depends who you ask," *ABC News*, October 15, 2018. https://abcnews.go.com/Politics/hackable-american-voting-machines-depends/story?id=58511054

"Hacking a Voting Machine is Getting Easier." *Fox News*, October 4, 2019. www.foxnews.com/tech/hacking-a-voting-machine-is-getting-easier

Halderman, J. Alex, and Jen Schwartz. "How to Defraud Democracy." *Scientific American*, September 1, 2019. www.scientificamerican.com/article/how-to-defraud-democracy/

Halpern, Sue. "How Voting-Machine Errors Reflect a Wider Crisis for American Democracy." *The New Yorker*, October 31, 2018. www.newyorker.com/news/news-desk/how-voting-machine-errors-reflect-a-wider-crisis-for-american-democracy

Keelty, Christopher. "Did Russians Hack US Voting Machines? Nobody Knows.," *Medium*, July 28, 2017. https://medium.com/@keeltyc/did-russians-hack-us-voting-machines-nobody-knows-9665a63b1514

Marks, Joseph. "The Cybersecurity 202: Voting machines touted as secure option are actually vulnerable to hacking, study finds." *Washington Post*, January 8, 2020. www.washingtonpost.com/news/powerpost/paloma/the-cybersecurity-202/2020/01/08/the-cybersecurity-202-voting-machines-touted-as-secure-option-are-actually-vulnerable-to-hacking-study-finds/5e14cc6e602ff125ce5bd747/

Morris, David Z. "Swing State Voting Systems Were Left Connected to the Internet for Months, Report Says." *Fortune,* August 8, 2019. https://fortune.com/2019/08/08/swing-state-voting-systems-connected-internet-vice-report/

Morton, Victor. "Indiana voting machines reportedly switching votes." *Washington Times,* November 5, 2019. www.washingtontimes.com/news/2019/nov/5/tippecanoe-county-indiana-voting-machines-switchin/

Newman, Lily Hay. "Election Security Is Still Hurting at Every Level." *WIRED,* June 6, 2019. www.wired.com/story/election-security-2020/

Niesse, Mark. "Hackers Highlight Vulnerabilities in Vote-Scanning Machines." *Atlanta Journal*-Constitution, September 27, 2019. www.govtech.com/security/Hackers-Highlight-Vulnerabilities-in-Vote-Scanning-Machines.html

Patterson, Dan. "Why voting machines in the U.S. are easy targets for hackers." *CBS News,* September 19, 2018. www.cbsnews.com/news/why-voting-machines-in-the-u-s-are-easy-targets-for-hackers/

Revell, Timothy. "Hacking a US electronic voting booth takes less than 90 minutes." *New Scientist,* August 1, 2017. www.newscientist.com/article/2142428-hacking-a-us-electronic-voting-booth-takes-less-than-90-minutes/

"Reliability of pricey new voting machines questioned." *Associated Press,* February 23, 2020. www.uticaod.com/news/20200223/reliability-of-pricey-new-voting-machines-questioned

Robles, Frances. "Russian Hackers Were 'In a Position' to Alter Florida Voter Rolls, Rubio Confirms." *New York Times,* April 26,

2019. www.nytimes.com/2019/04/26/us/florida-russia-hacking-election.html

Schwartz, Jen. "The Vulnerabilities of Our Voting Machines." *Scientific American*, November 1, 2018. www.scientificamerican.com/article/the-vulnerabilities-of-our-voting-machines/

"US mid-terms: Hackers expose 'staggering' voter machine flaws," BBC.com, September 28, 2018. www.bbc.com/news/technology-45680490

"Voting Machines: Last Week Tonight with John Oliver." *HBO*, November 3, 2019. Video can be viewed at www.rollingstone.com/tv/tv-news/john-oliver-last-week-tonight-election-security-voting-machiens-hack-907626/

Wilke, Jordan. "America's new voting machines bring new fears of election tampering." *The Guardian*, April 23, 2019. www.theguardian.com/us-news/2019/apr/22/us-voting-machines-paper-ballots-2020-hacking

Wofford, Ben. "How to Hack an Election in 7 Minutes." *Politico*, August 05, 2016. www.politico.com/magazine/story/2016/08/2016-elections-russia-hack-how-to-hack-an-election-in-seven-minutes-214144

Wofford, Benjamin. "The hacking threat to the midterms is huge. And technology won't protect us." vox.com, October 25, 2018. www.vox.com/2018/10/25/18001684/2018-midterms-hacked-russia-election-security-voting

Zetter, Kim. "The Crisis of Election Security." *New York Times Magazine*, September 26, 2018. www.nytimes.com/2018/09/26/magazine/election-security-crisis-midterms.html

Zetter, Kim. "Dan Rather Investigates Voting Machines—Uncovers New Surprises About ES&S Touch-Screens." *WIRED*, August 13, 2007. www.wired.com/2007/08/dan-rather-inve/

Zetter, Kim. "The Myth of the Hacker-Proof Voting Machine." *New York Times*, February 21, 2018. www.nytimes.com/2018/02/21/magazine/the-myth-of-the-hacker-proof-voting-machine.html

Voting Machine Companies

Aviv, Adam, et al. "Security Evaluation of ES&S Voting Machines and Election Management System." Department of Computer and Information Science, University of Pennsylvania. https://security.cs.georgetown.edu/~msherr/papers/aviv-evt08.pdf

Berkeley, Mike. "Dan Rather expose of Voting Machines & Chads." *Daily Kos*, September 14, 2007. https://m.dailykos.com/stories/2007/9/14/385221/-

"Bipartisan Group Calls on Congress to Hold Voting Machine Vendors Accountable." *Public Citizen*, August 27, 2019. https://yubanet.com/usa/bipartisan-group-calls-on-congress-to-hold-voting-maching-vendors-accountable/

Goodkind, Nicole. "Mitch McConnell Received Donations From Voting Machine Lobbyists Before Blocking Election Security Bills." *Newsweek*, July 26, 2019. www.newsweek.com/mitch-mcconnell-robert-mueller-election-security-russia-1451361

Gordon, Greg, et al. "Voting machine vendor treated election officials to trips to Vegas, elsewhere." *Impact 2020*, June 21, 2018. www.mcclatchydc.com/latest-news/article213558729.html

Halpern, Sue. "How Voting-Machine Lobbyists Undermine the Democratic Process." *The New Yorker*, January 22, 2019. www.newyorker.com/tech/annals-of-technology/how-voting-machine-lobbyists-undermine-the-democratic-process

Halpern, Sue. "The Iowa Caucuses and the Menace of Untested, Privately Owned Election Technology." *The New Yorker*, February 5, 2020. www.newyorker.com/news/our-columnists/the-lesson-american-voters-can-learn-from-iowa

Halpern, Sue. "Mitch McConnell is Making the 2020 Election Open Season for Hackers." *The New Yorker*, June 12, 2019. www.newyorker.com/tech/annals-of-technology/mitch-mcconnell-is-making-the-2020-election-open-season-for-hackers 12, 2019

Norden, Lawrence. "Voting System Failures." The Brennan Center, 2010. www.brennancenter.org/sites/default/files/2019-08/Report_Voting_Machine_Failures_Database-Solution.pdf

Parks, Miles. "Hacks, Security Gaps And Oligarchs: The Business Of Voting Comes Under Scrutiny." *NPR*, September 21, 2018. www.npr.org/2018/09/21/649535367/hacks-security-gaps-and-oligarchs-the-business-of-voting-comes-under-scrutiny

Starks, Tim. "Voting machine vendors under pressure." *Politico*, July 12, 2018. www.politico.com/newsletters/morning-cybersecurity/2018/07/12/voting-machine-vendors-under-pressure-277054

"U.S. election integrity is guarded by security-challenged firms." *CBS News*, October 29, 2018. www.cbsnews.com/news/u-s-election-integrity-is-guarded-by-security-challenged-firms/

Whittaker, Zack. "Senators demand to know why election vendors still sell voting machines with 'known vulnerabilities.'" *TechCrunch*, March 27, 2019. https://techcrunch.com/2019/03/27/senators-security-voting-machines/

Wilkie, Jordan. "'The selling of an election': how private firms compromised midterms security." *The Guardian*, August 1, 2019. www.theguardian.com/us-news/2019/aug/01/the-selling-of-an-election-dangerous-level-of-private-control-revealed-in-2018-georgia-midterms

Wilke, Jordan. "'They think they are above the law': the firms that own America's voting system." *The Guardian*, April 23, 2019. www.theguardian.com/us-news/2019/apr/22/us-voting-machine-private-companies-voter-registration

Zetter, Kim. "Critical U.S. Election Systems Have Been Left Exposed Online Despite Official Denials." *Vice.com*, August 8, 2019. www.vice.com/en_us/article/3kxzk9/exclusive-critical-us-election-systems-have-been-left-exposed-online-despite-official-denials

Zetter, Kim. "Top Voting Machine Vendor Admits It Installed Remote-Access Software on Systems Sold to States." *Vice*, July 17, 2018. www.vice.com/en_us/article/mb4ezy/top-voting-machine-vendor-admits-it-installed-remote-access-software-on-systems-sold-to-states

Other Reading of Interest

"9 Solutions to Secure America's Elections." Center for American Progress, August 16, 2017. www.americanprogress.org/issues/democracy/reports/2017/08/16/437390/9-solutions-secure-americas-elections/

Fandos, Nicholas. "New Election Security Bills Face a One-Man Roadblock: Mitch McConnell." *New York Times*, June 7, 2019. www.nytimes.com/2019/06/07/us/politics/election-security-mitch-mcconnell.html

Sanger, David E., and Catie Edmondson. "Russia Targeted Election Systems in All 50 States, Report Finds." *New York Times*, July 25, 2019. www.nytimes.com/2019/07/25/us/politics/russian-hacking-elections.html

Wickenden, Dorothy, and Sue Halpern. "Disasters at America's Polling Places." *The New Yorker*, February 6, 2020. The podcast can be heard online at www.newyorker.com/podcast/political-scene/disasters-at-americas-polling-places